LIFE & OTHER
HAPPY
ENDINGS

Melanie Cantor

BLACK SWAN

TRANSWORLD PUBLISHERS
61–63 Uxbridge Road, London W5 5SA
www.penguin.co.uk

Transworld is part of the Penguin Random House group of companies
whose addresses can be found at global.penguinrandomhouse.com

Penguin
Random House
UK

First published in Great Britain in 2019
as *Death & Other Happy Endings* by Bantam Press
an imprint of Transworld Publishers
Black Swan edition published as *Life & Other Happy Endings* 2020

A CIP catalogue record for this book
is available from the British Library.

ISBN
9781784164164

Typeset in 11.25/15.25pt Sabon by Jouve (UK), Milton Keynes.
Printed and bound in Great Britain by Clays Ltd, Elcograf S.p.A.

Penguin Random House is committed to a sustainable
future for our business, our readers and our planet. This book
is made from Forest Stewardship Council® certified paper.

MIX
Paper from
responsible sources
FSC® C018179

1 3 5 7 9 10 8 6 4 2

More love from readers

'Inspiring, joyous and funny.'

'It is beautifully written and is funny, sensitive and a page-turning story.'

'I invested in the characters and it's left me wanting more!!!'

'Can we have a sequel?!?!?!'

'Keeps your interest and keeps you guessing. Would definitely recommend for a holiday read.'

'Couldn't put this book down once I started it. Very funny and witty in parts. I did not want it to end.'

'Made me realize again the joy of getting lost in a beautiful book.'

'Cantor's novel celebrates women and their friendships, unfailingly an essential provider of the necessary support when life throws nightmarish challenges and heartbreaking events at them.'

'This is a lovely and entertaining read, full of warmth, humour and wit.'

'Brilliant book, making something sad and depressing into something quite marvellous!!'

'This book was the perfect escape from everyday life.'

'The storyline swept me up with its whirlwind momentum and I wasn't able to catch my breath until the closing chapter . . . It's an emotional journey of hope and happiness and I know I won't be forgetting this tale in a hurry, that's for sure.'

'Melanie's writing is captivating and intense.'

'There were several moments in this book when my eyes filled with tears and several moments when my heart felt like it was going to burst.'

'I laughed, I cried and I cried some more. A truly powerful story of a remarkable woman fighting against the injustices the world cruelly serves her.'

'A dark horse that utterly surprised and delighted me.'

'I want to stay with a good book such as this, and keep the characters with me for a while. Jennifer was brave, adventurous and a total inspiration.'

'It is life affirming, touching and very funny. The characters jump off the page.'

'This is a brilliant read! A story which perfectly combines a serious situation with deadpan British wit and a very likeable main character – it's a winner.'

'About courage, hope, love, family and realizing that in certain situations you just have to put yourself first. What a debut by Melanie.'

For my mother and father
Doreen and Eddie
Watching over me from their cloud

And for my sons
Alexander and Joseph
My happy endings

LIFE & OTHER
HAPPY
ENDINGS

'Somebody should tell us, right at the start of our lives, that we are dying. Then we might live life to the limit, every minute of every day. Do it! I say. Whatever you want, do it now! There are only so many tomorrows.'

attributed to Pope Paul VI

Part One

Part One

How it all begins

There are some people in this world to whom things happen. I am not one of them. I lead an ordinary life. I do regular things. That's not to say my life is boring, but it's not a life full of big 'you won't believe what happened to me' stories either. Until now. When this happened. Honestly, it really did . . .

'Are you with anyone, Jennifer?'

I smile apologetically. 'Erm no . . . still single.' Shuffle in seat. I hate this sort of question. 'I go out on occasional dates, Dr Mackenzie, it's just I'm not very good with this internet stuff. Besides, I've never known my left from my right.' I chuckle awkwardly then catch the look on his face. 'You don't mean that, do you?'

'No,' he says, scratching his chin. 'Are you *here* with anyone *today*?'

I'm thrown by this. For a moment, I thought he was about to tell me I had an STD, which under the aforementioned circumstances would give substance to my fear of public conveniences. 'Why?' I say. 'Should I be?'

'It would have been helpful. I asked the receptionist to suggest it.'

I think she did. I thought she was mad.

He takes off his steel-rimmed glasses and presses his palms against his eyes. 'I'm so sorry, Jennifer. It's not good news. You have a rare blood disorder.'

He looks grim-faced. I've never seen this expression before.

The room starts to throb disconcertingly. My ears throb. Everything throbs.

I try focusing on the doctor's face as he pinches the bridge of his throbbing nose, rubbing his pulsating spider-veined flesh. He casts me a furtive glance as if he's checking my response, then mutters some unintelligible name. I only catch the 'osis' at the end.

'What is that?'

This apparently warrants a biology lesson. A long and complicated lecture about platelets and white blood cells versus red blood cells. I've never been good with that stuff, least of all while the world is pulsating around me.

'That doesn't sound friendly,' I say.

'No,' he mumbles. 'Very unfriendly. And aggressive.' He fiddles with some papers, tapping them into neat alignment. He clears his throat. 'Untreatable.'

I'm not sure I'm hearing him properly. 'I don't understand.'

'I've looked into it extensively, Jennifer. This is such a rare condition, most haematologists in this country won't come across it in their entire career. I'm afraid there's no easily accessible treatment like, say, chemo. This needs time . . .' His jaw strains to the left then springs back as though hooked to elastic. 'Something I'm not sure you have.' He coughs. 'Three months at best.'

Now let's pause here. Did he actually say that? Slipping it in, the way a disreputable restaurant slips an extra bottle of wine on the bill, hoping you won't notice.

My ears are ringing. I try to ignore the bile that's rising in my throat but it's unrelenting. 'Dr Mackenzie,' I splutter. 'I think I'm going to throw up.'

He shoots me a panicked glance then makes an old man's slow-mo dive behind his desk, knocking his elbow. 'Ouch' – I feel his pain. He hands me a grey metal bin. I stare into it. He waits a polite moment.

My every cell is focusing on the bin. A discarded Snickers wrapper sits amongst scrunched balls of paper. I retch, then vomit. My head is pounding.

Dr Mackenzie passes me some tissues and a glass of water he has on standby. 'Take your time,' he says.

But I don't have any. I sip slowly, trying to take stock. 'So you don't think treatment is worth pursuing?'

'I've made some enquiries, Jennifer, but I don't want to raise your hopes. And I have to warn you, it's not a cure.'

His voice floats around the acrid air, landing in my consciousness in snatches: '. . . even if', '. . . it may only . . .' the words crashing against my ears. I don't want to hear them.

The walls of his office close in on me, grey and bleak, devoid of distinguishing features.

Like him.

He's been my doctor for more than thirty years, he was my family's doctor, and I know nothing more about him than these four grey walls. Oh, and he probably grabs Snickers bars for lunch. There's not a single family photo or pet portrait or anatomical diagram. Not even some terrible poster that might put me off smoking – not that I smoke, by the way, but still, it would have been nice to have something to distract my attention.

I've lost all track. He finishes. His voice is not one of enthusiasm. 'I'm trying to be honest with you, Jennifer,' he says, propping the glasses back on his nose. 'You need to understand the prognosis. You need to be prepared.'

For what, Doctor?

'Thank you,' I say.

Dr Mackenzie stands up and opens a window. I'm staring at the pale vinyl floor, turning back and forth in the swivel chair. I realize I'm still gripping the bin and put it down, sliding it away from under my nose.

'But, Dr Mackenzie, are you sure? I mean, I just feel . . . tired. No pain. Just tired. And maybe a bit bloated. Are you sure it's not IBS? Or ME or . . .?' I sound as if I'm making a plea for an acronym. I am! Anything but a bloody 'osis'. No pun intended.

'I have the results of your blood tests right here, Jennifer,' he says, holding up the neat set of papers, evidence for the prosecution. 'I wish I could tell you something different but I'm afraid it's very advanced.' Plea overruled. He emits a weary sigh then deals the guilty verdict. 'I'm so sorry. I wish you'd come in sooner.'

I gasp inside my head. I'm forty-three years old and I've just been told I'm not going to make it to forty-four because I missed a deadline. I want to cry. No! I *will not* cry. I mustn't. I'm trained. I'm in HR. I don't do conspicuous emotion. Besides, this must be tough for him. I don't need to make it any tougher. 'I'm sorry too,' I say.

He slides a clutch of leaflets across his desk like a croupier does his chips. 'These might help you,' he says, his voice mellowing. I smile stiffly and toss them carelessly into my handbag, preferring the bin, if I'm honest, and watch as he scribbles out a prescription. 'The chemist around the corner has everything. This should see you through for now.'

'For now,' I repeat, aware of how ominous that sounds.

I examine the shaky scrawl, hoping for a compensatory windfall: Valium or codeine or a drug I might recognize from my mother's long-gone medicine cabinet, her prized collection of everything anyone might ever need, particularly her. Nothing is familiar.

'What do they do?'

'They'll help with the fatigue. And the pain.'

I look at him curiously, a hint of polite doubt. 'But . . .'

7

His mouth twitches. I know what that means: *read the leaflets.*

He clears his throat, stands up with brusque finality. 'I'll need to see you again soon. Eunice in reception will find some available dates for you, so please see her on your way out. And don't forget to pick up the prescription, dear.'

He calls me 'dear'. He's never called me dear. I'm definitely going to die. He walks around the desk and accompanies me to the door, which is nice of him because I usually see myself out, then gives me a fatherly pat on the shoulder.

'Sorry about your bin, Doctor,' I say.

The countdown begins: Day 90

And that was it. 'Eunice in reception will find some available dates': the only kind of dates I have to look forward to now.

I avoid the front desk – I have no idea which one Eunice is anyway – I can't get out of that place fast enough. I walk home. I must have. I'm here. It's like when you've been out and got properly hammered yet wake up to find you managed to get home and in your alcoholic stupor still carried out all your normal rituals: put the front-door keys in the dish, took off your make-up, put your phone on charge. But you remember none of it. That was my walk home. I don't even remember walking into the chemist, but that crisp white-and-green paper bag on my kitchen worktop would suggest I did. There's a small bottle of whisky sitting alongside it. I don't drink whisky but in my haze of emotion, I must have decided I needed it. Amazing, the rational decisions you can make in a totally irrational state. Now I'm sitting staring into oblivion with a cup of tea in my hands. One I don't recall making. I think I may sleepwalk through these final months.

I am reeling. Where did this come from? This freeloader in my body who has squandered all my hopes of a future; one I no longer have because I left it too late. Because I didn't take my tiredness seriously.

What am I meant to do now? Sit and wait? Where is my mother when I need her?

I still haven't cried. It's weird, that. I can't. Not yet. It's as though my tear ducts refuse to believe it. I must be in the first stages of grief and this is denial. What's next? Anger? Probably. I can feel it sitting, waiting in the wings. But not yet anger. I like denial.

Still . . . I've got to be realistic. I should arm myself with every bit of information available so I understand what this 'osis' means (I will never call it by its full name. I will never, ever dignify this interloper with its title). I resolve to read the leaflets in my handbag then google my vile new bedfellow even though I'm well aware of the dangers of googling an illness. (I once had an overlong case of pins and needles and googled to discover I had MS. Except of course I didn't.) But googling this can't possibly terrify me more than it already has, and surely better to be prepared?

I go to retrieve the leaflets then stop mid-stoop, dropping my bag as though it's live. I can't do it. Determination deserts me. Knowing too much might risk manifesting the symptoms quicker than they would otherwise take hold. Like when you read all the possible side effects of a drug and you're doomed to get the stomach cramps, the diarrhoea, the skin irritation, the depression even before you start taking the damn things.

I scream inside my head.

If there is a God, please help me! Please tell me what to do.

I am lost.

I am scared.

I am dying.

I must have fallen asleep because I wake up with a jolt, curled in a ball on my sofa, freezing cold, with that horrible groggy feeling that seeps from your head to your stomach to your toes. To be honest, it's how I normally feel when I wake from a snatched weekend nap, but this feeling now terrifies me. I feel ill in a way I never felt before the diagnosis. I *mustn't* do this.

And then it happens.

I cry.

I cry with the abandon of knowing no one is listening and yet I so want to be heard. I want someone to hold me and tell me it's all going to be OK. But I'm alone in this. Suddenly I'm not so comfortable about being single. I feel vulnerable and exposed. But I am also pragmatic. I'm a list maker. Maybe that will help. I wipe my eyes, blow my nose, stop the snuffling and grab paper and pen.

Let's focus on the positives:

NUMBER ONE: I don't have to struggle through the shitty bits any more. And let's be honest here, the world is a pretty shitty place right now. No Bowie, no Leonard Cohen, no Maya Angelou. It's all algorithms, politics, no poetry.

NUMBER TWO: I've had twelve more years than my friend Vanessa. Vanessa was thirty-one when she died, and I've crammed a hell of a lot into those twelve years that she never had.

NUMBER THREE: I won't get Parkinson's like my father. Or Alzheimer's like my mother. I won't get wrinkles, or saggy breasts, or teeth that flop out at the mention of the word apple. And maybe I'll be remembered with the romantic grief bestowed on those taken too soon. It would be nice to think so. I hope I won't be easily forgotten.

NUMBER FOUR: I am not frightened of death. I've witnessed it. I was with my friend Vanessa when she died. It was peaceful. Beautiful, in fact. I was with my father, then two years later my mother. You see, there are the hand holders and the people who stay out of the room – like my sister.

I held their hands.
But who is going to hold mine? WHO?
I have no children. My three miscarriages are the reason my husband Andy is now my ex-husband. Supposedly, my insular sadness after each loss made him feel excluded. I could have included him if he'd asked, but he never did. Instead, he looked elsewhere.

At Elizabeth. Would things have been different if I'd made him mourn with me? I'll never know. Sometimes I wish I could rewind the tape. Never more so than now.

Saturday morning I take myself and my misery into Kentish Town and buy a wall calendar from the Pound Shop, each month illustrated by an English masterpiece. I could have got a Taylor Swift Official, but seeing her all vibrant and full of life seems counterproductive.

Dr Mackenzie's words ring in my ears. '*Three months . . . at best.*' I rip off January to August (an extravagant waste had it not cost 50p) to reveal a Gainsborough landscape, and start a ninety-day countdown, ignoring his miserable *at best* caveat. It's like making an advent calendar without the chocolates. If I'm lucky, I might scrape past Christmas.

But let's not get maudlin. It's not a science, it's a guide. Even an incentive. Something to encourage me to make the best of every day and, who knows, perhaps I can get beyond Day Zero. Maybe I'll see in New Year.

I hang the calendar inside my bedroom wardrobe. Two crosses. Today is the last day in September – a short month, which now feels even shorter. Gainsborough will be gone by tomorrow, and tomorrow is already day eighty-eight. I try to convince myself I am being proactive and that I'm facing my illness head-on, but I know full well it's a form of procrastination.

A distraction from my first hurdle. Telling people. Because no matter how much I try to deny it, once I tell someone, reality will kick in. And right now, denial holds an enormous amount of appeal.

Day 87

Monday morning. I drag myself into the office intending to tell my boss, which procedurally seems the right place to start, but when it comes to it, I simply can't say the words. Frank is the least sympathetic person I know, so hardly the best choice for first disclosure.

'Spit it out, Jennifer,' he says.

'Erm.' I'm literally trying to spit it out. His expression is making me so nervous I want to turn on my heel, come back through his door and start again; find my usual confidence. Instead I'm rooted to the spot, my mouth dry, my tongue having forgotten its purpose. 'I . . . I don't want to worry you . . . but I've been quite tired recently, unusually tired in fact.'

He throws me a classic Frank scowl that says 'We're all tired. Get over it.'

It freezes me. I'm having an out-of-body experience, looking down on my own performance and hearing myself going off-script. 'I . . . I think I'm in need of a holiday, Frank.'

He folds his arms over his chest. 'Well, book it in. You know the procedure – you wrote it.'

'Yeah . . . but . . . no! You're right. I'll book it in. I just thought I ought to warn you.'

I scuttle out of his office feeling sick and hopeless. I had no idea I was such a coward.

I wonder whether to break myself in more gently and tell Pattie, my best workmate. We joined the company on the same day sixteen years ago, which feels like both yesterday and a lifetime ago. Pattie's divorced too, only she has a son at university. We've spent many an evening together, ostensibly to discuss company grievances that, after a bottle of wine or two, would segue into our personal relationship woes. We're definitely work buddies but, like wine, sometimes things spill over.

I pass her office and hover momentarily outside her door, noticing she's on the phone. She catches my look and waves me in, signing 'Tea?' But there's an invisible barrier holding me back and I can't move. Instead, I check my watch somewhat over-emphatically. 'Later,' I mouth.

Back in my office, I pace the floor and decide I'm not a coward as far as Pattie's concerned. It was the right thing not to tell her. She can't bear the weight of my secret alone. It would be too hard for her to keep it to herself (everyone has to share a secret with someone, it's human nature) and if word got out, particularly before I'd told Frank, it would be wrong. For now, while I don't have any obvious signs, I might as well keep the news under wraps. And maybe if I behave normally, I'll believe I'm normal and stave off my symptoms simply by snubbing them.

I sit at my desk, staring at my computer screen, wondering what normal is now. I try to think about what would usually concern me.

'Jennifer?'

I look up, snapped out of my daze. 'Deborah. Sorry! Miles away.'

Standing in my doorway is Deborah Peevor, Ethan from IT's assistant. Been with us for two and a half years. Straight from university. Nottingham. 2:1 in Sociology. Broken engagement, to Paul, childhood sweetheart, but to be honest she was too young anyway. At least my mind is still working, I think, even though I'm embarrassed I can retain this stuff. It runs through my head like the ticker feed on a TV screen. Then again, it's quite an asset if you're in HR.

'Am I interrupting anything?' she asks. 'I mean, I realize we haven't scheduled a meet, but would it be OK if I come in?' The poor girl's face is bright red and her shoulders seem to be hugging her neck. 'It's a personal emergency.'

'Of course,' I say, a touch too brusquely. 'That's what I'm here for.'

She hesitates. 'Are you OK? I mean, if it's the wrong moment . . .'

I realize that it's going to be the wrong moment for the rest of my time here, so I might as well find out what her personal emergency is and hopefully put one of us out of our misery. 'It's fine, Deborah. I was immersed in a document. Tell me all.'

She comes in, sits down in front of me then bursts into tears.

'It's OK. Take your time.' I push my box of tissues towards her. She grabs one and her face dives into it. I want to hug her – I can't bear to see anyone cry – but it wouldn't be appropriate. My job denies you the ability to respond in the way you would if it were a friend. I have to stay in my seat, swallow my feelings and respect company rules, because in my job you can never afford to be compromised.

'I'm so sorry,' she sobs.

'Don't apologize.'

She looks at me with a downturned mouth. 'I want to lodge an official complaint against Ethan. He totally lost it with me. Became abusive.' She shudders.

Seriously? Ethan Webber? Been with us seven years. Three promotions. Quiet type. Geek. Head of Chess Club. Wouldn't have thought he had it in him. 'Can you describe abusive, Deborah?' I'm taking notes. 'Physical?'

'Verbal.'

'Can you tell me what he said?'

She gives an agonized growl. 'He called me something unrepeatable.'

'You need to tell me what he said, Deborah.'

'I can't.'

'Can you spell it?'

She takes a deep breath and her mouth stretches around the letters with distaste. 'C-U—'

'Got it!' I say. Wow! Ethan. What were you thinking?

OK. So when I said I'm in HR your eyes probably glazed over, but truthfully it's quite an interesting job. You get involved in people's lives, you get an insight into their psychology. You see the good and the bad. And you need to be strategic. It's more complex than you'd imagine. Plus, when the situation allows, you get to fight for justice. That's the bit that matters to me most. Justice in a world of unfair.

And now I care about justice for Deborah. I care that her feelings have been hurt because hopefully that's all this amounts to.

'Listen, Deborah. I'm not absolving his insult, but it's so unlike him. Do you have any idea why he might have said that to you?'

She coughs. 'Yes.'

I wait.

She gulps down some tea, coy now. 'I deleted an important file and then I panicked and blamed it on him. I mean . . . it's retrievable, for God's sake. We only need to get one of the specialist techies down. No biggie.'

'I understand, Deborah, I do. It didn't warrant that kind of reaction,' I say sympathetically. Then I explain the various ramifications of lodging an official complaint. It's not something you do blithely – not under any circumstances.

She listens, throws in a few buts, casts me a doleful look and shrugs. 'Yeah. Sorry, Jennifer. I guess I just

19

needed to blow off steam. It was either the ladies' washrooms or you. You won.' She cracks a smile.

'Thanks,' I say.

'So . . . I guess I should let it lie?'

'No! Not at all,' I say. 'We absolutely need to deal with this. Letting it lie is not what I had in mind. No, I'll have a word with Ethan.'

'That's so embarrassing.'

'Trust me, it's going to be a lot less embarrassing than lodging an official complaint. You deserve an apology. I'll deal with it. And maybe, if you feel this is the way forward, I can get the two of you in a room together to talk it out. So that he can make his apology official. To be honest, I'm sure he's already feeling remorseful, but that doesn't mean I shouldn't have words with him.'

She sighs. 'OK, then. If you think that's best . . .'

'I do. Now, why don't you take the rest of the day off? I'll speak to Ethan. Then both of you can sleep on it and we'll get it settled tomorrow. I'm assuming he's never spoken to you like that before?'

'Never.'

'It's going to be fine. Go home.'

'You're right. Thanks.' She presses her hands on her thighs and stands up. 'And I'll be happy to see him tomorrow. I'm sorry I provoked him. I guess I must be tired.'

'Honestly, Deborah, I totally understand.'

'Yeah,' she says, oblivious to the irony. 'And thanks

for talking this through, Jennifer. I know how busy you are. I really appreciate it.'

I watch her leave and think how 'cunt' doesn't sound quite so bad compared to 'rare blood disease'. I wonder whether everyone else's traumas will seem trivial to me now. Still, for a short moment, immersed in Deborah's problems, I've forgotten about my own and it occurs to me I should work for as long as is physically possible. I need to try and forget about me. But it's hard, I think.

'You'll get used to it,' I say out loud.

I recoil. Oh God! I'm talking to myself. I'm going mad. I have to tell someone. There's no way I can keep this to myself any longer. I need to exorcise this darkest possible of secrets.

Poor Olivia. What a thing to do to your closest friend. I'm so sorry.

I text her before giving it any further contemplation, so that there's no turning back.

Had some tricky news. Have you got time to pop round tonight?

I pace. Constantly checking my phone screen. Making sure my phone isn't on silent. Ten minutes feels like ten hours.

Ping!

Sure. How tricky? Should I bring cake?

Yeah ☹

Ohhhh. Got a meeting which should finish at 6.30 then I'll
be straight by. Cheesecake?

To be honest, cake is the last thing I want, but I
reckon Olivia might need it.

Nice

I can't get out of it now.

Back home, I stare at my reflection in my bedroom
mirror as if I'm checking this is really me. The same
person I saw yesterday and the day before and the day
before that stares back. But I am not the same. Everything has changed. The truth is I still don't accept it.
I'm clinging to denial because it's safe. Who can blame
me? But I have to open up to someone, and at the end
of the day, when you're single, that's what a best friend
signs up for: for better or worse, in sickness and in
health.

* * *

Olivia stands in my doorway, breathing sharply, as
though she's run all the way from the office. Her dark
red hair is tied back loosely, betraying her flushed
cheeks. She's dressed in silk khaki trousers with red
trim down the sides accentuating her long slim legs, a

white untucked shirt and open trench coat. Olivia works in fashion, which was always useful because I got to go with her to all the trade sales. So even though I'm stuck wearing office suits, at least they were beautiful ones. Note I'm already using the past tense.

She hands over a ribbon-tied box. 'Cheesecake,' she says. 'What's wrong? You look like shit. No offence.'

'None taken. Do you want a drink?'

'Yeah. Tea. Builder's, please.'

'I mean a real drink.'

'With cheesecake?'

'I'm having one.'

She appraises me with suspicion. 'This is not a cheesecake moment, is it?'

'Not exactly.'

'You're scaring me.'

'Oh, don't worry. It's nothing too awful.' I lie because her anxiety is instantly palpable. I'm not sure if I am properly prepared for this revelation. But then maybe I never will be. 'Whisky?'

'Shit, darling! We don't drink whisky! What's going on, Jennifer? Have you been fired?'

'First the drink,' I say. 'But I haven't been fired.'

We move with our inch of single malt from the kitchen into the sitting room and sit down next to one another.

She's staring at me, bug-eyed. 'Do we chat about the weather or can we dive straight in?'

I feel my cheeks spasm. My lips won't move. I sip the whisky for Dutch courage. What on earth does that mean? Dutch courage? My mind lingers over the definition.

'Jennifer?'

'Sorry. Sorry. Let's dive straight in.' And here I go. Diving from the highest board, my heart fluttering, stomach full of butterflies. I'm in freefall, waiting to feel the smack of water.

'You remember I went to the doctor the other day.'

'Yeah . . .'

'Well, I got the results of my blood tests. I thought he was going to tell me I was iron deficient or something, but turns out I have an unusual blood disorder.'

Olivia draws her chin into her long neck. 'Oh,' she says. 'I'm so sorry.'

'And it's terminal.'

'Don't be ridiculous.'

'I wish I was.'

She stares and waits. I can't think how to react. Is there some kind of etiquette for helping friends through this moment?

'Oh my God, Jen! You *are* serious!' She grips my hand and we stare at each other in a stunned silence, as if someone's hit the pause button. Then someone presses play. 'I'm so sorry, Jennifer. I'm not sure I know what to say.'

'I'm not sure either,' I tell her. I let go of her hand and pick up my drink for want of something less awkward to do.

'You need a second opinion,' she says, straightening her back as though she's preparing for battle. 'We need to find you the best blood specialist in the country. In the world!'

'Honestly, I'd do that, but Dr Mackenzie has looked into it extensively. It's incredibly rare. And if it's any reassurance, my mother called him our "gold dust"; the best diagnostician you could hope for, and you never doubted my mother. Besides, I'm not sure there's time.'

She scowls. 'Of course there is. How long are we talking here? Has that even been discussed?'

'It's months, Liv. Three. At best.'

She clamps her hand to her mouth. 'NO! Seriously. But this is from nowhere.'

'From nowhere. Well . . . I was tired.'

Her forehead furrows and she presses her lips together. 'Jennifer . . . ?'

'Yes?'

'Have you . . . cried?'

I point at my eye bags. 'The whole weekend. I think I'm all cried out. I'm so over crying.'

'Why didn't you call me? Why did you do this on your own?'

I shrug. 'I was frozen in panic. You think you'd do that – you know, reach out to your best friend. Pick up the phone . . . But you don't. At least, I didn't. I couldn't.'

She finally gives way to a body-racking sob. 'I'm so sorry. So, so sorry. Ohhh, Jennifer. What will I do without you? I shouldn't be crying, not with you being so brave and—'

'Liv?' Her name comes out of my mouth in a choked whisper. 'You know I said I was over crying . . .'

She shoots me a damp, question-mark face.

'Well, I lied. Will you hold me, please?'

She gives a tacit nod, shuffles her bottom towards me, opens her arms and draws me in. Finally, I am wrapped in love and I let it all go. We cry together, me into her perfumed neck, her into my stale grief-stricken hair, shaking and shivering as one. 'Life is so unfair,' she says. 'I'm not going to lose you. I'm not going to allow this to happen.'

'And I love you for that, Liv,' I say, staring into her watery gaze. 'But let's face it, there's no such thing as fair or unfair. Death is not discerning. My parents were good people who had horrible drawn-out deaths. At least mine will be quick.'

'Oh Jennifer! That's awful. You mustn't say that! You can't just roll over.'

'No, no. That's not what I mean. It's not a question of rolling over. Trust me, I've thought long and hard about this one. There may be treatment, but judging from what Dr Mackenzie said it's not a cure. It will only delay the inevitable . . . for what? To be sick for longer? To be given a few extra months of feeling lousy? No. That's not going to be my path. I'd rather enjoy what little time I have left.'

'Of course. But—'

'And I don't want to squander it on a hunt for some alternative nonsense that will give me false hope . . . like Andy Kaufman in that film we saw. Don't you remember what we said afterwards? We thought it was so sad.'

'But that was a film. That was some guy we didn't know. This is YOU!'

'Yes! And that's why I need to do what's right for me.' I take a deep breath. 'This is my choice. I've no idea how bad I'm going to be or how quickly it's going to take hold, but for as long as I can, I want to play normal.'

'God, that's so brave. What the heck is normal *now*?'

'Beats me. I guess we'll find out. But while I can manage, I don't want to be covered in morphine patches and pumped full of the drugs Dr Mackenzie's prescribed me either. I'm going to stay positive for as long as possible without chemicals. And you need to help me. No more crying. OK?'

'I'm sorry. I shouldn't have,' she snuffles.

'No, no! I'm glad you did. I'm glad we can cry together. But now we have to agree a deal. Stiff upper lip.'

She shudders. 'OK. It's your call. We do exactly what you want.'

'Thank you. More?' I hold up my empty glass.

'Under the circumstances, yes,' she says. 'Even though it's disgusting.'

'True. But it's numbing. I think that's why it was invented.'

I bring the bottle in from the kitchen and top us up.

'So, what *do* you want to do?' she says, sweeping blindly at the trail of mascara staining her cheeks.

'How do you mean?'

'I mean, how do you want to spend these three

months?' She shakes her head with a judder of her shoulders, slugging some whisky. 'I can't believe I'm even saying that. Shut me up if you don't want to talk about it.'

'Oh no, Liv. I need to get out of my head and talk.'

'OK, but you'll tell me if I'm pushing a boundary, won't you? This is uncharted territory.'

'Sure.'

'So . . . what then?'

'Well, I'm going to work for as long as I can.'

'Seriously? I mean, I get that you want to play normal, but you can't spend the end of your days working. That's like requesting beans on toast for your last supper.'

'I love beans on toast.'

She half laughs. 'Come on. I'm not going to let you get away with this. Isn't there anywhere you've always wanted to go?'

I pause for reflection. 'Cuba, Vietnam,' I say. 'Cambodia, Kyoto, Venice, Argentina. How long have you got? But I don't want to travel. I need to stay close to home. To a hospital. I'd be scared to get on a plane and risk being one of those poor bastards the captain has to make an announcement for: "Is there a doctor on board?"'

She nods. 'Yeah. I think I'd be the same.'

'I should have a plan, though, shouldn't I?'

'Other than work. I think that would be wise.'

'Right.' I nod. 'I should try to do something significant. Worthwhile.' Why haven't I thought about this?

Was I seriously thinking I'd simply carry on working, hoping it would all go away? 'OK. So, I'll give up work. When I'm ready.'

'Have you told them?'

'No. Not yet. You're the first. I tried telling Frank today and then Pattie, but I couldn't. The words got stuck in my throat. Probably just as well. I obviously needed to cry and I couldn't have done that in a professional space.'

'I don't think anyone's going to expect you to be professional now.'

'Well, I want to be. I don't want people's pity. I don't want to become that person they don't know how to talk to any more, who they avoid because they don't know how to behave around me.'

'People might surprise you.'

'I work in HR. Nothing surprises me.'

'So . . . what have you always wanted to do?'

I think for a moment but I'm stumped. I search for a reply. 'I've never had a bucket list. I always thought they were for pessimists.'

She smiles. 'Anything you regret *not* doing, then?'

'Oh definitely. Lots of regrets. I regret not eating more pancakes with maple syrup, and more chicken burritos. I regret saving my nicest clothes for *that special occasion*. As if I was expecting some knight in shining armour to show up and I'd throw on my best designer frock and he'd take me away from all this, even though I like all this. How stupid is that?'

'Not stupid. Very familiar. What else?'

29

'Well . . . I regret not helping Mrs Mumford with her shopping.'

'Who?'

'This woman in my street. She's lived here for ever. She must be well into her eighties now. Occasionally I'll see her shuffling along, struggling with one of those old lady trolleys full of shopping and I'll tell myself I should go out and help her, but I'm always on the phone or about to leave for a meeting and it's never the right time. Only now I realize there is no such thing as the right time. I should have made time. I should have fetched her shopping for her. But I never did.'

Olivia laughs. 'Oh my God, Jennifer! That thought wouldn't even occur to me. That's so considerate, you shouldn't feel bad. You meant well.'

'What good did that do her? And now there's no point in starting what I can't finish. Oh Olivia!' I tut. 'You don't need to hear my moans. Please make me shut up.'

'Absolutely not! You need to talk about this stuff. If anything, I need to hear more.'

I scoff. 'Oh, there's plenty more. I've been looking back and there are so many things I wish I'd handled better.'

'Such as?'

'Well . . . for starters, I wish I'd told Andy what I really thought when he announced he was leaving me that awful Saturday. You know, when he confessed to cheating on me with Elizabeth.'

'I always said you were too nice.'

'But he was crying. It made me feel terrible.'

'That was exactly what he wanted. So that you'd let him off the hook without a fight.'

'You think he was being manipulative?'

'Of course!'

'No,' I say decisively. 'You're wrong. Andy couldn't summon up crocodile tears if he was desperate. He was genuinely remorseful. But I shouldn't have let him go without making him think a bit harder about what he was leaving behind. I should have told him I thought we had a decent marriage worth fighting for and it deserved another chance. That even though I felt hurt and betrayed, I still didn't want to lose him. Instead, I stayed silent and listened.'

'Then you need to tell him this! Now!'

'Don't be silly. It's so long ago. He's been married to Elizabeth longer than he was ever married to me. Only now I guess I'm angry at myself for holding back. I wonder, if I'd told him how I felt at the time, he might have stayed. And then I'd have someone to go through this with.'

'I'm here for you,' she says, looking sombre.

'Yes, you are, Liv.' I squeeze her hand. 'Thank you. But you have Dan. I would have liked to have someone here twenty-four seven. Who knows me so well he doesn't have to ask how I'm feeling. Who can look at me and tell.'

'Was Andy like that?'

'No!' I hoot. 'But he might have been if he'd given our marriage a chance. And then there's Harry. I always felt we would get back together and now there's no hope. I've never stopped wondering about him; whether I could have handled things better. If I was too hasty to judge him.'

'Seriously, Jen! After he behaved so badly?'

'But did he? Maybe I should have believed him when he said he and Melissa were just friends.'

'You saw him on camera with her!'

'With his arm around her. It was hardly intimate.'

'Oh, come on!'

'OK, fine. But was it a deal-breaker? Who's to say we couldn't have got back on track? I know you never liked him, but he was smart and sophisticated and he was good for me. He gave me my confidence back.'

'You mean, before he took it away again.'

I roll my eyes. 'Anyway, I wish I'd given him more of a chance.' I throw my hands in the air. 'Oh, listen to me! I'm hopeless. My life has been one big round of repeat behaviours. I've never learnt a single lesson.'

'That's so not true.'

'It is true. I'm a coward. Never daring to confront people.' I nod my head in disappointment. 'And I think I must be lousy in bed. All men cheat on me.'

'That's because all men are cheats.'

'You think Dan is a cheat?'

'NO!' she says, affronted.

'I rest my case.'

'Anyway,' she rebuffs. 'You're not a coward. Look at how you're dealing with this news. You're brave and fabulous. You're witty and kind. You're the most genuine person I know.'

'Stop it!'

'No. Take it!'

'Thank you . . .' I ponder a moment. 'Admit it, though. I have been a bit of a coward. I've never fought for the things I wanted most.'

She brushes some non-existent creases from her trousers then takes my face in her hands and looks me in the eye.

'And that's why you need to tell those guys all the things you wish you'd said at the time. They need to hear that stuff. For their own sake as well as for yours.'

'Don't be ridiculous,' I say. 'I'm only telling *you* to get it off my chest.'

'Why is it ridiculous? What better catharsis? If you're going to face this illness head-on, you need to finish your unfinished business. You need to be at peace with yourself.'

'Listen to you! You're going all Anna Maria on me.' Anna Maria is the third point of our friendship triangle. The third Musketeer, if you will, only she's quite different from Olivia and me. She's into all things alternative. She wasn't always that way, used to be a bit of a party girl until one day she woke up with a man she didn't recognize, in a bed she didn't recall getting into. Finding herself alive and, subsequently, not pregnant was the moment Anna Maria found her spiritual side.

To be honest, I think we preferred her when she was a party girl. Being the school swots, having a wild friend made Olivia and me feel there was a part of us that must be a bit wild too. It probably worked in reverse for her. But I'm not sure what a friend who's into reiki and chakras and Tibetan singing bowls says about us, which probably explains why we don't see her quite as much. Once in a while is fun; too often and you start wanting to chew your sleeves. But, like family, there are some friends with whom you have an umbilical bond, and Anna Maria is one of them.

'Well, sometimes she has a point.'

'She's taken ayahuasca. She's done rebirthing. Three times. She's mad!'

Olivia laughs. 'I've been telling you that for years. So, who else would you like to take issue with?'

Her face has changed. She's animated. I decide to go along for the ride. I consider mentioning my oldest friend, Emily, who I've known practically since birth. She lived on my street. I saw her all the time. She was like family. But when we moved up to secondary school and I started hanging out with Olivia and Anna Maria, she never quite fitted. She drifted around us a bit, but mostly she and I would see each other outside of school. Then a few years ago, Emily dropped all contact because of something I said. She is the only friend I've ever fallen out with and, right now, drowning in nostalgia, I miss her. But it goes too deep to dredge her up and besides, Olivia was never keen on her. 'The doctor, for a start,' I say.

She looks surprised. 'Seriously?'

'Yeah. He was awful. He gave me this terrible news

then told me off.' I mimic Dr Mackenzie's reprimand. ' "I wish you'd come in sooner." As if it was all my fault that I didn't connect feeling a bit tired with something going horribly wrong with my blood.'

'I can't blame you for wanting to shoot the messenger.'

'And Elizabeth.' I'm on a roll now. 'After all, it wasn't only Andy who had the affair. She was complicit and yet she treated me as if I was the guilty party. She's so uptight and vindictive, she drove a wedge between me and Andy when we were trying hard to be amicable. She needs to be told she's an evil bitch.' I smile. 'Merely saying that feels good.'

'Way to go! You see!' She goes to high-five me then thinks better of it, diverting her palm towards a stray strand of hair which she sweeps behind her ear. 'So . . . Andy, Elizabeth, Harry and the doctor. Anyone else?'

'Isabelle.'

'Your sister?'

'Yeah. She may be my sister, and I love her – most of the time – but she can be pretty hurtful. And for whatever reason, I've always let her get away with it.'

'Well, if we're being confessional here, let's say it never went unnoticed. Even at school, I thought she was mean. Some of the things you've told me over the years, I'm amazed you've never had a falling out.'

I shrug. 'It's always been that way. My parents never said a word against her either. What does it say that I never told her about the miscarriages because I

35

thought she'd make me feel even more of a failure? My sister! She should have been my closest confidante. I had to swear my parents to secrecy. I'm so lucky to have you.' I squeeze her hand. 'So now you know everything about my dark side and I'm drained.'

She puts her arm around my shoulder, allowing my head to rest into her neck. 'Better to get it out into the light though, isn't it?'

I nod. I can even feel a smile. 'Yeah. Thanks.'

'So, how are you going to tell them all this, then?'

I pull back and catch her look. 'Come on, Liv. I told you. I'm not actually going to tell them.'

She frowns, genuinely shocked. '*Why not?*'

'Because it's *crazy.*'

She fixes me with a steely gaze. 'Jennifer. What are you waiting for? Isn't it time for a little bit of crazy?'

Day 80

They say you should write letters to the people who've hurt you as a form of catharsis and then file them away. Or tear them up. They being the gurus. Yeah, you've guessed it. I may not be as extreme as Anna Maria or Andy Kaufman but I've dabbled a bit. Read a few books, been on a couple of those motivational courses. Not the ones where you walk across hot coals – that's not my bag – more the ones where someone screams at you for a few hours and you scream back and promise you're going to change your whole life for ever, until you get home and within one night's sleep your whole life looks exactly the same as it always did – only you're a bit poorer because those things cost a frigging fortune.

Olivia is right. Now is the time to say all the things I should have said to the people who matter. I don't want to die weighed down with regret. I need to find peace. It may well be a crazy idea but I have nothing to lose. Right?

So if writing everything down is a form of catharsis then I've decided to write letters to everyone. Yes!

Old-fashioned letters. Only I'm going to post mine. What's to gain otherwise? Of course, I could always send emails, but emails get skimmed. Letters get read. The handwritten ones, anyway. They're such a rarity nowadays, they feel like something worth consideration. Well, that's what I'm hoping.

In the end, I only wrote three but they each took an eternity. I agonized over every line. Checked to ensure nothing had a double meaning or could be misconstrued. I wanted to be totally understood.

The first was to Andy and Elizabeth. In her last aggressive rant, when she was telling me to get out of their lives, Elizabeth pronounced them 'as one' so I've written to them 'as one'. Total transparency. I don't want there to be any secrets withheld from either of them about either of them. I wrote that I thought since they were the ones who had cheated on me, they could have been kinder. That my reticence at the time didn't mean I didn't care. It hurt. It still does.

I had just suffered my third miscarriage. I was sad and deep in grief but instead of working through it with me, Andy, and finding consolation in each other's arms, you went elsewhere. And Elizabeth, even though you didn't know me then, you knew exactly what you were doing: betraying the sisterhood at a time when I was at my most vulnerable. But the most galling thing you did was to lay the blame on me. I was the one who had been robbed of everything – my babies, my marriage, my confidence and my sense of trust – and you both behaved as though I deserved it. It was as if I'd forgotten to lock my front door, and this somehow entitled you to walk in and take whatever you wanted with impunity. And foolishly, by saying nothing, I became complicit.

Finally I told them I should never have had to spell everything out for them, but since I was dying I felt compelled to – over three heartbroken pages.

The letter to Harry poured out of me alongside the tears. I had to rewrite it a few times simply to ensure it was legible.

My darling Harry,

I am sure you will be shocked to see my handwriting and, just to warn you, it doesn't augur well. But I hope all is well with you.

For my part, I am truly sad to tell you that I have been given three months to live. I'm writing this because I didn't want you to hear the news via the grapevine and felt you deserved better, which is funny, bearing in mind how much you hurt me. Because you did hurt me, Harry. You'll probably say you never realized and you'd be right because I never told you. But you did. And now I'm telling you.

The fact is, I loved you and you betrayed me. I'm sure you will maintain you didn't, the way you protested at the time, but I think this is a moment for candour so I'm opening up my heart to you in the knowledge that it's now or never – literally.

My dearest Harry. I will never forget catching your eye that night in that chichi city bar and wondering if it was me you were looking at. Turns out it was. And you were so comfortable in yourself, strolling over to my gang of women the way you did. You immediately put me at my ease. I've never had anything like that happen to me before or since. It was magical.

I always told you, you were the man who gave me back my confidence, but you should know that when you walked out of my life, that confidence left with you. Betrayal does terrible things to a person, Harry, and what is worse, you knew it was my Achilles heel.

How often did we talk about it? That having been betrayed in my marriage, it was the thing I feared the most. And you were so understanding, so sincere, I felt I could trust you. But I couldn't, could I?

Call it women's intuition, call it what you will, but I knew Melissa was waiting in the wings, no matter how strongly you protested she was only a friend. Whoever believes that? Although I confess there have been times when I wish I had. But in that moment, during that awkward discussion, I didn't want to be the victim again. I needed to be in control – so I was the one who ended it.

Now I wish I hadn't been so proud. I was too hasty. All this time, I still wonder 'what if?' What if I had fought for you? What if I had told you how much you meant to me instead of pretending I no longer cared? What if I had believed you? Because we were good together. And that kind of relationship doesn't come easily. I miss you so much, Harry.

So there you have it. Full disclosure.

Finally, in the spirit of candour, despite everything I'd like to see you again, if you can bear it? One last goodbye.

Jennifer

Writing that letter completely emptied me, so it wasn't until a few days later that I was capable of addressing the one to Isabelle.

How do you tell the sister you love that you are dying? And then pull the pin on that grenade and let loose all the hurtful things she's done to you, which you'd previously left unchallenged? How do you justify bringing up old wounds she's not even aware she's inflicted because you've never been brave enough to tell her about them?

But that was what I did. I told her I loved her and then allowed all the old hurt to explode on to the page. I catalogued each duplicity:

Remember when you stole my boyfriend? And not any boyfriend. Neil! My first love. The one I thought was for ever. And you didn't even apologize. As though there was some medieval law that entitled you to purloin from your younger sister whatever took your fancy. I told you how devastated I was, but you just ridiculed me. It ruined so much. And I'm not going to hold you responsible for my lousy degree but I know I could have done better had I not been so heartbroken.

And on I ploughed. I told her that her actions stung and that her quick tongue hurt, too, and the fact that she was allowed to get away with everything didn't make it OK. Besides, I wrote, I wasn't the only one she treated that way. I'd observed things that were not mine to meddle in but now, under the circumstances, I thought she would benefit from knowing the repercussions. In fact, there were several people who might benefit from her knowing how I felt, even if I didn't.

I changed my mind about writing to the doctor. I don't want to shoot the messenger. I need him. I have an appointment in a couple of weeks – Eunice, the receptionist, tracked me down! – and I want him to behave like a doctor, not an apologetic victim. I guess he was only doing his job.

I've sat looking at these damned envelopes for days (too many crosses on my calendar). But, aware I'm wasting valuable time, I finally summon the courage to let them go and here I am, standing in front of a bright red post box.

If anyone's watching me, they're probably wondering what on earth I'm up to. I put my hand out to let go, then pull back. I stand and ponder. I count them in case I might have dropped one. I check the addresses. I question my motives. Do I really want to post them? Isn't it enough to write them; to observe the wisdom of the gurus and simply file them away?

And then I remind myself. I am dying.

So I get a grip and push the letters into the red slit of mouth.

And finally, with a flourish, I let them go.

It feels scary. My heart skips a beat, wishing I could climb in and retrieve them, but I turn around and walk back home.

I did it! I actually did it. And I feel brave.

Day 79

If the Royal Mail does its job, then my recipients should receive their letters today. Tomorrow latest. I'm nervous and anticipatory.

What was I thinking?

Evidently you don't suddenly become brave and thick-skinned overnight just because you're dying.

At four in the morning, I wake up in a hot sweat, panicking, wishing I could take every sentence back. Horrified by what I've done. But now, with dawn starting to break and the birds starting to sing, it doesn't feel so scary and somewhere deep inside me, I'm actually quite proud.

I wonder how they'll react. Will I ever hear from Isabelle again? Or will she be so offended by my honesty, she'd rather let me die than utter an apology? No. She wouldn't be like that. Offended yes, but silent, never. Will Harry think I'm an irrelevance from his past who should have said all those things at the time? Will Andy still be so intoxicated with Elizabeth's poison he won't feel a single ounce of shame or culpability or remorse? I can't imagine Elizabeth will feel anything other than disdain. But I can take that from her. I'm used to it.

Elizabeth is the needy type who sees all women as a potential threat, who flutters her lashes at men while flashing the evil eye at any woman who comes near. As soon as we started divorce proceedings she came out from the shadows, with the strut of entitlement, hell-bent on not leaving *her new man*'s side. Andy and I would meet to discuss arrangements and there she'd be, all wide-eyed and innocent, steely in her mission to ensure I didn't win him back. As if I was the one who deserved suspicion. It wouldn't have surprised me if she had written the parting speech he gave in the kitchen that dreadful day.

They married as soon as our divorce was absolute. Their vows included the line 'to the exclusion of all others particularly Jennifer'. Of course they didn't, but I wouldn't have put it past her. Anyway, now she knows exactly what I think. She's the only one I don't feel bad about.

I told my boss Frank about my diagnosis yesterday. Emboldened by posting the letters, I finally managed to spit it out. He was very nice about it. Caring, even. I never expected that from him. He said it was important I looked after myself and that everything else was secondary. He said it was my choice when to leave but that I should cut back my hours. Eleven o'clock to three at the most. He hugged me. Frank, the least huggy person in the world, hugged me! I think I welled up but then he got all fidgety and uncomfortable, so I pulled myself together. I told him the only other person I was going to include for the moment was Pattie. He said whatever I wanted would be respected because only I could decide what felt right for me. How nice is that?

I popped into Pattie's office immediately afterwards. 'You got a second?'

It was tough, far more painful than telling Frank. After all, she is my mate. She sat in stunned silence then fell apart. I requested her not to let the rest of the company in on the secret, not even my team. If anyone questioned why my hours had been cut back, she was to say it was because of a phasedown in HR and that I was completely comfortable with it. I told her I didn't want to make people feel bad.

'But we all love you here. People will want to know. They'll want to do whatever they can for you.'

'But there's nothing anyone can do for me and I don't want them to feel any obligation or make them feel awkward.'

'Are you sure? You may need more support than you realize.'

'If that's the case, I promise I'll ask for it, Pattie.'

She nodded sagely. 'You're very brave,' she said.

'If people keep saying that, one day I might believe it.'

'Believe it,' she said.

So from today, I start work at eleven. I no longer need to get up at seven but it's irrelevant. Waking up at six thirty, getting up at seven, is so part of my routine I'm going to wake up early whether I need to or not. This morning I wake up at six and for a moment I feel as though everything is normal, until I remember. Nothing is normal. Nothing will ever be normal again.

I don't want to hang around with these negative thoughts for bedfellows, so I decide to head into work anyway. A show of strength for Frank. What do I gain from delay? I get up only to be overwhelmed by that heavy sense of lethargy which is becoming more and more intense, seeping through my blood into my bones. I realize I have such low drive that even if I start to get ready now, I probably won't get to work until eleven anyway. Frank must have known something I didn't.

I sit on the edge of my bed and muster up my determination. I tell myself I have to get past this. Mind over matter. So I stand up slowly, head to the bathroom and take a long shower. I get dressed in a strange slow motion, putting on whatever's to hand, and make myself some tea.

I look at the clock on the kitchen wall. It's not even seven thirty. This is ridiculous. I need to find a purpose. I should think about putting my affairs in order. I've already made a will. I did that when I got divorced.

I suppose I should write my funeral service to make sure it happens the way I want. As if it matters. As if I'd know! But at least my friends won't have to wonder what to do with me. God, my funeral! MY FUNERAL. I've imagined it several times as a child in a game I used to play with Emily. In fact, she invented it. Should I get in touch with her? Is that what this is telling me? No. It would be too weird. Too much time has elapsed. But my funeral is no longer our silly childhood game. It's for real.

I go to my table and open my laptop. I stare as it fires up, then shut it down. I can't write my funeral service.

Not yet.

I'm not ready.

Maybe tonight.

Maybe tomorrow.

Perhaps I'll go for a walk. Get some fresh air into my lungs and give my blood a much-needed boost. It's a lovely time to be on the heath. It will be pretty deserted and I can catch the changing colours of the leaves and enjoy some solitude in nature. I can't take those things that are freely available for granted any more.

The heath has always been important to me. I grew up in Hampstead Village and the heath is a local treasure full of beauty and nostalgia. As a family, we used to come to the fair held every Easter and eat pink candyfloss, brave the dodgems, lose money on the one-armed bandits and watch my father try to topple coconuts to win a goldfish.

When I turned eight, my father would bring Isabelle and me to the mixed bathing pond, which was so deep and so cold you couldn't do anything but kick your legs and swing your arms for dear life. It would make him laugh as he held up our bellies. 'I'll make men of you yet,' he'd say.

Emily and I snuck our first cigarette hiding behind a massive oak tree, promptly declaring it our last as we coughed and choked. I even got my first kiss near the Vale of Health.

Andy and I would come here for romantic walks. He grew up in Hampstead too. I'd seen him around for ever, but he wasn't my type. He was tall and blond, and all the girls admired him. They thought he was sexy and funny, but I only saw him as arrogant and sarcastic. Then one Saturday we bumped into each other on the tube and had no choice but to make conversation – surprisingly we hit it off. He got off the train before me, at Tottenham Court Road, and asked for my phone number. I admit I was flattered. He phoned the next day. He showed up on time for our first date. He proved reliable and I liked that. Of course, I'd had a few boyfriends after Neil, bohemians and men who were totally unsuitable, so with Andy it was like slipping into comfortable flats after the agony of stiletto heels. He felt safe.

When we got married, I was desperate to stay close to family and Andy had no objection – it was his turf too. Happily, we found a wreck we could afford just up the road in Gospel Oak. Some consider it Hampstead, but don't ever say that to a real Hampstead-ite. To them, it's a million miles away.

Still, it's not as far away as the golf club suburb where my sister moved when she married her shit-hot lawyer of a husband, Martin. If it was inevitable that I would marry the boy next door, it was just as inevitable that

Isabelle would marry money. And that she would move somewhere grand. She was far more attached to status than she ever was to nostalgia.

Now, here I am on Hampstead Heath, facing my destiny, steeping myself in my past, in the only place I've ever truly known. I walk across this vast expanse of parkland, the early morning dew squelching underfoot like the slurps of someone enjoying a good steak. The leaves that cling to the branches of the trees for their final moments are all manner of gold and red and orange under the low sun. It's the most beautiful intense day. I feel as though I'm seeing the world through new eyes; appreciating the true glory of colour before it fades to grey and mulch to make way for spring and new life. I reluctantly acknowledge I won't see spring and a wave of sadness sweeps over me.

I push back the negatives and focus on the beauty and the silence. A tall male silhouette catches my attention, intruding on my solitude. He has an impressive outline, broad and distinct against the rays of sunlight, which throw a godlike glow across the landscape. A dog walker, I hope. But he has no obvious dog. My feminine hackles rise. As he comes closer into view, I feel uncomfortable, thinking I should take another path, but I don't want to be too obvious. We gain uneasy proximity and I can see he has dark curly hair that tousles over the upturned collar of a well-cut black peacoat. A sigh of relief. Surely he's too well groomed to be dangerous? Anyhow, he's deep in thought and unaware of me so I feel instantly bad for being suspicious for no reason. In fact he is rather handsome and I look away, regretting my absence of make-up and my untidy hair.

Laughing to myself at my foolish vanity, I carry on walking, not sure how best to pass him, whether to stare into the middle distance or at the ground – odd the way you suddenly don't know where to put your eyes in a vast open space. Before I've had a chance to decide, he says, 'Morning! Nice hat!'

I touch my head as if I don't remember I'm wearing one – a beret. 'Thanks,' I say, head dipped, hiding a smile.

'Beautiful day!' he continues, and he stops, which makes me stop too.

'Yes,' I say. 'So beautiful. Cold, though.' God, do I sound as though I'm complaining?

'So what brings you here at this hour? Dog some-where?' He glances around, checking the void.

'No dog,' I say, wondering if serial killers look like this. 'You neither, huh?'

'No,' he says. 'I needed to blow off the cobwebs, get some fresh air. Been a difficult morning.' He has the most alluring smile, instantly engaging. 'To be honest, it's nice to talk to someone. I've been so inside my head I'm driving myself crazy.'

'How funny. Same here,' I say. If he is a serial killer, he's a very nice one.

'Thank God you get it,' he says, 'and don't think I'm some kind of lunatic.'

I splutter uncomfortably. 'Oh, I get it,' I say.

'So why are you driving yourself crazy?'

It trips off my tongue, I have no idea why. His voice? His smile? My need to purge? 'Well, if you really want to know, I have seventy-nine days left to live.'

Whaaat? Why do I say that? Forget my precision (thank you, calendar) but why do I tell a stranger? I could have said anything. A work problem. A credit card fraud. Somehow I've come up with a total conversation killer.

He gasps with genuine dismay. 'That's awful!' He stares at me in shock. I look back at him in the same way, biting my lip, wishing I could swallow the damn speech bubble that's blazing over my head.

'Not great,' I say. 'Sorry. Shouldn't have said it. I wasn't looking for sympathy, though.' His face has melted into a compassionate frown. 'It's just . . . very much on my mind.'

'Oh, I can imagine. That's a blindsider, but don't apologize. I'm glad you told me. I'm the one who's sorry.'

The concern in his eyes makes me want to believe him.

We look at one another, not quite sure where this is going. Then something extraordinary happens, as though someone else has taken charge of the situation, and without thinking, I spring forward and kiss him. Literally. Right there! I meet his open face and kiss his surprised mouth.

And you know what? He kisses me back!

Yes!

He does!

And suddenly we are glued together, hugging, kiss-ing, his body curling around mine, warming me against the chill air. The kisses are lingering, tantaliz-ing. His mouth tastes of cigarettes and mint. We relax into each other with an ease normally born of famili-arity. He lifts me up and waltzes me towards the protection of a massive beech tree, throws off my hat, running his hands through my hair. We tumble to the ground, our mouths reluctantly parted as my head floats down to his chest. The amber scent of his soft woollen jumper alludes to the smell of his skin, which is deeply arousing. He reaches under my arms, draw-ing me back to meet his face, rolling me so that I'm on my side, propped against him as he stares into my eyes, stroking my cheek before tilting my mouth to meet his. It reawakens a part of me long forgotten as my skin responds to his touch, his gentle discovery as, in turn, my hands discover him. Our earthen mat-tress, hard and unforgiving, becomes a mound of feathers. Entangled in each other's clothing, scarves and belts, buttons and hooks become complex crea-tures needing unwinding, undoing. Layers are clumsily removed until flesh is pressing against flesh. We laugh between kisses, holding each other's gaze, the high of shock and enchantment outweighing all caution and danger. I have never felt so free.

'You OK?'

'Yes,' I say.

'Can I?'

'Yes.'

There's an awkward moment as he pushes inside me but then his hands intertwine with mine and we gaze at one another, unabashed, smiling, laughing, kissing and fucking as though this is how it always is. How it was always meant to be.

He moves his hands down to cup my buttocks, protecting me from the rub of soil, and the upward tilt of my hips heightens each sensation. I am totally in tune with his body, my mind immersed in the rhythm of each pulsating thrust. My breath quickens, my blood rushes through me, so alive, revived, until my whole body judders and I cry out with abandon, unshackled from a thousand woes. When he comes, he buries his face in my hair and his long cry crescendos against my skin. He kisses my neck, then flops the entire weight of his body on to mine.

We hold each other, our heartbeats, our quickened breathing the only things punctuating a stunned silence before he whispers in my ear, 'Fuck, that was good,' and I say, 'Yes, it was,' only I'm not sure I say it out loud because I'm grinning so broadly. He clasps me to him as if he'll never let me go and I don't want him to but then . . .

'I can no longer breathe,' I say, aware of being crushed where once he felt weightless. He lets out a deep laugh and rolls off.

'OK?' He grins.

'Better than OK.'

'Funny thing, sex, isn't it?' His voice has an incredible soothing burr.

'I've never laughed like that before.'

'Oh dear,' he says. 'Are you normally a lights-out kind of girl?'

'Yeah.' I giggle. 'Probably.'

He grapples for my cast-off beret, which he places over my face. 'Happier now?'

After days and nights of lonely introspection, this intimate stranger makes me smile. He takes off the beret and places a kiss on each eyelid with his soft, full lips. We lie under the heavy autumnal branches, smiling up at the light that shimmies through the leaves.

I reflect on what's happened, amazed to feel this comfortable. It was as if we were entirely private, not a thought to the prospect of passers-by. Passers-by! It would have been so possible. But nothing would have stopped us. Not even the threat of arrest.

I shiver.

'Cold?' he says.

'A little bit exposed, if I'm honest.'

He pulls his coat across me.

Our feather mattress is now restored to a lumpen mass of jumbled clothing and gritty soil, my feather pillow once again his arm. I feel the need to make myself decent and fumble for my knickers. He follows my lead, wriggles into the pants that are cuffing his ankles, pulling up his trousers.

'I think I'm wearing half the heath,' he says.

'I'm wearing the other half,' I laugh, inelegantly flicking away some grit.

He jostles inside his coat pockets, pulls out a squished packet of Marlboro, fishes out a cigarette with his mouth then shakes out a Bic lighter. He makes me cup my hands around his as he flicks the flint, the flame resisting before finally responding, and he lights the cigarette, drawing in deeply, his cheekbones sharp and defined, shaded by morning stubble.

He passes the cigarette to me and I take it as though it's the most normal thing I've ever done, trying hard not to make an idiot of myself, sucking on the filter, determined to keep the damn thing alight.

He scoffs. 'You've never smoked, have you?'

'You can tell?'

'It was a tough call.'

I laugh. 'Sounds stupid now, but I was always terrified it might kill me.' I look at the cigarette, take another drag and, as if to affirm his statement, the smoke hits the back of my throat and I break into a seizing cough.

'Breathe.'

'I'm trying to.'

He turns towards me, his face suddenly serious.

'Are you laughing or crying or choking?' he says.

'I'm not sure,' I splutter, sitting up as the pounding of a pair of joggers resounds in the distance. It silences me.

'Pinch me,' I say. 'Did we really do that?'

He reaches towards me and sweeps a strand of hair away from my forehead, his fingers floating across the curve of my cheek.

'We really did,' he says. 'And it was very beautiful.'

I feel myself blush. 'Yes, it was.'

'And I'm so sorry about your news. Truly I am.'

'Oh, don't be. You've made my day. And every day counts.'

'You shouldn't count them,' he says with a sombre shake of his tousled hair. 'You should live them.' He retrieves the cigarette from my amateur grasp, relights it, inhaling deeply with an air of exotic insolence, then hands it back to me as if to give me a second chance.

'I think I'll pass.'

He raises his eyebrows in a smile and lies back, cigarette clamped between his lips, looking up between the thick branches at the hints of clear blue sky. 'At least you can do all those things now,' he says.

'How do you mean?'

He pauses. 'You know. All the things you thought might kill you.'

Suddenly all I can think of is the letters; the brave, honest, foolhardy words out there, possibly held in the hands of their intended, and I shudder. He draws me back to lie down with him, tucking me into the warm curve of his body.

'For a start, you can become an eighty-a-day smoker,' he laughs, smoke dancing from his mouth. 'I envy you that.' He gazes back at me, the cigarette stuck in natural balance to his lower lip. 'Hmmm. I guess that's more my thing.'

'You should be banned!' I say.

'I should?'

'Yes! Because you make it look attractive. They should only allow people like me to smoke in public. I would be the best warning label ever. "Jesus, how off-putting is she? And she stinks."'

He gives a deep appreciative laugh, as if I'm the funniest person in the world. I don't care if he's faking.

'Do I stink?' he says.

'I like your stink.'

He snorts. 'I should give up.'

'Yeah,' I say, then grimace. 'Oh God, I sound like such an awful prude, don't I?'

He points at the lack of bedroom walls and grins. 'Nah. You're no prude.'

'Oh, I am,' I say. 'You have no idea how brave this is. I've never done anything like this before. Let alone no protection.' The thought suddenly dawns on me, but who needs protection now?

'It's not exactly a habit of mine, either,' he says.

'But you don't strike me as the conventional type. Unlike me. All my life I've stuck to the safe path. You've taken me off it and I needed to do that. To see how it feels.' I turn over on to my stomach, prop myself up on my elbows and gaze across at him. 'And you've made me realize something.'

He props himself up next to me, an elbow nudging against mine.

'I have?'

'Yes . . . Telling you I'm dying has freed me up to live.'

He lets out a mournful sigh and crushes the cigarette stub into the grass. 'You're welcome,' he says.

He asks for my number, but I tell him he doesn't need to be polite.

'I'm not being polite. I'd like to see you again,' he protests, fighting to brush the wet grass and mud flakes off his crumpled trousers.

'What's the point?'

'Come on,' he insists. 'See me again. We can do other things. Art galleries. Cinema. Pub darts. Speed dating as if there's no tomorrow – pun intended. Cram in whatever we can whenever we can! Or, we can just, you know . . .' He gives a cheeky grin, tilts his head to one side, '. . . fuck!'

I laugh, shocked by his easy candour. I like this man. I'm tempted.

'Come on,' he says. 'What are you doing otherwise? Twiddling your thumbs? Counting the days?'

This is agony. I long to have someone to hold and reassure me during the dark lonely hours, but somehow I don't feel that's what he's looking for. Besides, why would he want to get involved with a woman who won't be around much past this season?

'No,' I say. 'Let's leave it here. Why spoil the moment?'

'I was hoping to improve on it. A mattress and clean sheets, for a start. Sounds appealing, no?'

I smile. It is appealing. It couldn't be more so. But I'm doing him a favour; sparing him from something he couldn't possibly want to be a party to. 'It does. But this was special. It's how I'd prefer to remember it.'

He shrugs. 'Your call,' he says, peering at me as though he can see my quandary. 'Sure I can't persuade you?'

I shake my head. 'Certain.' I have never been less certain.

We hug each other like the friends we might have been. 'Don't be too good,' he says. 'You can let yourself off the hook sometimes, you know.'

'I'll try my best.' God, he's perceptive. Damn him . . .

I pick up my beret and walk away, clutching it to my chest, as though the imprint of his hand might stay with me for ever. I feel bereft, which is crazy, because I've known him less than an hour.

Is this what my life is going to be like now?

Full of loss and goodbyes?

I think he's watching me, you know how sometimes you feel it, but I resist the urge to turn round in case I'm wrong. I want to suppose he's holding on to the very last glimpse of me, the way I'm holding on to the final traces of him. Most of all, I want to believe I've imbued him with a lasting impression because that's all I have left to give.

* * *

I check my face in the lift mirror, on my way up to my office, having showered and changed and made sure all the grass and grit is out of my hair. Does it show? Will colleagues look at me and sense something's different? Or am I being ridiculous? After all, if they can't spot that I'm ill, how will they spot that I did something totally out of character? Maybe the smirk on my face is a giveaway. Stupid. Forget it. Yet, I feel there is a change – a new glimmer of defiance about me. Yes, I'm dying. Yes, it's terrible. But I'm not going to let it cower me. I feel good about writing those letters. I *am* going to let myself off the hook.

I turn events around in my head. I had sex with a stranger practically in plain sight. Me! The most law-abiding citizen ever! We could have been arrested, for heaven's sake. We got away with it. We were lucky. And I feel different. No longer in denial. Not angry or scared. Empowered.

Hang on a minute! What am I thinking? I can't go round having sex with strangers simply because I have an incurable illness. And yet . . . it was liberating. I'm glad I acted on impulse because, in the moment, it felt right.

I can't tell anyone. Not Pattie. Not even Olivia. If I share it, it might lose its heady magic. I want to keep it to myself like a piece of buried treasure. I've proven I can be wild and fearless but only I need know.

I hang my coat up on the stand and sit down at my desk, pull my phone out of my bag and check the screen. Nothing. Not a missed call. Not one response from any of them. Not even my sister.

What would Isabelle make of what I'd done? Her

goody-two-shoes, conformist sibling. Would I tell her? Probably not. But I'd quite like to, if only to prove a point.

They say the younger child is meant to be the more dynamic, less insecure one, but I maintain the younger child merely inhabits the space left by the older one, and Isabelle grabbed all the best bits. Extraordinarily pretty, all she had to do was smile and whatever she wanted was hers. Four years my senior, she seemed so sophisticated, so in charge. In our household, Isabelle was not only granted special privileges but any trans-gressions were conveniently overlooked. If Isabelle got a bad school report (frequent), it didn't seem to matter, but if I dared bring one home that was anything less than perfect, there was hell to pay. 'Isabelle has the looks but Jennifer has the brains' was said so regularly it was as though it was intended to bring comfort. It certainly did to my sister, who would go all coy, enjoy-ing the pronouncement, while I would swallow it like a disgusting medicine that was good for me.

Don't get me wrong, my parents weren't divisive tyrants. I'm sure they saw it as heaping appropriate praise on our individual strengths, doing their best to encourage us like all other parents. But they weren't like other parents – not the liberal, Hampstead types anyway. Deeply traditional, clinging to their own wartime upbringing for guidance, they had no truck with the progressive thinking hewn from the swinging sixties. My father was a city solicitor; his name came after the ampersand in the firm's title. My mother became his secretary from the day she left Pitman's College. When they married, she thought she was the luckiest woman in the Home Counties. She deferred to him on everything and my father duly rewarded her with a strict weekly allowance, which she never exceeded. Knowing the challenges of rationing, even when it was long over and those little blue books torn up and thrown away, my mother and father remained most comfortable living frugally. They were only extravagant in their love. They were each other's world and they put each other first.

Then came my sister. Then me. There was a definite pecking order, but for us it was normal. Any mention of favouritism was derided as ridiculous. Our family was run on harmony and respect. Thus they imprinted their disciplined beliefs into our DNA and I, being suggestible, followed their every rule. My sister, on the other hand, did not.

Isabelle was the canny one, always quick to spot an opportunity. Noting my conscientiousness, she decided I would make an excellent slave and I willingly obliged. It was not an entirely altruistic decision because being her slave allowed me to be around her friends as long as I fetched and carried and did their bidding. I was so in awe, I would happily have done whatever was necessary to remain in their company.

'Brush our hair!' they would say, and I would dutifully go round the circle with the Mason Pearson brush, being as gentle or as firm as instructed. 'Go get some biscuits from the kitchen.' 'Bring up the bottle of squash and a jug of water.' 'Bring up some cans of fizzy drink.'

Our mother was complicit in my slavery, preparing the tray, while I would to and fro, up and down our narrow Victorian staircase, juggling their requests, tongue clamped between my teeth, desperate not to fall or to spill anything on to the light beige wool carpet and incur her wrath.

'Now go and get some more!' Isabelle would instruct, and off I'd trot.

I was never allowed to sit amongst them or partake of any of the goodies I laid at their feet. Emily, back then my closest friend both in proximity and heart, would join me in my corner and we'd sit, holding hands, gazing with adoration at the sophistication that was my sister and her friends.

When Isabelle became a teenager, our parents in their even-handed wisdom decided it was time our rooms were redecorated. My mother brought home a book of Laura Ashley wallpapers she'd got on loan, which, judging from the look on her face, was the most exciting book Isabelle had ever seen.

The Laura Ashley tome was placed in front of us as we sat side by side at the old pine kitchen table. To add to the sense of treat, we were given a bag of Maltesers to share and invited to choose the design we most wanted.

'You can have them,' said Isabelle, pushing the Maltesers at me. 'No one will care if you get fat and spotty.' The bag remained untouched but oh so longed for.

Maybe to compensate for this mean-spirited jibe, she grudgingly said I could have first choice, which was so out of character in its generosity, I swiftly settled on a lovely blue and yellow floral before she had a chance to change her mind.

'That's so babyish,' she pronounced. 'You should have this!' She pointed to a burgundy and muddy green irregular stripe, which I didn't particularly care for but since I imagined her taste to be better than mine, I told our mother that was the one I wanted.

Finally, when our rooms were redecorated, mine looked dull and sensible and Isabelle's was bright and exciting . . . with blue and yellow flowers.

'I wanted that one,' I wailed. 'Why did Isabelle get it?'

'I got you precisely the paper you chose,' said Mother innocently.

'Isabelle chose it for me. I wanted the flowers but she said they were babyish.'

'Oh, don't whine, Jennifer!' she said. 'Your room looks perfectly lovely. It reflects your personality. I think Isabelle made the right choice for you. She's got a good eye.'

I wanted to punch that good eye.

'Isabelle . . .' I said tentatively to her reflection in the mirror as she sat at her dressing table, preening. 'Maybe . . . possibly . . . do you think we should swap rooms?'

'Jennifer,' she sniped. 'Maybe . . . possibly . . . you should have been born first!'

So I went and slumped on the floor in my bedroom, staring at my burgundy and muddy green stripes, wondering what they said about my personality.

Emily assured me that my room looked wonderful. 'Stunning. So smart,' she said, although I could see when we peeked into Isabelle's she was totally blown away.

'What are you two idiots staring at?' said Isabelle.

'Your room is so pretty,' Emily told her.

'I know,' she said. 'Now piss off.'

Isabelle's innate skills were soon transferred to the boys who pursued her. She could twist them round her little finger, be as beastly to them as she wanted, and they responded by being adoring. We all worshipped her, no matter what; she had the power to make us run around her and be grateful.

And then came my turn. Neil Abernathy. My first love. For me, Neil was 'the one' and to mess with a popular adage, 'It is a truth universally acknowledged that your first love is always the most significant.'

We met at university. He was in the same halls, his room a bit further down the corridor from mine. I noticed him straight away because of his hair. While most of the male students proudly cultivated Patrick Swayze mullets or ugly gelled quiffs, Neil had long glossy hair, which swung in curtains above his shoulders. I thought he was insanely handsome. Sadly, he never noticed me.

Until, one day, near the end of second term, I was dragged by a friend to a students' union meeting where

Neil was speaking. Afterwards, he came over and chatted to me and I was so flattered, I signed up there and then to be a member of the Labour Party, even though I had never given politics a second thought – it was a subject far too dirty ever to be discussed at home.

After attending several political meetings, I got what I wanted. Neil and I became lovers. Soon, we were a couple. He made me feel glamorous and rebellious, and I knew this was the man I wanted to be with for the rest of my life.

In the Easter break of my final year I brought Neil home, braving my parents' disapproval yet secretly craving it. Naturally, we were not allowed to share my bedroom, so Isabelle happily went to stay with her friend Miranda, and Neil got to stay in her blue and yellow floral boudoir.

'I'm not sleeping here,' he said, flopping back against her mound of plumped-up chintz cushions, kicking off his trainers and patting the bed for me to join him. 'Come the midnight hour, I'll be with you.'

'You have to sleep here,' I told him, sitting half on, half off the edge of the mattress, already uneasy at his suggestion. 'My parents will throw me out if they ever discover you sneaking into my room.'

'I'll be quiet as a mouse.'

'Don't even think about it.'

'Well, if they throw you out, you can come and live with me. You pretty much live with me now anyway.'

'Please don't, Neil. I'll be too uncomfortable to . . . you know, anyway. It would be pointless.'

'Jesus! What's happened to you? Show the adult her childhood bedroom and she becomes the child.'

'It's only a few nights.'

And so Neil behaved too.

I was disappointed that Isabelle wouldn't be around to meet my first official boyfriend. *My lover.* I wanted to show Neil off to her as much as I wanted to show her off to him. As luck would have it, though, curiosity got the better of her and she turned up for dinner on our last evening. I loved watching her stare at him when he talked politics, expounding on Thatcher's deserved downfall and how Major was a moron, as my parents' faces froze over. I knew Isabelle thought he was impressive even though he wasn't her type (she was into dating yuppies with fast cars and fat wallets), but what I really loved was the fact that Neil didn't even give her a second glance. This boosted him in my estimation and my confidence soared.

Turns out, people can be deceptive. Neil did not spend his last night in Isabelle's florals and frills alone. To rub salt in the wound, my parents didn't even notice what was happening on their watch. Didn't question why my sister was at the breakfast table in the morning, all pink and tousled, didn't doubt her explanation that she'd popped round early to say goodbye. Of course, had it been me, you could guarantee they'd have known and I'd have been sent to a nunnery.

On the train journey back to university, I had to endure two hours in a crowded carriage, listening to Neil declare his undying love for Isabelle, watching him simper like a lovelorn idiot, begging my forgiveness, telling me he was not worthy and I deserved better.

But I could see straight through all the fake remorse. He was no different from the rest. He had won the prize sister. He was loving every minute of it.

My last few weeks of that final term were spent back in my own room, in solitary confinement, sobbing over revision, determinedly avoiding my once true love.

That summer back at home, I finally worked up the courage to tell Isabelle how much she'd hurt me. She looked at me and laughed.

'You seriously imagine he would have hung around with someone like you?' she mocked. 'It was only a matter of time. If it hadn't been me, it would have been someone else. Better to keep it in the family, don't you think?'

She at least had the decency to hide the postcards Neil was sending. (My mother, on the other hand, felt it important to tell me about them.) When Isabelle was out, I'd sneak into her room, find them stuffed under a pillow and cry over the words he'd once reserved for me.

To add to my misery, a mediocre degree – when I had been predicted first-class honours – defied all expectations of my genius. My parents' disappointment could not outdo my own. I withdrew to my bedroom, refusing my mother's offers of food and Valium, preferring to beat myself up listening to Mariah and Whitney; all the romantic tunes I used to think were about 'us'.

Naturally, Isabelle went on to discard Neil the way you would a watermelon seed. This did not improve my feelings towards either of them. Neil broke my heart, but you can piece a young heart back together. Isabelle broke my trust, and once you've lost trust it's very hard to recover.

Apart from the loss of my babies, the fragile dishonesty of my relationship with my sister is one of the biggest sadnesses of my life. And yet I have never braved admitting this until now.

My mind floats back into the office and I automatically check my phone as though something might have come through from Isabelle while I was thinking about her. But why would we be telepathic when we're not even on the same wavelength? Come to think of it, I definitely wouldn't tell her I'd had sex on the heath. She probably wouldn't bat an eyelid at the idea, but she'd doubtless find a way to ruin things.

Day 75

Days pass uneventfully and I'm painfully aware of the silence that has met my letters. It's another weekend. What once was a happy relief, a time for friends and relaxation, has become a time of dread. I realize how important a distraction work is, for without it, I am lost. I tend to sleep a lot as a way of hiding from myself, because, left to my own devices, the fear overwhelms me.

I feel lonely and isolated although, to a degree, it's self-imposed. I turned down Olivia's brunch invitation today.

'You need to get out, somewhere other than your office,' she says. 'Dan wants to treat us to a trad English breakfast. Come on, Jen! Sausages, baked beans, fried bread. How can you resist?'

'Aw! No thanks, Liv. Thank Dan, but there's no way I can face the Saturday crowds any more. The noise gets too much.'

'We can go somewhere quiet.'

'Where's quiet these days? Coventry – where no one speaks to you?'

She laughs. 'But I worry about you, all on your own there. What are you doing?'

'This and that,' I say. 'Enjoying the newspapers.'

'Jesus. What's to enjoy nowadays? Oh, come on. Come out with us.'

'I'm fine. Honestly,' I lie.

' "I'm fine" doesn't wash with me,' she says. 'I understand that you don't want to be around noise and people, but if you want company, phone me and I'll be right there.'

That's true friendship for you. Someone who can see through the bullshit.

I spend the evening watching TV, but I'm not actually watching. Half of me is inside my head, wandering around my various thoughts, wondering why I'm of so little importance to anyone other than Olivia, wondering how I'm going to feel tomorrow, wondering when this weakness in my blood will finally beat me. Listen, I'm fully aware that being despondent isn't beneficial, it empowers my sickness, but sometimes I can't help myself. Sometimes you simply can't be brave. I grab a cushion and hug it to my chest, try to focus on the telly. The picture floats. Everything is floating.

There's a noise coming from somewhere. I look around, trying to discern the source of the buzzing, then realize it's my phone. I can't be bothered to get off the sofa. Who calls on a Saturday night? At first, I choose to ignore it then decide I might as well speak to someone, even if it's a robotic person who thinks

I've been involved in a car accident despite the fact I don't drive. How do these people get your number? I heave myself out of my cocoon of cushions and follow the sound, eventually realizing it's coming from the armchair across from me. I must have thrown it down and it slid between the gap. I fish it out. It stops. Typical! I check the screen. My heart lurches. It was not a cold caller. It was Isabelle.

Isabelle! Of all ironies! After days of obsessive checking, I miss her call.

I feel a surge of elation mixed with trepidation. I've been longing to hear from her and yet, when it finally happens, I'm panicked. I sit back down on the sofa and stare at my phone's screen as if it might tell me why she has waited so long to call. Siri! Why has my sister taken so long? Is she angry? Is she sad? Or is she just Isabelle?

Actually, I'm glad I've missed her. I need to be prepared before I speak to her. To be calm. To buy myself some time. If only.

My voicemail dings. She's left a message. She never leaves a message. I listen to my sister's voice. She's crying. The only time I heard her cry was at our mother's funeral. I find myself crying with her.

'Jennifer,' she sobs. 'I've just read your letter. I'm devastated. Martin does the post. He leaves mine for me in a pile to go through but I'm terrible. Always leave it for far too long. It's mostly boring stuff anyway, of no importance. But yours is so important. If Martin had put it on the top of the pile I'd have recognized your handwriting and opened it immediately. But he didn't so I have no idea when you sent it. Oh God, Jen! Call me back. Martin, sometimes I don't believe . . .' She disconnects.

I'm moved. Immediately desperate to speak to her, knowing that she's frightened and concerned. I'm relieved that there is a legitimate explanation behind the delay. I wipe away my tears then take a deep breath and dial her number. She answers straight away.

'I'm so pleased to hear your voice,' she says, then bursts into a torrent of tears. 'I can't believe your news,' she wails. 'I'm so sorry. I told you your lips were blue last time I saw you. I knew something was wrong but not THIS!'

'Please don't cry, Isabelle.'

She chokes back her sobs and stutters, 'How are you? If that's not a stupid question?'

'Strangely fine.' My tone is high-pitched. It doesn't sound like me. I feel as though my heart is breaking for her.

'Oh. I'm so pleased to hear that.' She swallows audibly. Her breathing is fast and shallow. 'Jennifer,' she says. 'Is it . . . is it . . . you know—'

'It's definitely terminal,' I say, trying to help her along.

'Oh, that's so awful,' she sniffs. There's a long beat. 'But . . . is it . . . erm . . . genetic?'

You see, this is why I needed to be prepared before I phoned her. It makes you smile, doesn't it? How some people can be so unashamedly transparent. How their first concern is not for you but for themselves. I'm tempted to frighten her and say, 'Yes, Isabelle. It is genetic! From our mother's side.' But I'm not the mean one.

'No,' I say. 'It's sheer bad luck. You'll be fine.'

'Ooof,' she sighs, all too plainly relieved. 'I'm not thinking about me, you understand. I'm thinking of the girls.'

'Of course you are,' I say. 'I completely understand.' And even though in a way I do, her relief is an aching disappointment, which confirms my worst fear: that she only absorbed the first part of the letter, the part that mattered to her.

'I'm truly sorry, Jennifer. Honestly I am. And I'd really like to see you. We need to talk . . . you know . . . about the other stuff. I'm . . . well, we need to talk.'

I can barely contain my delight. She must have read every word. She's opening herself up to discussion. 'Yes!' I say. 'I'd like that.'

'Oh good,' she says. 'I was afraid you might turn me down. When can you come round? Now? No, of course not. When? We'll have time together on our own but it would be nice for the girls to see you too. I mean, you saw them at the party, but it was only fleeting.' I went to my niece Sophia's tenth birthday party a couple of months ago. It was when Isabelle told me I had blue lips. I should have listened to her.

'You can get out, I assume?' she says. 'Sorry. I should have asked. You're not bedridden, are you?'

'No. Well, not yet.'

'Excellent. I'll organize a cab to bring you over.'

'It's fine. I'll get an Uber.'

'Don't be silly,' she says. 'It will cost a fortune. You need to allow me to look after you. I'll use Martin's account.'

I'd like to believe Isabelle wants to look after me, and maybe she does, but if she genuinely wanted to look after me, she'd come over here, wouldn't she? The truth is she never goes to anyone. You always have to go to her. I'm dying and she still thinks I should go to her.

To be honest, it works for me because even though the last thing I feel like doing is going over to her smart suburban splendour, it's better than her coming here, to the home she once pronounced as 'quite nice' even after Andy and I had finished the refurb. Now returned to a crumbling wreck, I don't want to be made to observe its faults, knowing she will highlight the long crack under my front windowsill, the pockmarked plasterwork, and will no doubt criticize the clunk of the worn-out boiler that never fully heats a room. I'm aware my life is different from her own cosy perfection. I don't need her to tell me.

So yes. I'm going over to Isabelle's next Friday. She's sending a cab and making me supper. It feels like the first positive result.

Day 73

Week two of my new office hours and I'm getting into a rhythm. Fatigue is so constant it has become standard. It's my new normal. But I'm buoyed by having heard from my sister although disappointed not to have heard a peep from Harry or Andy and Elizabeth. I keep reminding myself I mustn't expect anything.

I hang my coat on the stand, check my phone in case one of them has tried me (new habit), then sit at my desk feeling despondent. As I'm turning on my screen, Pattie appears at my open door.

'Knock, knock,' she says, then walks in, shutting the glass door, which instantly concerns me.

'How are you? You OK?' she says.

'Yes. I'm OK.'

'I'm glad. If you honestly mean that.'

'I do. I'm adjusting.'

She sits down in the chair opposite me and leans forward, her elbows on my desk, her hands rubbing at her mouth nervously. 'Listen, I don't want to worry you, but I think people are beginning to suspect.'

'Oh.' My heart sinks. 'Why? Has someone said something?'

'No,' she says. 'It's a gut feeling.'

I lean back. 'Pattie, it's because you know. Knowing makes you suspicious. You're looking for stuff that isn't there. Honestly, I've been at meetings, I've been with people, everyone acts normally around me. No one has spotted the Grim Reaper except you.'

She frowns. 'I'm not so sure.'

My stomach flips. 'You haven't told anyone, have you?'

'No, no! And I wouldn't. Not unless you said.' She sighs and cocks her head. 'Don't you want people to care about you?'

'Of course I do. But I've chosen the ones I want. It's easier that way.'

'Well, then I guess I should feel flattered.' Her teeth snag at her lower lip. 'And obviously I'll keep schtum.' She pauses and I'm waiting for the 'but'.

'But I want you to know I think you're amazing.'

I smile. This was not the *but* I was expecting. 'No, you don't. You think I'm odd.'

'That too. But amazing odd!'

We both laugh and she grins resignedly. 'I'd like to hug you, but I know you'll think I'm being over-emotional.'

'I'd let you, but I might become overemotional, and I'm avoiding that at all costs.'

She blows me a kiss. 'Take that for now then.'

I reach out as if to grab it. 'Thanks.' I blow one back, but she's already turned away, her shoulders hunched, her head down in sorrow. Exactly what I don't want to see. Exactly why I'm hanging on to secrecy.

I turn back to my screen with a heavy heart. The day has barely begun and already I'm depleted.

I still haven't taken any of the tablets Dr Mackenzie prescribed, determined to hold on to my vow for better or worse. And I don't yet need the morphine patches. I'm seeing him at the end of this week although I'm not sure I'll tell him I'm avoiding medication, even if it's not unusual for people given months to live.

Having avoided them at all cost, I'm afraid I've started to read some blogs about dying. There are so many out there once you start looking. Sometimes they're helpful, sometimes you'd rather not know, but reading them makes me feel I'm not alone, which gives me the strength to persevere drug-free while I can, encouraged that a lot of bloggers choose the no-drug route.

For now, while I can still get up, still walk, still make a cup of tea, I'm grateful. Those small things are important. They allow me to get through each day. For the most part, I'm OK, although, given half the chance, negative thoughts will find a way in whether I invite them or not, so I'm glad to keep working and hold them at bay.

They have their moments, though; they break in at night when the spectre of the letters looms largest. I lie there, stomach clenching at the thought of Harry sneering at my words, binning my letter like an unwanted flyer, or Andy and Elizabeth laughing together, in total disbelief that they are in any way guilty. Imagination can play dangerous tricks when you're robbed of sleep, robbed of so much.

Day 71

I've finally read those leaflets. A couple were about coping with terminal illness. Only one dealt with the disease itself. The symptoms are pretty scary. They include acute spikes of fever, bone pain, vomiting, easy bruising, bleeding gums, bleeding nose, rapid heart rate – I'll spare you the worst.

But these are yet to come.

For now, I'm just bone-achingly tired and the placebo of positive thinking is winning.

I phoned and cancelled my appointment with the doctor. It might seem a bit foolhardy on the basis of something quite so unscientific as positive thinking but, to be honest, I can't bear the thought of sitting in that surgery again, smelling that awful clinical smell, knowing what I know. I was perfectly straightforward about it. Told the receptionist – not Eunice this time – that I was doing well. I said that unless Dr Mackenzie had any particular concern, I'd rather leave it until I personally felt the need to see him.

My spirit has definitely been helped by Isabelle's

call. The downside is that hearing back from my sister has raised my expectations. And now, if I'm honest, more than ever, I want to hear from Harry.

I may be reinventing the past for my own self-esteem, but I've always felt Harry and I had some destiny to fulfil. That he still loved me. I've often gnawed at the notion that if only I'd handled things differently, been a bit less hasty, he would still be here today. Or that we would have got back together at some point in the future. The fact that I haven't heard from him yet isn't a great sign, but then again, he travels a lot. I'm not trying to cover for him. Most of Harry's work is abroad. What's more, he was always slow at getting back to me.

'How much time does it take to text "Yes" or "No" or "I'll get back to you"?' I'd say.

'I'm busy!'

'So am I. I still get back to you.'

'I get back to you when I can. I just don't get back to you exactly when you want me to. That doesn't mean I don't love you.'

You see? He would always draw me back in. But seriously though? How busy do you have to be to make typing a few words into your phone too demanding on your time?

So even though the signs aren't great, in my heart of hearts, I'm holding out for an answer from Harry.

As for Andy and Elizabeth, who knows? I've said what I wanted to say and maybe that's sufficient. But the curious part of me is intrigued to find out how my letter was received. I'd love to have seen the expression on Elizabeth's face as she read it.

Olivia is coming over later, once she's been to the gym with Dan. Thank God I never have to see the inside of a gym again. There are some things I have been spared.

She and Dan are great together. She's so relaxed with him. It's the first time I've seen her being totally herself. I'm convinced he's the one, although, to be fair, I thought Richard the advertising copywriter was the one. So did Olivia. She was with him for eight years and I was sure she would marry him. She's such a traditionalist, she's always wanted the fairy tale. Unfortunately, Richard decided he didn't buy the fairy tale, he only wanted to sell it, and that was the end of him. So I'm hoping it's what Dan wants.

Olivia sits opposite me in the armchair. Her feet are tucked underneath her green, pleated skirt.

'You're looking great,' she declares. 'And I'm not saying it to be nice. There's a gleam about you. A twinkle in your eye. I feel something's up.'

'I heard from Isabelle.' I flash my twinkling eyes.

'At last! What did she say?'

'Oh, nothing much. She was sad, of course. Said she knew something was wrong but hadn't realized it was this wrong. I'm going to see her for dinner on Friday. She sounded keen to talk. I mean, properly talk.'

'I'm pleased for you. Dare I ask . . . anyone else?'

'No. Not yet. And maybe not ever.'

'But at least you did it. That was the point, wasn't it?'

'Yes. Keep reminding me of that.' I lean forward. 'Listen! I need your help with something.'

'Sure,' she says. 'What you up to?'

I get up from the sofa and wobble, slightly losing my balance. Olivia's face goes ashen. 'I'm OK, Liv, honestly. That was a normal wobble, nothing to worry about.'

'Of course.'

I turn on my laptop. 'I've been planning my funeral.'

'Ohhh!' She shudders, as if she's tasted something disgusting.

'I'm not being morose, I'm being prepared. You'll thank me for it. I've opened a file stored on my desktop named *For When The Time Comes*. I'll leave a reminder for you and a note of all my passwords in that table drawer. Come here and see what you think.' I sit back down on the sofa and she comes and sits next to me. I click on the icon.

'I'm loving this already,' she says.

'I realize this isn't easy, but I thought if I told you how I'd like things done it would save you worrying about what I *might* have wanted.'

'Right. Sorry for being negative. Bring it on!' She rests her head on my shoulder.

'I've written an order of service detailing all my favourite hymns and readings. In fact, anything I can think of.'

'Right. Church service, then? I thought you didn't believe in God?'

'I don't. But I like his tunes.'

She smiles. 'Me, too,' she says. 'If he's a He.'

'He's not a great listener – he's definitely a He. Now, my favourite flowers are lilies and freesias and, of course, they must be white. And I want you to give the eulogy.' I check her expression.

'I'd be honoured,' she says.

'I've written out a few details that might help.' I show her the bullet points.

'Don't you think I know you well enough?'

'Of course. But there may be some things you weren't aware of. Haven't you ever been at a memorial service and heard things about the dear departed and thought, heck, I never knew that. I wish I'd known them better?'

'Yes. But not my best friend's.' Her bottom lip curls.

'Right!' I point at the screen. 'Number one: Did I ever tell you that when we were quite young, before I knew you, Emily and I found a stray dog? We remembered we'd seen the "lost" poster and trailed around Hampstead for hours, dog in tow on a piece of string, until we found the address. Our parents went crazy wondering where we were, but we were heroes to that family.'

'That's so sweet!'

'Number two: Did you know that when we were on honeymoon in Crete, Andy drove me mad to do a bungee jump with him and I didn't want to let him down, so I did it? Even after he'd chickened out.'

'He chickened out? What a muppet! No! You never told me that.'

I think back to that moment. I'd forgotten about it until recently. It reminded me how much I did for him and that I can be brave. I smile. 'To be fair, at the time I wanted to protect his dignity. Now, I don't care.'

'Oh Jennifer,' she sighs. 'This is making me so sad.'

'Me too. But we need to do it. Try and think of it as a normal conversation and forget the context.'

She takes quick, short sharp breaths. 'OK, OK! Normal. This is entirely normal. Like I'm making a speech at your birthday party.'

'That's good! Let's think of it as a party. Being upbeat and cavalier about this helps. I've got some money in savings to cover the cost. I thought it would be for my central heating or a bit of a refurb, but never mind. It's for a party!'

'Gotta hand it to you, girlfriend. You seem to have thought of everything.'

I *have* thought of pretty much everything. I don't need to share my wild imagination with Olivia, but I've even thought up funeral scenes. I have several variations. In one, Harry is there. Actually, he's always there. But in this one he's crying and sobbing, saying he wished he'd realized how wonderful I was and how he regrets ever letting me go. He says I will be a permanent mark on his conscience. He will never get over me. I like that version. And then there's the one where Andy is crying and sobbing, saying how he'll miss me for the rest of his days, with Elizabeth standing next to him, brittle as a cooked chicken bone, looking away with that tight pussy mouth of hers.

Shame, isn't it? The fact we can't be there on the one occasion we're centre stage and might enjoy the spectacle!

'Now, you're sure you don't mind being in charge of arrangements?'

Olivia swivels towards me. 'You can count on me. I promise. And thank you for being so straightforward. You're inspirational.'

I close the laptop and place it on the floor. 'OK, let's talk about something happy and properly normal. How's Dan?'

'Not that normal, thank you! That would be dull. But he's fine. He sends his love.'

'Do you think you'll marry him, Liv?' She appears flummoxed and uncomfortable, as though I've asked if they have anal sex. 'What's wrong?'

'Nothing,' she says, but she's so transparent.

'He's asked you, hasn't he?'

Her face scrunches up. 'Last weekend.'

'Why didn't you tell me?'

'I was protecting you,' she protests. 'I didn't want you to be upset because it pains me so much, the fact that . . .' She trails off. She doesn't need to elaborate. 'We're going to get married next spring. I'm so, so sorry.'

Bulbous tears scuttle down her cheeks and I grip her hand and tell her I'm so happy for her and she mustn't feel bad. But then I start crying too, even though I am genuinely happy for her.

'What happened to stiff upper lip?' she sobs. 'Are we allowed to cry now?'

'I give us permission!' I say, and so we do. We let it all go.

'I want to help you choose your dress,' I say, through snotty sobbing.

She gawps at me, startled. 'Are you sure you feel up to that?'

'Totally. I need nice things to do other than organizing my funeral.'

I feel Olivia's eyes burning into me. I'm disturbed to recognize the intensity of her stare. I did the same with my parents, at the end, when I would stare at them so hard, it was as though I could imprint their image on to my retina and never let it go. Now my friend's doing it to me.

I shake off her gaze. 'I want to know what you're going to look like when you walk down the aisle. I presume you're going to do the whole church, meringue dress, three-tiered cake thing?'

'Yes,' she says. 'I want to be a huge, mega-stylish meringue.' We force a laugh. 'And of all things, my father says he's been waiting all my life to give me a big wedding. He's never mentioned it before. Said he didn't want to put me under any pressure. I can't believe it's been so important to him. He loves Dan. I think my mother would have loved Dan too.' Olivia's mother died when Olivia was in her early twenties. She was the first mother of our friends to die. Her father has never met anyone else. Never wanted to. How romantic is that? I realize no one will ever feel that way about me. The way my parents felt about one another. The way Isabelle must feel about her husband Martin. It's a shame that being lucky in love is not genetic.

Olivia whispers a sigh then tips me a little nod of her chin. 'Jennifer, I can't think of anything more wonderful than choosing my dress with you. That's a beautiful, generous offer.'

* * *

When Olivia leaves, the pulsating upbeat excitement that came with her news leaves with her. The room tumbles into what I can only describe as a Sunday sadness even though it's Wednesday. Darkness is descending early and winter is approaching far too quickly. It will soon be time to turn back the clocks.

I can't go to bed so I lie down in front of the television. My eyes watch the screen while my head meanders, thinking about Olivia's wedding, thinking about the fact that of her oldest friends, only Anna Maria will be there because I'll be dead (that's a weird thing to hear myself say, even in thought) and Emily drifted away ages ago and they were never that close.

I wonder about Emily. Is she happy now? But then again, why would she be? She was never programmed for happiness.

Emily married her childhood sweetheart Michael about the same time I married Andy. We would see each other as couples fairly regularly. She seemed happy then. She would even do girls' nights out with Olivia,

Anna Maria and me until, for no apparent reason, she became obsessed with being ill. Emily had always been curious about illness and death as a child, but this was different. She started to conjure up a regular pot-pourri of afflictions, until she was ill more often than she was healthy. She would consistently cancel arrangements or simply be a no-show, which did not enhance her credibility or make it easy to feel sympathetic towards her. Olivia and Anna Maria despaired of her fairly quickly but having known her the longest, I felt a responsibility to accommodate her hypochondria so I played along, being nothing but supportive. I imagined it was a phase and would pass. But it didn't. The excuses became increasingly regular and more extreme, until one day I decided that colluding in her fantasy was ridiculous and the kindest thing I could do was to tell her to snap out of it. In as diplomatic a way as possible, I told her enough was enough. Years of manifesting illnesses was ruining her life and her friendships. She was becoming a recluse in her thirties – how much fun could that be? She should get help.

I never heard from her again. I tried to call her but to no avail. I even went round to see her a couple of times, but the door remained firmly closed. The brutality of her silence shocked and hurt me.

Now, knowing I'm dying, I've had a strange yearning to reconnect with my past, and Emily has been at the forefront of my mind. Never more so than when I was planning my funeral. After all, it was Emily who invented the funeral game.

She called it 'Deathopoly'. It seemed a normal game at the time, no less normal than Doctors and Nurses, but looking back now, how weird for children to be discussing such matters as dying and funerals. Still, how untroubled we were.

The first time I played Deathopoly was at holiday camp, a place that would make Emily homesick and morose. We were sent off every summer from the time we were both eight, together with Isabelle and John, Emily's older brother.

Our mothers requested Emily and I share a dormitory and my mother would tell me I should look after her because she was 'a child of a nervous disposition'. I always thought that meant she shook a lot, which I'd never noticed. Nevertheless, I took my role seriously.

Emily and I would share a bunk and I would always take the top because Emily said she was scared of heights. One night on our first ever camp, when I was sound asleep, I was suddenly aware of gentle breathing against my cheek.

'I can't sleep. Can you?' Emily's face is right up close to mine.

'I was asleep,' I yawn. 'But it doesn't matter. Climb in.' I roll over and make room for her and she curls up next to me.

'Can we play this game I've invented?'

'If you want to.' I'm so tired all I want to do is sleep but never mind, I have been given the responsibility of looking after her.

'It's called "Deathopoly".'

'That sounds awful.'

'No. It's fun. I play it with John some nights at home when I can't sleep.' She yawns. 'Move your fringe, Jen. I need to see your eyes.' The dormitory is pitch-black and we can barely make each other out barring the sheen of our whites.

'So . . .' she whispers. 'You have to tell me how you would like to die.'

'I don't want to die!'

'Not now!' she says, as if I'm being ridiculous. 'In the future. Like, when you're a hundred.'

'I've never thought about it.'

'Then think about it.'

I think hard and recall something I'd heard my mother say about Victor Beasley from up the road who died in his sleep very suddenly. I whisper, 'My mother says that a heart attack is the best way, although she says it's the worst thing for the people left behind. I'd feel bad about it, but I think I'd want to die of a heart attack. Preferably at a hundred and three. Because three is my lucky number.' I'm quite proud of this.

'I see.'

'And you? How do you want to die?'

Her eyelids flutter. She holds my face with her gentle hands. 'I'm going to have returned from a holiday in Africa and I'll have been bitten by a mosquito. I'll be terribly ill but no one will realize that I have malaria. By the time it's been diagnosed at the Hospital for Tropical Diseases, I'll be dead.'

'Wow! That's amazing. You've really thought this through. How on earth did you come up with that?'

'It happened to a friend of my mother's. Everyone talked about it for months.'

'You never told me.'

'I don't tell you everything.' She sighs, then jiggles my shoulder. 'Don't be upset. I tell you most things.'

'OK. Thanks.'

She continues. 'What hymns do you want played?'

'Erm.' I deliberate. She's taken this to another level. I have no idea, but I feel I should think of something purely to keep up. ' "Immortal, Invisible"?' I say, for want of inspiration. 'You?'

' "Amazing Grace". And I want John to play the guitar and his friend Michael to sing.'

'That sounds nice. And Michael is so handsome.'

'He is. And he has a lovely voice.'

'You're good at this, Em.'

'Now tell me what you would say in my eulogy,' she says. 'I want you to give my eulogy.'

'And I want you to give mine.'

'That won't happen,' she sighs with conviction. 'Because I'm going to die first.'

Emily liked to hear her eulogy because hearing nice things said about her made her cry and then she'd fall asleep.

As I told her all the lovely things I would say, she'd sniffle woefully into my pillow until the tears merged into the gentle sound of her steady breathing with the occasional rattle of a latent sob.

Once I knew she was settled, I would climb down to her bunk and lie there, wide awake, staring up at my mattress, thinking about Emily and how clever she was.

She got one thing wrong, though, didn't she? I'm the one who will die first.

Day 70

The following morning, I get a text from Olivia.

> Been thinking about your funeral. It's going to be beautiful.

I text back:

> Been thinking about your wedding. You're going to be beautiful. You win! ;)

I'm lingering in bed, finding it more and more difficult to garner the energy to get up and go to work. I apologized to Frank the other day for being tardy and he looked at me as if I was mad. 'Everything is up to you,' he says. 'Only you can decide what you're capable of. Take it easy!' Frank is a legend. I've discussed him with Pattie and she feels he's completely changed. Well, something good has come out of my predicament, then.

I hear the postman wrestling with my letterbox and know it's time to get up. I push myself out of bed and stagger to draw back the curtains. It's another grey miserable day. I labour one step at a time down the stairs and, body aching, bend to pick up my post, putting it on the side for my return from work.

And then I spot it peeking out. It's quite a shock. Handwriting. I pull it out from the pile. I recognize it instantly. It's my ex-husband Andy's. I'm rocked sideways, crippled with nerves. I'm holding the letter and I'm shaking.

I can't go to work yet. I make myself a mug of ginger tea, pour in a small shot of whisky, staring at the envelope, wondering about its contents, both nervous and elated. I sit down on the sofa, heart in mouth, blow on the tea, take a sip, sit back then slowly slip my finger under the flap and inch it open. I pull out the contents. There are two sheets (two!) of smart vellum paper, his swanky address embossed at the top of the first. He has proper continuation sheets. All Elizabeth's influence, no doubt.

I give both sheets a hasty scan. Then, knowing it's OK to proceed, I start to read:

My darling Jennifer

I cannot begin to tell you how devastated I was to receive your letter. I've sat here, day after day, wondering how to respond. I think that writing has to be the best solution even though my first instinct was to pick up the phone, but I didn't want to say the wrong thing which is why I've taken so long. So here goes.

Firstly, I'm so sorry. What a terrible shock. I can't imagine how you must feel or what torment you're going through. Awful. I hope you have someone to care for you.

About the end of our marriage, I think I can afford to be more candid now. You see, I was young and foolish and we were six years into marriage and as I told you, your sadness about the loss of our babies made me feel isolated and misunderstood. The thing is, I couldn't understand the depth of your misery. For me, it wasn't the end of the world, but for you it was, and so I felt you and I could no longer connect. I felt you were shutting me out. Which you were. We no longer had sex. A man needs sex and I felt really lonely. So, I guess I started to look around and see what else was out there. Someone who would understand my loneliness. I don't think I'd be the first guy to do that and I don't think I'll be the last, but I suppose that doesn't make it any better, does it? It's just you seemed to want to be left alone, in your own world, so I obliged. Sorry for being a prick about it.

I can honestly tell you I never intended to leave you. Is there any comfort in knowing that so many years on? Maybe not. But I didn't. All I wanted was to fool around – good word that, eh? Fool. And I never realized that was how you felt about my leaving. I thought you were relieved to see the back of me.

If it's any consolation, I feel trapped. Perhaps you'll think that's what I deserve? To be in a loveless

97

marriage with the woman with whom I cheated on you.

Jennifer, I wish I could rewind the tape but what's done is done. I'm so sorry. Nothing I can say will make you feel better but be assured I still care. Your letter brought that home to me.

By the way, I didn't know Elizabeth had called you and said we never wanted to speak to you again. It wasn't true. I would always have spoken to you. You were once my best friend.

I'll be in touch soon. It's just not easy. OK?

Please know that I did love you and always will.

Send in the clowns, baby!

Your sad fool, Andy

Send in the clowns. I sit and stare at those words. He remembers I love that song! In his own special clumsy way, I think Andy is full of regret too.

His letter has made me mourn my marriage all over again. Could it have been different? If I hadn't been so desperate for a child, would he have stayed? If I'd gone full term, would a baby have changed anything? Or is it true that I drove him away with my gloom, dragging him down with each gut-wrenching loss, making him feel worthless too?

How do you deal with trauma in a marriage so that it doesn't destroy you? I know that communication is all, but when you're deep in grief, or irrational with pain, how do you find the words? I couldn't. So I guess he's right. I did insulate myself. I needed to. And yes, we stopped having sex, but he went about it in such a clumsy way. If I'm honest, he started to repulse me. But I could have come back from that, I'm sure of it. If he'd only given it a chance.

Andy's letter makes it obvious to me that he hasn't told Elizabeth he's replied. I bet she would have told him not to. It would be typical of her. Selfish to the end. I'm glad I've heard from him though. And that he still cares. I ponder over that line. *I'll be in touch soon. It's just not easy.* Is his marriage over? I do hope not. No matter how much I dislike the woman, I wouldn't wish her that untold grief.

As I'm sitting mulling the possibilities, my mobile rings. I glance at the screen then do a double take. It's Harry. I mean, seriously! IT'S HARRY!

*   *   *

I truly believe that no matter how old you are, whether twenty-three or forty-three or eighty-three, when it comes to affairs of the heart, you are instantly a teenager.

'Hello?' I say, casually, as if I have no idea who it is. As though I haven't kept his number in my phone.

'Sally?' he says. Don't panic. He means me. Harry calls me Sally after my favourite movie. It's not that either of us resembles Billy Crystal or Meg Ryan, it was just something that started after I insisted he watch the film with me one New Year's Eve. Then the following one. It nearly became a tradition, except two years was all we could manage.

'Harry?' (sound surprised).

'Oh darling. I'm so pleased to hear your voice. What the hell has happened to you?'

'Oh God, Harry,' is all I can muster. I am already putty. That's what he does to me. He gets under my skin and I want to cry with gratitude that he's called. I sit up straight and pull myself together. I mustn't allow myself any expectations. Calling me Sally could simply be old habit. Although he might easily have called me one of his go-to favourites: darling or sweetheart or honey. He once confessed to using these variations because he knew so many women he couldn't possibly recall all their names. I used to be flattered he remembered Sally. As though it was a genuine sign of affection.

'I'd have called sooner, but I've been away. I've only just got your letter. Fuck, sweetheart! I wasn't expecting that.'

'Yeah. Sorry for that little number.'

'*I'm* sorry. Three months! That's awful.'

'Well, less now.'

'How are you, if that's not too ridiculous a question?'

'On and off. Today is on.'

'Good for you. I'm not sure if this will be any consolation, but when my aunt had some form of cancer, can't remember which . . . blanked it . . . she was great . . . literally until the last moment. If you didn't already know, you would never have known. Died peacefully in her husband's arms.'

'Thanks,' I say. 'That's strangely encouraging. Anyway, let's move on. Tell me about you. Are you well?'

'Yeah, great. Same old same old: work work work.'

Tell me about Melissa, I think, but then he says, 'Listen! Let's cut to the chase. I'm so sorry I hurt you and, if we're being totally candid, I have regrets too.'

'You do?'

'Of course.'

There's a second's silence and I panic he's said what he had to say and that's it.

Say it! Say it! I tell myself. *Before you chicken out.*

'Do you want to meet, then?' I bluster. 'To talk things through. Get the regrets off our chest. I for one will find it helpful.' I did it. I did it.

'I'd like that,' he says.

'You would? Thank you, Harry. That means a lot.'

'I'm going away again in the next couple of days and I have loads of prep.' My heart sinks. He's chickening out. 'I might sound as though I'm putting you off, but I'm not. I just . . . any chance we can meet tomorrow? Is that ridiculously soon?'

'Not with my timetable,' I say.

'So is that OK?'

And then I remember.

How does that happen? I mean, why? I'm meant to be going to Isabelle's tomorrow. Damn! People are like buses. There's nothing and suddenly they all come along at once. How the hell do I handle this?

I think on my feet. I'm sure Isabelle will understand. Actually, she won't, but you know what? I'll take the hit. This is important to me and you can be certain, if the boot was on the other foot, she'd blow me out.

'Tomorrow is perfect.'

'Great,' he says. 'Can you get out?'

'I need to. I'm sick of these four walls.'

'OK then. Let's free you of those four walls. Meet at the Shard, like old times? Seven thirty?'

'Sounds perfect. The Shard. Like old times.'

I put down the phone and practically dance around the room. Harry makes me feel amazing! If it weren't so essential to feel amazing whenever possible, I'd almost hate myself for allowing him to have this effect on me.

But it won't last. I have to call my sister. With every silver lining, there's always a damn cloud.

I dance a little longer, though. While I still can.

* * *

Isabelle sounds pissed off. 'But I've ordered in already. There's this great new deli on the High Street, does amazing meals. I know that sounds ridiculous. After all, I have a million cookbooks. But it's like a local Ottolenghi. Honestly, Jen, this area has changed so much. Can you believe our house has tripled in value? *Even* with Brexit. Crazy, huh? Anyhow, the deli opened three months ago. Bert's. Super hip and incredibly popular. You have to order in advance. I wish they'd deliver but they don't. Too posh to push a bike, we all say.' She laughs. 'And Bert has to like you. He always insists I pick up the order, not Martin.'

'He probably fancies you, then.' Flattery gets you everywhere with Isabelle.

'Don't be silly,' she giggles. 'He's gay!' But I can tell she's glad I said it so she doesn't have to. Her giggle segues into an irritated groan. 'Damn. He won't be happy I have to cancel.'

'I'm sorry, Isabelle, but I'm not feeling that great.' My fingers are firmly crossed behind my back. I know, I know. It's not very admirable but Isabelle will have no sympathy for the truth because her being put out overrides everything.

'I'm sorry to hear that. I realize I'm being selfish. I keep forgetting what's happening to you. I can't bear to remember.'

'Don't worry. I prefer to forget too. And I'm only postponing. Not cancelling. You understand that, don't you?'

'Oh, *I* understand,' she says. 'I only hope *Bert* does.'

I laugh, then she laughs. I'm relieved she can acknowledge the absurdity.

We refix for next Wednesday, but from now on there's an accepted caveat that I may need to cancel. It's a caveat I should affix to all my future arrangements. She calls to tell me that Bert has agreed to put the order back. Her voice is completely different. She sounds happy in her acquittal from being blackballed. 'We're going to have a beautiful chicken tagine with sumac and coconut couscous,' she sings.

'Sounds great.'

'And because I won't need to cook, I'll have more time for you. And I need all the time I can get.'

This is not the Isabelle I expected at all.

* * *

My sister's concern, Andy's letter and Harry's call have changed everything. I feel so much stronger mentally, so despite it getting tougher physically, I no longer feel as obliging when it comes to accepting my death. For all my initial determination to avoid quackery, I'm now wondering if one of Anna Maria's alternative therapies might help. With so much to live for, I'd like a little bit longer, please. I know, I know. I'm a hypocrite. I'm bargaining without much leverage because I've never paid attention to a *god* or to the *universe* but I'm hoping for some unconditional generosity and that one of them might spare me some extra time.

I leave a message on Anna Maria's voicemail apologizing for not having been in touch. She calls back immediately.

'Where have you been? I haven't heard from you since that day we had brunch. I've left you at least fifteen messages.'

'Have you?' I say. 'That's odd. I didn't get any of them.'

'You are so not tuned in,' she says. 'They were psychic ones.' She laughs. 'Oh dude!' she says. 'I'm kidding. I'm just pleased to hear your voice.'

'I need your help, Anna Maria.'

She drops her jovial tone. 'I'm here. What's the problem? Oh shit,' she says. 'I should have asked. Weren't you having a blood test?'

'Yes, but don't worry,' I cover. 'It was fine.' I find the truth impossible to launch into over the phone. I'd rather wait to tell her face-to-face, assuming I get to see her. 'But I'm feeling some negative energy!' I continue, amazed to hear myself speak her jargon.

'You are?' She sounds strangely thrilled; clearly she can't believe I'm talking like this either. 'What kind of negative energy? Bad spirits? What colour are they? Are you seeing them?'

'No,' I say, aware that her jargon remains foreign gobbledegook. 'I sense a dark cloud hanging over me. And I want to do something about it. It's making me horribly tired.' I'm quite pleased with that. There's a truth in it.

'Are you drinking lots of water?' she says. 'It's very important you stay hydrated. Drink lots. More than feels comfortable. That's the first thing.'

'OK,' I say. As it happens, I have been drinking lots of water. I feel thirsty all the time. I have this salty, metallic taste in my mouth that won't go away.

'Now I can send you reiki, but I think under the circs it's better we go to see someone.' Her voice is sounding more and more in charge. She sounds triumphant; after all, she's been proselytizing for years and thinks she's finally made a convert. 'There's a woman I know, an amazing reiki master, called Rita.

Does aura cleansing too. Totally picks up on what's floating around you. I haven't seen her in a while, but she's the best. I trust her. Some of them can't be trusted, you know. So many quacks out there.'

'Really? I'm surprised.' I must ditch the scepticism.

Anna Maria passes over it. 'But Rita's for real. When do you want to see her? I'll try and get her to squeeze you in. She's so in demand.'

I'm wondering what I'm squeezing myself into. 'I'm free next week,' I say. 'Except for Wednesday night, when I'm seeing my sister.'

'Well, the sooner the better. How about this Saturday, babe?'

'I can't do that either.' Olivia and I are going shopping for her wedding dress. Nothing takes precedence.

'Sunday then?'

'Yeah. Sunday's fine. If she does Sundays.'

'Dude! Energy never sleeps. She's twenty-four seven. She'll probably be booked up, she's so popular, but it's worth a shot. Charges forty of your earth pounds. You OK with that?'

'Sure. If it works.'

'Of course it works. You only have to believe. Right! I'll check if she's free and buzz you back.'

Ten minutes later she calls back. I'm already starting to believe.

Anna Maria says the universe is smiling on us. The reiki master has two free appointments from noon on

Sunday, despite being soooo popular, so Anna Maria's going to have a session too.

Rita lives in Neasden. Anna Maria is picking me up. I think she wants to make sure I don't change my mind. She has no idea how much hope rests on this. Changing my mind is not an option.

Day 69

I'm trying to stay calm. It's not working. I exit the lift, quickly checking my face in my pocket mirror, then walk, stomach aflutter, down to the Aqua Shard bar, peering through the open-tread stairwell exactly as I always did. Harry is already there, sitting by the window. There's a drink on the table, no doubt his usual vodka tonic. He's looking at his phone, his expression lit by the glow of the screen, silvered in the inky darkness of the room, his thick dark fringe flopping forward. He's in his casual garb. Round-necked black cashmere sweater, the hint of a long-sleeved white T-shirt at the collar, skinny black jeans. A surge of excitement rushes through me.

Deep breaths.

Deep breaths.

I walk towards him and he glances up as if sensing me, throws his phone down and leaps to his feet. He tilts his head, tentative, checking me, then, as if he's given himself permission to be upbeat, proffers a huge relieved grin.

'You look beautiful,' he says. 'I've been so worried.'
He draws me into his chest and gives me a hug. I smell
the familiarity of him and am reminded of everything
I've missed.

'Were you expecting me to be hunched and shriv-
elled?'

'I don't know what I was expecting. I'm just so glad
to see you. And you look defiantly gorgeous. How do
you do that?'

'Death becomes me,' I say. 'And trowelled-on
make-up and this dimmed lighting.'

He smiles. 'Good old Sally. Still able to make a joke
in a crisis.'

Is that what I do?

We sit down on the chenille velvet chairs looking
out over London, which sparkles like a million twinkling lights at our feet, as though responding to the
beat of the music that pulses through the bar. My
own pulse is in overdrive. Tower Bridge, beautiful in
daylight, is even more elegant by night, Tower 42 with
its green illuminated rooftop glows as brightly as a
polished emerald cube. I love this view. I love London.
More than I ever realized.

I turn to catch Harry studying me. He throws his
head back, laughing, managing to brush away what
for anyone else might have been an awkward gaffe.
'I'm sorry but I just . . . Maybe I'll stop there. *I just.*
End of sentence.' He nods, as though he's not quite
sure what's happening, as though this is a bit of a
dream for him too.

'That sentence works for me,' I say. 'Short perhaps, but I get it.'

'You always did, didn't you?'

There's this strange feeling bouncing between us, that this is so normal and yet so fragile. It's as if we both want to acknowledge how sad this is but we're afraid to say it out loud, in case we risk breaking the spell. For a brief moment we gaze at each other in silence.

'Can we not be sad?' I say. 'I'm not very good at it.'

'No,' he says. 'I guess I know that now. Can I just say it once then? That I'm really, really sad.'

'Ha! OK. Just the once. And in case you were wondering, I am too.'

He hands me the drinks menu. 'Sorry,' he says. 'Started without you. You ready for one? I'm ready for a top-up.'

'I'll have my usual cocktail,' I reply, not caring. I'm not into alcohol these days, but I guess it would be odd to come to a cocktail bar and not drink. Alcohol tastes like poison but I don't need to tell him that.

He nods, and I realize I've said it as though he should instantly know my usual.

'You remember?'

'Hello! How many times did we used to come here? You never once drank anything different.'

'And neither did you. I bet that's a vodka tonic.'

'Reassuring, isn't it?' he says. 'To know some things don't change.' He signs at a waiter.

Harry orders my Royal Julep and another vodka tonic. 'Oh, and a bottle of still water,' he adds, throwing me a look as if to say he remembers I'm a lightweight too. As though assuring me he remembers *everything*.

I can feel the muscles in my face tugging and know I must be one big eager grin. I can't help myself. Fortunately, his face is the same. Awestruck, open. His wide-set eyes, glossy and bright. And yet he looks different. There was a time, not so long ago, when I wouldn't have said anything out of politeness, I would have sat and wondered in silence. But my axis has shifted. There's no time to sit and wonder so I come out with it.

'You look great, Harry,' I say. 'But there's something different about you. What is it?' The directness feels liberating.

'There is?' He checks his face with the tips of his fingers, pressing his flesh. 'In what way?'

'I don't know. Something. Please don't say you've had Botox?'

'Do I strike you as the kind of guy who would have Botox?'

Yes! 'No,' I say. I'm not that brave. Then it occurs to me: 'What have you done to your teeth?'

'Ohhhh! My teeth.' He runs his tongue across his gleaming upper set, as if he's suddenly remembered they're there. 'I've got veneers.'

'Nice!'

'Thanks.'

'Why, though? I didn't think you were that kind of guy either.'

He shrugs his shoulders. 'Melissa thought I should.'

'Really?' I say, hackles instantly rising at the mention of her name. She's obviously still very much around. I'm annoyed by my reaction. What was I hoping for? Some happy reunion? 'I never realized your teeth bothered you.'

He notices the change of tone and leans back awkwardly in his chair, arm slung over the side.

'They didn't. They bothered her.'

'So if I'd asked you to fix your teeth, would you have done it?' Down, green dragon, down!

'Why? Did they bother you?'

'No. In fact, I liked them. That little crooked incisor had its own personality.'

He laughs. 'And that's why I'm here with you now.'

'Well, that . . . And the fact I'm dying.'

I can feel him struggling. I've had a few more weeks' practice at this.

'I'm so sorry, darling.'

'Let's change the subject. I didn't mean to bring it up . . . So where were you? On your trip.'

'Munich,' he says. 'Next stop Milan.'

'I love your life.'

'You're really making me feel bad now.'

'I don't mean to. I enjoy hearing about nice things.'

'It's all work though. Not that nice.'

'And how is Melissa?'

He all but jumps. I can't help myself. I have to know and I might as well ask while he's feeling bad.

He sweeps back his hair. 'I hear she's OK. We're not together any more. I thought you knew.'

My turn to jump. 'No. I didn't. I'm so sorry, Harry.'

'No you're not.'

'You're right. I'm not.' We both laugh, sharing a curious smile. How does this news feel? What does it mean?

'So what happened?'

'Nothing epic,' he says. 'It simply fizzled out.' He exhales deeply. 'Can we leave it at that?'

'Sure. It must still hurt.'

He throws me a bothered look. 'No. But I don't want to upset you with talk of her. I realize I've said too much already. Let's just say it wasn't my finest hour.'

'Oh?' I say. 'And I thought you reserved that one for me.'

He rotates his jaw and shifts uncomfortably as he remembers.

But I wonder if he remembers every word, every gesture, every nuance. The way I do. My mind wanders and I'm pulled back into the depths of that memory.

'I saw you on the local news today,' I say, not even allowing him to take off his coat. 'They were doing a report on shopping centres. You were in the background. And then the foreground.' I watch his face pale. 'You had your arm draped over some girl's shoulder. She looked very pretty.'

'I don't know what you're talking about,' he says. 'Why would I be in a shopping centre?'

'It's funny you should say that . . . I was wondering the same. But it was definitely you. Well, either you or a man impersonating you, wearing your khaki jacket and your orange trainers and YOUR FACE!'

He's standing there in his khaki jacket, with his orange trainers and his face is a picture.

'I'm sorry you had to see that, Jennifer,' he says. Bad sign. He only ever uses my name when he's angry. He takes off the jacket and throws it over the bannister. 'I mean, what are the chances? A local news programme. Anyway, she's no one. Just a business acquaintance who's become a friend. I would have told you about her, but there's never time to talk.'

'Are you serious?'

'Yes.'

'Then we ought to make time to talk,' I say.

And that's when we have *that conversation*; the one where he assures me that he and Melissa – the no one gets a name check fairly quickly – are honestly nothing more than friends.

'Men and women can't be friends,' I say. 'Because the sex part always gets in the way.'

'That's a line from a fucking film,' he parries.

'Fine,' I say. 'I happen to love that film. But I'm sad that you think there's never any time to talk.'

'Well, there isn't.'

'So . . . have you given up on us, then?'

'No. No! Not at all,' he says, all innocence. 'Not

unless . . . you have.' Which is how he betrays himself. He sticks his hands in his pockets and starts pacing. 'Is that what *you* want then? To give up?'

Well, that's my cue, isn't it? Because that's exactly what he wants, only he can't be the one to say it. That would label him the guilty party and no man ever wants that. So now I'm convinced I'm right about Melissa and I want to cut to the chase and get this over with.

I do my thing and make it easy for him. I tell him that yes, maybe he's right, there's never time to talk and perhaps that's a symptom of a dying relationship. I suggest that maybe subconsciously we've been avoiding real conversation because we're afraid it will end in tears. He listens, saying nothing, so I plough on and hand him his get-out-of-jail-free card and tell him that if he wants to be more than 'just friends' with Melissa then that's fine. He says that's not what he wants at all and he's not sure why I keep pushing her on him.

'I'm not. But I can't help feeling that maybe there's more to this than you're saying.'

'Well, you're wrong.'

'What does it matter? I'm right about us being over. Aren't I?'

'Yes,' he says, and my heart lurches. 'It certainly seems that's what you want.'

He turns it back on me again, ensuring it's my decision and now I'm past the point of no return.

We try to have a normal evening, pretending that

everything is fine and that we still care about each other and we're being very grown up about this and we'll talk more in the morning, but then he says, 'Maybe it's better I go home now. I mean, I can only play charades with you for so long. I just wish you'd trusted me.' And he puts his khaki jacket on and leaves.

Somehow I've manoeuvred myself into a corner and made myself history while handing him his future on a plate. Within a month, I hear he is with Melissa.

'Don't get upset, Sally,' he says. 'What does it matter now? We're here, aren't we?'

'Just about,' I say. 'But I need to talk about it. To get it sorted in my mind.'

'I understand,' he says. 'But I honestly thought you wanted out. Maybe I was being obtuse, but that was the message you gave me. I'm sorry I misread the signs.' He appears to be genuinely remorseful. He rubs his forehead and sighs. 'Sitting here now, it all seems quite ridiculous, doesn't it? I feel . . . so foolish. Your letter made me feel awful.'

'I didn't write it to make you feel awful. I wanted you to know, that's all.'

He shrugs. 'I'm sorry. Trust me. I've never been more sorry.'

'Ditto,' I say. 'I don't know why I was so scared to fight for you, to tell you how much I cared. I guess I didn't want to be made to look a fool and yet, you're right, look at us now.'

He nods sadly in agreement. 'So you really wanted to fight for me?'

'Yes. But I wanted you to fight for me too.'

'Oh Lord,' he says and runs his hand down my cheek, his fingers following the line of my jaw, the gesture so tender it hurts.

I've imagined the possibility of this moment a thousand times, long before I became ill, but I never dreamt Harry would be as warm and sensitive as this.

Our drinks are put down in front of us and Harry hands me my cocktail. He holds up his glass. 'To old friends,' he says.

'Old fools,' I say, and he laughs.

We sip. It makes my tongue curl.

'There's a plant pot over there,' he says. 'Shall I?' His eyes crinkle with a sad smile. He makes a show of surreptitiously pouring away the cocktail and comes back. 'My aunt couldn't do alcohol either. It robs you of everything, doesn't it?'

Veneers or not, he has me. He's right back there under my all too delicate skin. I don't think he's ever not been there. Why is it that some people can do that? Occupy a space they don't necessarily deserve.

'So,' he says, pouring me some water. 'How are all the old friends?'

'Olivia's great. She's getting married.'

'No! Crazy fool!'

'She's very happy.'

'I bet she's been shattered by your news.'

I nod, unable to speak for a moment. 'And Anna Maria is, well . . . Anna Maria.'

'Ah, Anna Maria. She always made me laugh.'

'I think she has that effect on everyone.'

'I'm sure.' He sips his vodka and stares into the glass. 'So . . . what are you going to do with your time?'

'Well, for now, I'm still working.'

'Seriously?'

'Yes. I have to. Well, I don't have to. I want to. It's good for me. I do fewer hours and I'll probably stop soon but, for the moment, it gives me a purpose.'

'Jesus, that's pretty stoical. I think I'd want to run away to some beach and drink myself into a coma.'

I laugh. 'Yeah, well . . . we all think we'll do something along those lines, but when it happens, we don't do that at all. We cling on to what feels safe.'

Harry takes my hand. 'Come on, let's live dangerously and move over to that sofa. It's just become free.' He signals to the waiter to take our drinks. I walk with him, loving the feel of my hand in his and we sit down on the long sofa. He puts his arm around me and I curl into the shape of him, exactly as I used to. As if nothing has changed.

'I'm so glad we could do this, Harry,' I say. 'But so sad that this is it. The end of the road.' I can't help myself. A single warm tear trickles down my cheek.

'Hey! What happened to the woman who doesn't do sad?'

'The man next to her is being too nice.' It comes out in a muffled whisper.

'I will never be nice again,' he says, wiping away the tear. 'Shit! Fuck! Damn! How the hell did this ever happen? To you of all amazing people?'

'Because shit happens. Even when you're this amazing,' I josh.

He pulls me in closer. 'You always did make me happy.'

'I did?' Against my will, the tears take over. 'Stop being nice!' I'm practically bawling now. 'Harry, you never once said that to me when we were together . . .'

'Yes, I did! I always told you I loved you.'

'That's different,' I say, through my sobs. 'People can be tearing each other apart and still say "I love you". As if that makes everything OK.'

He hands me a paper napkin. 'Here.'

'Do I look like shit?'

'Yeah.'

'Thanks,' I say. 'Keep that up.'

I dry my eyes and blow my nose as inoffensively as I can. 'Most of the time I'm fine. I'm not like this at all. Honestly.'

'What are you saying?' he asks, taken aback. 'You don't have to be fine. This is awful. You're allowed to cry.'

'I know, I know. But I don't want to. Not here with you now! I'm such an idiot, Harry. How did I ever let you go—'

'Please. Don't upset yourself.' He kisses my damp cheeks, then looks at me hesitantly. 'Here's an idea. And you don't have to answer now, but . . . will you let me help you? I want to be there for you. If you want me to.'

OK. We need to pause here. Did you hear that? Please bear witness to this in case I start to think I imagined it.

'You mean that?' I say. 'I mean, really be there for me? Through all the shitty, messy, ugly stuff?'

'Well, maybe that's taking it a bit too far!' He laughs. He's playing absently with my fingers, the way he always used to. 'YES!!! Through all the shitty, filthy, stinking, ugly, disgusting—' He catches my expression. 'OK, now I'm the one taking it too far.' His eyes smile. 'But seriously, yes! I would. I mean, obviously while you're still working, I still have to work too . . . but when you need me, I promise you, I'll be there.'

I swallow. 'Oh my God, Harry. I never thought I'd hear you say that.'

'Why? Am I *that* awful?'

'No! No! Of course not.' And I castigate myself for my misplaced suspicion all over again.

* * *

Harry offers to drive me home. 'And don't look at me like that. I'm completely sober.'

'It's fine, I'll take an Uber.'

'Aw, come on, Sally! You don't have to do your "I'm so self-sufficient" number any more. I'm here now. I'm not going to be here again for at least ten days. Accept my help while you can.'

'Ten days?' I sigh.

'Sorry. You know how it goes. But I can come back at any time.'

I nod. He's being so sincere. 'OK, driver!' I say. 'Take me home, please. Same address. Nothing's changed.' Nothing, I think. Absolutely nothing. Not now.

We leave hand in hand, smiling and comfortable, as though we've rewound the clock and no time has elapsed. For a brief moment, I can pretend I feel well again. My hand wrapped in his helps me forget.

We walk down the street together and he puts his arm around me, protecting me from the wind and damp of autumn, towards his building, a converted industrial warehouse. We walk through the modern atrium and wait for the lift.

'I'd invite you up, but you look pretty wiped.'

'I am,' I say.

We take the lift to the basement car park. There it is. A vintage Mercedes, sitting in its regular spot.

I flinch.

'You OK?' he says.

I've remembered his car is the most uncomfortable coupé ever built, its suspension long shot. It should be sold for scrap. Expensive scrap, of course, but nonetheless. I think Harry loves this car more than he's ever loved a woman. It's probably the longest relationship he's ever had.

'You never liked this car, did you?'

'Never.'

We bump and jolt our way across London and he pulls up in a rare space outside my house.

'I'd invite you in,' I say. 'But I may have to throw up.'

'Oh, I'm so sorry. Are you going to be OK?'

'As soon as I get out of this car and breathe some fresh air I'll be fine.'

'I should have thought of that. I should have taken an Uber with you.'

'I'm exaggerating. It's not that bad. Good night, Harry.'

He leans over, turns my face towards his and briefly kisses me.

'Can you do that again?' I say. 'I've waited a long time for that to happen.'

He cups my face in his hands and his mouth meets mine. My body relaxes, as though there has been no time lost. No heartbreak. No pain. I am here with him, right where I should be, and the thrill of our first kiss comes flooding back.

I'm celebrating in a city bar with my team. It's one of those bars with lots of glass and chrome and the newly fashionable exposed light bulbs with designer filaments. We're celebrating winning an employment tribunal. It's a significant victory so the company is paying for a night out.

'That guy keeps looking at you,' says Aoife.

'Don't be silly . . .' I glance over fleetingly. I know who she's talking about. I've noticed him too. Hard not to. He's very handsome. 'It's definitely not me he's looking at.'

'It totally is. He's been ogling you for ages.'

I was vaguely aware of it but thought I was being crazy. 'Should I do something about it?' I say.

'Yes! Smile back at him!'

'I can't. That's way too obvious.'

She lets rip a boozy cackle. 'For goodness' sake. Men only understand obvious.' She has the confidence of youth and beauty.

'I feel too awkward.' I'm talking under my breath, like all of a sudden he can hear me even though he's the opposite side of the crowded, noisy bar.

'What are you two talking about?' says Pattie.

'Shhh,' I say. 'Keep your voice down.'

Aoife is enjoying this. 'Don't look now, Pattie, but the guy over there keeps on giving Jennifer the eye.'

'Don't look,' I say sharply.

Too late.

He picks up on the fact that we are talking about him. Smiles and raises his glass. I turn away, mortified.

'Shit,' I say. 'He knows we know.'

'Smile at him, Jennifer.'

'Don't be ridiculous.'

As if to save me, Mia comes back from the loo. 'What have I missed?'

'Nothing,' I say. 'Let's go.'

Aoife is not going to let anything go. 'No way. Not yet. The boss has a task to perform.' Mia looks confused. Aoife nods her head at the sweet spot. 'See the fit guy over there?'

'Don't look!' I say again.

Too late.

'He's been making eyes at our Jennifer.'

'And you were thinking of leaving?' says Mia. 'Go get him!'

I fish into my bag for the company credit card. 'We're leaving.'

'For God's sake, woman, what have you got to lose by smiling at him?' Aoife is like a dog with a bone. 'Smile!' she instructs. 'Do it for us. Do it to prove you can.'

I smile. I feel ridiculous.

Blow me down, he gets up and wanders around the bar to our huddle. I want to fall through the floor, beyond embarrassed.

'Hi. I'm Harry,' he says, cool as anything. 'Can I buy you all a drink?' He's so handsome. Too good for me. What was I thinking?

'Thanks, but I'm just going,' says Pattie.

'Me too,' says Aoife.

'Me too,' I say.

'No, you're not,' says Mia. 'You have to pay the bill. We three have to dash. See you in the office tomorrow.'

And with that, they bundle up their stuff and leave.

I watch them go, feeling I've been left behind with a prize, not necessarily a good one. Like being left with a box of Krispy Kremes.

Harry leaps on to the bar stool next to me, all confidence, no self-consciousness at all. I smile, feeling tongue-tied and pathetic.

'I'm Jennifer,' I say, for want of anything more original.

'Nice to meet you, Jennifer. Is it your birthday? You looked as though you were celebrating.'

'Were we being that loud?'

'No!' he says. 'Not at all. You seemed very happy.'

'Oh right. We've just won an employment tribunal. I'm in HR. Are you bored yet?'

'Not quite, but carry on like that and I could be.' He flashes an amused smile. He has a nice mouth, good teeth but with one crooked incisor, as if the rest have refused it room. This is a relief. Otherwise he'd be too perfect. 'Congratulations!' he says. 'For winning.'

'You're too kind.' I flick my hair. I never flick my hair. 'So what do you do?'

'I'm an art curator.'

'Really?' I say.

'Yeah, really. Don't you believe me?'

'Oh no, of course I do. It's just . . . I wouldn't have guessed that.'

He laughs. 'What would you have guessed then? Insurance salesman?'

I'm flustered. 'No! No! Absolutely not . . . I just wasn't expecting something so different. I mean, you're here and you're not a banker. You must be pretty unique.' I might be digging myself into a deeper hole.

'Thank you. I'll take that. I am a pretty unique art curator. But I do work for a few of the big city banks. So you were almost right.'

'I'm glad I was wrong, to be honest.'

'Do you have something against bankers?'

I pull a face. 'Doesn't everyone?'

He laughs. 'So I guess you don't work for a bank then?'

'Construction company,' I say. 'I think that probably puts paid to any further discussion about my job.'

'Not at all. You have an important role to play in people's lives. All I do is buy them paintings.'

'Maybe, but in the end, HR is HR and paintings are art. You bring joy. Oh my God! Listen to me. I think I've had too much champagne.'

'And I was going to offer you another glass.'

I smile. 'Rude not to,' I say. I'm enjoying this.

We drink Moët. He asks me about my taste in art and I say I like Warhol and Monet and Hockney, then panic that I'm being too clichéd but he talks me through the background to their histories and I'm hooked by his knowledge, held by the sound of his voice. He could talk about anything and I'd be hooked. We are huddled together, not allowing anyone to invade our world, only emerging when they start to close up the bar. I hadn't noticed the time; I realize that at least two hours must have passed.

'There are some Hieronymus Bosch paintings I need to see at the Saatchi Gallery,' he says. 'Would you like to come with me?'

I have no idea who he's talking about. 'Yes,' I say, thrilled that he's not going to leave me wondering if I'll ever see him again. 'That would be great.'

'You haven't a clue who I'm talking about, have you?'

'None whatsoever!'

'Don't worry, I can tell you everything you never wanted to know about him. How about Sunday?'

'Sounds perfect,' I say, trying to sound casual while my flushed cheeks are giving the game away.

Harry insists on paying for all the drinks, including my team's. Won't hear of it when I remind him it was a work celebration and I have the company credit card. He takes my number. 'I'll call you,' he says. 'But save Sunday afternoon for me. And don't google Hieronymus Bosch.'

'I can't even spell it, let alone google it.'

'Good. I want to see your reaction when you see his work for the first time.' He flashes that smile.

'I definitely won't google. I won't google ever again.'

He hails me a cab and, as I'm about to get in, he pulls me back and kisses me. He has the confidence of a man who knows how to kiss. I am putty.

And here we are, sitting in his car, kissing, and I am putty all over again.

Later, in the quiet stillness of the early hours, I lie on my sofa, staring at the ceiling, reliving our evening. I go over and over it, re-examining everything Harry said, every promise, every word. I knew it. I knew it. I allowed my friends' negative view of him to influence mine and I panicked, presuming him guilty for the sake of my pride. But he's back in my life and I'm grateful.

Eventually, I crawl up to bed and fall asleep. In my

dreams I'm being held in someone's arms. I look up, expecting to see Harry only to see my mother. She's smiling at me, welcoming me in, but I tell her I'm not ready to join her yet. She nods as though she understands. And then she lets me go.

Day 68

Olivia has been given a private appointment in a bridal shop in Mayfair. That's what you get when you're in fashion. I'm relieved she's already there when I arrive, otherwise I'd feel awkward and out of place, the way I feel in smart hairdressing salons. She rushes towards me and gives me a huge, excited hug.

I can't help but notice her ring, a beautiful solitaire diamond with emerald baguettes, as it catches in the light.

'God, it's gorgeous,' I gasp, as I grab her hand to give it closer inspection. 'That man's a keeper. Does it feel real now?'

'Almost. Trying on a dress will definitely make it feel real.'

The personal assistant is charming. She helps Olivia choose from the abundance of dresses available, pointing out styles that might suit her as she flicks along the clouds of silk and chiffon, and hanging the ones Olivia likes on an allotted rail. I sit down, quietly observing her excitement.

'Can I offer you ladies a glass of champagne? Or maybe you'd prefer still or fizzy water?'

'Champagne for the bride, please,' says Olivia.

'Still water would be great, thank you,' I say.

'You OK?' whispers Olivia. 'You're very quiet. Have I been insensitive? Shoving my ring down your throat?'

I roll my eyes. 'Don't be ridiculous. I love your ring. I'm simply enjoying the show.'

The assistant returns with champagne and water. 'Oh, that's one of my favourites,' she says, looking at Olivia, who is admiring a cream satin off-the-shoulder dress embellished with feathers.

Olivia turns towards me and holds it against her. 'What do you think?'

'Oh Liv,' I gasp. 'It's beautiful. It's a yes from me.'

'OK. I'll try on all of these, please,' she says, pointing to the rail she has been amassing.

The assistant gathers up half the frocks. 'I'll take these through first. Come this way into the private salon where it's more comfortable.'

Olivia throws me a look. 'Oooooh,' she says, picking up her champagne. 'Come on! We're going fancy.'

We follow the assistant into an extravagant room decorated with a crystal chandelier and several gilded mirrors, in the style of a French boudoir.

She hangs up the dresses then pulls a pink velvet curtain in front of Olivia, who makes a huge show of disappearing behind it to change. Through the chink of light, I catch a glimpse of her in sexy cream-coloured lingerie. I'm wearing big black knickers. Underwear says so much about where you are in life.

She comes out suddenly transformed in dreamy organza. She looks like a film star. The dress fits perfectly to the body then kicks out at the knees with wave upon wave of translucent cream fabric.

'Liv! You're a vision,' I say. 'How are we ever going to choose? You're going to look stunning in all of them.'

'Jennifer is my biggest fan,' she tells the assistant. 'And I am hers. We've known each other for years.'

'How lovely.'

'It is,' she says. 'Special.' My heart swerves.

She checks herself in one of the mirrors, biting her lip as though she can't believe it's her reflection. She does a twirl, examining herself from every angle. 'It's gorgeous,' she says. 'But not quite right. I'm sure we'll know "the one" when we see it.'

'I saw Harry last night,' I say, which stops her in her tracks.

She throws me a look in the mirror akin to horror. 'Harry?' she says, spinning round, hands on hips like she's been left at the altar. 'When were you going to tell me?'

'Now!' I say.

'Bloody hell.' She walks up and down, unable to resist giving a bit of a sashay. 'OK, hold that thought. I want to be able to concentrate entirely on you when you tell me about him. We're discussing this over lunch.'

'Fine by me,' I say. 'I want to concentrate entirely on you.'

She turns to the assistant. 'Is it OK if Jennifer takes photos? I did check with Venetia and she said it would be fine.'

'She told me. It's completely fine,' says the assistant.

'Thank you.' She turns to me. 'Can you use your phone in case I inadvertently show one to Dan?'

'Of course.' She stands in front of me in each dress, giving different poses. I pretend for a moment that I am present at her big day. I could be sad, but Harry is back in my life and I am determined to stay happy.

The receptionist at the Arts Club is gracious and welcoming. The place smells of glamour and wealth; of expensive candles layering the air with the scent of cinnamon and cloves, of heady aftershave and rich perfume. I'm sure it's lovely, but for me, it's a bit overwhelming. I feel giddy.

We're shown through to an elegant room buzzing with the hum of conversation, following the sharply dressed hostess's Louboutin red-soled clip-clip, across a polished black-and-white marble floor. We pass a sumptuous bar, its leather stools occupied by young off-duty bankers still in their regulation suits, eating oysters, drinking champagne, their faces glued to their smartphones for fear of missing out.

The place is gleaming with money, full of Russians, Americans, Arabs and Europeans. I feel as though

I'm being gifted a parting glimpse of Olivia's glittering world.

We're shown to a table. Our order is taken.

'Right! Tell me about Harry,' says Olivia.

'He phoned me.' I'm smirking.

'When?'

'I don't know. A couple of days ago, maybe. Invited me out for a drink.'

'And you didn't call to tell me immediately?'

'I knew you'd worry about me.'

'Why? Should I be worried?'

'No. He was amazing.'

'Great,' she says.

She swigs some champagne and eyes the breadbasket. 'There are no carbs in French bread, are there? What the heck.' She takes a piece and starts buttering it. 'So define amazing in relation to Harry.'

I tut. Olivia will never like him. Not even now that he's called me. 'He seemed genuinely concerned for me. Really kind. Just lovely.'

She chews ravenously. 'Well, who'd have thought it? Old Harry's crawled out of the woodwork and he's doing the right thing. Not necessarily what I would have expected.' Her words sound so brittle that if you could hold them in your hands they would snap. 'So where's Melissa? Dumped her too?'

'In a manner of speaking.'

'Still the commitment-phobe then?'

I glare at her.

'Oh, come on,' she says. 'Take off those rose-tinted glasses. He has issues, does he not? I mean, let's not eulogize the shit. He's nearly fifty, he's never been married and he was a shit to you. You were broken for months after he left. Or have you forgotten that?'

'Thanks for the memo,' I say. 'Has it occurred to you that maybe we all got him wrong? That he wants to be there for me? To look after me. And I want that too.'

She grimaces. 'Does he?'

'Yes!'

She tilts her head with surprise. 'Oh right. Ignore me. Sorry, sorry, sorry.' She drags her teeth across her bottom lip. 'Ach, Jen. I'm such a big mouth. It's just, it's kind of weird. I'm still angry with him. And it's been odd trying on those wedding dresses and . . . knowing you're not going to be there . . . And . . . I don't know. Harry. Of course it's great if he's going to be there for you. I'm pleased. Honestly I am. I know how much that piece of shit means to you!'

I scoff. 'Thank you, I think.'

The waiter puts down our salads.

Olivia picks at some lettuce. 'I want the best for you, that's all,' she says. 'Go carefully.'

'You're like a parent. You say the harshest things but only in my best interest.'

'Well, someone needs to. Now, can we check out the photos? We need to decide which of those gorgeous frocks is the one for me.'

We debate each dress as we eat, then enter our

separate worlds of contemplation. She sighs intermittently and polishes off her champagne and orders another glass.

'You're drinking quite a lot,' I say. 'Is everything all right?'

'You're not drinking. That's why you're noticing. Anyway, I'm fine. More importantly, are you OK? Because if I'm honest, you look tired.'

'That's my permanent look. Get used to it.'

'We should get you home,' she says.

'I'd rather be out with you than contemplating my navel at home, that's for sure.'

She flops back in her seat and stretches out her long legs. 'Shit, Jennifer! We're making this feel so normal, I almost forget the horrible reality. It's as if we're starting to believe alternative facts.'

'Maybe we should. Whatever helps.'

'True.' She fiddles with her engagement ring, gives a little smile. 'The letters have helped, haven't they?'

'They have. Thank you. You were my inspiration.'

I think to mention that I'm going to a reiki healer with Anna Maria tomorrow then think again. I know Olivia will say I'm mad and not long ago, I would have agreed. But what if I'm not mad? What if Anna Maria's the one who's got it right?

Day 67

Anna Maria's driving is shocking. She pulls out in front of an articulated truck and swears at the driver animatedly, as if it's his fault. He gives her the finger and she honks her horn.

'Fucker!' she cries.

'Jesus, Anna Maria,' I say. 'You nearly killed us!' I realize I must be determined to live because being bumped off by a lorry is a swifter solution and yet I'd still rather not.

'Nah,' she says. 'I'm going to live till I'm ninety-five. It's written in my birth chart. I wish you'd have done one. You might have been better prepared. You might have been able to shift your destiny.' I've told Anna Maria my news.

'Thanks a lot,' I say. 'But you might want to get a second opinion.'

She groans like I'm being ridiculous. 'So might you,' she says. 'I mean, doctors aren't always right, you know.'

I laugh wistfully. 'And that's why we're going to see Rita.'

'To Rita!' she says, in a celebratory toast.

Anna Maria is not the least bit perturbed by my news, which in one way is refreshing and yet somehow oddly irritating. She says everything is curable with the right healer. She refuses to accept there is anything that can't be fixed by energetic help. The first thing I have to do is drop my negative thinking, she says, and have an open mind.

I tell her my mind is totally open. 'Could have fooled me,' she says.

Somehow, we make it to Neasden without incident. We draw up outside an ordinary row of terraced houses with net curtains and rusting wrought-iron gates.

Anna Maria tries to park her car. She drives, front first, into a massive space then stops, as though she's had quite enough of the hassle. 'We're here,' she announces, turning off the engine. The car's rear end is sticking out into the road like a Kardashian's. She pushes in her wing mirrors, as if that makes all the difference.

I follow her down a narrow path with crazy paving, and instinctively avoid all the cracks. At the yellow front door there's a rainbow-coloured picture propped up against the window. 'Love Lives Here' it reads. 'And so does Rita.' I breathe a sigh of relief. Rita has a sense of humour.

'You nervous?' Anna Maria says.

'Why? Do I look it?'

'Oh dude,' she says. 'This is going to do you a world of good. Rita has been known to cure cancer. If she can do that, she can cure anything.'

A tiny woman with grey hair opens the door and the smell of incense hits me.

'Hello, my dears.' She smiles and gives a little bow, her hands pressed together. 'Namaste.'

'Namaste,' says Anna Maria, returning the bow. I mutter the word under my breath and do a kind of bob.

'Rita!' says Anna Maria reverentially. 'Thanks so much for seeing us at such short notice.'

I smile. 'Yes, thank you, Rita.' Another bob.

She is wearing a patterned pink kaftan and a row of purple beads. Her face is naked of make-up, nothing to mask the lines and wrinkles, as if she's saying, What's to hide? She has bare feet. I clock her toes, crooked and misshapen with yellowing nails. Perhaps there are some things worth hiding.

Anna Maria removes her trainers and I start to do the same. I guess it's what you do. I hope I'm wearing decent socks. Who am I to judge Rita? Anna Maria removes her socks and reveals a beautiful pedicure. I leave mine on. I realize in that weird moment I will no longer need pedicures, or manicures or facials, and it saddens me even though I hardly did them anyway. Funny, those silly, inconsequential things that suddenly seem to matter so hugely.

Rita leads us down a dark hallway. The smell is quite overpowering. An incense stick, tip aglow, sits on an ormolu-and-gilt side table. Surprising what one little twig can muster. Alongside sits an olive green Trimphone with an old-fashioned dial. I haven't seen one of those phones in years. I imagine upstairs is an avocado bathroom suite with pink tiles. This house is frozen in time. Seventies aficionados would pay good money to come here. And not for the reiki.

We follow her into a small lounge. The walls are covered with brightly coloured pictures of Indian gods. There is another incense stick puffing away. It makes me feel slightly sick.

'Can I offer you some chai?' she says.

'Yes please,' says Anna Maria. She turns to me. 'You'll love Rita's chai. You've never tasted anything like it. She refuses to give me the recipe, don't you, Rita? She shares her powers but never her potions.'

Rita smiles. 'I have to keep something for myself.'

We sit in silence, waiting for Rita to return. Anna Maria has closed her eyes, her hands are held out, thumb and fingertip touching. I think she's meditating.

'Should I tell her what's wrong with me?' I whisper.

'You don't need to tell Rita anything,' she says, eyes still tightly shut. 'She probably already knows. She's *that* good.'

'Wow!' I say. I'm starting to get into this.

Rita comes back with a small gold tray and two cups of chai. She sits very straight-backed, breathing deeply as she watches us sip. There is a crack in the rim of my cup and I try to avoid it. Anna Maria is humming with appreciation.

'This is lovely,' I say to Rita, like I'm attempting to gain favour.

She waits for us to finish. The dregs at the end are unpalatable but I swallow them, convincing myself they are delicious.

'Who wants to go first?' she says.

'Let Jennifer go first,' says Anna Maria. 'She's the important one. If you run over the hour, just carry on. I don't mind having a quicker session.'

I throw Anna Maria an appreciative smile, still trying to consume the sandy residue. 'Bless you,' I mouth. Suddenly I'm all spiritual.

'Follow me then, dear,' says Rita.

We go upstairs to a back bedroom and there's a large massage table which practically fills the room. It has a white towel neatly draped across it. The room is cosy and warm with the mandatory incense stick puffing trails of grey smoke. There's a tiny sink in the corner. She turns down the lights. I need to lie down. Now.

'Have you had reiki before, dear?'

'No. Never.'

'OK. Lie down on the table and we'll get you comfortable, then I'll explain.'

'Do I have to take anything off?' I ask.

'It's entirely up to you, my dear,' she says. 'This is not a massage. I hold my hands above your body and move around your aura. I work on your spiritual self, not your physical self. I will only touch the back of your head. You might want to take off your cardigan in case you get too warm.'

I take off my cardigan and throw it over the chair, and then I climb on to the massage table and lie back.

'You're tense, dear,' she says. I wonder if she's reading my face or my mind. If she really is *that* good. 'Try to relax. If you get uncomfortable I can stop.'

She squeezes past the table and washes her hands in the sink. Then she squeezes back.

'Now, dear, take a deeeeep lonnnng breath in . . . and out. In . . . and out.'

I do exactly as she says. It's strangely calming, as is the timbre of her voice.

'You're going to enjoy this,' she says. 'I've never had anyone leave after their first experience and not feel that something remarkable has happened.' Her voice sends tingles down my arms and I find myself letting go of my fears, unwinding into her care.

I close my eyes. I hear the flick of a switch and the sound of something akin to whale music whirrs into the room. It's eerie yet soothing. Rita is standing over me. I hear her whispering and open one eye in case she's speaking to me. She has her hands clasped together in prayer, her eyes tightly shut. I quickly close my sneaky eye.

She moves behind me and places her hands below my chin, close enough for me to feel their warmth. I can smell the herbal scent of her soap. 'I want you to think of your intentions, dear,' she says. 'I want you to ask for what you need.'

I give it a moment's consideration. 'I think I'd—'

'Not out loud, dear. Keep your thoughts in your head. You're speaking to the energy.'

I nod. I must be open-minded, I instruct myself. I

must speak to the energy. Hello, energy, I think. Would you mind finding a cure for me? If at all possible? I hope I'm not being greedy but I'd like to stay around a little bit longer. And if that's too much to ask, then perhaps you could help me sleep without waking up at three in the morning. That would be a good start.

Rita's herbal hands move over my cheeks. They hover there for a few minutes. Then she moves them above my forehead. Eventually, she slips her hands under my head. She is touching me now as she said she would. She's so gentle it feels gratifying. I'm starting to unwind.

She stands there for what seems an age then shuffles back to my side and I'm aware of a strange, magical warmth over my stomach. Even though she's no longer touching me, I feel each movement, I relax under the heat of her palms.

The next thing I know, she is gently shaking my shoulders.

'Wake up, dear,' she says.

The whales have stopped singing. Rita places a cup of chai on the side table next to me. And a glass of water.

'You were in a deep sleep,' she says. 'I'll let you recover and then we can talk. I'll tell you what I felt. I'll leave you for a few moments. Please drink.'

I feel woozy. I breathe slowly and deeply, feeling myself coming back into my body. It's the strangest sensation. 'Thank you,' I say out loud to the empty room. 'Thank you, energy.'

I sit up and look around. I have completely lost myself here. Let go of fear. It's amazing. I drink as I'm told. I'm sipping the tea which tastes delicious without my needing to convince myself it does. Everything feels right. Rita comes back in. She slowly turns up the light with the dimmer switch and my eyes adjust. I'm keen to hear her findings.

She passes me my cardigan. 'Put this on, dear,' she says. 'Your body temperature will drop now. You might get cold.' She sits down in the chair, close to my side.

'You have not been well, my dear,' she says. 'I feel you have been very tired.'

'Oh, Rita. That's amazing,' I say. 'That's very true.'

Her eyelids flutter, as if to tell me she knows this and I shouldn't interrupt. 'But you are a strong person,' she continues. 'People will always suck your energy. Weak people are like vampires,' she says. 'They suck the energy of the strong. Someone has been sucking your energy. Who is it?' she says.

I'm dumbfounded. I'm not quite sure. I wait to see if she's going to tell me. She just stares.

'I don't know,' I say.

'Think!' she says firmly. 'There is one person. A relationship. It has made you sad.'

'Well, there's Harry—'

'Yes,' she says, her hands going up in a hallelujah! 'That's him! Harry. That is the name that came through.'

I feel a bit freaked. 'But I don't think Harry has got

anything to do with how I feel now. I mean, time wise—'

'Energy does not understand time,' she says. 'You are suffering because of this man. He has been a negative force. Your body is acknowledging it. It is in shock. Trauma.'

'Yes,' I say. 'You're right.' She nods at my acknowledgement. 'Though I still don't think it's because of him.' I kind of mumble that as a stubborn aside.

Her expression darkens. 'It *is* because of him!' she shouts. 'Harry! That man has sucked your energy. It is obvious to me. But he is DEAD now!'

I scream from the depths of my soul. Rita puts her hands over her ears.

'NO!' I howl. 'But I saw him. Friday!'

'He is dead to *YOU*, dear,' she scolds. 'You must not think of him any more. I have shifted the damage he has done. He is a vampire. He has been sucking you dry. He is dead to *YOU*.'

I'm shaking. 'That's a terrible thing to say, Rita.'

She tuts. 'I am not here to tell you nice fairy stories, Jane.'

'Jennifer.'

'I have a job to do.'

'But still.'

Rita stands up abruptly. Her knees brush my toes and I recoil.

'Sometimes it's hard to hear the truth,' she says, pushing back the chair.

Oh, don't you know it, I think.

I'm finding her quite scary. I'd like to leave but I'm rooted to the table.

She draws in a deep breath, then releases it slowly. 'You will probably feel bad tonight.' Her tone is mellow again, as though she's turned a page and this is a new chapter in our story. 'You will have a bad headache. The bad energy will be escaping. You must drink lots of water. In two days you will feel like a new woman.' She whisks the cup away from me as though I have lost the right to drink her celebrated chai, let alone have the recipe. I have the distinct feeling Rita is someone who doesn't like to be contradicted.

The smell of the incense is making me feel nauseated. The chai is making me feel nauseated. All the good feelings I had only a moment ago are making me feel nauseated. 'Should I get Anna Maria?' I say, shivering.

'Take the time to consider what I have said. I have cleansed your aura but some resistant energies can hang on. If they do, then you must come back so that I can remove them. Now relax here for a moment until you feel steady. I'll wait for you downstairs. With Marianna.'

'Thank you, Ria,' I say, with intention.

'Rita,' she corrects.

I wait for her to leave, ease myself off the table, and pace the tiny space between the table and the wall, hugging my sides, trying to calm down, to warm up, until I think I've paced for long enough.

I want to make a run for it. I can't sit for one more

second in that funny little front room with its sickly smells, its cheap prints staring down at me as if they know I'm a non-believer.

I quickly descend the stairs, walk back into the room and the two of them stare at me, Anna Maria all bright and cheery, enthusiastically nodding at me as if she wants me to tip her the wink that I feel a bit better, Rita serious and calm. I fumble in my handbag and give Rita my £40. 'Thanks so much, Rita. I'll definitely be back.' I ask Anna Maria for the car keys. 'I need to go for a walk. I'll wait for you in the car.'

She flashes me a curious look. 'Did you scream?' she whispers.

'With delight.' I smile.

Anna Maria is grinning wildly, secure in the knowledge this has been a success. She gives me a knowing nod then follows Rita.

I walk out into the cold autumnal air and draw it deeply into my lungs. The world seems to spin, making me grab on to a tree before throwing up over the kerb. I sit down on a low garden wall. The cloying smell of incense is still hogging my nostrils. The taste of chai sticks to the back of my throat. I will never be able to go near a health food shop again.

I return to the car and get my bottle of water. My clothes stink. My hair stinks. The first thing I'm going to do when I get home is have a bath.

I lie back in the car, retching and shivering, until eventually Anna Maria opens the driver's door and jumps in behind the wheel.

'She's amazing, isn't she?' she says.

'Amazing,' I say.

'It's quite draining though, isn't it?' she says cheerfully, putting the key in the ignition. 'You might feel odd for a day or two. It's your first time. It's like a drug hit. The first is always the strongest.'

'Yeah,' I say, even though I've never taken a drug stronger than ibuprofen in my life. Anna Maria's wackiness suits her, but I don't think it suits me.

She barely glances over her shoulder as she reverses out of the space, then straightens up and drives straight ahead, her wing mirrors still turned in.

'Your wing mirrors, Anna Maria,' I say. It's an old car, some kind of Morris Minor, not one where you can reach out and adjust the mirrors from inside.

'Shit,' she says. 'I always do that.' She bangs on the brakes, stops the car dead in the middle of the road, jumps out and flips her wing mirrors. 'Thanks,' she says, climbing back in. 'I'd have driven all the way home without even realizing.'

'Good to know,' I say, resolving never to allow Anna Maria to drive me anywhere ever again. She might live to be ninety-five, but I'm not sure she'll be in one piece.

Anna Maria raves about Rita the whole of our torturous car journey home.

'You're going to feel better, Jennifer,' she says. 'I feel it. You look better already.'

I check myself in the wonky mirror on the sun visor. She's either lying or she's blind, which is possible, judging from her road sense.

'Did you tell her what was wrong with me?' I ask.

Her face becomes thoughtful. 'I didn't know what was wrong with you, did I? Not until today.' She turns her head towards me, her eyes now wide with excitement.

'Watch the road, please,' I say.

She instantly obeys but her eyes are still squeezing sideways at me.

'Did she get it right, then?' she says. She doesn't wait for my response. 'She did, didn't she!!! That's why you screamed! She's so amazing, isn't she? I can't believe that woman.' She thumps the steering wheel. 'She has X-ray vision.'

'She was pretty unbelievable,' I say.

We're back on the main road now, which is fairly straight. A relief. I don't want to distract her from driving but I have to ask her. 'So what did you tell her about me then, when you booked?'

'Nothing,' she says. 'Why?'

'Just curious,' I say.

She hums. 'Well . . . I might have told her you had some negative energy around you. Like you told me.' She trumpet blows her cheeks and glances in her rear-view mirror, which I think is a first. 'And I think I might have mentioned you'd had a toxic boyfriend. You know. Harry. Eugh. But that was all.'

'Oh,' I say. 'Right.' It starts to fall into place. Anna Maria never liked Harry either. I turn away and stare out of the window, watching the grey blur of houses speed by.

'I'm going for some thermo-auricular therapy next week. You should come,' she says.

I have no idea what she's talking about. 'Thanks, but I think I'll pass.'

'Fair enough. But if you change your mind . . .' She turns on the car radio. 'Spice Girls! Tune!' she shouts. We listen to some obscure station which plays upbeat retro pop for the remainder of the journey. Anna Maria sings along. You can take the girl out of the party but you can't take the party out of the girl.

As soon as I'm through my front door, I run a warm bath overloaded with bubbles and lie under the water, staring through the iridescent shimmer, totally miserable, reflecting on what I've done.

What was I thinking? There is no hope. Face it! No reiki master, no aura cleanser can change my destiny. Anna Maria can believe in what she likes because she has nothing to contest her faith. When things are good, what's to prove? We only find out how effective any-thing is when we hit a crisis. But still, I understand her. Because I wanted to believe in Rita too. I wanted to be open-minded. It gave me hope. But it gave me expect-ations and they're the worst possible thing I can have at this juncture in my life because they can only lead to disappointment.

I grip the sides of the bath. Face facts:

I am not the master of my fate. Reiki will not cure me.

Day 64

Harry is still in Milan on business and very much alive. It is Rita who is dead to me. I've heard from him several times. I've even called him a few times. My calls to him go automatically to voicemail but he always calls me back. There's a comfort in knowing this is how we operate.

I'm on my way to dinner at Isabelle's in a limo booked on Martin's account. I insisted I get an Uber, but she won. She always wins.

When I arrive, she opens the door before I've even rung, as if she's been tracking me in the cab, which possibly she has. She pulls me into her. 'Oh Jennifer,' she says and gives me a big tight hug. I hug her back then she holds me in front of her, inspecting me as though she was expecting someone different to show up. 'You don't look sick. A bit pale maybe, but nothing a bit of decent make-up couldn't help. This isn't fake news, is it?'

'I wish.'

'Yeah. I wish too.' There's an air of relief as we take each other in. It feels safe to be here. With family.

Even though I'm not sure how the mood might develop.

'You look good,' I say, even though she doesn't. She looks puffy, her beauty oddly distorted.

'No I don't,' she replies.

'Hello, Auntie Jennifer.' Cecily and Sophia sidle across the marble hallway from the kitchen, wearing shy smiles. They each give me a little embarrassed hug then cling to either side of their mother like parentheses. It's obvious that Isabelle's already told her daughters my news.

'Hey, girls!' I say brightly to dispel their unease. 'These are for you.' I hand them a bag full of gummy sweets and watch their eyes widen as they pull out the different megapacks. It's a relief. I wondered if brightly coloured snakes and bottles and bears might be an insult to girls of such maturity as thirteen and ten and that I will have proved I completely misunderstand children – as my sister so often reminds me.

'Wow!' they exclaim, looking at each other excitedly then at their mother. 'Awesome!'

The person I've misunderstood is Isabelle. She is not thrilled at all. I hand her a box of Belgian chocolates.

'Thank you,' she smiles. 'Not necessary. Off to your rooms now, girls. Homework! I'll call you when supper is ready. And I'll take those.' She extracts the bags of sweets from their hands.

'Ohhhhh,' groans Cecily. 'But they're for us!'

'Come on, Mummy!' says Sophia. 'Please. Can't we have a few in our rooms?'

'You know the rules,' says Isabelle.

'Fine,' says Cecily. 'But I've done my homework and I want to stay down here and chat with you and Jennifer.'

I'm so glad she's dropped the 'Auntie'. It makes me feel ancient.

'Me too,' says Sophia. 'I want to chat.'

They're both so adorable it saddens me.

'You can chat with her over dinner. Now, go upstairs and . . . do something . . . I don't know. Tidy your rooms. Watch something on your iPads.'

Cecily is about to protest when Isabelle throws her such a dark, scary look, they both turn on their heels and stomp upstairs. 'And don't stomp,' she says.

She turns to me and rolls her eyes. One eyelid appears to be stuck but I daren't mention it. 'Kids!' she exclaims. She holds up the chocolates. 'You don't mind if I put these away, do you? I'm on a diet. Martin and I are doing the 5:2. But tonight's a five. We can eat anything. Not chocolates, though. Or sugar. I mean, you can but they're so unhealthy.' She nods to the bags of sweets and looks at me, with a non-verbal tut-tut. 'Can I get you a drink?'

'Erm. I'm not drinking.'

'Oh, come on. What harm can it do now?'

'Well, a very small glass of red then. Literally a drop.'

Her neck tightens. 'Awk-ward!' she sings, turning it into two highly complex words. 'I should have said. We don't have red in the house any more. It's sooo bad for your teeth and Martin and I have just had ours whitened.' She gives me a demonstrative grin.

'Oh right! They look good. I guess I don't have to worry about those things now.' I pause, wondering if everyone is obsessed with teeth. 'Not that I ever did.'

'No, indeed,' she says, matter-of-fact.

'Then I'll have whatever's open,' I say.

She swings round towards the kitchen. 'Martin,' she shouts. 'Pour Jennifer a glass of the organic Chardonnay.' All I hear is 'Poor Jennifer' and then the correct word registers. 'And one for me of course. We'll be in the drawing room.'

I can see Martin's silhouette moving back and forth as he's laying the table. He's probably trying to avoid me. He's not the most comfortable human being at the best of times, let alone when having to confront his dying sister-in-law.

Martin turns round, looking towards us, shading his eyes as if he's wondering who's out there when he knows exactly. With a play of spontaneity, he bounds out of the kitchen like an overgrown puppy, a tea towel tucked into the waist of his trousers. 'Hi, hi, hi!'

'Hello, Martin,' I say.

He's at sixes and sevens, hugs me at a distance, then all but pushes me away. 'Sorry,' he whispers. 'Very sorry.'

'Thanks,' I say.

When he first started dating Isabelle I found his gaucheness quite attractive, although I'm not sure that's what attracted Isabelle. Now it just seems odd.

He's lost most of his once thick dark hair and his blue pinstripe shirt betrays a beer gut, which must account for the 5:2 because Isabelle is slim as anything, so I'm assuming she's only doing it to support him.

'How are you?' he says, clearly trying to change the subject and failing. His white teeth gleam at me.

'I'm good, thank you, Martin. And how are you?'

'A bit of gout, but can't complain.' He raises his eyebrows. 'Nothing to quite match what you've got.'

'Martin!' Isabelle groans. 'For God's sake!'

'What?' he says. 'I didn't mean to offend.' He clasps his hands together. 'I think you're better off with me out of the way. I'll sort the drinks and leave you to your chat. Are you drinking, Jennifer?'

'Yes,' Isabelle says, with marked impatience. 'I told you. Chardonnay. The organic one recommended by Bert. There's already a bottle opened in the fridge. We started it yesterday.'

'And we didn't finish it? Were we not well?'

'We were on a two.'

'Ergh. The terrible twos,' he groans. 'Well, it's a high-five tonight, darling!' He holds up his palm, which is met by hers.

'Thank God!' she says, laughing, her snappiness eased by the prospect of a decent meal.

Martin scampers back into the kitchen and Isabelle leads the way across the large square hall into the drawing room, for *our chat*. It feels uncomfortably ominous, as though everyone knows what's in store except me.

We sit opposite one another on huge grey velvet

couches which flank either side of the massive ebony marble fireplace. There's a tall glass vase of scented lilies on an elegant console table that sits behind Isabelle against the wall overshadowed by an imposing oil painting of the family. They've lit a fire and the room smells and feels like a beautiful country hotel. It's all very cosy, in a grand way, but still welcoming. I appreciate the fact they've made an effort. Or maybe it's always like this. Luxurious. Scented. Ordered. Everything in its place.

I look across at my sister, fascinated by her face. Her forehead appears stretched and shiny. Her cheeks seem bumpy. Her right eyelid has this mild droop.

'In case you're wondering,' she says. 'I've had a bit of intervention.'

'Oh? You can't tell.'

She stretches out her long neck. 'Don't humour me. I don't tell everyone. In fact, I don't tell anyone. I mean, normally it's so natural.' She sighs, pressing her fingertips over her cheekbones. 'I had it topped up last week. It went horribly wrong. Dr Miller says it'll settle down in a few more days. You should have seen me before. Thank God you cancelled. I looked like a freak. I haven't dared venture out. I've been a prisoner in my own home. It's been awful.'

'I can't begin to imagine.'

Martin brings in the wine. He exchanges glances with Isabelle as if he's giving her encouragement, which only adds to my concern. 'OK, I'll leave you to it,' he says, standing there hovering as though he might be invited to stay after all until Isabelle shoos him out as if she's dismissing the maid.

We hold up our glasses to each other as the door clicks shut.

'Thanks for inviting me over,' I say. 'Your house looks lovely.'

'Yes,' she says. 'Not overrun with kids like the last time you were here.' She takes a sip of wine and puts down her glass on a black and gold patterned china coaster sitting on the oversized zebra-skin ottoman that serves as a massive coffee table. Huge art books are neatly positioned in the centre. They look untouchable but I don't think they're there to be touched. There's a small pile of china coasters, all in different colours, and she pushes a turquoise and gold one across to my side.

'If you wouldn't mind,' she says.

'No problem.' I guess if I had beautiful things, I'd do the same.

She clasps her arms across her middle. 'Now,' she pronounces. 'I want to discuss your letter.'

I wasn't intending to drink my wine but I hadn't expected *our chat* to be quite so immediate. I take a large gulp, instantly regretting it. 'Sure,' I say.

She looks past me, over my shoulder, as if she's staring at someone else in the room. 'Firstly, I'm devastated by your news. You have no idea. I still can't take it in. And you being here now, looking pretty normal, makes it even harder. And then there's the rest of your letter.'

I'm holding my breath.

'It makes me so sad, Jennifer,' she says. 'That we've wasted all this time not talking to one another. I mean, I know we talk, but we don't *talk*, do we? Not really.'

'No,' I say, letting the breath go. 'It wasn't a family trait, was it? Let's be honest.'

'I think you've misunderstood me and I've obviously misunderstood you.' She faces me head-on and my skin prickles. 'You're right. Mum and Dad made me the pretty one and you the clever one. It was how it was. I would never do that to my kids. It's so divisive. But I realize now they were only doing their best. That's all we can do as parents. The funny thing is, as much as you hated being the clever one, I hated being the pretty one. It made me feel shallow and pointless. I wanted to be clever. But that was your department.'

I can feel my jaw dropping. I've never thought of it that way.

'I was always envious of how bright you were. How Mum and Dad would put you on a pedestal because you got such great exam results. How they encouraged you with your studies, which only belittled mine. I didn't need exam results, was the message they gave me, I would always succeed on my looks. Have you any idea how bad that feels?'

I shrug. I have no idea whatsoever. I might have liked to.

'But they made us play to type, didn't they?'

I nod, yes, still passively listening.

'And we played the roles we were given because we didn't know any better. But it set us against one another.'

I sit up. 'It never set me against you,' I say. 'I adore you, Isabelle. I've always adored you.' I feel a rush of the old feelings pulsing through me. For the first time ever she seems vulnerable.

'I know,' she says. 'And I took advantage of that. I'm *so* sorry. I took your love for granted.'

This is overwhelming. She's never uttered sorry to me in her life.

'Thank you, Isabelle,' I say. 'I really appreciate that.'

She swooshes the wine around her glass then sips it and draws in a deep breath, her lumpy cheekbones sharpening. She hesitates, gazes up at the ceiling then looks back at me. 'I'm sorry about that idiot, Jennifer. When I read his name in your letter I had to think hard about who the hell Neil was and I can tell you, he wasn't worth it. But I could have made it easier by not seducing him. I was always looking to prove my worth, but that's no excuse. I could have apologized instead of dismissing you. I was crap at saying sorry.'

'Thank you.'

'And . . . and . . .' Oh my God, her eyes are welling up. 'And I am just the most sorry about the babies. How did it get to the point where you couldn't even tell me about something so major? That's awful! I mean, I know we lead different lives, we're different, but I would have been there for you, Jennifer. I promise you. I would have.'

'Isabelle?' I say, voice trembling. 'Do we have to sit opposite one another? Can I come and sit next to you?'

She nods. Choked up. I walk around the ottoman and sit next to her.

She looks directly at me, tenses her shoulders. 'I'm going to miss you,' she says, her eyes fluttering. 'You're all that's left. No Mum, no Dad. Just you. And now this. You should not be the one to go first. When I got your letter it was like a dagger plunging through my heart. I'm gutted by your news.'

I swallow hard. 'I'm sorry I wrote rather than telling you face-to-face, but I needed to say that stuff. I thought reading it in a letter would give you time to think about everything. And I was scared. It was such a difficult, emotional thing to do. I'm glad you were able to take everything the way it was meant. I'm glad to hear your side. I'm so sorry to be the bearer of such lousy news.' I stare at her, holding my gaze in an attempt not to cry.

'Does my face look that terrible?'

'No! No! Not at all. Was I staring?'

She shakes her head. 'I'm such an idiot, Jennifer. All this stuff I do: hanging on to my beauty for dear life. And now look at me.' She groans. 'It'll sort itself out, though. The doctor said it'll settle down. Oh, listen to me harping on. As if any of it matters.'

'It does matter,' I say. 'Everything still matters.'

She studies me for a moment and nods her head. 'Oh God, Jen. You're so kind and thoughtful. You got given the gentle genes as well as the smart ones. Anyhow, you do know you're beautiful, don't you? You scrub up really nicely. Look at you. You're sick but you look amazing.'

I scoff at the backhanded compliment. 'But I could still do with a bit of decent make-up, right?'

'Yeah. Wouldn't hurt.' She laughs at herself then lets out a groan. 'What a waste, Jennifer. Of a life. Your life. Of our sisterhood. We wasted so much over trivia.'

'Hubris,' I say, her unforeseen warmth playing havoc with my emotions.

'There you go with your big intellectual words.' She smiles.

I laugh awkwardly, trying to push away the tears.

'Don't cry,' she says, which is always my cue.

She gets up and fetches me a Kleenex. 'I didn't want to make you cry. I only wanted to apologize.'

'And you didn't think that would make me cry?'

'Oh, don't get me going.' She flings her arms around me, breaking down into big, ravaging sobs. And there we are. Sobbing in each other's arms. Letting go together. Aware of love and regret. This feels like what we should have had. What we could have had. It feels like the release of years of pent-up disappointment. The recognition that two lifetimes that should have been running together in parallel somehow forked at the crossroads and lost their way.

Martin pops his head around the door. He appears perplexed at the sight of us. We're slumped back in the couch, me lying against Isabelle, hugging her waist, her arm draped around my shoulder. It's how I always dreamt we'd be.

'Dinner's ready,' he says uncomfortably. 'When you are, of course.'

'We'll be out in a second,' says Isabelle, still managing to bark at him through her sobs.

'OK,' he says, quickly backing out of the door.

'Oh dear,' she grimaces. 'Listen. I know in your letter you said that I should be nicer, but sometimes he needs to be told.' She laughs. 'But he means well. And he's a great dad and a great lawyer. You can't have everything.'

'You've not done badly,' I say. 'That's a nine out of ten by my reckoning.'

'A seven,' she says. 'The sex has gone. Make that a five.'

'Sex is overrated.'

'Telling me,' she says with a giggle. 'Actually, it's a relief. What with kids, you're always so tired.'

'I see,' I say.

'Oh no!' she says, shaking her head. 'It hasn't always been like that. Martin was great in the beginning. He was so fit, you remember? So good looking. But he's let himself go. It's difficult to eat healthily in his job. Out with clients all the time. But sex gets dull anyway, doesn't it? After a while.' She pauses in contemplation. 'Same old, same old.'

'It's been so long since I've been in a long-term relationship I don't remember. But thanks! You're a great advert for staying single.'

'I envy you that.'

'Don't be silly!'

'Really,' she says. 'I do. Your life always sounded so exciting. So free . . . after your divorce. And Mother always went on about how amazingly well you were doing in your job. Unlike me. Stuck at home. I was so short-sighted back then. Always in a rush to have a family and then that didn't happen quite as quickly as I'd hoped. I wish I'd got some qualifications first. I've never worked. I've achieved precisely nothing.'

'Oh, Isabelle. Don't be ridiculous. You have two beautiful daughters. What could be better? What have I got to show for myself? A list of failed relationships, an average degree, for all that mega brain power I supposedly had.'

She turns my face towards hers. 'I love you, Jennifer,' she says. 'And I'm truly sorry.'

'I love you too,' I say. I don't think we've ever said that to each other. So many firsts, too late.

'Thanks for writing the letter. It was very brave . . . I'm not a complete bitch, am I?'

'No, you're not,' I say. 'Only half the time.' We laugh and share a forgiving smile.

I feel amazing. I've made this happen. I've done something good between Isabelle and me. Not that I think she's a different person. She's exactly the same as she ever was. I can see that over the family dinner. She's bossy and controlling, but I see how her husband and children work around her. They take her for who she is and they love her for it. It's fascinating to watch from a place of acceptance instead of resistance and awe. Her behaviour has taken on a different quality. And it's not because I'm looking at her through rose-tinted glasses. Or that I'm trying to whitewash the past. It's simply that I understand her so much better now.

She smiles at me across the table. She's luminous. And that's how I want to remember her. I hope she'll remember me that way too.

Day 62

Every night, before I climb into bed, I cross off another date on my calendar, reminding myself of my ever-looming deadline. Of course I know some people defy these deadlines, but somehow, with the creeping tiredness and Dr Mackenzie's unshakable conviction, I don't feel I'm going to be one of the lucky ones. To be honest, I'm not convinced the counting is doing me any good. I feel I'm gamely watching the days slip by. But I'm committed to my calendar now, too frightened to stop in case it's an omen.

Harry is due back soon, which lifts my spirits, but no matter what my mood, sleep as always is hard to come by. Tonight I toss and turn, lie quietly for a bit, focus on deep breathing, but it's all hopeless. I decide to drag myself from the warmth of my bed, wrap myself in a blanket and lumber downstairs like some frozen somnambulist. It's so cold. So cold! I boil the kettle and make a herbal tea, then stumble back to bed, clutching it to my chest. Eventually, tea consumed, I close my eyes, at last heavy with sleep. Yet as soon as I feel I'm dropping off, my mind switches back on again. I think about work and Isabelle and Harry and what the end will feel like. My thoughts drive me to distraction.

Against all the wise counsel of the sleep sages, I brave the cold again, groan my way to my desk and retrieve my laptop, then crawl back up to bed. I google alternative advice for sleep and find myself listening to some weird crackling noises which are meant to be soothing. As I am trying to enter a form of meditation, my phone rings. It takes me by surprise. I check the screen and my heart skips a beat. It's Harry. I love the effect that seeing his name has on me.

'Hey! Where are you?' I say. I turn off the crackling, relaxing into the far more soothing sound of his voice.

'Still in Milan,' he says. 'I was going to leave a message. I thought you'd be asleep.'

'Chance would be a fine thing. Tell me nice things.'

'Tell me how you are.'

'Tired. Missing you.'

'I'm missing you too, but unfortunately I'm held up out here. Will you be OK for another week?'

'Oh no, Harry,' I sigh. 'That's so disappointing. I mean, time is not exactly on our side.'

'I'm so sorry, Sal.'

I groan. 'It's fine. It's just I was so looking forward to seeing you.'

'I was looking forward to seeing you too. I promise I'll make it up to you. I'm coming home next Friday. I'll pick you up Saturday morning and take you away from it all.'

'OK. Well, that's a nice thing! Sadly, I'm busy.'

'Seriously?'

'Of course not. I have no plans for the rest of my life.'

'Well, you do now. Be ready early. Pack light. You'll mainly be wearing a towelling robe. And I promise the time will fly by. It will be next Friday in a blink.'

'That's lovely but I'd like to hang on to time, if it's all right by you.'

'Of course you do. Stupid thing to say. Now, promise me if things change and you need me, you'll call. I swear I'll be there at the drop of a hat.'

Things change every day, Harry, I think. I just prefer not to talk about them.

'Promise,' I say. 'I've got you on speed dial.'

'Good. Now try and get some sleep!'

'Good night, Harry.'

We hang up and I put my laptop on the floor, all interest in crackling noises gone. It's as though someone is teasing me, keeping Harry at a distance, the way he always used to be in my dreams. But still, I get a weekend away with him. I should be grateful.

Day 56

This week has seen a sudden rush of activity, like my symptoms have finally woken up and remembered they have a job to do. On Monday a dark depression overwhelmed me like an unstoppable wall of water. Barely able to put one foot in front of the other, I retreated to bed, just about managing to send a text to Pattie to tell her I wasn't coming in. Work wasn't an option.

Tuesday, Day Fifty-eight, felt a bit lighter. I could still feel the misery in my soul but sensed it was losing its power. I waded through it, determined to go back to work, not to let it claim me, telling myself that so many good things had happened and there would be more to come; even in the short space of time I had left. I had to believe this.

I made myself see the bright side: I have Harry returning this weekend, taking me away because he cares about me, and Isabelle, who is coming over after I finish work on Friday, something she hasn't done in years. It's symbolic. Huge, actually! She needs to see that my life hasn't been the big, riotous singleton extravaganza she imagines and then maybe she'll accept that she's done pretty well, even on five out of ten.

But things are on the move again. From my bed of misery to the recovery of optimism, Wednesday began with full-blown, head-over-the-toilet vomiting. I've been feeling nauseated for a while but actual vomiting is a new development. And the nosebleeds have started. The information in the leaflets is becoming all too real.

Then today, Day Fifty-six, the worst happened. I can no longer use work as a diversion. I was resisting it for as long as possible, but Frank took the initiative. He took me aside in his office after morning conference where an untimely nosebleed seemed to startle everyone despite my protestations that it was nothing.

'You don't look good, Jennifer. I think you might be pushing yourself too hard.'

'I'm fine, Frank. That nosebleed was unfortunate.' I don't want to tell him I'm being sick too but it's as if he can see through me anyway.

'I don't want you to struggle. I want you to go home and take care of yourself.'

'I need to work, Frank. I need the distraction.'

'I understand. I do. But it's not helping you right now. You'll find better distractions at home.'

'But what about everything I'm involved in? What about my team?'

'We'll get cover, Jennifer. It's only temporary. I'm not saying this is for ever, because maybe the rest will do you good.'

I can see he's trying to be nice, cushioning the blow. 'It's not going to happen though, is it, Frank? It's going to be permanent. Once I leave . . .' I feel faint. 'That's it. Isn't it?'

'Oh, Jennifer,' he says. He sways disconcertingly and I swear he's trying to stave off tears. He lets out a huge sigh. 'I'm so sorry. Truly I am. But you never know. Things may improve. Don't give up without a fight. That's not your style.' Frank knows nothing of my personal life.

'Thanks, Frank. For everything. I hope you're right.'

He puts his hand on my shoulder and gives it a firm squeeze. 'We'll make sure you're looked after. Anything you need, and I mean anything, call me. We'll still keep your news to just Pattie and me. I'm sure no one will associate a random nosebleed with anything and, knowing what people are like, they've probably forgotten about it already. And don't worry, I'll keep Pattie in check. We'll think of a way of explaining your absence. Compassionate leave, maybe. No one ever questions that. It will account for the suddenness. And the lack of the usual party and cake.'

'Makes sense,' I say. 'Although I'll miss the cake.'

He gives a wry smile then grabs me in one of those unexpected big hugs. I smell the sweat of his armpits. Poor Frank. He must have hated doing that.

I'm crying all the way home. I know I'm being irresponsible and should go back to the doctor – I haven't rescheduled that cancelled appointment – and maybe I'm still in denial, but I'm hoping a couple of days with Harry at a spa will help. Of course if nothing changes, then I'll go and see Dr Mackenzie next week, but all he'll do is insist I start taking the drugs. And perhaps I'll have to. Maybe I'll even want to.

I text Harry.

I've had to give up work. I'm devastated.

To my amazement a reply pings straight back.

Even more reason for me to spoil you x

I take comfort in his immediacy and long to be held in his arms. But the onset of my new symptoms couldn't be worse timing. I wish they'd waited until after this weekend when he'll undoubtedly be away again. It's trivial in the scheme of things, but I don't want them to spoil our limited time together.

Truth is, Harry was never one for sympathy, even when I had nothing worse than a cold. Or a headache. Or, heaven forfend, period pains. I'm not sure why I'm putting all my deathbed expectations on to him. But credit where it's due, he's definitely more considerate. The shame is it took a terminal illness to change him. Why do we only appreciate what we've got when it's put at risk?

Day 55

Today Isabelle is coming over, which is a real turning point. I told her I'd stopped working and she's coming round earlier than planned, allowing herself time to get home and pick up the girls from school.

I've tidied up the house as best I can, vacuuming and polishing, even though it's draining me. I don't want the place to disappoint her.

She brings me a beautiful bunch of flowers. We exchange hugs and wander through into the living room. 'Last time I was here was aeons ago,' she says, giving everything a cursory glance. 'I don't remember it at all.' She goes to take her coat off, then changes her mind. 'It's bloody freezing in this house, Jen. Maybe that's why you got ill.'

'I've not got the flu, Isabelle.'

'No,' she says. 'Obviously not. Sorry. Listen, I don't know whether I should say this, but are you aware your eyes are bloodshot?'

'Strain of vomiting.'

'Oh, Jennifer,' she says, failing to muffle a gag. 'That's awful. You poor, poor darling.' She shudders.

'Sorry to be a pain, but have you got a hot-water bottle? I'm not used to the chill and I can do without catching a cold.'

'Sure. That would be annoying.'

We stand in the kitchen and she chats away about nothing while the kettle boils. I'm making her a coffee with her hottie.

I peel some ginger. 'You having ginger tea?' she says.

'Yeah. Want some?'

'I love ginger tea.'

'I don't know you at all, do I?' I say.

In the living room, she sits huddled in the armchair with the hot-water bottle stuffed inside her coat, cupping her mug close to her, warming her hands. 'This is quite a lovely room, Jennifer,' she says, looking around.

'You're being polite.'

'Maybe,' she says. 'A little bit. But at least I'm trying.' We both laugh. 'So how are you coping? I mean, how on earth can you be doing this on your own?'

'I'm not on my own any more,' I say. 'Harry and I are together again.' Her eyebrows strain upwards. 'I sent him a letter too. He's been quite wonderful. He's taking me to a spa tomorrow.'

'That's so lovely,' she swoons. 'I'm so pleased for you. You need someone. Everyone needs someone. I just hope he's kinder to you this time.'

'Not much harm he can do in fifty-five days,' I say.

She chokes on some tea. 'Are you counting down the days?'

'Yes.'

'Why? That's awful. I mean, that's like . . . being on death row.'

'I am on death row.'

She looks away. 'It just seems wrong,' she huffs. 'Listen, I was going to suggest you come and stay with us. I'll take care of you. Unless Harry's living with you, of course?'

'That's really kind. Thank you.'

'Well, it would be warmer.'

'But I'd rather stay here. Not that Harry's living with me. His work takes him away a lot. He's abroad more than he's home and, besides, he has a beautiful flat in the city. He has this amazing view of the Shard.'

'Gosh!' she says, as though she's impressed. 'Think of the pollution.'

I snort. 'Yes. I'm sure he does.'

'Oh well! The offer is definitely open, should you change your mind. You ought to do something about your heating though.'

'I'm fine, Isabelle. I'm used to it. Honestly, I don't even notice the cold.'

'So who else did you write to?'

'Just you, Harry, Andy and Elizabeth.'

'Andy and Elizabeth. Did you hear back?'

'Yes, actually. Andy sent a lovely letter. In an Andy kind of way.'

'Can I see it?'

'No! It's personal.'

'Oh, go on.'

'You can see it when I'm dead. If you can find it.'

'I'm not going to wade through your things. What about Elizabeth?'

'Nada.'

'Ah well. Not much she can say really, is there?'

'You mean apart from sorry.'

She shrugs. 'Maybe she's not sorry.'

'Ouch.'

She picks at some ragged loose threads on the arm of the chair. 'Not everyone's kind like you. In fact, I think you're the exception that proves the rule. Most of the women I know are real bitches. I'm aware you think I am too, but some of the mothers at school are far worse than me. You're lucky you've never had to deal with any of them.'

'I don't think you're a bitch,' I say. 'But I'd have quite liked to have been a mother. Even if it meant dealing with some bitchy ones at school.'

She shakes her head. 'I can't believe I thought you never wanted kids. Shows how wrong you can be. And I'm so sorry that bugger cheated on you because of it. I guess we can't always know what drives people into other people's arms when everything seems fine on the surface.'

'Did it seem fine on the surface?'

'Always. I was shocked when you told me. Mum and Dad were shocked too. So upset for you.'

This is a revelation to me. 'They never said as much. It was like, Move on. Let's not discuss it. He's not worthy.'

'Well that's classic Mum and Dad. They never liked discussing uncomfortable stuff. They probably thought they were being helpful by not bringing up the subject.'

'I know. But why? Look how long it's taken us to have a real conversation. And look how good it feels. I loved them but seriously, they were hopeless at dealing with shit.'

I point to a black-and-white photo of them that sits on my sideboard, dancing together at some ball, happy and relaxed. 'They were such a beautiful couple,' I say. 'A shining example of a perfect marriage, and that's all they ever allowed anyone to see. Did they never falter? I certainly never heard them argue.'

'Nor me.'

'It was as though they didn't want us to find out that life is messy and people screw up.'

'Damn! You found out!'

'I still miss them,' I say. 'Do you ever think about them?'

'All the time. The fact they can't see the girls growing up.'

'Yeah. That's tough. But I'm glad they're not here for this. I wouldn't want them knowing about me.'

'They'd never have coped. Never!' She gives a little shiver. 'Anyway. Let's be more Mum and Dad. Talk about nice things. So where do you think Harry is going to take you for your spa weekend?'

'Not a clue. He wants it to be a surprise.'

'Oh, how lovely and romantic. Martin used to do that sort of thing for me. In the good old days! Before the kids. Gosh. You make me realize what we've allowed to let go. It's so sad when you lose the magic.'

I want to say something encouraging, like the magic will return, but before I have a chance to say anything, she lets out a little mew and bursts into tears.

I'm thrown. It's totally unexpected. From nowhere. I'm not sure what to do. I go over to the chair and place my arm around her shoulder. She fans her hand in front of her face. 'Oh, don't worry about me,' she says. 'I'm so sorry. I promised myself I wouldn't do this.'

'It's fine,' I say. 'Isn't this precisely what we were talking about?'

She puts down the tea and grapples for her handbag, pulling out a tissue.

I dash into the kitchen and come back with a half-empty box. 'Here,' I say, putting it down next to her. She's properly sobbing now. She leans over, grabs at another tissue, dabs her eyes, delicately blows her nose, then starts sobbing again.

'I don't know what this is all about,' she says. 'I feel ridiculous. I'm sorry. It overwhelmed me. Maybe it's talking about Mum and Dad. Maybe it's knowing I'm going to lose you.' She lets out a plaintive wail and I kneel at her feet, resting my chin on her knees, looking into her pale wet eyes.

'But that's not the only reason, is it?'

She glances down at me, then closes her eyes as if to say, Don't go there. 'Oh God, Jennifer,' she jibbers. 'It's so difficult. When you've got children, all the endless obligations. Always dashing from this activity to the next, worrying that you're neglecting one child or favouring the other or neglecting your husband when really the only one you're neglecting is yourself. I've forgotten the person I used to be.' She looks back at me. 'And I have no romantic weekend to look forward to. Ever!' She throws her head over her knees and her hair flops forward. I massage the exposed nape of her neck, trying to calm her.

'Don't be silly,' I say. 'You're amazing with the girls and Martin merely needs a nudge. All men do. Look at me, I have to die in order to get a spa weekend.'

She snorts into her lap. 'Not funny.'

'And I completely understand how difficult it is. Juggling the way you do. I admire you so much, how you've kept everything together. Your children are adorable. A real credit to you.'

She composes herself. Her bottom lip trembles, her face is streaked with make-up. She hugs the hot-water bottle like a child does their teddy bear.

'Shall I refill it? It must be cold now.'

'It's fine . . . it's fine . . . oh God!' she cries. 'I shouldn't tell you this – I swore I wouldn't but I can't keep it to myself a moment longer. And I know I shouldn't need to ask you to swear to secrecy but—'

'I swear I will take whatever secret you have to the grave.'

'Don't keep saying things like that,' she says. She looks me in the eye and snivels. 'You mustn't talk that way. It's awful.'

'OK. I won't. Now tell me what's wrong.'

'Oh, Jennifer. I wish I didn't have to involve you. Can you bear it?'

'Of course.'

She bites her lip. 'No,' she says. 'No . . . I mustn't! I'm sorry. I'm being so selfish. You don't need to be burdened with my pathetic story. You have quite enough worries of your own.'

I give an exasperated sigh. 'Actually, I'd quite like to worry about something other than myself for a change.'

She looks at me imploringly. 'Is it wine o'clock?' she says.

'Does it have to be?'

'No,' she smiles. 'Not in my household.'

I go into my kitchen and scurry around trying to find a bottle of white wine, but I've only got a couple of bottles of red. I've hardly been intending to replenish my stock. 'This is embarrassing,' I say from the kitchen. 'I only have red wine. Or whisky.'

'Red wine is fine,' she says. 'And maybe some water.'

'What about your teeth?'

'That's what the water's for.'

'Of course,' I say.

I unscrew the bottle and pour her a large glass. I pour us both some water and wander back into the sitting room. She's checking her face in a little mirror, removing the rivers of mascara. She quickly flips it shut and puts it back in her handbag. 'Thanks,' she says, taking the glass of wine from the tray and I put the water down on the floor next to her.

'Who is he, then?'

She looks back at me, startled. 'What makes you say that?' she asks, but her stunned expression has already told me everything I need to know.

'Because I'm not sure what else it could be. I don't think you've got a rare blood disorder, have you?'

'No,' she says, snivelling. 'No. Obviously I haven't.' The glass of wine judders against her lips and she takes a lingering breath followed by a long slow sip. 'You're right. You must have a sixth sense,' she says. 'He's a teacher at Cecily's school. I don't know what to do.'

'And you're having an affair?'

'Yes,' she sniffs. 'Don't judge me. I know it's your bugbear.'

I take stock. 'So how long has it been going on?'

'Not long . . . a year, I guess. He was Cecily's form teacher.'

I'm trying not to look too surprised but I think I'm failing. 'Martin doesn't suspect, does he?'

'No.' She thinks for a second. 'Well, if he does he's keeping it very close to his chest.'

'The girls?'

'No. We're very discreet. And if the school bitches suspected, I'd know because everyone would bloody know.'

I pull my knees up to my chest. 'So, apart from the obvious, what's the problem?'

Her face stretches into a silent scream. 'He wants me to leave Martin.'

'Hmmmm . . . Do you want to leave Martin?'

'No . . . I mean, I'm not sure.' She throws her hand to her forehead. 'It's an impossible situation.'

'It's far from impossible, Isabelle. Is he married?'

'No. He's twenty-nine. Never been married.'

'Wow. Young!'

She tries to hide a coy smile.

'So it'll probably fizzle out,' I encourage.

She looks horrified. 'Why do you say that?' she says, and I realize she's serious about this man and fizzling out is definitely not a consideration.

'I don't know.' I deliberate. 'He's young. He'll probably want to settle down.'

'I told you! He does. With me.'

'And have children.'

'Yes! With me!'

'I hate to point this out, Isabelle, but you're nearly forty-eight. It's hardly likely, is it?'

'It's totally likely. Not by the normal route, obviously. The menopause has done for that, but that's not what I'm saying. I mean, he'll have the girls. He loves Cecily. I'm sure he'll love Sophia too.'

'So you're going to leave Martin?' I feel inordinately sorry for the geek.

'No. I couldn't do that to Cecily and Sophia.'

'I'm confused then. What's the issue?'

'I don't want to leave Barry either.'

The sound of my laughter surprises us both. 'Isabelle! You cannot have an affair with someone called Barry. That goes against all the rules.'

She's glaring at me. I can see she doesn't see the

funny side. 'What's the difference between Barry and Harry?' she snarls.

A consonant, I think. Oh, the power of a consonant. 'You're right,' I say.

'Anyway, if you met him you wouldn't say that. He's so handsome, the name becomes handsome too.'

'I'm sure. So, why do you have to do anything?'

She looks across at me, eyes narrowed. 'Because he's threatening to tell Martin if I don't,' she hisses.

I feel the room shift. 'Oh my God, Isabelle!' I say. 'That's awful. That's blackmail. Doesn't *Barry* realize how terrible that is? What that will do to the girls? Their schooling, their relationship with you, with their father? With him? That'll ruin everything!'

'Oh God! Will it? You think?'

'Well . . . yes. Don't you?'

'I'm trying not to think about it.'

You see, that's the problem when you've led a charmed life. You simply haven't a clue how to deal with things when they don't go your way.

'Do you think he'll carry through with the threat?' I say. 'He must surely be risking his job? You think he's *that* reckless?'

'Oh God, Jennifer. You're panicking me. I don't know. I've never even considered that. It's all too awful. I want to curl up and die!'

'Want to swap?' I say.

She tuts. 'I didn't mean it that way. You know I didn't.'

'OK, OK.'

I draw my legs tighter to my chest. Isabelle drains her wine.

'Do you want a top-up?'

'No. I'm driving. Maybe I should have come by cab, but I have to pick the girls up from school don't I?'

'Is that when you see Barry?'

'No!' she says with distaste, like it's an unconscionable suggestion. 'No! I told you. We're very discreet.'

I raise my eyebrows.

She puts down the wine glass and leans forward to take a long sip of water. She fiddles with her perfectly highlighted hair, drawing it over her shoulder and twisting it into a plait. 'There is something you could do to help, though,' she says.

I sense danger. I recognize that look. 'There is? What?'

'You could meet Barry. With me, obviously. Prove to him that you're dying.'

'What?' I can't believe she said that. 'What on earth for?'

'Oh, please don't be upset with me, Jennifer. I don't want you to be offended.' Her eyes tear up and she blots them with a fresh tissue.

'I'm not offended,' I say, which is the truth: I'm horrified. 'But why on earth would you want me to prove I'm dying to Barry?'

'You promise you won't get annoyed?'

'I'll do my best.'

She looks nervous. 'Well . . .' She winces as though I might hit her. 'I told him I would agree to leave my husband but that I had a sister who was dying and that I couldn't possibly do anything so unsettling for the time being. Not under the circumstances. The girls and I would need to recover from our loss before I could bring any more changes into our lives.'

'Thank you,' I say. 'Such a sweet thought.' I feel like I'm overhearing a conversation at my graveside.

'I hoped it might put him off doing anything for a while. I hoped then maybe he'd forget and we'd slip back into normality.'

'It has the ring of normal.'

'Only he doesn't believe me.'

'I'm liking the sound of Barry a lot.'

'He says I've never even mentioned a sister before, so why all of a sudden?'

'He has a point.'

'So I need you to go and see him. To prove that you exist.'

'What? And take my blood tests with me?'

'No, Jennifer. Don't be ridiculous. Why are you making this so hard for me?'

I shake my head at her myopic pig-headedness. 'I'm not. I'm trying to make it easy for you, Isabelle. How does "no" sound?'

She stares at me, checking I'm being serious. 'No? You mean . . . you *won't*?'

'That's right. I won't.'

She's amazed. Amazed to hear me speak that way – to her, someone I've never said 'no' to in my entire life. It's a critical moment. Not one that makes me feel good, because that would mean I have no feelings for Isabelle's situation and I do. But I don't want to be a pawn in her game any more and for once I'm not going to allow myself to be manipulated. For all her vulnerable beseeching.

'Look,' I say. 'Either he believes you and trusts that you have a sister who's dying, or he doesn't trust you, in which case the relationship is doomed anyway. But you've got yourself into this mess, Isabelle, and you're going to have to be the one who gets yourself out of it.'

'Jennifer!' Her red-raw eyes glower at me. 'But I've been so supportive of you. Can't you at least find it in your heart to be supportive of me?'

I gape at her with incredulity, realizing she genuinely believes what she's saying.

'I'm hugely supportive of you, Isabelle. I've always been supportive. You know that. But you have a lovely family and I'm not going to help you destroy it. And it's not because he's called Barry. And it's not because I disapprove. I think everyone is entitled to seek happiness in whatever form it takes, so long as they accept responsibility for the fallout. What I'm saying is, you can't drag my dying into this. It's absurd.'

We are staring at each other, in uncharted territory. Her expression is that of a woman deeply misunderstood.

'Fine,' she says. 'Fine! If that's what you think.' She throws off the hot-water bottle, stands up and shakes out her hair, pushing her chin forward with stubborn resolve. 'In which case, Jennifer, I think it's possibly best we go back to how things were. We have to accept we are different people with different lives. I hoped I'd get more compassion from you, but I was wrong. I thought you would understand my feelings, but you're still that same goody two shoes you always were.'

'Oh, I understand your feelings all too well, Isabelle. It's a shame you can't understand mine.' My mouth is dry. 'I told you, I'm not judging you. And I mean it. I'm not. But I'm not going to collude with you in your deception. There will be somebody else out there who will happily do the job for you, but it's not on my bucket list. Thank you all the same.'

She picks up her handbag, flounces towards the door, yanks it open, hesitates, slams it shut, then swivels round on her heels and collapses to the floor in a heap. Her coat pools round her like a protective moat.

I'm fixed to the spot. 'You OK?'

She glares back at me. 'What do you care?'

'Oh, stop it! Of course I care.'

She puts her head in her hands. 'Damn you, Jennifer,' she says. 'You're so annoying I want to punch you. Why do you have to be so goddamn moral? Do you have any idea how frustrating that is?'

I can't help myself any longer, it's as if a tornado has been whipping up inside me for years.

'Do you have even the faintest idea how irritating it is for me to hear you say that?' I yell. She stares at me, open-mouthed. 'I'm fed up with that attitude. I'm bored with being labelled a goody two shoes! I'm bored with having to be nice and sensible. What good did it ever do me?'

'God! You're so angry.'

'Too right I'M ANGRY. Wouldn't you be angry? Here you are with your whole gilded life ahead of you, willingly messing it up, and God knows it will probably all go right for you in the end. And look at me. All I've ever wanted is to be decent and kind and fair and this happens. OF COURSE I'M ANGRY!'

Her face pales. 'Hush, sis,' she says softly. 'It's OK. It's all going to be OK.'

'NO, IT ISN'T!'

'You're right,' she says, struggling to her feet. 'It isn't. But I'm still going to hug you whether you like it or not. Even if you kick and scream and try to get the fuck away!'

She walks towards me, arms flung wide, then envelops me inside her coat.

'You said the F-word,' I say. 'Mum and Dad would soap your mouth out for less than that.'

'I hate to remind you, but they're not here. You can say it now. You can say it as loud and as often as you like.'

I let go of her and scream 'FUCK!' at the top of my lungs and she starts to scream with me.

'FUCK FUCK FUCK FUCK FUCK!'

We're shouting with laughter, holding on to one another. Bouncing up and down like a couple of crazy kids.

I lean against the wall, holding my aching sides. 'God, that felt good!' I say.

'It felt FUCKING GOOD,' she yells, getting her breath back, smiling. Her face changes. 'Oh, why has it taken us so long to be sisters?' she says. 'This is such fun.'

'I should have written that letter years ago,' I say.

'And now you have a damned illness. Go away, you parasite! Leave my sister alone!'

'Thanks, Isabelle! That's worked.'

'Excellent. Then maybe you owe me one.' She simpers up to me and puts on a silly girl plaintive voice. 'Would you see Barry for me?'

I gawp at her. 'You are joking, aren't you?'

'Kind of . . . Oh, don't fret! Of course I'm joking. And yes, I got myself into this mess, blah blah blah. Point taken.'

I smile. Relieved. 'But I'm here if you need someone to talk to. For the time being anyway.'

'I know,' she says, kissing my cheek. 'Stick around, kiddo! And now I have to go and be a grown-up and collect some kids who call me Mummy. Let me know about your weekend. Hope it's somewhere fabulous.'

I watch her leave. I've never been more sad to see her go.

Day 54

The rumble of a car announces Harry's arrival before he even rings the doorbell. Once then twice. I have one last gargle of mouthwash, shove it in my carry-on and rush to the door. A quick glance in the mirror to check my eyes aren't bloodshot and I open up, ready to go. He's wrapped in a navy scarf, his face working its instant magic. I feel happy. Excited. This is a special treat intended to help me forget the bad stuff and I'm going to try my damnedest to ensure it does.

Yesterday morning, I called the doctor's surgery to tell them I was going to a spa and to ask if there was anything I should avoid. I'm put through to a nurse who checks my notes and says I should probably avoid saunas and jacuzzis, anything that involves a lot of heat or could hold bacteria, but otherwise she says she's sure it will do me the world of good. Whatever helps improve my state of mind is as beneficial as any medication. I tell her my state of mind is pretty sound and she says she's glad for me. She has no idea that my state of mind is called Harry.

'My favourite Sally!' he says. 'Your carriage awaits you.' He points at a shiny Range Rover. 'Check it out!'

'Is that yours?' I say.

'For the weekend. I could hardly take you in the old banger. I don't want to make you more ill.'

'Oh, Harry!' I jump up to his cheek and kiss him. 'That's so thoughtful.'

He opens the door for me then grabs my carry-on and puts it in the boot.

'It's like the interior of an aeroplane,' I say as he climbs in.

'I could probably get used to it,' he smiles. 'But I wouldn't want to turn in the old lady.'

'Of course not.'

Ten minutes into the journey, I say, 'So fess up. Where are you taking me?'

'Come on! It's a surprise,' he says. 'You'll have to wait till we get there.' He smiles across at me. 'You feeling OK? Do you want me to open the sunroof for a bit of air?'

'No, this is perfect. This is luxury.'

Having expected to suffer in the old banger, I've brought a tin of travel sweets, the kind my parents always had for car journeys. I dig around in my handbag and pull them out, struggling to unscrew the lid. This was always a good game in our family. I can hear Isabelle in my head.

'Jennifer, give it to me! You're useless.'

'No. I felt it twist. I've nearly done it.'

'Give it to your sister, Jennifer. You've had your turn. You've been trying for quite long enough.' That would be my mother.

'Ta-dah!' says Isabelle as the icing sugar bursts out in a puff of the sweetest white smoke.

'But I was the one who made it twist,' I'd say.

'What are you laughing about?' says Harry.

'Travel sweets. Want one?'

He looks across. 'Oh my God! I haven't had one of those for years. My parents always had them in the car for long journeys.'

'So did mine,' I say. 'That and Dramamine. My mother was never without her disgusting pink Dramamine. What colour do you want?'

'Red, please.'

'Reds are mine,' I say, immediately coveting what was once always reserved for Isabelle. I'm sucking fervently, thinking they used to feel so much bigger. 'You'll have to fight me for a red one.'

He snorts. 'You sound like my brother!'

'Actually, I sound like my sister.'

'OK, since it's you, I'll have a purple one.'

I pop a purple sweet in his mouth and his lips get a white dusting. I stare at him and smile. He looks adorably silly.

'Lick your lips,' I say, and he does.

'Now make your tongue touch the tip of your nose.' He goes to attempt it and I laugh. 'You're very well behaved this morning.'

'Very funny,' he says. 'But it's nice to see you happy.'

'Sometimes it's the simple things in life that bring the most satisfaction. That and pratfalls.'

'Ah,' he says. 'Your love of slapstick.'

I realize we're heading south. 'Are we going to Brighton?'

'Maybe,' he says, his smile the giveaway.

'Oh, I do like to be beside the seaside. I do like to be beside the sea.' I'm singing. Happy, happy, happy.

'I do like to stroll along the prom! Prom! Prom!' he rejoinders. 'But today is for special treats. Maybe tomorrow.'

It's not too long before he pulls into a sweeping driveway and we cruise down an elegant avenue of trees. In the distance is a magnificent stately home, the kind you see in the dusty copies of *Country Life* left in doctors' waiting rooms, my least favourite place.

'Honey, we're home,' he says, looking across at me. 'Well, let's pretend we are. For a couple of days.'

'I can do pretend,' I say.

'And we can pretend the other guests are our servants. Watch the horror on their faces when we ask them to bring us tea. "Oh, I'm so sorry. I thought you were a member of our staff."'

I laugh. 'First one to do *that* wins a tenner.'

'Oooo. High stakes,' he says.

He grabs our bags from the boot and we crunch across the gravel, up some wide limestone steps into a grand reception hall. It smells of wax polish and lilies. 'Our' staff are warm and charming, talking us through everything. After check-in, we are shown to our suite,

191

which is vast and luxurious, full of silks and velvets and piles of perfectly plumped cushions covering the four-poster bed, which beckons me. I throw off my shoes and lie down on the bed, closing my eyes, listening as Harry pads about, inspecting everything. My head starts to fool around. Is this what it would have felt like if we'd held on to our relationship. Fun? Cared for? Special?

'You dreaming?' he says. I open my eyes and he takes a photo of me on his phone. 'Pretty,' he says, then jumps on the bed. 'Selfie, please,' and he holds out his phone arm and we both smile. 'One more.'

'Let me see first.' He shows me. 'Jeez, my hair!' I smooth down the back. 'OK, ready!' He takes several of us making ridiculous faces then passes me a brown leather sleeve. 'For my darling,' he says. 'You'll need to get going.'

'I don't have an ounce of get going in me, but I'll do my best.'

I open the folder. There's a long list of luxurious treatments. No expense has been spared. 'Thank you, Harry. That's amazing. Are you not having any?'

'No. You go and enjoy yourself. I'm going to have a power nap and then maybe I'll go for a long walk. Plus, I've got a bit of work to do.'

'Werk, werk, werk. But if you change your mind . . .' I retreat into the bathroom, get into my fluffy white bathrobe. I check my face and smile. I remember you, I think. That's your happy face.

'See you later,' I say, passing through the bedroom.

'Get some relaxation. That's what you're here for.'

'Really,' I say. 'You're sure that's all?' I playfully inch open my bathrobe to reveal a set of black lacy underwear discovered when I was organizing my clothes for charity. Wrapped in tissue at the back of a drawer, it was gathering dust hoping for a special occasion. I found it just in time. For dinner this evening, I've packed a beautiful dress I've owned for years but never worn. From where I stand now, I would definitely tell my younger self to wear whatever she wanted, whenever she fancied. I'd tell her that if she felt so inclined, she should wear her best dress to the supermarket. That she shouldn't waste her time waiting for that special occasion because the occasion doesn't matter. And she should always wear pretty underwear because she deserves it even when she feels she doesn't.

Harry raises his eyebrows. 'Put that away now or you'll be late and that sweated-over schedule will go up the spout.'

'You sweated over my schedule?' I smile. 'That's such a flattering and yet somehow disturbing thought.'

'So don't waste it.'

'Now I feel as though you're trying to get rid of me.'

'Hardly. I want you to be around for as long as possible.'

'I set you up for that one, didn't I?' I say.

I take the sweeping staircase down to the basement where the whole atmosphere changes. The decor is modern and minimalist. The air feels warm, humid in fact, and I follow the scent of aromatic oils towards the spa.

The rest of the day floats by like an enchanted illusion. Every bone in my body is so tired, so infused with bad blood, I happily doze through all the treatments, sleepwalking from one to the next. I drift through my deluxe massage and my purifying facial. I float above the clouds during my signature pedicure, my head nods off embarrassingly during my manicure. I achieve my objective to forget that I am ill until a thought flutters through my brain. *At least I'll have perfect fingers and toes when I go to my grave.* Sometimes my head messes with my best intentions.

I return to the suite feeling polished and shiny, trying to ignore the tiredness that permanently hovers, like tinnitus, in the background.

I open the door to our suite and hear voices. For a second I panic that I've walked in on something then realize it's the TV. The curtains are drawn, Harry is lying on the bed in his bathrobe. He quickly shuts his iPad like he's guilty. My feminine hackles jump to attention but I push them back down. I don't want my suspicious self to ruin this. I'm too happy.

'Look at you,' he says. 'All pink and glowing. Have you had a wonderful day?'

'You have no idea,' I say. 'Thank you so much. It means a lot.'

'Come and lie down then before dinner.' He pats the bed and invites me to crawl into the crook of his arm. 'Fancy watching something?'

'What, you mean the football is on?'

'No!' he says. 'But then again . . .'

'I don't mind,' I say through a yawn. 'I can fall asleep. I'm exhausted.'

'From all the sleeping?' he laughs.

'How did you guess?'

He kisses my cheek. 'You smell nice. All herbal and oily.'

'I am an oil slick. Wanna slip off me?' I may not be able to get very far but I'm not going to miss the opportunity to at least attempt make-up sex with Harry before I die.

'Not if you're going to fall asleep,' he says.

I start to untie my bathrobe. 'See what you can do to hold my attention.'

He turns towards me and runs his finger down my sternum. My flesh tingles.

'Are you sure?' he says. 'I mean, honestly, I didn't get you here to fuck you. I wanted to give you something that would make you feel good.'

'Fucking me will make me feel good.'

He gives an uncomfortable laugh.

'Don't you want to?' I say, embarrassed.

'Of course I want to,' he says. 'I just wasn't sure you'd be . . . you know . . . up to it . . .'

'I'm not sure either, but let's give it a try. Go gently.'

He reaches towards the side of the bed and dims the lights.

'Let me take your bathrobe off,' he says.

I lie there in my black lingerie, looking back at him as he throws off his robe.

'Beautiful,' he says, stroking me. He leans in and butterfly kisses my face. 'Gentle enough?'

'Yes.'

He wets his forefingers and runs them across my skin. 'Do you know . . . you have the sexiest . . . goosebumps.'

I laugh and close my eyes, taking in the sensation. 'Don't let that distract you,' I say.

I allow my senses to follow his touch, his fingers drawing my curves until he traces down my stomach, circling my belly button, slowly reaching between my legs. 'This OK?'

I merely nod, I can't speak now. I'm in raptures. His mere touch has always had this effect on me. Can it be this way for ever, please? For ever isn't long.

He stops mid-arousal, his tongue slowly lingering up my body.

'How are you doing?' he whispers.

'I'm good.'

'Then I'd like to fuck you.'

'I'd like that too.'

He leans across me, his hand grappling in the bed-side drawer. 'Hotel supply. They think of everything.'

He tears open the foil of the condom and holds it up to the faint light, slipping it over his erection with theatrical aplomb. I smile. I'd forgotten his condom performance was worthy of Shakespeare.

We make love in a way that is familiar yet new. The smell of him, the taste of him, the tenderness of his kiss, transports me to a place of utter bliss.

'You OK?' he gasps.

'Yes,' I sigh. 'Now really fuck me.' We make love with all the intensity of two people who know this time might be their last.

We lie there afterwards, tucked into each other, spooning, recovering our sense of reality.

'Wow,' he says. 'That was unexpected.'

'Not for me.'

'Temptress!'

'Yeah, I've found my inner Mata Hari.'

He laughs, swoops up my hair and kisses the nape of my neck.

'I like your inner Mata Hari,' he says and rolls on to his back. 'Just forty winks,' he mumbles and he's asleep.

I feel woozy: whether with love or sex or massage oils. I fumble to the bathroom and lock the door, leaning up against the double basin unit, pressing my head against the cool of the mirror. I take some deep breaths then study my reflection. My hair is wild, my cheeks flushed. A smirk appears across my face. 'Well, what do you know, Jennifer?' I say. 'You just made love to Harry and he's asleep in that bed. The one you're going to climb back into. Whoever's in charge up there has just granted your wish.'

* * *

We get dressed for dinner.

'You look lovely,' he says. 'New dress?'

'Yes,' I say. I don't need to explain my recent resolutions.

We walk into the wood-panelled restaurant that is full of diners and yet somehow so quiet you can hear a pin drop. Even the waiters seem to whisper.

'Wine, sir? Madam?'

'You drinking, Sally?'

'Not tonight, thanks.'

'Do you mind if I do?' he asks.

'Of course not.'

We eat our meal, staring across at one another like two young lovers at the start of a budding romance, holding hands, tasting from each other's plates, which is good because I can hide the fact I'm barely eating. Not hungry at all. And then, as if to say this is going far too well, my body decides to show me who's boss. I excuse myself from the table and dash to the cloakroom, feeling hot and weird. There is a ribbon of sweat across my upper lip. I quickly drench one of the towels in cold water and press it over my face, hoping to cool down. 'Don't do this to me, body,' I plead. 'Not now. Don't let me down. Allow me some last moments of pleasure. Please. And if you do, I promise when the time comes, I'll go quietly.' My nose starts to bleed. Shit!

'You OK?' Harry says with a look of concern when I return to the table. 'You were gone for so long, I was wondering if I was going to have to break into the ladies' loos.'

I smile at the thought. 'Yeah. I'm fine now. Panic over. You're not going to have to save me.'

After dinner, we wander back through reception and I'm expecting to go up to our room when Harry says, 'Stop a moment.'

I frown at him.

'Relax,' he says. 'You're going to like this. Now turn around.'

'What have you got up your sleeve?' I say as he twirls me round.

'Magic.'

I'm aware of him fiddling in his pocket, then some silk presses against my eyelids and he ties it behind my head in a blindfold.

'Harry! You can't do this in reception.'

'Stop worrying about everything. Now hold my hand.'

I reach for his hand and walk with him blindly, not having a clue where he's leading me. I imagine we're going down a corridor because the sounds change and I hear him open a door. He walks me through it and the click of the latch makes my heart lurch.

'Where are we?'

'Ready?'

'I'm not sure.'

'Well, ready or not,' he says, and he removes the blindfold.

I blink for a second. I'm standing in what appears to be a small private cinema. There are four red velvet love chairs, little couple sofas. I look around, open-mouthed.

'What have you done?' I say.

'*Match of the Day* is on.'

'Be serious.'

'Just sit down and get comfortable.' He points to a sofa.

My jaw remains firmly open as I sit down and he sits next to me. 'Right,' he says and starts fishing around on the floor.

'What are you doing?'

He bobs back up and passes me a neatly wrapped rectangular box. 'Because I love you, Sally.'

My eyes light up and I shake it, smiling. I'm overwhelmed.

'Open it.'

I tear back the wrapping. 'Oh. My. God!' I gasp. '*Mallomars. The greatest cookie of all time*,' I quote, my eyes gleaming in wonder. 'Are we going to watch *When Harry Met Sally*?'

'We certainly are. We're going to have our very own New Year's Eve together – come what may.'

'Oh, Harry!' I say, welling up, swinging my arms around his neck and kissing him. 'This is the nicest thing anyone has ever done for me!'

'Now hold that thought,' he says as he gets up and disappears for a minute, and I reflect on how lucky I am and how crazy this is.

He sits back down. 'Right, phones off, please. The movie's about to begin.'

'My phone's been on silent all day.'

'Good. I don't want you shaming yourself.'

The lights go down and he reaches across and holds my hand. I pass him the box of Mallomars.

'Want one?' he whispers.

'Not yet.'

We watch together, my face entranced as if I've never seen it before. Harry munches on Mallomars. I join in with all my favourite lines, squawking 'Pecan Pie. Pecan Pie', and he squawks with me when before he always took the piss. We sing along to 'Surrey With The Fringe On Top' and 'It Had To Be You'. Tonight he joins me in my every foible.

By the time Billy Crystal is rushing to Times Square to catch Meg Ryan before the New Year ball-drop, I'm in tears as though I think he might not make it. When he says the iconic line – *When you realize you want to spend the rest of your life with somebody, you want the rest of your life to start as soon as possible* – I am completely done for.

Harry puts his arm around me. 'Sorry,' he says. 'I didn't remember that one.'

'It's beautiful, Harry,' I say. 'Don't worry.'

As the credits roll, I turn to thank him. 'Wait,' he says. 'It's not over yet.'

I watch as the credits fade and my eyes pop out as a photo of him from a few years back appears then a photo of me followed by the title 'When Harry Met His Favourite Sally'. A slow montage of old photos of us, some I've never seen before, starts. His thoughtfulness and effort are so touching, I'm deeply moved. Finally, the shots he took of us on the bed this morning appear and I'm dazzled by the unexpected thrill of it all. I'm so glad I never challenged him when I came back from the spa. I guess he was doing something wonderful.

'You've just done the impossible,' I say. 'You've made me love you more.'

'Happy New Year, Sally,' he says, and his eyes water.

'Happy New Year, Harry.'

We stroll back to the room, gazing into each other, not wanting to let go of the romance of the moment. Finally, we fall into bed and he holds me close, telling me he loves me and he wishes he hadn't eaten so many Mallomars. Almost mid-sentence, he falls asleep. Tonight I forgive him everything.

Day 53

I'm woken by the early-morning light and that queasy feeling I hoped I would be spared. Harry is on his side, turned away from me, the gentle rise and fall of his shoulders telling me he's still sleeping.

I slip quietly from under the covers and tiptoe into the bathroom then fall on to my knees, throwing my face over the lavatory bowl and fumbling for a towel to put over my head in a desperate attempt to muffle the sound. I stay there, shivering, staring into the sullied bowl waiting for it to be over. I flush, cringing at how intrusive the noise of water sounds.

How long, Lord? How long? What do I have to do in order for you to allow me some final moments of unencumbered joy? What? Tell me, Lord, universe, whoever the hell's in charge, and I'll do it.

There's a knock at the bathroom door. 'You OK?'

'Don't come in, Harry,' I plead. 'It's a war zone.'

'Can I get you anything?'

'No, no. I'm OK now. I'll come out. Just give me two.'

I stagger to my feet, throw water over my face, check

my nose isn't bleeding – it isn't – brush my teeth then gargle with my mouthwash.

Harry is standing by the door waiting for me, his face ashen.

'Oh baby,' he says. 'I'm so sorry. Come back to bed.' He lifts me in his arms and puts me back under the covers then climbs in next to me.

'I had no idea,' he says. 'You cover up so well.'

'I didn't want you to have to witness that. Honestly, I'm trying to keep the gruesome parts from everyone until I have no other choice.'

'You don't have to keep them from me,' he says, looking into my eyes. 'That's what I'm here for.'

'What you did for me last night surpasses everything.'

Before leaving for home he drives me down to the beach for our Prom! Prom! Prom! He parks up and we wander along the seafront, under a grey sky, wrapped up like people parcels in scarves and hats and our huge parkas, taking in the fresh sea air amid the squawk of swooping gulls. He hugs me the entire way, saying I mustn't catch cold, he would never forgive himself.

'I'm going to miss out on so much,' I say.

'I'm going to miss out on so much of you,' he replies. 'I already have.'

A feeling comes over me whispering in my ear: You're frightened, admit it. You're scared! I don't want to be won over by it. I put my hands over my ears. 'This wind is so penetrating,' I say.

The drive home is strangely uneasy, despite the comfortable luxury of the car. I'm filled with that horrible childhood Sunday gloom, knowing tomorrow is a school day and I want it to be the weekend for ever. Worse, I'm not going to see Harry for another whole week because he is working abroad again.

'I'd invite you to stay at mine,' he says, 'but I have to get this car back and then be up horribly early for the flight to Berlin, plus I've got a lot of prep to do. Do you mind?'

'Of course I do,' I say. But I smile in a way that lets him off the hook.

Harry accompanies me to my front door and we kiss on the doorstep. He hugs me for a long moment and I know I'm going to miss him badly. That I'm connected to him now as profoundly as I ever was. If not more. I don't want to let him go.

But I have to.

There's a pain in my heart as I watch him leave. An actual physical pain. Heartache means what it says on the tin. I hesitate on the doorstep, not wanting to go in, not wanting to face the emptiness on the other side. It's dark in every sense of the word and I don't want to breathe in the pain and sorrow that occupies the air in those cold, lonely rooms.

But I have to.

I open my front door, hit by an awareness of everything I'm going to lose and everything I've squandered. I throw my case into the hall and stomp. For the first time I'm properly angry. Angry at myself. Angry that

I never went after what I wanted when I had the opportunity. For thinking that I was being good and kind and non-confrontational when all I was being was a considerate coward. I'm angry that I've come too late to the party. That I've only now learnt to accept that I'm loved. And that I am worthy of it. And that's the most beautiful and painful realization of all.

I no longer want to roll over and allow my illness to do its work. I don't want to be gracious in defeat. I'm not going to go quietly. I want to rant and rave and kick and scream. I'm going to miss out on so much. On Olivia's wedding. On Anna Maria's carefree adventures. On my sister's future. On my nieces' futures. On my own future. Why do I have to pretend to myself that it's OK? That the world is a lousy place and I'm better off out of it. I love this lousy world. I want to enjoy every lousy thing it has to offer.

And I miss Harry. More than anything right now I really miss him. Damn him and his work! I MISS HIM! I wish he'd turn round and come back and say, 'Sod the prep, I want to be here with you because I love you!' Damn him for being so disciplined.

Tonight I am not disciplined. I slam doors. I throw my clothes out of my case on to the floor. I'm not going to pick them up. I'm not going to wash them. Why bother? What's the point? I've enough clean clothes to last me until I no longer need anything more than whatever they're going to bury me in.

I yell and thump at the walls.

I don't want to die.

I DON'T WANT TO DIE.

'I WANT TO LIVE!' I scream.

I'm throwing myself around the room, not knowing what to do with myself, when I notice the blue light on my answerphone. The flashing riles me; it has no right to intrude on my drama. I hit the playback button with impatient fury just to stop the damn flashing. What bloody ambulance chaser is calling me now? What refund for PPI am I entitled to that I've never even taken out? I listen distractedly, my finger ready to press delete.

You have three new messages.

Three?

I'm amazed to hear a real voice. I've a missed call from the surgery. Three, it would seem. The receptionist asks me to call her as soon as I get the message because I need to fix an appointment with the doctor. Why? When I phoned on Friday they didn't ask me to make an appointment. The urgency is worrying. I press delete for the sheer hell of it, yelling at the world for being so inefficient and why couldn't the receptionist be more specific instead of leaving me to guess the urgent nature of her call. And why didn't she call my mobile?

I check my mobile. She did call. My phone is still on silent since the spa treatments and the movie. I've even missed a call from Harry. I phone him back immediately.

'Hey,' he says. 'Where were you?'

'In hell,' I say, lying back on my sofa. 'I miss heaven.'

'It was a beautiful weekend,' he says. 'Special. I will miss you terribly this week.'

I want to tell him to stop saying he'll miss me. That it's unfair. That it frustrates me. But of course, I want to hear him say it over and over again and I'm annoyed at the conundrum.

'Then don't go away,' I say.

'You sound angry.'

'I *am*.'

'Good,' he says. 'That's healthy.'

'I'm not fucking healthy!' I yell, sitting up. 'That's the point!'

'I know,' he says. 'I know. I'm just surprised—'

'At what? That I'm angry because I'm dying?'

'No. No! I guess I thought you'd be further along—'

'Along what? What the hell are you talking about?'

'I'm sorry. Forget it. You have every right to be angry.'

'No, seriously. Further along what?' I stand up, rigid with tension.

'You know . . . the stages . . .'

'Stages?'

'Of grief.' He coughs.

'Are you kidding me? What are you saying here?' I'm pacing the room, phone clamped to my ear in disbelief. 'That I'm so near the end I should be at acceptance? Is that what you're saying? You think all us poor dying souls sit there ticking off each stage, going thank God that one's over, what's next?'

'Obviously that's not what I mean.'

'Well, I can assure you we don't. Sometimes in fact

we get a whole clusterfuck of stages. And today I'm angry and I'm depressed and I'm bargaining with myself because no one else is listening—'

'I'm listening!'

'Then I'm telling you here and now that I've ticked off denial and I AM NEVER, EVER GOING TO TICK ACCEPT.'

'I'm so sorry. I just miss you and—'

'Stop saying that. I'm still here. I'm still on the end of a phone. You can still see me. And if you genuinely missed me you'd drop all your prep and you'd stop going away.'

'I'm coming round,' he says.

'Please don't,' I say, my tenor reverting with a jolt, trying to recover my composure, shocked by my own reaction. I sit down again. I don't want to sound like that. Ungrateful. Not to Harry. Not after everything he's done this weekend. If he's being clumsy it's because being around someone who's dying is clumsy territory. It's all too easy to slip up. But now I know he's thoughtful and caring too, so clumsy mustn't matter.

'Just prepare for Berlin,' I say, letting it pass.

'No, no, I'm coming over.'

I smile sadly because that is exactly what I wanted him to say.

'Please don't, Harry,' I say flatly. 'I realize you have to work. I'm not at my best, but I'll get through this stage, I promise.'

'Don't say that. It makes me feel foolish. Please let me come over.'

This is a revelation. Here I am, showing my anger and he's not running for the hills, which was always my greatest fear.

'No. I'm fine. I've calmed down now. I'm fine. Honestly. Thank you.'

He sighs. 'Well, only if you're sure . . . ?'

'I'm sure.'

'Right then. I'll call you tomorrow,' he says. 'I'll check in as often as I can. And if you're not feeling great I'll come straight home.'

'Thank you.'

'And . . . I do love you. Even though I'm a foot-in-the-mouth fool sometimes.'

'But you're my fool, Harry. That's all that matters to me now.'

Day 52

I phone the surgery first thing. 'It's Jennifer Cole,' I say. 'Someone asked me to call in for an appointment. I'm Dr Mackenzie's patient.'

There's a strange silence at the end of the phone.

'Ah yes,' the woman says gently. 'Jennifer. I'm so glad you've called. We've been trying to reach you.'

Her knowledge of me immediately puts me on high alert. 'Is there a problem?'

'No. Not a problem,' she says. She clears her throat. 'We need you to come in and see the doctor. When are you available?'

'Can you tell me why?' My mind does an instant round-up of possibilities.

'I'm afraid I have to leave that to the doctor.'

Now I'm becoming properly suspicious. There's something wrong. I feel it.

'What time can you come in?'

'Today? Any time.'

'Ten o'clock suit you?'

'Yes.' Shit! I'm being given an emergency appointment. Why? Why the urgency?

'Excellent,' she says and I hear the tapping of the keyboard. 'We'll see you then.'

I put the phone down. I should have said I can come in right away. An hour feels like a long wait, wondering why on earth the doctor wants to see me. But then, what can be so bad? He's already told me the worst possible news. What on earth can he tell me that might top that?

Maybe he's traced the treatment. What does it matter now if he has? It will only prolong this emotional torture.

I pace, nervously starting chores but not finishing them. I pick up the clothes from my bedroom floor, hanging up the dress, throwing the rest in the washing machine. It is too depressing to look at them. They symbolize defeat and even though I am defeated, I don't want it staring me in the face. I find the empty box of Mallomars. My keepsake. I clutch it to my chest, reminding myself of that evening. I try to forget I'm scared.

Harry texts me to say he has landed safely. I'm glad to see his name pop up on my screen. I text back a thumbs-up. It's all I can manage in this state.

I get to the surgery early. The receptionist greets me warmly, making me ever more ponderous. I sit down and flick through endless pages of an outdated magazine, more occupied with the receptionist, listening to her taking calls. I hear the mention of my name. 'Yes,' she says. 'I'll tell her.' She looks across at me. 'Jennifer. Dr Mackenzie will see you now.'

It's still not ten o'clock. He never sees a patient early. I'm shaking inside.

I knock, then peek round his door and Dr Mackenzie, his steel-rimmed glasses balanced on the end of his nose, glances up from his desk. 'Ah, Jennifer,' he says. 'Good to see you. Come in.' He types something into his computer and turns away from the screen to study me. 'You're looking well.'

I wince. 'I bet you say that to all your patients.'

He clears his throat. 'Sit down, dear.'

Can I just interject here? I really hate it that he calls me dear.

I slide into the chair, put my handbag on the floor next to me and clamp my cold hands together, trying to calm them. 'It's cold in here today,' I say.

'Is it? I hadn't noticed. I can put the blow heater on, if you want?'

'It's fine, Doctor.'

He has my file open in front of him. He plays with a few papers, a serious expression on his face. This is not good. I shift uncomfortably in the swivel chair. We're both uncomfortable but he has the advantage: he knows why. There's a silence of maybe three seconds but it feels laboured and heavy.

'I have some news for you,' he says.

I sit up. My mouth is so dry I can barely separate my tongue from the roof.

'There's been a mistake.'

I stare back at him. I'm rigid. It's as if I've turned to stone, yet I'm still flesh and blood because my heart is

213

beating at a hundred miles an hour. 'What kind of mistake?' I say.

He holds up a bunch of papers and bounces their edges on the flat of his desk, squaring them into neat alignment. Why does he always do that? Hurry up!

He hums.

'A good one,' he says. 'For you anyhow.' He sits very upright and I find myself doing the same. He coughs, licks the tip of his finger then quickly flips through some pages of the file. 'It would seem . . .' He coughs again.

'Yes, Doctor?'

'Well, it would seem . . . that unfortunately, although fortunately . . .'

What is wrong with him?

'. . . you were given the wrong blood-test results . . .'

My mind falters. I can hear the droning of his voice in the background as if he's talking to me but I'm not in the room; his words slide away from me. Things start to swim, to left and right, the room is a blue blur and the next thing I know, Dr Mackenzie is leaning over me, slapping at my cheek, breathing his sour breath in my face.

'Are you OK, Jennifer?' he says.

I allow my eyes to settle so that he comes into focus. 'You tell me, Doctor,' I say, rubbing my cheek.

He smiles with obvious relief. 'Yes,' he says. 'Yes, you are.' He takes my hand and pats it. 'Let me help you back into the chair.' He lifts me unsteadily, my arm around his shoulder, then plonks me down awkwardly and walks back behind his desk, rubbing the base of his spine. He pours us both a glass of water. He takes a gulp. I guzzle mine, finishing it in seconds.

'I'm very sorry we put you through this ordeal,' he says, and he keeps on talking, not allowing any gaps for any questions I might have. 'I'm just so glad to be able to tell you we got it wrong. For once. So much better this way round, Jennifer. You will obviously need time to recover from this *excellent* news and I'm sure you will be very angry with me, but I have to apologize and just say, my office staff is human. If it weren't for the nurse you spoke to before you went to your *spa*, we may not have spotted the error.' He says this as if to imply I was having a nice time anyway, so where's the problem? 'That is, until your unexpected survival might have drawn us to it. Or . . . well, never mind.'

I am in shock. I'm not quite sure how to react. I'm going to live. But that means someone else is going to die. How awful! But then, get a grip, I'm the one who is going to live. And that's a good thing. Isn't it? But that poor woman. She'll have even less time than me to tell her family. To decide how she wants to spend her final weeks. And now I, who have usurped her precious days, have all the time in the world and I feel as though I've lied to everyone. I'm so confused.

'So what's wrong with me then, Dr Mackenzie?'

'Nothing,' he says with a larky lilt. All of a sudden he's so upbeat. I'm sitting here in turmoil and he's unashamedly cheery. How dare he!

'But I feel so ill,' I say. 'I've been regularly sick, I'm tired beyond belief, I have nosebleeds, I've had bouts of depression. All the things those leaflets said.'

His face darkens. 'Which of the drugs I prescribed have you been taking?' He's speaking in that same accusatory tone. I'm pushed to my limit.

'Why do you always make it sound like everything is my fault? If I don't come in soon enough, it's my fault. If I take the drugs *you* prescribed, it's my fault. Well, I haven't taken a single one of those drugs on that prescription, Doctor. And I'd say that was your lucky break. Because, let's not forget, this is your fault . . .' I don't enjoy watching him squirm, but frankly! 'And to think my mother thought you were some kind of god.'

He splutters. His Adam's apple bounces. He knows he has no rebuttal.

'I wish the mistake hadn't been made, and for that I'm very sorry.' He blows out a quick puff. 'I only asked about the drugs because you could have been having a contra-reaction.'

'Obviously not.'

'Hmmm,' he says, his mouth turned down. 'Of course, these things could well be psychosomatic. The mind is very clever.'

Is that what he's telling me now? That I'm conjuring up a fake fatal illness because I've been told I have one?

Then I remember Emily and her hypochondria. I wonder whether her symptoms are as real to her as mine are to me? That, to be fair to Dr Mackenzie, maybe he's right on this one. Is there such a fine line between what's real and what we make real?

'So what did my actual blood tests show?'

He clears his throat. 'You are anaemic, hence the tiredness. I've prescribed iron tablets. And you're entering menopause.'

I'm staring at him aghast. 'Are you saying I'm nothing other than menopausal?'

'Yes!' Gleeful – again! 'Perimenopausal.'

'But I'm so sick.'

'Well, it's no picnic.'

'Thanks, Doctor!'

He shakes his head, smoothing an eyebrow. 'I'm sorry, Jennifer. But it could be psychosomatic.'

'I am not inventing it,' I say, fighting for my credibility, as though it matters more than my health.

'Hmmmm,' he says.

We stare at one another. Taking stock.

'So what happened to the person whose results I got?'

'I'm not in a position to discuss that with you, dear. Let's focus on the positives. You are going to live.'

'But how did she take it? By my reckoning, this error has denied her half the life she had left. I mean, do you not think I should go and see her? To maybe—'

'I understand your concern, but patient confidentiality means that is not possible. You are getting your life back. Let me take responsibility for the rest.'

I stare back at him. Right. I must think positively. 'So I'm going to live.' It's as if I'm testing the sound of the words. 'And of course that's a good thing. So why am I feeling so damn awful?'

He scratches his head. 'The menopause is not easy. But to put your mind at rest, would you like me to run more tests?'

I throw him a look.

'It was a bad mistake, Jennifer. It won't happen again. The woman who put the wrong test results in your file has been dismissed.'

'Oh,' I say. 'That makes me feel doubly terrible.'

'You should feel fantastic. You must go home and celebrate.'

'Seriously? I think I'll be the first woman to celebrate her menopause.'

He laughs. Dr Mackenzie actually laughs. I'm grateful. It defuses the tension. 'I'm going to take another blood sample. We should find out why you're being sick. Just in case.'

'In case of what?' I say. 'I don't want any more bad news. I'd rather live in denial.'

'It's up to you,' he says, unhooking his glasses and rubbing the bridge of his nose. He raises his bushy grey eyebrows in a way that says it's not up to me at all and he's made the decision.

'OK, Dr Mackenzie,' I say, rolling up my sleeve. 'Do your worst.'

But we both know he already has.

Part Two

Part Two

1

You're probably thinking I should be elated: celebrating my good fortune, as instructed by Dr Mackenzie. But it's not that simple. For six weeks or so I've been mentally preparing for my death. It's a shock to discover I'm going to live. A good shock, of course, but no less traumatic. I feel guilty. Perhaps it's survivor's guilt because what about the woman who should have got those results? I know Dr Mackenzie said I should let him take responsibility for her, but still. The very notion of her haunts me. Did she get the chance of a dying wish? Is she already dead? Did anyone hold her hand? It's too awful to contemplate.

I also feel weirdly embarrassed. I can't decide how to handle this news. How am I going to tell people? 'Oh, by the way, I'm not dying after all. I'm perimenopausal.' Did it have to be quite so prosaic? Could it not have been a little more spectacular? I feel ashamed, foolish. Mortified, in fact.

And there's something else that might seem odd and churlish. I realize that I'm going to miss the attention. I appreciate this might sound ridiculous, but when people around you think you are dying, they put you centre stage. You become the person they'll drop everything for. They think about you more than they normally would and, if I'm being candid, I liked that. Now I'm worried people won't be interested in me any more because I'm just me again. Plain old boring Jennifer from HR. Listen, I know I'll adapt to normal life, the way you do after a great holiday, but at this moment in time the thought of going back to an unremarkable normality feels pretty unenticing.

My mind is going over and over everything, trying to make sense of it. If nothing else, I think I might have post-traumatic stress. Dr Mackenzie's surgery certainly seems to think so. They have given me a year of free psychotherapy. 'It might help you to talk this through with someone,' Dr Mackenzie said. What does that tell you?

But I don't feel like talking to anyone, let alone a therapist. I've turned off my phones because if anyone calls I'll have to tell them the truth and I'm not ready. The mistake wasn't mine, but I feel like a fraud all the same.

Olivia won't think I'm a fraud. She's going to be thrilled. But what about the others? Will Frank be embarrassed about showing his vulnerability, letting down his guard? Will he let me have my job back or will he no longer be able to look me in the eye?

What will Isabelle think? Will she regret telling me about Barry, since I won't be taking her secret to the grave? Did she admit more to me than she would if I wasn't going to die? And if I ever bump into Andy, will he be shocked and annoyed, thinking he was emotionally blackmailed into admitting the truth about his marriage?

But oh, agony and shame! Will Harry still love me? Oh, please let Harry still love me.

Let's face it, would I have written those damn letters if I hadn't thought I was dying? Of course not. But perhaps that's the point. Making a stand for yourself is worth the risk. More important than your pride. More important than your fear of losing your dignity. Even when you're not dying. I need to convince myself of that.

I open up my laptop and start wantonly googling *menopause*, knowing the dangers. I have to. I need to see precisely what it means. What is the significance of *peri*?

There are myriad sites. I pick the one that seems the most user-friendly and scroll down to 'Symptoms'. The number of parallels with what was once my 'oh so rare blood disorder' are ridiculous. Sweats, dizziness, depression, lack of sleep, mood swings. OK, so it never gets as bad as fever and delirium, it never quite reaches vomiting blood or coma, the things the leaflets told me about my 'osis', but no wonder I never questioned anything.

You should see the plaintive cries on this forum I'm reading. There are women going through menopause who feel as though they *are* dying. Sometimes they even want to die. There's no reason to think my suffering has been psychosomatic. It gets *that* bad.

I should have been prepared. But I've never been prepared for anything hormonal. My mother would never discuss our bodies. When Isabelle and I were old enough to learn about sex, she simply handed us the book *Where Did I Come From?* I learnt the rest from changing-room gossip at school. Sometimes I think she wished she'd had boys so she could have left the intimate stuff to my father.

It should be a mother's duty to warn her daughters of all the potential hazards of being a woman from puberty onwards. And to do it in a way that Google can't. Because googling any kind of medical ailment makes you want to blow your brains out. A mother can hold your hand, look you in the eye and discuss everything openly so that when it happens you can remember the file she so diligently placed in the back of your brain and think, Ah yes! I will survive. After all. Look at Mum. She was on HRT and she was just tickety-boo.

Of course, I have no idea if my mother was on HRT. I imagine she was. It was medication after all and my mother was one of life's great pill poppers. She didn't understand the notion of stoical suffering. Antibiotics are bad for you? Nonsense, she'd say. But why couldn't she talk to us about bodily things? Why were *sex* and *vagina* and *menopause* such dirty words that she couldn't even utter them? What was she so afraid of? Our wrath? That we might hold her responsible for our gender?

I need to talk to Isabelle. I must ask her how she's dealing with her daughters. I hope she won't make the same mistake as our mother. Daughters need to be empowered. In all things. Now more than ever.

I check the time. It's one o'clock in the morning. I've spent hours staring at a screen. I have to go to bed and somehow get myself ready to face life and tell everyone my illness was a fraud. No! Not a fraud. A mistake!

I get undressed and stand in front of my bathroom mirror, preparing to brush my teeth. I tell my reflection I am well. I am merely entering a new hormonal cycle, horrible though it is. And I am a good person. My friends will get past this error, they'll be thrilled for me. Still, I'm not going to fool myself into believing it'll be plain sailing. This is going to be the biggest test of love and friendship I've ever been through. Thank God I never allowed Pattie to convince me to tell everyone at work.

And then I pull myself up. I'm going to live.

I'M GOING TO LIVE!

I asked for it and either a compassionate god heard or it was serendipity. And none of the people I hold dear to me will be anything other than over the moon. I have to stop being so negative.

I go to bed and resolve that tomorrow I will deal with reality. I will start to tell the ones who matter my good news.

Tomorrow it will all be tickety-boo.

2

I slept fitfully last night, dreaming of the moment I told everyone it was a mistake, staring out at a crowd of anonymous faces, listening to them cheer, only to wake up and realize my big reveal is yet to come and I can't put up the banners yet.

They should be phoning me from the surgery today with my latest results. Dr Mackenzie said he would put it on fast track. I wonder why I haven't heard from them?

Shit!

I'm such an idiot. I've forgotten I unplugged my house phone and turned off my mobile when I didn't want to speak to anyone. When I was in my hole. I mustn't do that any more. I can't simply burrow away from the world while I decide how to confront my future.

I turn on my mobile phone. It pings several messages. My voicemail starts ringing and just as I'm listening to the woman's voice telling me I have twenty-one missed calls – twenty-one! – my doorbell goes. I am glued to the spot, looking wretched in my dressing gown, torn between my phone and the front door, not knowing which to deal with first. The doorbell rings again, frantically. Whoever it is is holding down the buzzer. I throw down my phone. Who the hell can it be? The postman is never this aggressive. I peer through the spyhole.

OH GOD!

It's Olivia with Dan. She looks grey and frightened. I immediately register why she's there.

I want to skulk away and hide but I owe her more than that. I open the door . . . slowly . . . guiltily.

'Jennifer! Shit, Jennifer! I thought you were dead!' Her face has now turned as red as her hair. She's hysterical. 'Where have you been? Why haven't you answered your phone?' Dan is standing with his arm protectively round her as though I am the enemy.

'Come in,' I say. 'I'm sorry. Everything's OK.'

'Well, obviously!' she says tearfully. 'What the hell is going on? I mean . . . Oh God, I shouldn't be angry, Jennifer, forgive me. I'm sorry to sound harsh, but we've been worried sick about you. You go away and then no reply.'

'Did you think Harry had murdered me?'

'Don't joke. I thought I was about to find you spreadeagled on the floor. This is not a good time for you to cut yourself off from the people who care about you. It's not fair.'

'I know, I know,' I say. 'I'm sorry. Really I am.'

'Well, OK then,' she says, drawing a jagged breath. She clutches my arm, her mouth downturned. 'I'm just glad I've had the opportunity to be angry with you.'

I give her an apologetic hug, feeling more ashamed than ever. She's about to say something but I stop her. 'Olivia,' I say. 'I owe you a huge apology. I'm sorry to have put you through that worry.'

She smiles half-heartedly. 'Apology accepted.'

'And we all need a cup of tea and to put things into perspective because something rather weird and wonderful has happened.'

Olivia's face registers curiosity. 'It has?' She stretches her long neck, shaking her head and rolling her shoulders to relieve the aftermath of worried tension. 'What? What's happened? You're going to marry Harry?'

I scoff. 'I'll tell you when we're sitting down. Go into the sitting room and I'll put the kettle on. How do you take your tea, Dan?'

'Milk no sugar,' says Dan.

Olivia stares at him as if he's lost his mind. 'You're talking tea?' she says. 'I want to hear what's happened!'

'Tea first,' I say. 'Go and relax in the sitting room.'

'*Relax?* I want to know. Now!'

'Sitting room!' I say, trying to josh her. 'Behave, please.'

She looks at me with suspicion. 'I'm not sure who should be told to behave. I mean, I'm not going to lie to you, but when I saw your face at the door, I felt like throttling you.' She takes Dan's hand. 'Come on. Let's leave the lady with the funny hair in the bathrobe to her teabags.' She's still pissed off.

I take in a tray with three mugs of normal tea and

put it down on the sideboard. I'll never touch ginger tea again. It tastes of death. It's time to get back into my old routines.

Olivia and Dan are sitting tightly next to one another on the sofa, Dan looking out of place and uncertain, Olivia eager and restless. I hand them each a mug and Olivia's eyes follow me wildly. 'Well?' she says.

I sit down in the armchair, sip some tea, shut my eyes for a second, then blurt it out. 'There's been a mistake,' I say.

Silence. I look at both of them. Their faces are a picture.

'What do you mean?' says Olivia. 'A mistake. What mistake?'

'A medical mistake. A good one.'

From nowhere, a wave of relief washes over me. I put down my mug, bury my head in my hands and burst into tears.

I hear Dan whisper, 'Should I go?'

'No!' Olivia mutters. And then tentatively she says, 'What is it, Jen? Is it what I think?'

'They gave me the wrong test results,' I splutter. 'I'm not dying. Of all things, I'm entering the frigging menopause, Liv. I'm going to be hot and sweaty and moody and unpredictable, but I'm going to LIVE!'

She puts her tea down on the floor and throws her hands in the air. 'I don't believe it. I don't bloody believe it!' She stands up and starts doing high knees on the spot. 'Come over here, you silly old meno-pausal woman, and give me the biggest hug ever. What were you waiting for, Jennifer? Were you going to wrap up the news and give it to me for Christmas?'

'Christmas,' I say. 'I'd forgotten about Christmas. I'm actually going to see Christmas.' And I let out a visceral whoop.

We're waving our hands in the air with joy and Olivia grabs me and rocks me from side to side as if we're doing a bad jive.

'I can't believe it,' she sings. 'It's like a dream.'

'Tell me about it,' I say. 'I'm not sure I've woken up yet.'

'Oh, you're awake all right,' says Dan, reminding us of his presence.

'Come on, Dan,' I say. 'This calls for a group hug.'

'Wait a moment, darling,' Olivia says to him. 'I want this woman all to myself for a few seconds more. I need to feel her pulsing life force and know the nightmare is over.' She's kissing my forehead like some angry chicken pecking for seed. 'God, I love you,' she says, in between lip strikes. 'I had no idea how much until now. I think I was holding back the true depth of my feelings, hoping it would be less painful to lose you. And now I don't have to. And I don't have to worry about your fucking funeral. I'm going to have you for a whole lot longer.' She nestles into my neck, hugging me so tightly I am almost struggling to breathe.

'I think you might just kill me in a minute, Liv,' I splutter.

She holds me away from her and smiles. 'Sometimes

you have to suffer for love,' she says. 'Isn't that right, Dan? Now, time for that group hug.'

He frowns at us, bewildered. 'I'm not sure I should intrude,' he says.

'Aw, come on,' I say. 'Don't be such a spoilsport. Get tucked in.'

Olivia and I open a chink for him in our circle.

He stands up. 'OK!' he says. 'I've always wanted a threesome.'

'Keep wanting, honey!' says Olivia, and we all three hug as tightly as we can.

3

'I can't believe you felt bad about telling us such amazing news,' says Olivia, sipping her tea. 'What did you think was going to happen? Did you think we'd all go, "Oh no! I was looking forward to your funeral"? What on earth must you think of us?'

'I needed to get to grips with it myself. You have no idea what a shock it is.' I cringe. 'I've done things I *never* would have done if I'd thought I was going to carry on with a normal life. So I needed to hide away. Work out how I felt. And I feel foolish and ashamed.'

'The letters?' says Olivia.

'Yeah, the letters.'

'What letters?' says Dan.

'You didn't tell him?'

'He wouldn't understand.'

'What?' says Dan.

'I'll tell you later,' says Olivia.

Olivia and I stare across at each other.

'Everyone will be fine,' she says, nodding in agreement with herself. 'Things happen for a reason. It's brought so much good into your life and, loath as I am to admit it, Harry for a start. And Isabelle. They'll be thrilled. And what about Andy? Have you heard from him since he wrote?'

'Not a thing.'

'OK, so screw him. He doesn't matter any more. That was the point of the letters. To flush out the ones who genuinely matter.'

Dan and Olivia gaze at each other and exchange a smile.

'And of course I will now be at your wedding. If I'm invited.'

Olivia's eyes light up. 'Of course! You forgot about Christmas, I've forgotten about our wedding.'

'Great,' says Dan. 'That's encouraging.'

She gives him a playful poke. 'You know what I mean.' She looks at me, beaming. 'And now I have my maid of honour. You will be my maid of honour, won't you? Or my best woman? Pick a title. Any title.'

'Am I forgiven, then? For not being in touch.'

'What do you think?'

'I think I'm going to be your best woman.'

'Oh, Jennifer,' she says wistfully. 'You have no idea. I'm guessing you haven't told Harry yet?'

My stomach does an instant somersault.

'Have you been on radio silence with him too?'

'Oh shit,' I say, examining my phone. 'He's texted me four times. I'd only just turned my phone back on when you knocked. I'm such an idiot. And I've had twenty-one missed calls.'

'I think Olivia made twenty of them,' says Dan.

'I think you'll find I made all twenty-one,' she retorts.

'But I'm not going to tell him until he's back. I need to tell him face-to-face. It's too big a deal to say over the phone.'

I study the details of the missed calls. 'I ought to check my voicemail. The doctor should be calling me too. I need to get the results of my latest blood tests.'

'Oh,' says Olivia, frowning. 'Why more?'

I flick my hand dismissively. 'It's precautionary. Honestly, Olivia, I understand Emily so much better now.'

'Emily? Why?'

'Because I think a lot of my symptoms might have been psychosomatic.'

'Oh, spare me. What's happened to you is nothing like Emily. She's just a self-obsessed drama queen who invents illness for sympathy. She certainly got none from me.'

'Maybe that's how we all saw her, but I feel differently now. I mean, look at me. The doctor, a man whose word I trusted, says I'm terminally ill, so in my head I become terminally ill and my body dutifully responds. Why should it be any different for Emily?'

'Because she has a relationship with illness the way some children have an imaginary friend.'

'Well then, she's genuinely sick, isn't she? Mentally. So we should be just as compassionate if not more so.'

'Call her!' says Olivia. 'Ignore my scepticism. If this bothers you, you should call her.'

'I'll write her a letter and then leave it up to her.'

'Ha! I guess the letter thing has worked rather well for you.'

I smile. 'Yup. Until everyone finds out I wrote under false pretences.'

'Don't be ridiculous. It was a mistake. Hardly false pretences.'

I stretch my arms in the air, let out a yawn louder than intended. 'Sorry,' I say. 'I'm just so tired. I've barely slept.'

They both look at me, lost for words. I don't think the sympathy is as forthcoming as it might have been at the beginning of this conversation. It's back to business as usual. No special dispensations any more. And maybe it doesn't feel so bad after all.

4

To: frank@thearkhouse.co.uk
Subject: News!

Dear Frank

I wanted to write and thank you for being so understanding about my terrible news. I couldn't have hoped for a kinder way to exit from the job and the people I love.

I hope you're sitting down as you're reading because what I have to tell you will probably come as much of a shock to you as it did to me. It seems my doctor's surgery mixed up my file and I was given someone else's results. Turns out I'm badly anaemic (I know!).

So, once you've picked yourself up off the floor, I was wondering whether it would be OK to ask for my job back? I'm hoping the temporary replacement is just that and you'll see a way forward for me. I'm glad we never told anyone. If you believe in fate, perhaps that's why.

As you can imagine, I'm keen to hear from you, but in the meantime, thank you again.

Jennifer

I read it, re-read it then press send.

5

I've taken myself in hand, convinced that if my mind can make me manifest bad symptoms then, by definition, it can make me manifest good ones too. I'm ignoring the nausea in the hope it will eventually get the hint, pack its bags and move on.

For the first time in weeks I've put on full make-up and blow-dried my hair so that it actually looks decent. I'm wearing a dress I'd saved for best because that whole notion has gone out the window. I've put on heels, a spritz of perfume and most symbolically of all, on my way out I throw away my calendar. I don't need to see that miserable reminder ever again. It's put me off Constable and Turner and Gainsborough, but there are plenty more where they came from. Harry's taught me that. And now I'm on my way to see Isabelle to tell her the news.

I haven't warned her I'm coming. I know she doesn't like people dropping in, but this is not any old casual visit. If I warn her, she'll only work on me until she's dragged it out of me over the phone. And I want to see her face.

As soon as Olivia and Dan left, I replied to Harry's anxious texts (I love it that he's anxious!). I told him that I'd forgotten to put my phone on. I apologized, saying that all is well, which is nicely euphemistic if you think about it. He said he wants to take me out this weekend, but I'd rather stay at home. Better to tell him the news in the privacy of my own sitting room, then we can celebrate freely.

I'm seeing Dr Mackenzie tomorrow. I have a four o'clock appointment to get the results of my blood tests. There was no sense of urgency in the receptionist's voice, which I take as a good sign.

The Uber draws up outside my sister's house. My mental attitude is in full positive throttle but, annoyingly, I haven't quite convinced my body. I guess the iron tablets will take a few days before they kick in.

Isabelle's doorbell responds loudly to my touch. My heart is thumping in my head, in my stomach, in my legs. I want to keep a poker face, but my excitement won't let me.

Martin opens the door. His expression, understandably, is one of bewilderment.

'Surprise!' My mouth has formed a rictus grin. I probably look most odd. *Get a grip. Get a grip.*

'Certainly is,' he says. 'Erm, do you want to come in?'

'Well, that would be nice,' I say, sensing resistance. 'Is it a bad time? Am I disturbing you?'

'No, no, come in,' he says.

The girls shout, 'Who is it, Dad?'

'It's Aunt Jennifer,' he says.

239

They charge out of the kitchen and come rushing towards me. I fear I'm about to be rugby-tackled, only to be given the sweetest double hug.

Cecily peers at me strangely, as if she's amazed this is what I can look like. 'You look lovely,' she says.

Sophia grabs my hand and swings my arm back and forth. 'Mummy looked lovely too. Did you want to come and see us first, then?'

'Of course I did.' I ruffle the top of her head. 'Where *is* Mummy?' I turn to Martin and then it registers. My thoughts scramble into shape. I can tell a cover-up is in order. 'Am I not meant to be meeting her here?' I say.

'No,' says Martin. 'She said she was meeting you in town somewhere. A halfway house.' His voice sounds tight and distrustful. I need to play this really well.

'Oh, my memory!' I say. 'It's just hopeless. I could have sworn I was meeting her here.' I feel as though I've popped out of a cake naked and found myself at the wrong party.

'You're not well, Jennifer. It's understandable. Let me sort you a cab. I guess you'd better call her. She must be wondering where you are.' He still looks unconvinced as he grabs the telephone from its cradle in the hallway. He feels in his shirt pocket then taps the top of his head and replaces the phone. 'One of you two fetch me my glasses, please, off the kitchen table.' Both girls rush into the kitchen, Cecily elbowing Sophia out of the way.

'Don't be mean, Cecily,' she yells.

'Behave, the two of you, please!' says Martin. 'It's a pair of glasses, not a medal.'

I make out I'm phoning Isabelle. 'She's not answering,' I say, knowing I'm not good enough to pretend to have a conversation with her. 'I'll just get an Uber and text her from the car.'

'You'll never get an Uber here. I'll call you a cab. Where are my glasses, girls?'

'It's fine,' I say. 'My car's probably still quite near. He can come back. Don't worry, Martin.' I don't want to have to tell him where I'm meant to be meeting her. Who knows what Isabelle might have said?

Cecily jumps back into the hall in front of Martin, wearing a winner's smile, and hands him a pair of half-moon glasses which he wraps around his ears. 'Please allow me to book you a cab. You've come all this way, it's the least I can do. Now where are the two of you meant to be meeting? She did tell me but I—'

'Oh look!' I yell too loudly. 'My Uber's coming. He'll be here in . . . er, one minute.' I quickly hold up my phone screen then retract it. 'He's nearing the top of your drive. I'll text Isabelle to let her know I'm on my way.'

The girls stare at me, fascinated. Martin rolls his eyes, replacing the phone. He's agitated, shifting listlessly the way people do when they can't quite pinpoint what's bothering them. He takes off his glasses and slips them into his shirt pocket. 'Fine,' he says. 'Anyway, it's good to see you – even unexpectedly. Tell my wife not to get too drunk or to be home late.'

'I will!'

He twitches a smile. 'You look well,' he says. 'Surprisingly well.'

'Thank you.'

'Looking like that, I can't imagine you get much sympathy.'

'I don't want sympathy, Martin.'

'No. No. Not your style.'

I kiss the girls and give Martin an awkward peck on the cheek. He stands there stiff as a board.

I run down the drive, cursing my high heels. I'll never get an Uber. Martin was right. This is not their terrain. I'll have to walk to the station and pick up a local cab. I text Isabelle, cursing her too. I know exactly what she's up to.

She doesn't reply.

There's a line of cabs outside the station with a small queue of commuters waiting. I'm freezing. I hadn't planned on this. Eventually I get to the front.

'Hampstead?'

'You've got to be kidding.'

'Please, I'm desperate. Gospel Oak end.'

'Go on then. You've caught me in a good mood. Jump in.'

My mind is whirring the entire journey home. I move between anger and panic. I need to talk to her. I need to warn her even though she deserves to be found out. But I don't want her to be. I love and care for her too much. God, I'm furious. How could she do this to me? Put me in this predicament. But then, why would she ever expect me to turn up at her home unannounced?

I call several times. I text her. She's not responding to anything. I leave a voicemail, another text, telling her to call me no matter when. We need to coordinate our stories. I'm so worried about her I've actually forgotten the reason I went to see her in the first place.

I call again in desperation, expecting to hear her voicemail, when I realize it's her actual voice.

'Isabelle?'

'*Jennifer?* What's up? Are you OK?' she slurs. Drunk.

'I've been trying to get hold of you.'

'So I see,' she says. 'Do you need me, *darling sister*?'

She's beyond drunk. 'No! You need me. You need to listen. OK?'

'It's my sister. I told you I had one!'

'I take it you're with Barry?'

She sniggers. 'Secret squirrel!' She must have put her hand over the phone because her voice sounds vaguely muffled but I can still hear her. 'I think she knows,' she says.

'I think everyone knows,' I say.

'What's wrong?' she slurs.

'I went over to your house tonight.'

'You did WHAT? *Why?*'

That sobered her up! 'It doesn't matter why. Obviously, Martin and the girls were expecting me to be with you.'

'Shit!'

'Yes. Shit! But I think I covered well. I told them I'd

made a mistake and thought we were meant to be meeting at yours.'

'Did they buy it?'

'I think so.'

'Thanks,' she says. 'You're a gem. You're going to say I should have told you.'

'Yes,' I say. 'You should have. I asked you not to use me, Isabelle.'

'I guess that's why I didn't tell you. Are you angry? Don't be angry with me, Jennifer. Life's too short. Oops!'

'I'll ignore that,' I say.

'Why did you go round? What on *earth* made you do *that*?'

'Does it matter? What matters is we sort out this mess. We need a story.'

'Go on then.'

'Right . . . Where shall we say we met?'

'Ham Yard Hotel.'

'Is that where you are now?'

'Yes, Miss Marple.'

'Do you know what the bar looks like or just the bedrooms?'

'I'm not answering that,' she says. 'You're being judgemental.'

'I'm not being judgemental, I'm being practical. We need to get our story straight in case *your husband* asks. Which I'm sure he will. So this is our story . . . we met in the bar.'

'Fine. I'll check out the bar before I leave.'

'I was very late and you couldn't get hold of me. Bad signal. You'd already ordered a bottle of wine – white, obviously, a Sauvignon—'

'Jesus, Jennifer. He's not going to need details!'

'Maybe not, but *we* need them. Detail will help us be authentic. And you had practically finished the bottle while you were waiting for me because I was so late. Which is why you're DRUNK!'

'OK,' she says. 'I'm sober now, trust me!'

'You're sure you'll remember?'

'Jennifer, I'm not an imbecile.'

'Yes, you are, Isabelle.'

'Fine. I'm an imbecile. If I can work out how to use a phone, I'll call you tomorrow.'

'Make sure you do.'

'Thank you,' she says. 'I owe you one. Love you!'

6

The cab turns into my street and I notice a dark figure lurking outside my front door.

'Drive slowly, can you?' I tell the driver. 'And keep going if I say so.'

I peer through the window, trying to see who it is. It's disturbing. I'm ready to call the police. As we approach, the figure turns round, puts his hand up to shield his eyes from the glare of headlights and I realize, with both relief and shock, who we're dealing with.

'It's all right,' I say. 'You can pull over. It's my ex-husband.'

'You're having quite a night of it,' says the cabbie.

'You have no idea.' He must have listened to every word of my conversation with Isabelle while I thought he was listening to angry voices on LBC.

I gather myself together, wondering what the hell Andy is doing at my house at this strange hour, jump out of the car and walk towards him.

He realizes it's me, smiles and opens his arms. He's shivering.

'Jennifer,' he says, and bursts into tears. His head

drops on to my shoulder, his whole body racked by sobs. I prop him up, my heart aching. I hate to see him cry.

'Andy. What's wrong?' He stinks of booze.

'I'm so sorry, Jennifer. I had to come and see you. I've been so worried.'

I am moved by his pain. His unexpected concern. I thought he'd forgotten about me. 'Let's go inside,' I say, freeing myself from the weight of his bulk, allowing him to wobble while I hunt in the dark for my key. 'Argh!' I sigh, fishing around in my handbag. 'I hate this bag. Where's my key?'

He snorts. 'Nothing changes.'

'Thanks,' I say, recoiling at his breath. 'Wow. Your nose is bright red.'

'I've been standing outside in this fucking weather at least an hour.'

'Why didn't you call?'

'You're ill. I assumed you'd be in,' he says, snivelling. 'And Elizabeth checks my phone.'

'Got it,' I say, finding the key and jiggling it in the lock.

He's standing so close behind me I can feel the brush of his breath on my neck, cloying and claustrophobic. I hurriedly push the door with my shoulder, ramming it because it swells in the damp.

'Same crap door,' he says. 'Shrinks in summer, bloats in winter. A bit like me,' he laughs.

He walks into the house, straight past me into the kitchen as if he still owns the place and starts banging around the cupboards.

'God, it feels weird being here,' he says, poking his head into the shelves, shifting tins and condiments.

'What are you looking for?'

'I need a drink. Is this all you've got?' He holds up a bottle of red wine. 'Anything stronger? Whisky?'

'No. You're too late.'

'Can I open this then?' He's already picking at the foil.

'Be my guest.'

He clatters around the drawers, hunting for the corkscrew. 'Jen!' he says. 'This house is an icebox. It's colder inside than out. I thought we put in a new boiler?'

'That was over ten years ago!'

He shakes his head, muttering to himself. 'No wonder you're fucking dying.'

'Excuse me?' I say, my skin crawling. 'I'll turn the heating back on in a minute but it's going to take at least an hour to crank up and I was planning on going to bed.'

'Well, I'd appreciate your turning it on.'

'How long are you planning on staying?'

'How long have you got?'

I can tell I'm going to regret this visit before it's even started. I dash upstairs to turn on the heating, go into my bedroom and pull a cardigan from a drawer. I grab a scarf for Andy.

'Aha!' I hear him cry. I guess he's discovered the corkscrew. 'Aw, fuck that!' He's discovered the wine is a screw-top. It gives me a moment's pleasure.

When I walk back into the kitchen, he's pouring

himself a healthy slug of wine which he knocks back like it's a shot before pouring the same again. 'Man, I needed that,' he says. He looks at me. 'Sorry. You want a glass?'

'No thanks,' I say, wrapping the scarf around my own neck, deciding not to bother to extend the gesture to him. His concern for my welfare seems to have taken a back seat rather quickly. 'Did you come because you'd run out of booze? In which case, you can take the bottle and go.'

He throws me a wild look. 'God no,' he says. 'I wanted to check up on you. I care about you, Jen. I wanted to see how you are. I mean, time is passing and . . .'

'I'm fine. In fact—'

His face does a weird gurn. 'I need to talk to you.'

'Oh.' I feel my whole body sink.

'Can we sit down?'

'Sure,' I say. 'I need to talk to you as well.'

'Oh dear,' he says. 'I hope you're not going to have a go at me too.'

I think I can guess what's coming. I follow him into the sitting room, wondering whether he was always this irritating. Wondering if nostalgia has made me romanticize the past and I've rewritten my marriage the way people rewrite the memory of an abusive parent who, in death, becomes a saint.

He throws himself on the sofa, forgetting he's clutching his glass of wine and spills a drop on his trousers. 'Shit! Aw. Bloody hell!'

He searches for somewhere to put the bottle down.

'When are you going to buy some bloody side tables?' he grunts.

'Oh, come on,' I say.

'Right. Pointless now, eh?' He puts the bottle on the floor and peers at my face, which is deadpan. 'Sorry, that was meant to be a joke.'

'It wasn't funny.'

'No. Cheap. That's what it was. Cheap.' He shudders, examines his lap and rubs at the stain, then looks up. 'You go first,' he says.

'No,' I say, sitting on the edge of the armchair. 'You go first.'

I'm shocked to see the state of him, his face blotchy, lit by the unforgiving light of the overhead spot, his nose a purple red. His hair is starting to thin and he's grown it long as if to prove he's still got hair. It's no longer blond, more a dirty grey, flicking into a curl above his shoulders.

'I'm a mess, aren't I?' he says. 'I'm such a fucking mess. You look good, though. In fact, all things considered, you look great. You been out celebrating?' He starts to sob again.

I get up, go into the kitchen and fetch the exhausted box of tissues. 'Here!' I hand him one and put the box down next to him. He blows into it with great effect. 'What's going on, Andy? What's wrong?' I ask, sitting back down and kicking off my heels.

'Everything!' he says, slurping the wine. 'And you're the only person I can talk to. You're the only one who'll understand.'

'Must be my lucky night.'

'Yeah,' he sniggers. 'You deserve a bit of luck, don't you?'

'I don't have to put up with this.'

'Soz, I'm drunk.'

'Don't state the obvious. So what do you want to talk to me about?'

'Elizabeth. That's what.'

I guess that was obvious. What a night, I think. 'What's happened?'

'She got into my phone. Must have worked out my passcode. She's seen all the texts and emails.' He stops there, assuming I know what he means.

'You mean there's another woman?'

'Women,' he corrects.

'Oh. I see.'

'And there are some pretty special photos.'

'Do I need to know this?'

'I'm not boasting,' he slurs. 'Truth is – and don't cry for me – I'm trapped and I'm fucking bored. These girls make me feel better. Where's the harm in that?'

'You're reckless, Andy.' It must be a full moon. Everyone's behaving idiotically tonight.

He flashes me his hurt look.

'Listen, I'll call you an Uber. I think you should go home. You can't run away every time there's a problem.'

'I can't go home. Elizabeth has changed the locks.'

'Wow! Good for her!'

'Why are you on her side? You hate her, don't you?'

I groan. 'I'm not on anyone's side, Andy. And no matter what I think of Elizabeth, I understand her. You ruined our marriage because you couldn't keep your dick in your trousers and now you're about to ruin your second marriage. I'd say, for once, Elizabeth deserves my sympathy.'

'Pah! You have no idea how difficult she is.'

I laugh. 'Is that how you justified cheating on me? "You have no idea how difficult Jennifer is? She's always so miserable." Is it only ever someone else's fault?'

'Jesus, you've changed. What's got into you?'

I lean forward and look into his tiny drunken eyes. They are the eyes of a cheat.

'I've just taken a big dose of clarity.'

He blinks and turns away. 'Stop looking at me that way. You're making me feel uncomfortable.'

'Were you hoping I'd make you feel better about yourself?'

He shrugs, rubbing the arm of the sofa. 'I thought you'd understand,' he says. 'You were always so understanding. I was going to ask if I could stay. Take care of you for a bit.'

My mouth drops open.

'But don't worry. I'll get one of those Airbnb things.' He jumps forward as if there's a wasp in his pants and the wine spills a second time on to his trousers. 'Fuck!' he says and stands up, reaching into his back pocket. He pulls out his phone. He holds the screen right up close to his face, then at arm's length. 'It's her.'

'Which one?'

He tuts. 'Elizabeth. Who do you think? What should I do?'

'Talk to her.'

'But what should I tell her?'

'I don't know! Try the truth, if you can remember it.'

His eyes shut as if he doesn't want to see himself take the call and he sits back down. 'Darling,' he says, cringing.

I can hear a high-pitch tirade. He listens, his hand stroking his straggly hair, saying, 'I'm sorry, I'm sorry' at various intervals. I walk out of the room feeling I should give him some privacy but after a long five minutes I remember it's my house and I can be where I want. I walk back in and stand in front of him, my arms folded, hoping to hurry along the conversation.

He glances up at me and mouths 'Sorry', pointing at the phone and nodding his head, rolling his eyes, before his expression suddenly becomes awkward. 'I'm with Jennifer,' he says. He looks horrified. 'Nothing! She's dying, for Chrissake. You think I go round schtupping everyone?'

I decide it's about time he booked his Airbnb.

'I think you should go, Andy,' I say.

He holds up his index finger. The 'one minute' sign. 'Listen, I'm coming home. OK?' He moves the phone from his ear to the front of his mouth and says, 'Stop crying, darling, it's OK.' He starts to whisper into it. 'Yes, yes. I promise I'll behave. I promise . . . Yes. I'll delete everything. In fact, I've deleted everything. Yes . . . You know I love you. You know you're the only one for me.' He turns back to me with a face that says, What can I do?

He could leave for a start.

I'm hating this. I don't want to be privy to his lies and fancy footwork. I don't want to witness how he operates. And I don't want to know that on the other end of the phone Elizabeth, the woman with no compassion, might actually be winning some compassion from me because she's falling for this bullshit.

Finally he ends the call. He stands up awkwardly, rubbing his neck. 'You'll be pleased to hear I'm going home,' he says.

My arms are still tightly folded. 'So she's taking you back?'

'Seems that way.' He straightens up with a kind of swagger, his ruddy, forlorn face now bathed in a patina of triumph.

Despite myself, I feel genuine pity for Elizabeth. How awful to be so scared of being alone that she has to plead with this fraud. But that's the trouble with unreliable men. You cling to the times when they're nice and funny and sober and you forgive them.

Andy pats his pockets the way he always used to: his phone, wallet, keys routine. 'Oh well, toodle-oo!' he chirps. 'Best get home, eh? Keep her happy. Thanks for the vino, Jennifer. You're the best. I'm just so sorry. About everything.'

His cheery hypocrisy pushes me over a line. 'You know what?' I say. 'You're the best too. Certainly the best thing that's happened to me tonight.'

'I am?' His eyes flash with boyish glee.

'Yeah. It's been eye-opening watching you operate. Because witnessing your little performance, I see you for who you really are.' His face retreats with suspicion into his neck, making him resemble a turtle. 'I was so pleased to get your letter, Andy. It made me feel that our years together had not been wasted. I appreciated your candour. But I've just witnessed your MO. You only say the right words to serve a purpose. You don't mean them at all. You're not sorry for any longer than it takes you to say the word sorry.'

He goes to interject but I hold up my hand and he snarls.

'And please tell Elizabeth she is welcome to you, because frankly I wouldn't *schtupp* you if you were the last man on this planet.'

His head lists from side to side, like he's readying for a fight. 'It's lucky it's not an option then, isn't it?' He sashays towards the door then swings round, pointing an accusatory finger at me. 'I don't know what's got into you. I come round to see how you are and to talk to you. To share a problem. And you practically throw me out. You've definitely changed,' he says. 'You're bitter. Yeah! That's what it is . . . bitter.'

Send in the clowns. Don't bother. They're here.

7

I wake up feeling slightly sick about the events of last night and squirm as I recall my outburst at Andy. My discomfort with confrontation is back, if it ever went away. Then I chastise myself. If there's one thing I need to take from this whole massive blunder, it's that sometimes telling people how you really feel is healthier than letting them off the hook. And if it's uncomfortable, you roll with the punches. But better to get in the ring than throw in the towel.

And being honest, I doubt Andy remembers any of it this morning, in his squall of a hangover. It will have been wasted on him. Elizabeth will be there, all fawning and grateful, yet terrified every time she hears his phone ping. At least I've been spared that.

I get out of bed. The nausea is still there and despite trying to ignore it, I feel better once I've thrown up. I make myself a cup of tea and sit in front of my computer, waiting to log into my emails. I start deleting all the junk in the hope of making my computer speed up and just manage to stop myself from deleting an email from Frank. I take a deep breath then click on it.

Jennifer, forgive the delay in my response but your personal email went into spam. That's good news. Of course your job is here for you. Let me know when you are ready to return.

Frank

I'm thrilled. Frank is back to his normal curt self. I email Pattie. I relay my news unsensationally, and ask when might be convenient for me to come back. Frank won't be thinking about any of the formalities so it's best I sort it with her.

The phone rings and I grab it, hoping it's Isabelle. I still haven't heard from her since yesterday despite her promise to let me know she's OK, but it's Pattie. She's called me back immediately. She's one of a kind.

'I can't believe it!' she says. 'Such amazing news.'

'I'm so embarrassed, Pattie,' I say.

'Oh, stop it! And stop worrying about formalities,' she says. 'Joan is still on temporary cover. I think she was hoping it would become permanent, but maybe we can find her something else.'

We agree that I'll return in the New Year to allow Joan a Christmas bonus and a generous notice period in case they can't find her another position. I'm relieved. This time of year always goes so quickly, New Year doesn't seem far away. I realize the passing of time is no longer the threat it once was.

I need to get my test results this afternoon so I can move on knowing I have my old job to look forward to and will truly have my life back. Then I can properly enjoy some time off and sort myself out.

I keep checking my phone to see if there's anything from Isabelle. But there's still nothing. It's deeply disconcerting. I put the phone aside and resolve to do something I've been intending to do for days but have been putting off because it's going to be hard.

I sit down with paper and pen and commit.

Dear Emily,

I imagine you're going to be in shock when you realize this letter is from me. It's been so many years since we last spoke. How can time fly by so quickly? It feels like only yesterday we were skipping together in our back gardens. I guess I'm feeling very nostalgic and if you manage to forgive the fact that this is from me and read through the whole letter, then you'll understand why.

I had something rather shocking happen to me, Em. I was given three months to live by Dr Mackenzie. Remember him? He's still going, although I wouldn't necessarily describe it as strong. He told me I had some rare blood disorder and I'd taken too long before going in to see him. I thought I was tired. No way did I expect that news.

So over the last couple of months, I've been preparing to die. It's been very difficult. I've been regularly sick, experienced all manner of symptoms and yet, would you believe it? – they got it wrong.

258

Mixed up my results with some other poor woman's. I'm merely going through a horrible menopause. And now I'm left feeling guilty for all the sympathy and care I received.

It made me think of you and my lack of empathy when you were ill. I feel bad about what I said. I realize how awful that must have felt and now I completely understand why you dropped our friendship. I really do. How could I have been so insensitive? You were suffering and I got pissed off because you kept cancelling arrangements. I'm so sorry.

I would like to see you and apologize face-to-face, Emily. It may not be possible to get our friendship back to where it was but it would be so good to see you again. If you can forgive me?

I wait to hear from you. I hope that you and Michael are well and that life has been kind to you both.

Much love and shame,
Jennifer x

I affix a first-class stamp to the envelope and post it. It's done. And if I hear nothing from her then at least I tried.

8

'Dr Mackenzie will see you now, Jennifer.'

I climb the stairs of dread to the doctor's surgery and knock on his door.

'Come in,' he says. He looks up. 'Ah, Jennifer, sit down. Good to see you. How have you been?'

I sit. I want him to cut through the niceties. I want him to give me the results so that I can get out of this place.

'Let's just say I'm a lot better than I was.'

'Still being sick?'

'Yes.'

'Hmmm,' he says. 'Well, I think I might know the reason.'

He looks concerned. '*What is it?*' I say, instantly fearful.

He coughs awkwardly and I tug at the sleeves of my jumper, pulling them down over the tips of my fingers. He makes me feel as though I'm sitting in the headmaster's office and I've done something wrong.

'It would seem you're pregnant.'

I burst into laughter. I mean, it's the only response

that preposterous statement deserves. 'Don't be ridiculous,' I say. 'I'm in the menopause, remember?'

'You are *perimenopausal*, Jennifer,' he corrects. 'It's a time when some women are highly fertile. Think of it as your ovaries having their last hurrah.'

'You mean their last laugh.' I fall back in the swivel seat and the wheels roll with me, my arms dangling at my sides. I no longer know what to think, battered by every punch thrown at me. 'But that's impossible.' I shake my head impatiently. 'I really think you ought to get your house in order. This is becoming a joke.'

He strokes his upper lip and frowns at me. 'Really?' he says. 'Impossible?' He leans back. 'Well, I remember you said you weren't with anyone. Should I assume that means you haven't had sex?'

I stare out of the window at the grey winter sky. I don't want to have this conversation with him. I allow a silence to hang in the air, as does he, and then I concede to the inevitability of a response. 'If you must know, I have. But only once and we used protection.'

'Protection can fail.'

'Well, it hasn't. I'm sure of it. My partner is vigilant.' The doctor doesn't seem convinced. 'We were together for two years and contraception never let us down. We had a bit of a break and now we're back together.' I pause to give myself a moment's reflection. Oh God, Harry! What have we done?

'No, it's nonsense, Doctor,' I say, rolling the chair back towards his table. And then it occurs to me. A thrill of realization. 'Hang on! I started being sick

261

before we had sex. Definitely.' A sigh of relief. 'So that makes it utterly impossible. I am perimenopausal. No doubt in my mind.'

He frowns, picks up a pen, twirling it between his fingers.

We stare at one another. I can't believe he's humming. It sounds like Frank Sinatra's 'My Way'.

I'm uncomfortable as hell but I'm not going to sit here any more allowing him to play Russian roulette with my life. I can't deal with another one of his surgery's mistakes. It really is becoming a joke. At my expense. I'm actually angry at my mother – my poor dead mother – for making me trust this fool.

'OK,' he says, as he scribbles some notes and closes the file. He fixes me with an expression that says, Fair enough, and turns to his computer screen. 'Well, I was going to suggest this anyway.'

He rubs the bridge of his nose, props on his glasses and turns to look at his screen. 'I think you should have an ultrasound. Just to be sure. Hormones can be very tricky at this stage. Let's make sure they're not misleading us.'

I smile triumphantly. I knew this would not be a cast-iron result. 'That would be a good idea.'

'There's an ultrasound clinic I use that specializes in early gestation. They're normally heavily booked in advance, but I can try to get you an emergency appointment, if you'd like? Or you can book it yourself. It's up to you.'

I take a moment to work out what I want to do. It's

an unexpected conundrum. I'm seeing Harry tomorrow night. I was hoping to tell him positive news, not greet him with 'What do you want first, the good news or the baby?'

'It's OK, Doctor. I'll book it myself,' I say, still unconvinced it's even an issue. 'But thank you.'

He swivels round, picks up a pad and pen and starts writing a letter in large black scrawl, ending with his scribbled signature. He writes the address of the clinic on an envelope with the phone number and the website and slides the letter inside. 'Don't leave it too long. Let's get this sorted. Then come back and we can discuss the result either way. And give them this when you get there.'

'Thank you.' I slip the envelope into my handbag. 'Am I the most challenging patient on your books, Doctor?' I sigh.

'Far from it, Jennifer. But you've certainly been among the most challenged.'

9

On my walk back home from the doctor's it dawns on me. What was I thinking? Of course it wasn't Harry. That was far too recent. I was thrown by Dr Mackenzie's news, and as often happens when you're looking for something under pressure I couldn't see it even when it was right under my nose.

Quick snapshots hover in front of me.

Hazy black and white.

Then vibrant colour.

But surely not?

It was ONCE! One reckless, untypical moment on the heath. What are the odds?

I wrap my coat around my middle and tuck my chin into the folds of my woollen scarf protecting myself against the cold, mean chill of possibility. I'd accused Andy of being an idiot. Isabelle too. The doctor. Who's the idiot now?

I stop for a moment and lean my back against a brick wall, pausing for breath. An old woman passes in front of me, grey-haired, tweed coat, hunched over a shopping trolley, the wheels squeaking and lurching with every tug. She stops and cocks her head. 'You OK, dear?'

'Mrs Mumford!' I say, embarrassed. 'Yes, I'm fine. I've been meaning to come and see you.'

'Are you from Social Services?' she asks, bemused.

'No. I live on your road.'

'Well, you might want to go and see a doctor. You don't look well, luvvie.'

'I will, I promise. And I'll pop by soon. I'd like to help you! With your shopping.'

She gives me a strange look. 'That's very kind, dear. But see a doctor first.'

She trundles off and I make a mental note to ensure I see through the promise I made to myself. No more empty excuses.

But what's my excuse for unprotected sex on the heath? Which I initiated with my foolhardy kiss. I haven't thought about that stranger for ever. Carelessly forgotten; so quickly replaced by Harry.

I all but take myself by the scruff of the neck. YOU DO NOT FEEL PREGNANT, I say inwardly. You know what that feels like, and this has not been the same.

Or has it?

I wander past the chemist, hesitate for a moment then decide against it. I need to be patient. I don't need to pee on a stick. I'll book an ultrasound. I don't want to ruin my weekend with the man with whom I've been given a second chance. The man I love. Who loves me . . .

Despite my resolve to be patient, as soon as I get through my front door I rush to the kitchen and throw off the dustbin lid. It's practically empty. I remind myself I threw a full bag out the other day – the one with my calendar in it. I go outside to the wheelie bin. But the council has done its job. It's empty. Now I have no conclusive evidence of when that heath aberration happened. It seems like it was years ago, in another life. If only it was. I wish my mind could chuck the entire interlude in a wheelie bin so it could be taken away. Then I could forget it ever happened.

I lie down on my sofa, needing to take stock.

Truth is, when I was pregnant all those years ago I suffered from morning sickness. Back then I thought being sick was good. Because that was what I had read. Or someone had told me. Being sick is a sign that my pregnancy was strong. It was fact.

But the signs lied. The facts lied.

Three times they lied to me.

'I'm sorry it wasn't viable,' the nurse said after the first miscarriage, while I was getting dressed, sobbing. 'Sometimes it's for the best. Nature has a way of rejecting the ones that shouldn't survive.' She said it as though she was offering me something to be grateful for; as if I should be relieved not to have gone full term with an imperfect baby. As though it's not possible to love imperfection.

'I hate nature,' I sobbed.

Andy took my hand and I flinched because although I wanted to be kind, although I knew he had suffered loss too, I really didn't want to be touched. Not then. Not when it had just happened. I was too sensitive. My nerves were raw wires, ready to flare. Besides, I was trying so hard to keep myself together, any show of kindness might have torn me apart.

The second time, Andy was sympathetic for a while – until he wanted sex, of course. And by the third time he just said, 'Oh well,' dismissing it the way he might an ill-chosen meal that would be set to rights by the next one.

But I couldn't let go of it like that. With each pregnancy, I had a visceral connection to the life growing within me. Dependent on me to keep it alive. And I had failed. I couldn't simply move on the way Andy could.

I tried my best. I really did. I wanted to be happy, to make Andy feel OK about everything, but I longed for a baby to nurture and to love and to connect us as a family. I felt sorrow beyond words.

Today, although I'm being sick, it doesn't feel the same. Surely if I were pregnant it would have had an air of familiarity, like a scent that transports you back to a memory long forgotten. And my body would look different.

It's another mistake. I'm certain of it. I only hope it's not mine.

10

I decide to carry on my evening as originally intended and start my preparations for dinner with Harry tomorrow night. First, though, I want to see if I can get hold of Isabelle. Her lack of communication is becoming more and more disconcerting. I hope she's OK and I haven't messed things up between her and Martin.

I retrieve my phone from my bag and call her number.

'I can't talk,' she says in a whisper.

'Is everything OK?'

'No,' she says. 'I'll call you later.' She disconnects. I stare at the phone. This is not good! I'm worried. She sounds stressed.

I go to dial my mother, then recoil in horror.

It's the first time I've done that in years. Four years on and it's still possible to make that mistake. It shocks me. I realize I want to hear her voice even though part of me knows she wouldn't necessarily say the words I needed to hear. I bury my head in my hands. I would really like today to go away.

I dial Anna Maria. I've behaved badly towards her, ignoring her calls since the reiki session, knowing she was looking for reassurance that Rita's powers had helped. I can hardly criticize Isabelle for not calling me when I've left Anna Maria dangling. At least now I can tell her in all honesty I'm healed. She doesn't need the precise details.

'How are you?' she says. 'I've been so worried I haven't heard back from you. You're always so good at getting back.'

'I'm so sorry,' I say. 'It's been a difficult couple of weeks but I have good news.'

'You do? Go on. Tell me. No, wait!' she says. 'I know what you're going to say. I can feel it.' There's a beat. I can almost hear the light bulb flick on in her head. 'You're healed, aren't you?'

Yes! Exactly to order. I'm thankful for her unerring confidence in the esoteric. 'I am,' I say. 'Rita must have worked her magic. She's amazing.'

Anna Maria lets out a scream that pierces my eardrum. 'DUDE!' she screams. 'That Rita. She's a master. I KNEW IT. I'm thrilled for you. I'm so excited. You wait until I tell her. She'll put you down as another of her success stories. You *will* write a testimonial for her, won't you? Because, you know what?'

'What?'

'If you write your story, you will probably NEVER have to pay for another session again. Lifelong reiki. For free. Have you any idea how much that's worth?'

'A lot of £40s,' I say.

'When can we get together?' she says. 'We need to celebrate and see Rita. You should be the one to tell her the news.'

'I'd rather just see you, if that's OK. For now, anyway. I'm taking my recovery slowly.'

'And so you should. Holy moly!' she says. 'Got to run. I'm late for my spiritual healing night. You should come sometime. They'd love you. Inshallah!'

'Physician, heal thyself,' I say.

'Oh, I do,' she says. 'I'm working on myself all the time.'

I laugh as I disconnect. Anna Maria is so unremittingly upbeat I wonder whether there isn't something to be said for what she does, a joy to be gained from an unerring faith in a belief system. She probably *will* live to be ninety-five.

11

Somehow I get through the rest of the evening, occasionally stopping to consider how I feel, questioning if my body is behaving differently in any way. I check my face for signs. There is nothing. I peel the potatoes in preparation for tonight's fish pie and pop them in a bowl of water and into the fridge.

I watch the *Ten O'Clock News* but give up halfway. It's all too depressing. More worrying still, I haven't heard back from my sister. I daren't phone her again. I go to bed hoping to find solace in sleep but there is no respite. My dreams are full of babies. I leave them on buses or forget I'm cradling them and drop them from my arms.

My hormones are seriously up the creek.

It's six o'clock in the morning and there's no point in trying to get back to sleep. I lie there, mulling everything over, knowing I'm going to be sick, which now bothers me for a very different reason.

I dare myself to check my boobs and examine my waistline. There are no tell-tale signs and I'm not sure whether to be relieved or disappointed. I tell myself this is the last time I'll do this otherwise I'll drive myself insane.

I check my phone for messages. There's a text from Harry saying he loves me and is looking forward to seeing me tonight. Normally this would make my heart sing but this morning it makes me squirm. Nothing is straightforward any more. I have good news to tell him, I should be excited, but the phantom of pregnancy is overshadowing everything.

And still nothing from Isabelle. This doesn't bode well. I can't be the one to keep calling and messaging her. I wonder what's stopping her from calling me? I sense disaster.

I sit down at the table with a notepad and make a list of everything I have to deal with.

In no particular order I write:

Isabelle ☹

Harry ☺ *or* ☹

Fish pie

And then I write, in tiny letters so it doesn't seem too daunting: *book ultrasound*.

Why couldn't it just be simple? Suddenly the prosaic menopause has a whole new charm.

The ring of my mobile releases me from my pondering. Isabelle, I think, at last. But a name flashes on my screen that I haven't seen in years. It's Emily! I certainly wasn't expecting to hear from her quite so quickly. My letter worked. I take a deep breath and pick up.

12

I call Olivia immediately. I'm in shock.

'What's wrong?' she says. 'What's happened?'

'I wrote that letter to Emily,' I tell her.

'And?' she says, dropping her concern.

'Michael called me today. I thought it was Emily but he was just using her phone for my number.'

'So typical. Gets her husband to call because she's too pathetic to call herself.'

'No. That's not it. Michael had read my letter.'

'That's a bit unscrupulous, isn't it?'

'Under the circumstances, no. Emily is in a coma.'

'What! That's AWFUL! What happened?'

'She tried to kill herself.' Olivia gasps in the same way I did. I'm relieved her lack of feeling towards Emily does not limit her compassion. 'Took a massive overdose, but luckily Michael found her just in time. He said he's wondering whether he's done her a disservice by trying to save her. He said he's sure she wanted to die this time. THIS TIME. Apparently, she's tried twice before. How awful is that? Our friend, Liv! Did we ever realize how sad and desperate she was? Why did we never take her seriously?'

'It's terrible. I feel awful now about everything I've said. It goes to show, we never really know people.'

'Poor Emily. Poor Michael. What a shocking thing.'

'Thank God, in a weird way, you wrote.'

'Yes, exactly. Michael asked would I mind if Emily's mother called me, and of course I didn't. She was my "Auntie" Marion. I loved her. So we spoke and she asked if I would go and see Emily in hospital. Talk to her. See if it helps. I told her that we had fallen out and she said it didn't matter. We had shared history and the memories are what count. They're what might help. She was so lovely and calm, even though she must be in a terrible way.'

'Terrible. So are you going to go? It's going to be very traumatic. Haven't you been through enough?'

'I must.'

'Do you want me to come with you? I can go get a coffee while you're with her. You might need support when you come out.'

'That's so thoughtful. Thanks. I'll let you know.'

'And you must stop worrying about her. Isn't tonight Harry night?'

'Yes. And I have to bake a fish pie.'

'You're cooking for him? Is that wise? Why don't you just order in?'

'Because I'm trying to put together a romantic dinner.'

'Good luck. But if the way to a man's heart is through a fish pie, I'll eat my veil.'

13

As I'm making the cheese sauce for my pie, I get a bit hot and bothered, wondering why it refuses to thicken. Eventually, it starts to take and I breathe a sigh of relief. It's a sign that everything's going to be OK – Emily, Harry, Isabelle – and all I need is patience.

As if to confirm my rationale, Isabelle's name flashes up on my phone. At long bloody last. I grab it.

'Isabelle!'

'Sorry! Sorry! Sorry! I know, I should have called you back, but it's been crazy,' she says. 'I haven't had a second. Getting costumes organized for the girls' Christmas plays has been a nightmare. And I have a terrible headache – dinner party last night. Late one. I think I might be coming down with a migraine so don't shout at me. I've phoned even though I feel terrible. You see! I can do nice.' She lets out a groan. 'Oh, my poor head. Are you OK?'

'Are you serious?' I say. I couldn't care less about her head.

'Why wouldn't I be?' She gasps, acknowledging her oversight. 'Oh sorry, Jen. I'm *really* sorry. Are you all right? I'm not thinking straight. The girls said you looked *great* when they saw you the other night. Amazing, in fact. Why did you come round, by the way?'

'Where are you?'

'Lying down on my bed in a darkened room. Waiting for the pills to kick in.'

'Where's Martin? What's happened?'

'Nothing. He's taken the girls ice skating.'

'So what happened after the other night?'

'What do you mean, what happened?'

'When you got home the other night? After Barry.'

She sounds mystified. 'Nothing much. I came home, Martin was half asleep. Told him we'd had a nice evening and he went straight back to sleep. Well, straight back to snoring, if you want the full details. I know how accurate you like to be!'

I'm starting to get a headache too. 'So why when I called and asked if everything was OK did you say "No"?'

She's silent. She puts on her innocent voice. 'I don't know what you're talking about. When did I say that?'

'I asked if you were OK and you said, "No. I can't talk right now." '

'Did I?'

'Yes! You did. And I've been off my head with worry.'

'Oh Jennifer,' she says. 'Stop worrying. My marriage is fine. The last thing Martin wants to do is to find out about Barry. He trusts what I tell him.'

'Well he didn't seem too trusting when *I* saw him.'

'He hates it when I go out without him.'

'Can you blame him?'

'Ohhhhhhh!!' she drawls. 'Ohhhhhh, Jennifer. I'm so sorry. Ohhhhhh deeeear. I've just realized what you're talking about. What a mix-up,' she snorts. 'It was Sophia. She was having a tantrum about her costume for the play. She didn't want to be a pink fairy. She wanted to be a purple one. It was all a bit intense. I mean, that's the way it is with kids sometimes. Oh hun!' she says. 'That's why I couldn't talk. I'm so sorry. Nothing sinister.'

I glare at the phone like it's her face. That's it? Oh hun! The colour of Sophia's costume has been responsible for hours, days no less, of panic and concern?

'Anyway, you haven't told me why you came round.'

I'm speechless.

'What's wrong?' she says, uncomfortable with my silence.

I let it go. Wasted energy. And breathe.

'My friend Emily's in a coma. Attempted suicide.'

'Oh, Jennifer. I'm so sorry.'

'But that's not why I came round.'

'Oh?'

'Actually, there's nothing wrong with me. I came round to tell you I'm not dying.'

'Don't mess with my head, I can't take it.'

'It's true. I'm not going to die.'

'What?' Her voice changes, no longer languorous. I feel she's sitting bolt upright now, paying full attention. 'Tell me honestly. You're not fooling with me because you're pissed off?'

'I'm not that petty, Isabelle. The doctor's surgery made a mistake. They gave me someone else's results. I'm not dying.'

She screams.

'Your head must be really hurting now,' I say.

'Are you kidding me? Forget my head. This is the best news ever. You're serious? Dr Mackenzie made a mistake?'

'Yes.' I feel uplifted, enjoying the mistake with her.

'That's outrageous,' she says, and screams with delight. 'Honestly. Mum's good old Dr Mackenzie! What a major cock-up – but I couldn't be more pleased.' She draws breath. 'It's almost funny. I hope you're laughing. We must celebrate. Can you come round now? No, don't – I'm in no state for champagne. When, then? I know. Come for Christmas. Come and stay. As long as you want. It will be the best Christmas ever. Promise me you'll come and stay.'

'Yes,' I say, smiling along with her joy. 'I'd love to.'

'You must bring Harry too.'

'He goes to his mother's at Christmas.'

'Come alone then. It'll be such fun. This is the best news ever. Wait till I tell the kids. They're going to be so excited.' She falters. 'Hang on a minute. If you're not dying, then what's wrong with you?' Another beat. 'Anything?'

I garble. 'Early menopause.'

She splutters down the phone. 'Seriously?' she sniggers. 'Oh bravo, Jennifer. Welcome to my tribe.'

14

The signature growl of Harry's car announces his arrival and I fuss at organizing the table. I need to light the candles! I strike a match, which instantly disintegrates. 'Bugger.' Fumble with another and try again, struggling to control the involuntary shake of my hands, willing each wick to take. 'Come on! Come on!' At last!

His car engine stills, followed by the beep of his alarm. I'm quivering. Jittery. It's the moment of truth and I'm scared and excited in equal measure. I'm uncertain what the truth is but I'm going to give Harry my version of it and hope it turns out to be correct. My thumb starts to burn and I blow out the match I've forgotten I'm holding.

The fish pie is baking in the oven. Not particularly romantic, I know, but it's cold out and we need nice warming comfort food.

I'm freezing. I'm wearing lots of layers but I'm still cold. Nerves.

Harry rings the doorbell.

This is it. Prepare yourself.

I open the front door and he's standing there, wrapped up against the chill, looking cold and kind and adorable. His outline is backlit by the street lamp, giving him a golden aura as his breath leaves ghostly blue clouds in the freezing night air. He pulls a bunch of flowers from behind his back.

'For the lady of the 'ouse,' he says, in mock cockney. 'And this, my good woman, is for the gentleman of the 'ouse.' He pulls a bottle of wine from his coat pocket and I'm expecting it to be followed by an endless trail of coloured scarves and white doves.

Suddenly I'm terrified. Terrified of losing him. He's completely lovely. His every mad gesture, so caring and thoughtful. I find myself bargaining again. Please let everything go to plan. Just for once. Please!

He steps into the porch and draws me to him. 'Quick, cuddle me. I'm freezing but most importantly . . . I've missed you. God! I've missed you.'

'I've missed you too.' I love the smell of him. The touch of him. The everything of him. Is it possible to love someone too much?

'Are you feeling better?' he says.

I gulp. 'In what way?'

'You were so angry last time.'

'Oh. Yes. I'm not angry now. I feel a lot better. You can relax.'

He kisses my forehead. 'Good. I'm pleased.' He holds up the bottle of wine and turns the label towards me, like a sommelier hoping for my approval. 'I bought it on the recommendation of a German art dealer. I remembered you prefer red so I got it in case you might fancy a sip. He says it's from one of the best vineyards.'

I relieve him of the flowers. 'It's perfect,' I say. 'But I've made fish pie. Isn't that breaking the wine rules?'

'To hell with that,' he says, throwing off his coat. 'Let's make it a night of breaking rules. Let's be crazy people.'

'You're happy,' I say.

'I am now I'm here.'

I try to smile but my mouth will only twitch.

He grabs my shoulders. 'Listen, Sally, I was seriously bloody frightened when you weren't returning my calls. You had me properly panicked. Can you please not do that again? Promise me you'll always keep your phone on.'

'Sorry,' I say. 'I didn't intend to panic you.'

'Good. Well, now you know.'

But you don't, I think.

He walks through the house into the kitchen, an air of relaxed acquaintance with his surroundings. As much as Andy irritated me, I love to watch Harry behave as if he's at home.

I find a vase and fill it with water. Start to cut the ends off the stems.

Harry opens the tall kitchen cupboard and grabs a couple of glasses. 'Corkscrew?'

'Drawer.'

He finds it immediately. 'I'm wrecked. What a week! And now I'd like to unwind and relax with *you*! Put it all behind me.'

'Why the bad week?' I say.

'Oh, you know, clients,' he says. 'Usual crap.'

I arrange the flowers and put the vase on the windowsill. 'They're lovely. Thank you.'

There's the satisfying sound of the cork leaving the bottle.

'I've had a bad week too, to be honest,' I say.

He glances up from pouring the wine.

'My friend Emily took an overdose. Her husband found her just in time, but she's in a coma.'

'Bloody hell! Poor bastard.' He frowns. 'Emily? Did I ever meet her?'

'No. I fell out with her a while ago over something ridiculous. But it doesn't make it any easier. In a way, it makes it worse.'

'I'm sorry to hear that. That's hardly what you need, is it? I mean . . . well, you know what I mean.'

'Yeah. We need to talk about that.'

'Yes, we do!' he says emphatically. 'But first we need this.'

'Listen,' I say. 'Don't waste good wine on me. I saw the doctor. He advised against it.' Why did I have to say that?

'Spoilsport,' he says. 'I mean the doctor, not you. Just a dribble? What's the harm?' He's insistent. He hands me the glass and opens his arm for me to slide into. 'So what else did he say?'

The oven timer dings. Saved by the bell. 'Fish pie's ready,' I say, grabbing the oven gloves. I open it to a whoosh of steam which instantly clings to my face.

'Ow! What the hell?' I despair. I'm so keen to keep things under control I'm managing exactly the opposite. I put the burning dish down on the metal trivet. My hands are shaking with nerves.

'You OK?' he says.

'Heavy dish.'

'Shall we move into the other room? I'm starving. You carry the glasses, I'll grab the pie.'

He takes the oven gloves from me and picks up the pie dish.

'This is all very romantic!' he says, nodding at the candles on the table, sitting down, placing the pie between us. 'Great-looking pie, Sally-o!'

I'm not sure if his cheerfulness will play for or against me. I sit down opposite him and tuck the serving spoon into the pie, releasing a puff of steam.

'I think this is the most heat I've had in this house all day,' I say, serving him a generous portion.

He rubs his hands together over his plate, warming them. 'This can't be good for you,' he says. 'This cold.'

'Do you want to talk about your bad week?'

'Nah. Boring! Just some pain-in-the-ass clients.'

'Go on. I'm interested.' I'm playing for time. I know I am. I'm getting more and more agitated.

'Well, OK . . . so there's this wealthy couple, I mean BIG-time, fuck-off wealthy, who are getting tetchy . . .' I'm not really interested. My mind is elsewhere. I'm just staring at him as if I'm listening. He picks up his fork and toys with the potato crust. I watch as he sips his wine. '. . . and there's a painting they want in

California . . .' He looks over at me and I sit to attention. 'But I told them they're going to have to wait because I had to see you.' He smiles.

'Thank you.' My stomach clenches. 'How did they take it?'

'They were livid, but don't worry. I'm here, aren't I? I can handle them. I've told them the dealer's a mate, so it's not going to be a problem even if they have to wait a month or so.' He checks my face again. 'Stop worrying. Waiting is good for them. They're like spoilt children. They need to be shown who's boss.'

'Right.'

'Anyway,' he says. 'I've been thinking . . . about us.' His expression changes. '. . . And I've come to a decision.'

I absent-mindedly sip the wine. It catches the back of my throat and I feel I'm going to choke. 'Give me a second.'

I run into the kitchen, stick my mouth under the cold tap and guzzle, a technique my father taught me. It works. I lean my back against the warmth of the oven, wiping my mouth with the back of my hand. This is going to be embarrassing. I can feel it in my bones. I take a deep breath, dab my face with some paper towel and walk back in to see his anxious face.

'That's better,' I say, sitting down.

'Sure?'

'Yes.'

'This happens a lot now, doesn't it?'

'No, no. In fact—'

'So let me tell you my decision.' He clears his throat and breathes in sharply. 'I've thought about what you said . . .'

I must appear puzzled.

'That if I genuinely missed you, I'd give up work.'

'Oh Harry, I was upset and—'

He holds up his palm. 'Let me finish! I need to say this.' He gets all choked up. 'Last weekend together was so special—'

'It was.'

'And I want to be free to do more things like that with you. To make the time we have left even more special . . . .' He gazes at me with morbid longing. 'So I'm going to take a sabbatical.'

My eyes widen. 'Seriously,' I gulp. 'I mean, are you sure?' Suddenly, I am hugely encouraged. He must love me if he's prepared to give up work for me.

He squeezes my hand. 'I couldn't be more certain. It's taken a weight off my mind. I only want to make you happy.' He sits back. He looks raw with emotion.

'You do make me happy, Harry,' I say. 'And I know what a huge decision that is for you.' Beat. 'But you might be here for me in a different capacity from the one you're expecting.' I grin stiffly.

His eyebrows shoot up. 'Meaning?'

'Meaning, I have some news.'

'You do?' The soft lines around his eyes fan into deep crinkles.

'Yes,' I say. 'Good news.'

15

I'm watching him closely, trying to discern his reaction in the candlelight.

'A mistake?' he says, in an odd voice.

'Yes,' I say.

I've said it now.

It's out there.

'They mixed up my file. Can you believe it? They gave me the results of someone else's blood test. They got it WRONG!'

I'm expecting him to scream the way Isabelle did. Or bounce up and down and hug me like Olivia. After his thoughtful declaration, he might even burst into tears of joy or burst into song. What I'm not expecting is for him to fold his arms and rock (quite precariously, I think) on the two back legs of his chair.

'You *are* fucking kidding me!' he says in a kind of deadpan.

'No,' I say, shocked. 'I'm not.'

His chair slams down. 'Jeez, Jennifer. That sure is one hell of a mistake!'

Bad sign! He's called me Jennifer.

He makes a puffing sound like it's quite ridiculous. And I can't blame him. Because it is. BUT STILL. 'You're not messing with me, are you?' he says.

My face falls. 'Why would I mess with you on this, Harry?' I dig my fork into the potato crust and the cheese sauce oozes out like pus from a wound. 'It's true,' I say. 'I got someone else's results. God knows what's happened to her.'

'Bloody hell,' he says and shovels some food into his mouth.

'But it's good news for us, isn't it?' I say, feeling the need to prompt him.

He flaps his hand in front of his mouth. 'Hot!' he says, hand still flapping. He blows out quick breaths, swallows, grabs his wine and knocks it back. 'I think I burnt the roof of my mouth! Fuck!!' His eyes are watering, this time from pain. He gargles with the wine then looks across at me, clocks my horrified gaze, knowing I'm waiting for a more appropriate response.

He gets his composure back. 'Yes!' he says. 'That is good news.' He's staring uneasily, puffing and blowing. 'Sorry! But fuck! Painful mouth. Yeah. Good news.' He smiles a big fake grin.

'You don't sound that thrilled, or maybe this is you breaking the rule which says you should be nice when your girlfriend says she's not dying?' I don't care about his burnt mouth. All I can see are his veneers glowing in the dark.

He nods his head in exasperation. 'Of course I'm thrilled! *I am*,' he says. 'If I sound otherwise it's because . . . well, you caught me unawares. I mean, it's a major surprise, isn't it?' He leans in. 'But I'm thrilled *for you*.'

'What about for *you*?' I say.

'Yeah, yeah. For me too,' he says. 'Of course I'm thrilled.' He looks down at his plate then starts cutting up the fish from under the potato the way you would a child's. 'But it changes everything now. Doesn't it?'

'Yes,' I say, trying to be upbeat. 'It does. For the better.'

'Yes. Of course, for the better,' he says. He blows at a forkful of potato and smoked haddock and puts it cautiously into his mouth, chewing slowly. We sit in ominous silence. I'm not going to be the one to break it. He owes me an apology.

He's staring at his plate. 'So I guess I should cancel my plans for a sabbatical then?' he says.

I stare at him, aghast. 'Is that the nicest thing you can think to say?'

He shifts uncomfortably. 'Sorry. Sorry,' he says. 'Forgive me. This is coming over badly. I'm tired and I need time to properly absorb your news. That's all.'

'Sure,' I say. 'Trust me. I've needed time to properly absorb it too. But for now, can you at least pretend to be happy about it? Treat it like good news as opposed to an inconvenience!'

He rubs his temples. 'Oh shit, sweetheart. I'm sorry. I've been ungracious. Look – I've had a tough week. Just ignore me.' He stands up. 'I need more wine. What about you?' he says. He can barely meet my eye.

'I'm fine.' It's obvious my glass has barely been touched.

He suddenly stops in his tracks and turns back, staring at me, accusation bulging from his eyes. 'So why the doctor's orders?' he says. 'Why can't you drink if you're OK now?'

I want to kick myself. Why did I have to say that? Now he's smelled the rotting rat.

'Because I'm still . . . because the doctor needs to check my blood. He's not entirely happy even though there's absolutely no doubt I do not have the "osis".'

'So there might be something else?'

'Oh,' I say. '*Now* you sound thrilled!'

His eyes do a strange pirouette. 'This is all going horribly wrong,' he says. 'I'm getting the wine.'

'Bring in the damn bottle,' I say. 'Maybe I need to get drunk after all. One of us should celebrate my good news.'

He lets out a frustrated sigh and walks towards me, crouches at my knee and props up my sullen chin. In any other circumstances, I'd think he was about to propose.

'Don't be like that,' he says. 'I'm sorry. I didn't mean to sound anything but thrilled. It's just . . . what can I say? Unexpected.' He gives me a big cheesy grin. 'Good, though,' he adds hastily. 'Unexpectedly good.'

He's placed a wretched feeling in my stomach that's going to be hard to shift. This was not how it was meant to be.

'I'll get the wine,' he says.

I sit there, waiting for him, recovering from the upset. I try to tell myself I'm overreacting, that he's entitled to feel shocked, to feel doubt. He's tired and uptight. He's had clients on his case. It's knee-jerk, of course it is, and I should forgive his clumsy reaction.

And then I wonder, If I'm pregnant – if that crazy possibility is true – will Harry forgive *me*?

'Listen,' he says, returning with the wine. Looking contrite. 'Will you forgive me—'

'Of course I forgive you—'

'No,' he blusters. 'I mean, will you forgive me if I don't stay the night?'

'Are you going now?'

'Not immediately, no, but I'm tired.'

'So stay!'

'I can't,' he says. 'Too much to do. Can I take you out to celebrate properly tomorrow? When I'm less stressed? You choose where. Tomorrow night will be better. I'll be in a better frame of mind.'

I suggest Ham Yard, which seems to be in the fore-front of my mind. If Martin brings it up over Christmas then at least I'll know what I'm lying about.

'I'll book,' he says. But he doesn't seem pleased about it at all.

* * *

Our dinner at Ham Yard goes better than I could have hoped. Harry is back on form. He's had time to absorb my news and he's decided he can cope with the fact it was all a big horrible mistake. I stop worrying about his inelegant reaction. I understand.

'Isabelle has invited me to spend Christmas with them this year. She's invited you too, but I told her you go to your mother's.'

'That's kind of her,' he says. 'In fact my mother has asked if I can stay with her longer this year, she's getting old, Sally, it's sad.'

'I'm so sorry.'

'I was going to ask if you wouldn't mind doing Christmas earlier, like a pre-Christmas Christmas, before I go and see her. You don't mind, do you? We've done our New Year's, after all.'

I smile at the memory. 'That will always be my best New Year's ever. Of course I don't mind. Anyway, the earlier I can start celebrating Christmas, the longer it will last.'

We go back to mine and he leads me by the hand up to my bedroom and we make love. He's armed with the obligatory protection.

In the morning when I wake up I reach across the pillow but he's already left. There's a sweet note apologizing for his early morning getaway. He says he'll call.

As I'm making the bed, I notice something on the sheet. My heart misses a beat. It's blood. Not much but enough to panic me. I clasp my hand to my mouth. Maybe I am pregnant? Am I going to lose it? Probably. But no cramps yet. I sit down and place my hands protectively across my stomach. And that's when it occurs to me that I know exactly what I want.

I want it all.

16

'I'm going to put some gel on your tummy, and it's going to feel quite cold. OK?'

I want to tell the sonographer I've done this before but I don't feel inclined to say anything. I'm frozen with fear. My tummy is exposed. Lying down it looks pretty flat. Empty.

'OK,' I say, only it comes out more like a squeak.

'Right then, I'm going to move this around your stomach and let's see what happens.'

I close my eyes as she rolls the probe across the cold gel, then slowly peel them back, staring sidelong at the screen, watching without any comprehension of what I'm seeing.

'Well,' she says, all merry and sing-song. 'There you go, Mummy. Clear as anything.'

'What's clear? I can't see anything.'

She points at a blurry grey blob as it shifts shape, looking completely meaningless and I feel the strangest sensation as she sweeps her hand across my stomach.

'There's Baby,' she says, and I lurch.

'Are you sure?'

She laughs. 'Positive. Look! See its little heartbeat!' She pushes quite hard into my stomach, making deep circles, and I feel a little bit sick but I'm trying to see a heartbeat. Then she travels over my tummy, making a massive whoosh as though she's shifting my insides. 'And here's the head. Look, Mummy!' She's staring at the activity on the screen, lapping it up as if it's a revelation to her too.

I swallow the lump of anxiety that's gathered in my throat. 'Listen,' I say quietly. 'I know it's all very lovely, but would you mind not calling me Mummy. Not yet.'

'Oh,' she says, sounding a bit taken aback. 'Oh! I'm sorry. Most women get excited when I say that.'

'Yeah, maybe,' I say. 'But most women probably aren't forty-three, nearly forty-four, thinking they're in early menopause.'

'Oh dear,' she says. 'I'm so sorry. I had no idea that's what . . .' She's prattling, pedalling anxiously. 'I'm very sorry. Someone should have told me.'

I shake my head. 'It's OK,' I say. 'It will be OK. It's a bit of a shock, that's all.'

'I understand.' Her voice mellows, sounding less effusive, probably more like her own voice.

Silence. Just the sound of whooshing coming from the speakers on the screen.

'Do you want to know how many weeks?' she ventures.

Please don't tell me. Just say it's not true.

'No,' I say, then I put up my hand. 'And I don't want to know the sex either.'

'That's fine, it's too early for that.' She carries on in an uncomfortable silence. She stops and then starts again, then stops and turns towards me. 'Listen. This is not my business, but I hope you don't mind my asking. Do you want this baby?'

I feel it rising, that sense of fear, that sense of not knowing what's happening to my body. One minute I'm dying, the next I'm creating life. I'm aware of the responsibility. A new life. One I wasn't expecting. It's so confusing. Of course I want it. But under these circumstances?

'I don't know,' I say.

She takes my hand. 'Well, that's perfectly fine. Not everyone is sure. And it's been a real shock for you. Think carefully. You may never be totally sure but be honest with yourself. You've still got time if you want to do something about it.'

'If Mother Nature doesn't get there first.'

Everything crashes down on me. Every shock, every high, every low of the past few weeks. It's all too much. I burst into tears in front of this stranger.

To my surprise, she takes me in her arms and I sob on her shoulder. 'I'm so sorry,' I say. 'This has all been so overwhelming. It's been an emotional few weeks.'

She holds me until my sobbing subsides, then looks at me, taking my hands in hers, her eyes brimming with sympathy. 'It's OK,' she says. 'You mustn't feel guilty about not wanting it. It's your body. Your right.'

'No,' I say. 'Maybe I do want it.' I'm shaking her hands with emotion. 'But maybe not. I mean, I've always wanted a baby, but this is so not what I was expecting. Not now. Anyway, I daren't allow myself to believe that I'll be the one to make the decision.' I swallow hard. I start to sob again. 'I normally lose them in the first few weeks.'

'Oh, I'm so sorry,' she says. 'But let me reassure you on that one. There's a foetal heartbeat. That's a good sign. But I completely understand where you're coming from.' She gives me a hug and looks me in the eye.

I nod. 'I'm OK now. Thank you.'

She grabs some paper towel and wipes the gel off my stomach, then from the front of her white coat where I've rubbed against her. 'Let me get you some water.' She pops outside and the door swings softly shut behind her.

I blow my nose, glad that this woman has been so understanding. I guess she sees people like me all the time. She walks back in and hands me a plastic cup of ice-cold water.

'I might have had a tiny show, last night,' I say, knowing I should tell her.

She eyes me with that same concern. 'How tiny?'

'A drop. Literally a drop. But fresh blood.'

'Well, it could have been the placenta shifting. If that happens again, you should come in straight away.'

'I had just had sex.'

'That's OK,' she says. 'The biggest indication is the heartbeat. Just go easy.'

'You mean no more whips?'

She all but recoils.

'I'm kidding,' I say.

Reality is, I might never have sex again. Not if Harry knows I'm pregnant. I'll be waving him good-bye, that's for sure. He won't want a baby, least of all someone else's. Or will he? God, I don't know. I don't know anything right now. I need time to collect my thoughts.

The sonographer is standing at the sink, scrubbing her hands. 'Well, I hope this works out, whichever way you want it.' She gives me the sweetest smile. 'And maybe I'll see you again. Can you find your way out?'

'Yes,' I say. I unhook my cardigan and my coat from the back of the door and throw them over my arm.

As I wander through the reception out into the street, I think on that encounter.

I'm glad I asked her to stop calling me Mummy. Before, I would have stayed silent, allowing her to trill on merrily, her hand rolling across my exposed stomach making me feel vulnerable, getting silently pent-up. I would have festered all the way home and we wouldn't have had the important conversation we ended up having.

If there's one thing I've learnt from these last few weeks, the more I speak up, the more I make myself heard, the better people seem to respond. Good people. The rest of them – the ones who get defensive and mean and bitter – those people don't matter.

But what *does* matter, what matters overwhelm-
ingly, is
I.
Am.
Pregnant.

17

Olivia and I are doing our Christmas shopping, hoping that Sunday will be less busy than Saturday except, by the look of things, everyone else has had the same idea. I'm excited, though. Only recently I never thought I'd get this opportunity. I have a long list of silly presents to buy; a celebration in itself.

It's slightly overshadowed by the fact that I need to tell Olivia the news that I'm pregnant. The whole truth. I have to own up to sex on the heath. It all feels a bit tawdry and ridiculous now. I'm going to bide my time. Shopping first.

I get to Selfridges early and gather up a few small gifts, piling them into a basket, ticking the recipients off my list. I'm standing in line waiting to pay, finding my head immersed in my confused thoughts.

'Jingle bells,' says Olivia, right in my ear, making me jump. 'Sorry,' she says. 'Didn't mean to frighten you.' We kiss. 'How are you?'

Pregnant, I think. 'Fine,' I say. 'Hope you don't mind. I've made a head start.'

'Snap!' she says. 'So have I!' She holds up some carrier bags.

The queue moves forward.

'So what are you buying Harry?' says Olivia, peering into my basket.

'Oh, these aren't for him. I'll get him something ironic. What are you buying Dan?'

'We've agreed not to buy each other anything this year. We're putting the money we might have spent towards the honeymoon fund.'

'Oh, Liv!' I say. 'You can't do that. Let's go to Primark. Buy them both a terrible Christmas jumper.'

'Ha!' she says. 'I love that idea.'

I pay at the till and we make our way out of the store, battling through the crowds, across the road, to fight for a couple of silly jumpers.

'What do you think?' says Olivia, holding up a black sweater with stars.

'Absolutely not,' I say. 'That's almost *nice*. It misses the point.'

She looks at me as if to say, Seriously?

I pull out another one in vivid green with a cartoonish reindeer's face and big red nose. 'Here!' I say. 'Couldn't be more embarrassing.'

'Brilliant,' she says. 'I hate it.'

I grab a red one with a massive Christmas pudding decorated with holly and icing. It's perfect for Harry.

'Sorted!' I say. 'Listen. Have you got time for a coffee?'

'Sure,' she says. 'Desperate for one.'

We go to a café she knows along Bond Street which is noisy and very Italian. 'They do the best, strong stuff,' she says as we sit down.

'Good,' I say. 'You're going to need it. Now please don't scream.'

She looks at me like I'm mad.

'I'm pregnant.'

'You're WHAT?'

I flap my hands, telling her to keep it down. 'I'm pregnant,' I say out of the side of my mouth.

'Blimey. Harry's a fast worker.'

'It's not Harry's.'

'Is this conversation happening?'

'Yes. It's not his, Liv.' I hunch towards her across the table. 'I have a confession.'

'Go on.'

My voice drops to a hurried whisper. 'I had sex with a guy on the heath when I thought I was dying.'

'You WHAAAAT?' she yells.

'Shhhhushhh. Exactly what I said. Don't make me say it again.'

'And you never told me?'

'It didn't feel necessary.'

A waitress hovers into view.

'Two cappuccinos, please,' Olivia says with a huge smile then turns back to me and gawps. 'But now it does?'

'Obviously. I'm pregnant!'

'How many weeks?'

'Not sure. I told the woman who did the scan I didn't want to know.'

'Why?'

'I wasn't ready. Anyway, the doctor will no doubt tell me. I have to go back to see him. It's early, though. It may not . . .' There's no way I can relax. Not even in the knowledge that a foetal heartbeat is a good sign.

'I understand,' she says. She squeezes my hand, biting her lip. 'So, was it a total shock? Didn't you have any clues?'

'I wasn't looking for clues. I thought I was dying. I thought that was why I was being sick.'

She exhales. 'Of course. But what the fuck?' she scoffs. 'Sorry, not funny,' she adds.

Our coffees arrive and we sit there, spooning the froth into our mouths. Olivia is smirking.

'So, this secret man on the heath. Are you still in touch?'

'God, no!'

'Who is he, then?'

'No idea.'

'SHUT UP! You're having a laugh.'

'If only.'

'Harry must be thrilled.'

'He doesn't know yet.'

'Awkward!'

'Just a bit!'

'When are you going to tell him?'

'Soon.'

'You mean before he works it out all by himself.'

'Sooner than that. He's going to California on a long trip. When he gets back we're doing an early Christmas before he goes to his mother's. If I manage to hold on to this little one, I thought I could make it his Christmas present.'

'He might prefer the sweater,' she laughs.

'Don't laugh. You might be right. Oh Liv! But I really want this baby.'

'More than you want him?'

'I don't know. Our relationship is good right now. I mean, he's thrown himself back into work and he's away a lot, but that was always how it was, only now he keeps in touch regularly, better than he ever did and I'm hoping . . .' I intuitively place my hands over my stomach. 'Hey! Let's not talk about him.'

'Fine by me. Let's talk about the man on the heath. What was he like?'

I roll my eyes. 'I can't remember.'

'Well, try!'

She's not going to let this one go. 'All I can remember is that he was kind . . . and tender . . . and funny. And he smoked.'

'Jennifer! That's on everyone's wish list. Apart from the fag breath. Why on earth did you not stay in touch?'

'Because I had a date with destiny and I didn't feel it fair to two-time him.'

'Don't you think you should try to find him?'

'Why? As back-up?'

'No. Out of fairness.'

'Are you mad? I don't know his name and I can't even remember what he looks like. That's called a needle in a haystack. I'm keeping my hopes pinned on Harry.'

'Oh right! Because he's always been so reliable.'

'Olivia!'

'I'll drink my coffee and shut up,' she says.

18

'Let me know if there's anything you want me to bring you back. Text me. Or email me. And give me a clue as to what you'd like for Christmas.' Harry is calling me from the airport. I can hear the tannoy announcements in the background. I can't think of anything more alluring right now than jumping on a plane and heading off for a bit of sunshine in California. But Harry never invites me on his work trips. Not even now when I'm free to travel.

'Bring me back sunshine,' I say. 'On second thoughts, don't. I'd like a white Christmas.'

'OK, Bing Crosby!' he says. 'And don't forget. They're eight hours behind so I'll keep in touch via email because I'm going to be charging around and might not get time to call when you're awake. OK?'

'OK. Have a good trip.'

Harry's suggestion suits me. I'd rather communicate over email than talk to him if my conversation with myself is anything to go by. I know how many weeks I am now – Dr Mackenzie confirmed it – and the dilemma of telling him sits firmly at the forefront of my mind.

Head: We're nearly eight weeks pregnant. Don't you think we should tell Harry?

Heart: No. Wait until we're sure, when we see him at our pre-Christmas Christmas.

Head: We're only delaying the inevitable. That's not fair.

Heart: No, we're not. We're being cautious. And we want to see him when we tell him. And there's never been a convenient time to say anything. Which has been convenient in a way.

Head: We can't have this baby and have Harry. It's just not going to happen.

Heart: Who says Harry isn't going to fall in love with the idea? Who says he isn't so in love with us he'll refuse to give us up and agree to father the baby.

Head: Get real.

Heart: You're just a horrible sceptic.

Head: And you're a deluded romantic.

And so it goes on. So emails are just fine because my head might say something my heart will regret but I can keep my fingers from blabbing.

19

She looks like she's asleep. Peaceful. Content. To be honest, if it weren't for the vaguely perceptible rise and fall of her chest, for all the wires snaking around her and the beeps and flashing of the equipment next to her, I'd think she was dead. But she's not. Emily is just in a very, very deep sleep. Let's not say the coma word. Let's be hopeful.

The nurse had made it sound so simple. 'We'll go in and you'll tell her who you are and then you just talk to her like normal,' she says. 'Sit and chat.'

'Like normal?'

'Yes. Behave as though you're having a one-sided conversation. Talk about anything you used to do together. The things you remember about the two of you growing up . . . her favourite music or places you visited, things that made you laugh—'

'Right.' I've suddenly forgotten everything about our past. Like I'm on a radio phone-in competition and every thought in my head freezes. 'Do you think she can hear me?'

'We believe so. Talk to her as though she can. And watch for a response. Of any kind.'

'Has she responded before?'

She shakes her head. 'Not so far.'

I gather my strength. 'People do come out of this type of coma, don't they?'

'We never give up hope,' she says with a placatory smile, opening the door into Emily's private room.

'Emily!' she trills. 'You have a visitor, darling. Aren't you a lucky girl?' She talks as if Emily's sitting up in bed, bright as a button.

I'm shocked to see her from the other side of the glass pane. The horror of her condition seems more real. I pull myself together and try to adopt the nurse's tone. 'Hi, Em!' It comes out shakily. 'It's Jennifer. Erm . . . Jennifer Cole. Your old friend. Remember me?' I feel ridiculous.

The nurse smiles at me, then says, 'Try to chat. Be natural,' and she closes the door. I'm alone and there's nothing natural about it. I sit down and look around. It's a small clinical bedroom. A high bed with white metal frame, neatly tucked-in sheets and blankets that remain undisturbed. It's not dissimilar to the hospital rooms you see in the movies or on TV when there's someone attached to wires and machines, lying in a coma. Only it's my friend who's attached and it's real. Even though it's surreal.

In a weird way she looks exactly like she did as a child. There's something so innocent about her.

I wonder where to begin.

'How are you, Emily?' That's a stupid thing to say for a start.

I watch her, scrutinizing her passive face the way you can when you think someone isn't looking. She seems so stress-free and unlined. Not in an Isabelle way, more natural, like the years have drifted away and left no trace.

I begin telling her the thoughts I've prepared. 'Do you remember when we used to dance around your room to Queen?' I say. 'And Duran Duran. You always said you were going to marry Simon Le Bon.' This feels so bizarre. 'Remember your brother's hair? How he used to make you backcomb it and spray it with your mother's hairspray until it was stiff as a board. Your father would go crazy and call him a poof!' I'd almost be enjoying myself if it wasn't such a one-sided conversation.

I take her hand in mine, watching, waiting. A twitch would be enough. Maybe a flicker of her eyelids. Isn't that what happens in the movies? I stare at her, willing it. Give me something, Em. Anything.

But there's nothing. No miracle.

If I stop talking the room becomes eerily silent. Barring the beep of machines.

The interminable beep.

I carry on. Despite my long rendition of retrieved memories, the things so personal to the two of us, her face doesn't move. Nothing moves. I'm horribly aware that I'm going to let her mother down. I think she truly believed that I might be the difference. That my

309

letter was a sign. I hear the nurse's words, *we never give up hope*, yet I seem to have done precisely that.

Beep

Beep

Beep

'Em? Do you remember that holiday in Ibiza when Anna Maria stayed out late because she met some awful guy and wanted to see where it might go? And when it went nowhere she came home but she'd forgotten her key and had to sleep on the landing because we'd all passed out and didn't hear her ring?' I check her expression. 'Do you remember how we all laughed when we found her lying in a ball in the corridor snoring?

'Em? I wish you'd laugh now. Please. Wake up. You're one of the only ones left who remembers this stuff. And you're the only one who remembers my childhood. Well, apart from my sister, of course, but she saw it through different eyes. I'm so sorry I let you down, Em. For getting impatient with you. Can you forgive me? Please? It doesn't matter that we haven't spoken. Because, like your mum said, we have history. You can't buy that. You can't friend it on Facebook. That means something, doesn't it?'

Beep

Beep

Beep

I'm running out of inspiration.

'It's Christmas soon. You love Christmas. Remember how we'd sing carols really loudly in school assembly?

I bet we were embarrassing.' I snort at the memory. 'Remember your favourite? Come on, Em. You must remember that.' Nothing. Not a twitch. Not a blink.

'Well, here's a little reminder just for you.' I clear my throat, 'Ahem!' as if I'm about to start an important performance.

'O little town of Bethlehem . . .' I gaze into the empty expression on her face. 'How still we see thee lie,' I say, bringing the song to an abrupt halt.

This is not working. I have nothing more to give. I squeeze her incongruously warm hand and try to transmit all the love I possibly can.

'Choose life, Emily,' I say. 'Please. Choose life.'

20

I've told Pattie I'm pregnant. She sounded shocked, even though she didn't say as much – pregnancy is never great news for an HR department – but I think she was delighted for me personally. I didn't give her the full explanation, nor did she ask for one. I'm guessing she thinks it's Harry's.

'I can't believe this crazy turnaround in your life,' she says.

'I'm sorry for throwing this into the mix. I'm so embarrassed.'

'Why? I am aware people have sex, you know. I just wish I was one of them.'

I laugh, grateful for the left of field riposte. 'There's always Tinder, Pattie.'

'I'm on Bumble. Fat lot of use it's done me. Obviously, we'll have to accommodate your pregnancy in your package, but don't worry, we'll sort something.'

'Thanks,' I say. 'I hope it's not going to cause too much grief.'

'Less grief than your previous condition, that's for sure. Leave it with me,' she says.

Harry is back from California. He wanted time to recover from jet lag but today he's coming round for our pre-Christmas Christmas. I'm so looking forward to seeing him, desperately trying to build up heaps of good cheer. And a huge dose of courage.

My gifts are wrapped and ready. Everything for Isabelle's family is in a big carrier bag by the front door and Harry's is under an acrylic Christmas tree that I bought at the Pound Shop. It's genius, already decorated with baubles, tinsel and multicoloured fairy lights. You simply plug it in and it's instant *Ding Dong Merrily on High!*

Harry's present looks lonely, but I have the surprise gift to save till last. Of course it could end up being a bad joke from a cheap cracker. But let's think positive. The man loves me. He is more committed now than he's ever been.

The Christmas pudding jumper is wrapped in black and gold foil, tied up with gold ribbon and a gold foil rosette making it appear fabulously expensive. I want him to think I've made a supreme effort and think it's something extravagant. Then he'll get the joke.

It's one of those grey, foggy days when the sky feels as though it's about to fall in on you because the cloud is so low. I bet Harry can't see the top of the Shard. I only hope he can see his way over here. Hopefully the fog will start to lift and it will be fine before gathering again as night falls, meaning, with a bit of luck, Harry will have to stay after all. He's intending to head off to his mother's straight after our little party for two

313

(or three) and has to hit the road by six because the motorways will be empty at that time, he says.

If it's miserable outside, I've made it cosy inside. I've draped loads of red and green paper chains everywhere. There are plastic holly and berry garlands and trailing tinsel that I've taped to the walls. There's a sign that lights up flashing HoHoHo which I've propped against the window ledge. And there are a few strategically placed bunches of mistletoe. All from the Pound Shop. I even bought a fan heater, but it seems to only manage to heat the area of the room directly in its path. I have to keep changing its position.

I've laid out a Christmas picnic on a rug in front of the sofa. Chicken wings, cocktail sausages with spicy tomato sauce, and mince pies with a can of whipped cream to add to the fun. There's a CD playing Christmas songs on repeat. I refuse to be short-changed on atmosphere.

Harry's bringing Prosecco. I'm going to allow myself a glass. Special dispensation. Then we're going to watch *It's a Wonderful Life* – a Christmas classic for a change. I don't think he'll mind a bit of schmaltz. I'm alive and we're together! That's what matters.

I'm around ten weeks pregnant now. I'm thrilled even though I have moments of tears from time to time. It's silly, but I can't seem to help it. Sometimes, I feel more emotional looking back at what I went through than I did when I was going through it. But I'm becoming less retrospective and starting to look to the future. I've seen the doctor and put the arrangements for the birth in place. I've been assigned a midwife at the hospital. It's significant. Particularly for me. I'm so thrilled to have scraped past my danger zone. I still worry it's vulnerable, but I'll probably worry about that the entire pregnancy. And in between worrying, I tell myself it's going to be OK. Everything is going to be great. Because *it's the most wonderful time of the year.*

I'm wearing a onesie. It's a good solution when you don't know what to wear and you're about to tell the man you love you're pregnant. With someone else's baby.

So I'm dressed like a bunny, with big white and pink ears and a bobtail that I have to move every time I sit down because otherwise it feels as though I'm sitting on someone's foot. Yes, I look silly but why not? It will make Harry laugh and I might need all the laughs I can get.

Harry stands on the doorstep, a big bag in his hand, and studies me as though he's not sure whether to laugh or cry. 'Nice outfit,' he says.

'Thanks,' I say. 'It's a bugger when you need to go to the loo, but it does mean I can eat all the pies.' I hold out the pink fluffy fabric of the tummy, proudly demonstrating the amount of spare room.

'Impressive.' He doesn't sound impressed. He takes off his overcoat, strolls past me into the sitting room, looks around, checking out my decorations, taking in the picnic. 'What's with the oh oh oh in your window?'

I point to the illuminated sign. 'Now read it from inside!'

'Oh right!' Not even a chuckle.

He's odd. Definitely odd. He's not ready for Christmas.

'Hug?' I say. 'Nice to see you too.'

'Sorry,' he says and gives me a hug. He smells different.

'New aftershave? It's nice.'

'It's what I always wear,' he says.

'No, it isn't.'

'OK. It isn't.'

What's his problem, I wonder, but I don't want to know. Not today. I don't want to know about another bad week. Or his failure to secure the painting in Santa Barbara. I don't want to know anything bad. I want this to be a wonderful day of happiness and laughter and goodwill to all men. And women. And babies. Especially babies.

He's wearing a thick-ribbed black polo-neck sweater and black wool trousers. He's come prepared for my freezing house. He's probably wearing thermals. He opens the bag, pulls out a couple of bottles of Prosecco without any theatre and says, 'Jesus, it's stuffy in here,' running his hand around his polo neck, loosening the ribbing.

'*Voilà!*' I say proudly, pointing at the whirring heat monster in the corner. 'Pound Shop. I blew the budget. Bought everything there.'

'Yeah,' he says, looking at my HoHoHo and then

my flashing tree. 'I guess I know what to expect in that then.' He points to the lonely parcel.

'Not that!' I say, sounding appropriately insulted. 'I didn't get your present from the Pound Shop.'

'Here,' he says, and he hands me a small purple gift bag with a silver bow. 'Merry Christmas.'

'Merry Christmas!' I say, shaking it. 'Don't tell me. It's a gold Mallomar?'

'Don't be ridiculous.'

'Silver then. Perhaps gold was being greedy. Oh, come on, Harry, laugh.'

'It's actually a beautiful gift. I went to a lot of trouble to find it.'

'Ooops. OK. Thanks.'

Jet lag. I think. He's still jet lagged. I'm going to have to work on him to get him into my happy mood. I don't think he's quite got into the swing of goodwill. When we did Christmas combined with New Year we were all festived out. He's never witnessed how much effort I put into the celebrations before they start to pall. And this year I'm super pumped.

I hand him back his purple gift. 'You have to put it under the ironic tree. We'll wait until we've finished the picnic and then we can open our *plethora* of gifts.'

He groans impatiently, bends down and puts the gift under the tree, throwing me a look that says, I can't believe I'm doing this. ' "Good King Wenceslas",' he says, picking up the background music over the hum of the heater. 'You're serious about this Christmas malarkey, aren't you?'

'Totally,' I say. '*One Hundred Christmas Songs*. Part of my outstanding collection of CDs no one else wanted.'

'Why am I not surprised?' he says.

I laugh, hoping he might too. But he doesn't. 'You ready to picnic?'

'Sure,' he says. 'You ready for Prosecco? Or is the bunny drinking carrot juice?'

'HoHoHo,' I say.

I'm playing at being flippant and silly and am about to bounce into the kitchen but then I catch that look on his face. The one I hate. The one that says he has something to tell me but doesn't know how.

'What's wrong?' I say, before remembering I don't want to know. 'No, don't tell me. Let's just pretend everything's fabulous and full of good cheer.'

He walks up to me and takes me by my acrylic fur paws.

'Oh, Jennifer,' he says. 'I knew you'd guess. I knew you'd drag it out of me.'

'Have I?' I gulp. 'Am I Jennifer now?'

'I'm not sure how best to say this.' His eyelids flutter as my bobtail droops into my rabbit feet. 'I thought I'd wait until we'd opened our presents and then you would know how much I love you and how much this pains me.'

'What pains you?' I say. 'Arthritis? Please tell me it's arthritis.'

'Come here.' He leads me to the sofa and sits down,

bidding me to sit next to him. I shift my tail and shuffle back against the arm, keeping a bit of distance.

The room is crowding in on me. Everything is starting to look cheap and nasty instead of fun and frivolous.

His lips ruffle. 'You do believe me when I say I love you, don't you?' he says.

I remove my hands from the mittens. Suddenly I'm very hot. 'It depends what follows,' I say.

'Jesus,' he says, puffing his cheeks. 'For once it's hot in here.'

'I'll turn off the blow heater.'

'No, don't,' he says. 'Just listen.'

'I'm all ears.' I hold up my pink and white bunny ears.

He reverse rotates his shoulders. 'When I got your letter,' he says, 'I was devastated. Devastated that you were going to die. We hadn't been together for some time and it surprised me how much it got to me. So I called you and we met and that's when I decided I wanted to be with you. Until the end. Which I did, darling. I really did.'

'Get to the "but", Harry. I feel I need to hear the "but".'

He rolls his eyes. 'OK.'

Nooooo. There *is* a 'but'. 'Jingle Bells' starts playing. It sounds tinny and threatening and wrong. I want to close my eyes and shut my ears.

'I told a little white lie.' He shakes his head, trying to appear remorseful. He looks back at me as if he's waiting for my probe. I stare right back at him.

'You remember I told you Melissa and I were no longer together?'

I continue to stare.

'It wasn't exactly true.'

I twitch. 'What do you mean? Not exactly?'

'Exactly that,' he repeats. He looks away.

This is not good, my head is saying. This is not good, my heart is saying. For once they agree.

'We were still living with one another.'

'Fine. So you finished with her after we'd talked?'

He pushes back his hair. His face is flushed. There are beads of perspiration breaking out on his forehead and his upper lip.

I get up. I want to turn off the heater, not because I want to spare him the sweat but because the noise is getting to me. My nerves are jangling.

'Just sit!' he says. 'Please.'

I sit back down again, right on the bobtail. 'Ouch.'

'I'm really sorry. Truly I am. I had no idea this was going to happen.'

'Harry, I don't understand what you're saying. What was going to happen?'

'You still don't get it, do you? Melissa and I. We're still together.'

I fall back on to the arm of the sofa. 'Don't be ridiculous. How can you be?'

He reaches out, puts his hands on my knees, gazes at me all forlorn. 'We are. She lives in my apartment. Well, she has a key.'

'So get it back!' I realize this is not the point. I push

320

away his hands, stand up. This time I'm ignoring his instruction. I turn off the heater and turn off the CD. Everything's getting to me now. I can barely bring myself to look at him even in my peripheral vision. I pace. 'But, *we've* been together. Whenever you've got back from a trip, *we've* been together. Don't tell me the trips were a lie?'

He sits there, his head now in his hands. 'They were real. I promise. And yes, we have been together. I wanted that. And Melissa understood. She wanted me to be with you.'

I look at him and he looks back at me, pleading.

'Whoa. Hang on a minute. Did you say what I think you said? Melissa understood? Melissa wanted you to be with me?' I'm trying to absorb this. The pieces of the puzzle are starting to fall into place. He never once invited me back to his flat. He took me away, to be out of the way. 'That's very kind of her,' I say. 'How extraordinarily generous.'

'She is kind—'

'Oh shut up, Harry!'

'Sorry,' he says.

I'm pacing back and forth, up and down and across the room in my ridiculous onesie, feeling entirely ugly and fat and stupid and mortified. I accidentally upset the bowl of chicken wings, then purposefully kick them across the rug.

'Sweetheart! Don't be mad.'

'Don't you dare "sweetheart" me. What should I be? Thrilled for you? Oh, congratulations, I hope you'll both be very happy? I couldn't be more mad. Now let me get this straight. *Melissa* let you be with *me* because I was dying. She was letting you hang out with me until the end, the end you wanted so desperately to help me through, because she knew that once I was dead you'd be back?'

'God! You make it sound . . .'

'Disgusting. Right? So she let you have sex with me because I was nearly a corpse?'

'She doesn't know about the sex.'

'Oh right! Oh, that's OK then. Well let's just keep that little intimacy to ourselves, shall we? I suppose it was her idea to give me a private screening of my favourite film? Which you've now ruined.'

He lets out a frustrated sigh. 'That was my idea.'

'Well, you're full of them, aren't you?'

I take my arms out of the sleeves of the onesie. I'm down to my T-shirt and I'm sweltering. I'm sure there must be patches of sweat under my armpits. I bet Melissa doesn't sweat. I bet she'd never wear a cheap onesie. I tie the arms around my waist and the rabbit paws flap in front of me with every step I take.

'Sit down, Jennifer!'

'Stop calling me that. You don't need to keep rubbing it in.'

'Please sit down.'

'No!' I swing round, hands on hips, giving him full-on eye contact. 'Now I get it. Now I've heard it all. That's why we're doing Christmas early, isn't it? Because you're spending New Year with her.'

He looks guilty.

'Arrrrgggghhhhhh! I'm such an idiot. That must have been so inconvenient for you when you heard I wasn't going to die. No wonder you behaved the way you did. No wonder you were so horrified.'

He's speechless. His body language says it all.

'But you recovered really well, didn't you? You took me out for a pity dinner and a pity fuck while you were trying to work out how you could extract yourself from this relationship. You've even bought me a pity present.' I stride over to the tree and pick up his pathetic little purple package with its pathetic little bow and throw it back at him. It falls at his feet and he picks it up and places it on his lap. He reminds me of Gulliver with a Lilliputian suitcase, packed and ready to go. 'Well, I don't need your consolation prize, thank you.'

He rolls his eyes. To him, I'm just a woman overreacting.

'Do you know what?' I say, taking him in. 'I actually fell for it. I believed you truly loved me and wanted to be with me until my dying day. I fell for all the *When Harry Met Sally* and Mallomars schtick. And when you were horrified when I told you I wasn't dying, I believed you were entitled to take your time to absorb the news because it was a shock for me, too. I actually felt sorry for you because I understood how difficult it was to rationalize such a huge UNFORTUNATE MISTAKE.'

'Not unfortunate. Don't be like that.'

I hoot. 'Not for me. But oh boy, did it put a spanner in the works of your little plan. There I was, happily celebrating our love when all the time, Melissa was lying in your cosy bed, counting the days until she could have you back in her arms – as soon as mine were cold with rigor mortis.'

'You make it sound so horrible.'

'It is horrible!' I stamp on a chicken wing. 'Fuck!' I grab my foot, rubbing the sole, hopping to maintain my balance. 'It's worse than horrible. It's . . . it's . . . I can't even put a label on it, it's that bad.' I release my foot and steady myself.

'No, it isn't,' he protests. 'You have to understand. You have to trust me. It was done with good intentions.'

'Oh Harry. The road to hell is paved with good intentions.' I stare him down. 'And I will never . . . ever . . . trust you again.'

'I think I'll go.' He stands up and I push him back on the couch with such unexpected force he tumbles awkwardly and drops his Lilliputian case to the floor.

'No, you won't,' I say. 'You're going to sit right there and listen to ME now!'

He looks back at me. 'What the fuck?'

'Don't you "what the fuck" me! Last time I let you go all too easily. In fact, I cleared the path for you. This time is different. This time you're going to hear me out.'

'OK, OK,' he says, holding up his hands.

'And shut up with your patronizing gestures.' I kick

the food aside and walk the short length of the wall, pulling at the red and green decorations, ripping them from where they had been taped with festive optimism and love, like I'm ripping up my heart. I can feel his eyes follow me, waiting for a gap to appear so he can make a sudden break for it.

I lean against the wall and pull some mistletoe from its post above my head, tearing at the leaves, bursting the white berries. One by one.

'The truth is, Harry, I sensed there was something wrong with your reaction the night I told you there'd been a mistake. My head knew it, but my heart didn't want to believe it. So I let you off the hook. I always let you off the hook. You must think I'm really stupid. And I don't blame you. Because I've behaved like an idiot. An idiot who loves you. And I thought you loved me.'

'I do love you.'

'How can you say that and still happily tear me apart? What kind of love is that?' I hold on to my anger. It's my one moment. I'm not going to waste it this time. 'I've always believed we were meant to be together and when you came back because of my letter, I knew it was destiny. That you would be there for me until the end. And you told me this great new yarn about Melissa. And yet again, I believed you. But we weren't each other's destiny. Ever! Were we? You were only passing time with me. It was only ever about you and your heroic journey. It was always about you. You're a self-serving narcissistic illusionist and I fell for the pretty smoke and mirrors.'

'Hang on a minute! You wanted me! You needed me!'

'Get over yourself. Yes, I was thrilled that you wanted to be there for me. Yes, I wanted you to hold my hand. I was frightened. And maybe if I'd died, you would have been seen as this martyr, this knight in shining armour who made the end of my life a decent one. But I didn't die, did I? You were outed. And that's why I can't see anything good in your intentions. In fact, you make me sick.'

He folds his arms across his chest and sneers, flashing his annoying white veneers. 'Well, that's OK, then, isn't it?' he yells. 'Because now we don't have to pretend to each other any more. You don't have to pretend you're dying and I don't have to pretend to love you.'

'WHAT?' I feel my breath quickening, my heart is pounding so fast it might gallop out of my body. I move towards him. I need to eyeball him. 'You think I was pretending?'

He eyeballs me back. 'What else? No one makes that kind of mistake. You did it purely to get me back in your bed. You thought you'd be able to keep me there, once you had me hooked. You wanted a pity fuck.'

I let rip a burst of laughter. 'Are you mad? You think I'm that desperate?'

'Deny it.'

'Fuck you, Harry! Do not flatter yourself. Go back to Melissa. The two of you deserve one another. You can enjoy looking in the mirror together, admiring how wonderful you both are.'

He stands up and I feel the air shift between us. 'Do you know what? That's precisely what I'm going to do.'

I step back. 'Good! And you can take your gift with you. I'm sorry you went to so much trouble. And whilst you're at it, you can take these too.' I bounce down and grab the bowl of cocktail sausages. 'Here!' I throw them in his face. There's an adrenalin rush of pleasure. It emboldens me. 'And here's some relish to go with them!' I pick up the spicy tomato sauce, throwing the bowl at his fake white teeth. 'And no double dipping! I know what you're like now!'

He ducks awkwardly so that it bounces off the top of his head and flips over. The sauce trickles down his face, into his eyes and on to his shoulders and he stands there, spluttering, looking like a burst blood boil, slopping it away. 'That fucking stings, you stupid bitch! And this is a Prada jumper!'

'Gee. Sorry about that.'

He's rubbing his eyes. 'You see this!' He shakes the bloodied gift bag at me. 'It was a token of my generosity. But you wouldn't understand that, would you?'

I dash to the tree, its lights still flashing festive joy, oblivious to the carnage, and grab his Christmas pudding jumper, clutching it to my chest like he's going to have to fight me for it. 'Oh no? Well, now you'll never know the extent of my generosity either.'

'Perfect,' he says, flicking off more sauce from his jumper. 'Just perfect.' He picks up the bottles of Prosecco and shoves everything back in his bag. 'And I'll take these home for Melissa. Although I'll leave you one. You probably enjoy drinking alone. You must be so practised at it.'

'Well, well, well!' I sneer. 'You can be a right little bitch when you show your true colours, can't you?' I'm at boiling point. 'But take it. I won't be needing it, thanks all the same. Want to know why?' I'm so past caring now.

He gazes at me, locking horns, his face streaked red and fierce. 'You know what, Jennifer Cole, I couldn't give a damn.'

'Well, Rhett Butler, I'm going to tell you anyway . . .' I throw his gift back towards the tree. Its branches teeter and flicker. I put my hands on my hips, allowing a dramatic pause. 'I'm PREGNANT!'

His eyes burst out of their sockets. He rubs them with the heels of his hands and groans in pain. 'You're WHAT?'

I stand there smiling, the revelation feeling more satisfying than I could ever have hoped. 'I'm UP THE DUFF,' I say.

He gives a derisive snort. 'Well, there's no way it's mine.'

I stare at him, saying nothing.

He rolls his eyes. 'I repeat. There's no fucking way it's mine!' Steam is practically coming out of his ears.

I throw him a look of contempt. 'Did I say it was?'

Confusion washes over his face. He's open-mouthed. 'Well, isn't it?' he blusters.

I casually examine my fingernails.

'Whose is it, then?'

'I don't think you have the right to ask me that question.'

'Jesus, you're such a fuck-up.'

I fix him with a glare. 'And you're not? You've got it so right?'

He shrugs.

'Well, Mr Wrong, I'd like you to leave.'

'You don't have to ask,' he spits. 'I'm off.' He gathers his pride and picks up his bag. 'Tally Ho Ho Ho,' he says. His one flash of humour.

'Just go!' I say and throw a further handful of sausages at his back.

He grabs his coat, slams the front door behind him and I hear the beep of his car alarm, the heavy thud of his car door.

I rest my back against the door and slide down it. I sit staring at nothing, then burst into hysterical laughter, the chill of cold air blowing from under the weather strip, before dissolving into hysterical tears. What just happened? What the hell just happened?

Eventually, I pick myself up and wander back into the sitting room. I look at the detritus of our hoax love affair, pick up the can of cream and spray it everywhere. For a brief moment, it feels good.

'Well, that's one hell of a mess,' I say and sit down on the couch, my tail between my legs.

I gaze around the room in sad contemplation.

That's it then, I think. It's over. Everyone dealt with. Harry, Andy, Elizabeth, and pretty much Emily, too. I've lost them all. In different ways, but they've all gone. The only one who has stuck by me is Isabelle. Who'd have thought it?

I think back over everything and weirdly, I know I will miss them. Because you can't end relationships, no matter how toxic, and not feel some kind of grief.

But with all the loss and grief, I have this. I place my hands over my stomach. Yes, this.

What's meant for you will come to you.

'You'd better stay in there, little bunny,' I say. 'You'd better stay right where you are.'

21

'Come in, come in,' says Isabelle. 'Let me take your bags.'

'Thanks,' I say. 'All the presents are in the big plastic one.'

'Oh, how exciting,' she says. 'You take that one then. Lay them out under the tree in the drawing room. We don't open presents until tomorrow. After Christmas lunch.' She looks at me. 'If you can wait?'

'I think I'll manage,' I say. 'You were the one who could never wait.'

'I still can't,' she says with a mischievous giggle. 'I've already sneaked a peek at what Martin's bought me. Very, very generous, I can tell you.'

'Lucky you!'

'Don't tell him, though, will you?' She's momentarily panicked. 'I'll act surprised when I open it. And don't make me laugh.'

There's something reassuring about her behaviour. The fact that as we get older, at Christmas we can still be the same child. Cheeky and silly and ridiculous, and we can throw sausages and – oh, never mind.

Isabelle's house is decorated beautifully. Far more sophisticated than I could ever imagine let alone achieve. More sophisticated than our family home ever was. It smells delicious: oranges and cinnamon and cloves. There are scented candles burning everywhere. There are decorations beautifully draped over doorways, along the dado rails and up the wooden bannister. I have a feeling she didn't buy any of them from the Pound Shop.

I wander with the heavy bag into the drawing room where the biggest tree I've ever seen is sitting in the corner by the French windows, laden with baubles, all white and silver and wonderfully coordinated like something out of a magazine. The white fairy lights are elegantly trailed around it, in such a way you can't see the wire (how does she do that?), and there are literally mounds of presents pooling from the large pot base, as if Santa's entire sack has burst in their house.

Back home I threw out all my decorations, the picnic, everything. I just grabbed a bin liner and shoved it all in. Christmas tree included. I am broken. I wanted to throw out Harry's jumper, but I managed to stop myself and relabelled it to Martin. And then I sat down and cried my way through *It's a Wonderful Life*.

I start laying out my gifts underneath Isabelle's tree. Martin's present stands out as the most glamorously wrapped of my collection. I wish I'd at least rewrapped it. It brings back too much of what I want to forget.

How did I ever allow Harry back into my life? Believing in him all over again.

Because the truth is, people don't change. It's our perspective that changes. We see what we want to see and I only wanted to see the best in Harry. I didn't want to see the lies. I could have said all the things I regretted not saying the first time around, but the end would always have been the same. Because Harry never really loved me. He was just a convincing charmer. And that's tough to acknowledge. There will be no third time. It's really over.

But hey! It's Christmas and I'm alive and even though I'm hurting, holding together what's left of my heart, I'll pull through. Because that's what you do.

I fold up the empty carrier bag and stand back, looking at the tree. It's so beautiful. It lifts my aching heart. 'Jennifer,' I say out loud. 'It's all going to be fine.'

'What's going to be fine?' says Isabelle.

'Jesus! You startled me.'

'Do you talk to yourself a lot?' she says.

'No idea,' I say. 'No one's around to tell me.'

She comes over and puts her arm around my waist. I rest my head on her shoulder and we both stand there looking at the tree. 'You've done a beautiful job,' I say. 'You're quite good at this, you know.'

'Thanks,' she says. 'Not just a pretty face.'

'Oh, I've realized that for quite some time,' I say.

She squeezes my waist. 'Ooooh,' she says. 'I feel a little bit of menopausal thickening. You need to start doing yoga. You should deal with it sooner rather than later. Later it all goes to pot.'

'I'm pregnant,' I say flatly. Just like that.

She laughs. 'Shut up!'

'I am.'

'Pah!' she says, turning me round to face her. 'Don't joke.'

'I'm not.'

'Holy cow!' she says. 'You are just one miracle after another.' She pulls me in to her skinny frame. 'I can't keep up with you. One minute you're a goner, the next minute you're perimenopausal, and now you're eating for two.'

'I hope so,' I say. 'I'm around ten weeks. I've never gone this far before.'

'Why didn't you tell me sooner?'

'I didn't want to jinx it.'

'Ten weeks is OK,' she says. She breaks away and we look at one another. 'So how does Harry feel about it?'

'Well . . . How do I put this . . .'

She sees my discomfort. 'Is this a conversation we should be having when everyone's gone to bed?' she says. 'Before Santa comes down the chimney, knocks back the sherry and tries to fuck me.'

I make a half-amused grunt. 'Yes, I think we need to have one of those conversations.'

Her face falls. 'Just tell me you're OK with it.'

I nod. 'I am. I'm very OK with it.'

Isabelle's eyes glisten. For a second, I see a glimpse

of our mother. She kisses my cheek. 'Come on,' she says. 'Let's go and have dinner. Would you mind if I tell Santa and the kids?'

'Go ahead,' I say. 'What's the point of secrets? Apart from yours, of course.'

I give her a playful nudge. I'm thinking about Martin's present but she says, 'Shush, I need to talk to you about that too. It's all over. I did it.'

'With Barry?' I mouth, amazed.

She shakes her head, yes. 'But hold that thought!'

'Holy cow!' I say.

We all sit round the table and Martin pings on his wine glass with his knife.

'Announcement!' he says, and the two girls sit up straight, paying full attention. He smiles grandly. 'Let's welcome Jennifer to our Christmas Eve dinner,' and he glances at each member of his family in turn, finally resting his gaze on me. 'Now, Jennifer, let me tell you that on Christmas Eve we eat all the girls' favourite dishes. Don't we, girls?'

They nod.

'So tonight's dinner is prawn cocktail followed by spaghetti bolognese and then there's a surprise pudding.'

'Ooooooh,' we say, playing along.

'But first, let's put our hands together and pray.'

I flash a look at Isabelle.

'He finds God at Christmas,' she says, and I try to keep a straight face.

Martin peers over the top of his half-moon glasses. 'Better Christmas than never,' he says.

'Just get on with it,' says Isabelle. 'The prawn cocktail will get cold.'

The girls giggle, then stop themselves, putting their hands over their mouths, quickly putting them together again in prayer.

Martin takes a deep, theatrical breath and clears his throat. 'For what we are about to receive, may the Lord make us truly thankful.'

'Amen,' we say, putting down our hands, but he continues in a kind of evangelical boom. 'And thank you, Lord . . .'

Isabelle stares at him across the table, like this is not part of his normal performance. '. . . for allowing Jennifer to be with us and for making her illness a mistake. We have a lot to be grateful for this year, O Lord. We have *all* made mistakes. Forgive us the error of our ways and grant us the strength to be your *loyal* and *humble* servants.'

I'm struggling to stop myself from laughing. I take a surreptitious peek at Isabelle and my glance meets hers across the table. We share a moment of childish bemusement while her daughters, serious-faced, eyes tight shut, play at being adults.

'And please, dear Lord—'

'Amen!' says Isabelle, standing up, her chair scraping across the floor. 'Let's eat. Help me serve, girls!'

The girls flash a look at their father, then jump up and follow her. Cecily brings me a prawn cocktail from the breakfast bar. It's beautifully presented in a cocktail glass, the prawns arranged on a bed of shredded lettuce, dressed in Marie Rose sauce.

We eat to a clatter of cutlery, then Isabelle and the girls clear the table. Isabelle won't let me do a thing. 'You're our guest!' she says. 'Sit down!' She serves up the next course. The girls express their delight at the spaghetti bolognese and Martin tells them how lucky they both are and how he never had Christmases like this when he was a child.

Isabelle looks at me, shaking her head. 'He says the same thing every year,' she whispers. 'Another ritual.' She rolls her eyes.

'Do you have something to say, Isabelle? If so, perhaps you'd like to share.'

'Oooooh, Martin. You're scaring me!' she says.

I look at Martin. Whatever has happened with Barry, whether he knows about him or not, he senses something has changed and he's strutting like a peacock.

We polish off our bowls of spaghetti. 'Right,' says Isabelle, patting her mouth with her napkin. 'If everyone's finished – girls, collect up the plates and I will serve dessert.'

The girls do as they're told while Martin sits there, watching them with a satisfied smile. This must be the one time he lets everyone else do the work. Either that or Isabelle is having to earn some points.

She disappears into the utility room and returns with a huge pavlova laden with strawberries.

'My favourite,' says Cecily. 'Thank you, Mummy!'

'Mine too,' says Sophia.

'I arranged the strawberries,' says Martin.

I smile to myself. Maybe one day, I think, I'll serve up my child's favourite dessert and they'll say, 'Thank you, Mummy,' and I'll be relieved there's no one there to say, 'I arranged the strawberries.'

In amongst the heartache, I'm allowing myself some tempered excitement. This little person growing inside me is the most important thing in my life now. It's the one thing I mustn't lose. It makes everything that's gone before, all the pain, the trauma, the loss, seem unimportant.

'There's good news,' says Isabelle and all eyes turn to her. 'Auntie Jennifer's pregnant.'

The girls yelp with excitement, rush round and hug me. Martin raises his eyebrows, eyeing me with suspicious bewilderment. 'Congratulations, Jennifer,' he says, his lips stretched into a tight smile. 'You're a walking miracle.'

'Thanks. It's early days,' I say.

'It's very exciting,' says Isabelle. Her face drops. 'Oh, sis!' she sighs. 'What a shame Harry has to spend Christmas with his mother. He should be here with us. They should both be with us. We're all family now.'

'We need that talk.'

'Oh!' she says. 'Right.'

We all help with the clearing up – I have to protest to be allowed: 'I may be a guest but I'm here for a few days and I don't want you moaning about how lazy I am when I've gone!'

'As if!' says Isabelle.

Martin gives us stage directions: how to fill the dishwasher, which plates should be rinsed first, what pot goes where. I start to understand the appeal of Barry.

When everything's cleared away, Isabelle announces we're going to have a sisters' chat in the drawing room.

'What about the presents?' says Sophia.

'You'll have to wait until tomorrow. You know that. It's the rule.'

'Ohhhhh,' the girls cry.

'Go and watch *The Princess Diaries* in the media room. And take Daddy with you. Here,' she says, looking at Martin, pouring a glass of sherry. 'You'll need this.'

'Don't be too long,' he says.

'We'll be as long as it takes.' She gives him a kiss on the lips and his eyes brighten. I'm fascinated. That's all it needs, I think. One kiss and his chest puffs right out. Men are so simple. If only I could fathom them.

Isabelle looks at me. 'Fizzy drink, Jennifer, or water? What's your pregnant tipple?'

'I'm not sure I have one. Perhaps I'll have some fizzy water.'

'Well, let's go mad and add a splash of lime.'

We wander into the drawing room, the Christmas tree sparkling, its presents in waiting, and lie down, our heads at opposite ends of the sofa, feet entwined, hands cupping our glasses.

'So tell me,' she says.

She listens with rapt attention as I tell her about Harry and his massive deception. 'What a bastard! That's outrageous!' Then about the guy on the heath and my massive deception. Her eyes are wide as though she can't believe what she's hearing.

'That's epic!' she says. She sits up for a moment on her elbows. 'So you're going to have it?'

'Yes,' I say. 'If it will have me.'

She leans back down and sips at her drink. 'Well, good for you. You're very brave, doing it on your own. You've certainly got guts. But this time I'm here for you. No more secrets.'

'Thank you,' I say. 'I've had my fill of those.'

'Cecily and Sophia will make perfect little helpers. They'll be begging to come and see their cousin all the time.' She laughs. 'And you of course.'

'It will be all about the baby from now on, won't it?'

'Yes. 'Fraid so. Say hello, back seat!'

I smile. I'm trying not to get over-excited, but now I'm talking about a baby cousin, making it real, it's impossible not to.

'And what about you?' I say. 'What happened with Barry?' I'm whispering, even though there's not another soul near by. Even though that soul is on the other side of the hall, sipping sherry and watching *The Princess Diaries*.

She groans. 'Oh don't,' she whispers. 'What a mess I've made.' She pushes against my feet, and we start playing air bicycles the way we did as kids. 'He insisted I leave Martin before Christmas and I couldn't think of a more selfish time for him to ask me to go. I mean, the girls need Christmas together as a family. And then I thought, What am I thinking? It brought everything into sharp focus. The girls don't just need Christmas together as a family. They need a family. They need Martin. They need both of us. We're not just for Christmas. I knew then I couldn't break up our unit. I had no choice but to end it.'

'You see! You're brave too.'

'And the truth is, annoying though he can be, Martin is steadfast and he loves me. Far more than Barry would ever be capable of. I guess I got tired of all the dreary responsibility and looked for some excitement elsewhere, but in the end, if I left Martin, the dreary responsibility would simply be shifted along to another name. And what's in a name, huh?' She gives her best attempt at a wink. 'A terrible name at that. And it was the right thing for the children.'

'You must love Martin, though, Isabelle. That's the most obvious thing to me in all this.'

'Yes,' she says. 'In a funny kind of way, I guess I do.'

'Does he suspect?'

'He senses something, I'm sure. He's behaving so weirdly.'

'I noticed.'

'He's never asked me anything, though. Never once said, "What's wrong?" '

'Possibly for the best.'

'I know,' she says.

'So how did Barry take it?'

'Not well. How does anyone take that kind of thing?'

I laugh. 'Yeah. I threw some sausages over Harry and then a bowl of spicy tomato sauce.'

'You did not!'

'I did!' I'm remembering the pathetic expression on his face. I have to hold on to that look when the surge of sadness overwhelms me.

She gasps. 'Didn't it ruin the carpet?'

'Only you could say that,' I say. 'My carpet is long beyond ruin. But I think it might have stung Harry a bit and it probably didn't smell very nice on his Prada jumper.'

She smiles then lets out a sigh. 'I wish I'd have had some spicy tomato sauce to throw at Barry. What an arse. He made his usual threat to phone Martin and when I told him, "Go ahead, phone him," and handed him my phone, he just backed off. He's such a coward. They're both cowards. Throwing sauce must have felt wonderful.'

'You have no idea.'

She squeezes my feet affectionately, her toes tipping over the top of mine. 'The annoying thing for me,' Isabelle says, 'is that I'll have to bump into him for a few more years while the kids are at school. But so what? I'll take up bridge and knitting and have average sex once a month. What's not to love?'

'Sounds blissful,' I say.

'Marriage,' she says. 'Why are we so conditioned to want it?'

'Not sure I am . . . Besides, my appalling taste in men makes me better off single. The joke is, I'm so sussed in my job. I mean, I see people for exactly who they are. I can spot all the good traits, all the negatives, and yet when it comes to my own personal life, I'm hopeless. All I want to see is the handsome prince.'

'I blame Disney. You always loved that crap. Anyway, I think you're pretty normal.'

'Harry told me I was a fuck-up.'

She sniggers. 'What does that make me then?'

'A more mature fuck-up!'

She holds up her glass. 'To mature fuck-ups everywhere!' she says. 'Merry Christmas!'

Part Three

Part Three

1

Goodbye, last year. I'm glad to see the back of you. Hello, New Year! It's just another day but somehow a new number feels like the chance of a fresh start. That was my *annus horribilis*. This is going to be my *annus* of hope. Come to think of it, I always say that. But up until last year I had no idea how *horribilis* an *annus* could be. You can't really say that out loud, can you? Not even the Queen should say that out loud.

I saw the old year out on my own. Not for lack of invitations. From Isabelle (Christmas was amazing but I didn't want to outstay my welcome and I wanted to be at home), Olivia and Dan who were having friends over to dinner and invited me (she's already so married and she's not even married), and Anna Maria who suggested I should go with her to Glastonbury (you can guess my response).

So I stayed in.

Alone.

And I felt fine.

Optimistic.

Because that's what the New Year is about, isn't it?

Optimism. So no matter what happened to disprove it in the year just gone by, I'm always prepared to believe that this year will be better. And I'm still pregnant. So far, so good.

New Year, New Me! Harry is so last year.

It's the weekend before all the schools start, before the return to work becomes the return to normality. Bye bye, festivities. Bye bye, quiet London. The roads will be jammed again, the tube packed. Life goes on.

Today I'm meeting Pattie for a long overdue catch-up and to talk about my return to work. I'm hoping they're going to be fair. I reckon sixteen years of service should stand me in good stead. Although I shouldn't assume anything. I'm not exactly clued up on how you deal with someone who left because they were dying, then wants to come back because it was a mistake and then declares they're pregnant. I don't suppose any law accommodates that. But I need to get out into the world again and work. I need to stop focusing on my pregnancy. Happily, the sickness has stopped but I go to the loo far more often than I need. This did not go unnoticed at Christmas.

'She's going *again*?' Sophia would whisper loudly behind her hand and the girls would giggle furtively as though the observation was their little secret.

I couldn't help it. I'd convince myself I felt something like a trickle so I had to check it wasn't blood. Had to! Otherwise I'd have sat there panicking quietly inside. I'm trying meditation. Anna Maria has given me a CD and some lessons in 'om'. It's working but not quite as intended. I find it hard not to laugh.

Pattie and I have agreed to meet in a café in Primrose Hill. I squeeze past tables full of families, couples with their faces glued to their smartphones, their children's faces fixed on their iPads. Not one table is engaged in conversation. I sit down at a table for two in the corner, vowing to myself this will never happen in my family. My family! It gives me such a rush when I allow myself to believe it. My family of two. But then again, who knows what kind of mother I'll be? Maybe . . . well, let's just wait and see. Let's not get ahead of ourselves.

Pattie walks in, looks around unsure. I wave and she spots me straight away, rushing towards me, her arms open wide. I stand up and she grabs me to her.

'You look bloody marvellous,' she says. She steps back and examines my face. 'Yeah, you look really, really well. And what about the bump?'

I push my stomach forward. 'There's nothing there yet. Just a very thick waist.'

'You'll get that back in no time,' she says.

I'm in no rush, I think.

We order her coffee and my tea. I've gone off coffee. I realize there is a fine line between the symptoms of menopause, pregnancy and maybe even dying. Your nose, your taste buds, your senses do weird things. No wonder it all merged. I could have been any of those things but I think I drew the best straw.

'God, I've missed you!' she says. 'The office hasn't

been the same without you. Although the biscuit supply seems to last longer.'

'Ha! Thanks,' I say.

'Look at you though. You look great, bearing in
mind everything that's happened to you. I always eat
my way through trauma,' she says. 'I'd be three stone
heavier by now if I'd gone through what you've been
through. You couldn't make it up, could you?'

'Well, some people thought I did.'

'Why would anyone make that up? It was shocking.
But I guess there's always some conspiracy theorist
somewhere.'

'Like my so-called boyfriend.'

'Harry?'

'Yes. Him.' I can see the shock register.

'So how's he coping with the pregnancy?'

'He isn't.'

'If I'm honest, he never seemed the fatherly type.'

'Then it's lucky it's not his.'

Her jaw drops. 'It isn't?' Her eyes brighten with
the promise of intrigue. 'Can I ask whose . . . ?' she
says.

'You can. But I don't know the answer.' For some
weird reason, I want to laugh. I can see she wants to
laugh too. So we both start laughing.

'What have you been up to, Jennifer Cole? I know
you're trained in the art of discretion but now I feel
you've surpassed yourself.'

I tell her the story of the heath and her expression
betrays a shimmer of bemused awe.

She pulls out her phone. 'Let's google him. I want to see what he looks like. What's his name?'

I wince. 'I told you. I have no idea. I never asked.'

She screams with laughter. The other tables look across at us.

'Sorry,' she says. 'I'll calm down.'

'You don't have to. Not on my behalf. At least we're engaging in conversation.'

'You know what? If I thought I was dying and some gorgeous guy appeared like an apparition on the heath, I'd have done exactly the same. I'd have opened my legs and said, "Take me to eternity, you hunk."'

'I think I said that!'

'You did?' she yelps, then puts her hand over her mouth, shoulders still bobbing.

I snort. 'No! Of course not.'

'Wow, Jennifer! Wow!'

'And to think I used to believe nothing ever happened to me.'

'Yeah well, I reckon you've now had your lifetime's quota.'

'Hope so. So are you ready for me to come back to work? I know I am.'

Pattie fiddles with a paper serviette and her expression instantly becomes more serious. 'Are you sure you want to come back? Of course you can, and you have every right to.'

'I couldn't be more sure.' Her hesitancy makes me nervous.

'Great. Well, I've put various packages together:

financial proposals for the different options, including part-time . . .'

'OK. I understand. I'm happy with that.'

'We've been fairly flexible. You need to decide which one is the best way forward for you.' She feels inside her coat pocket and pulls out an envelope that she places on the table in front of me. She shifts awkwardly in her seat.

'Tell me something. Would you rather let me go?'

She rolls her eyes. 'No! Of course not. We kept your post open for you when we thought you were dying, that's how much you mean to us. But there's an opportunity here for you – and us – to make sure that when you do come back – particularly after you've had the baby – we're all properly geared up for it and it's on the right terms.'

'What you mean is, you can't ask if I'm going to come back once I've had the baby but you'd like to know my intentions.' This is uncomfortable. I hadn't expected my pregnancy to be such a problem. I'm an idiot. Pregnancy is always a problem!

'Jennifer! Stop being so defensive. In a way that's true. You know about this stuff more than anyone. But we want you back. And we want it to be set up in the right way so that you want to come back. So take your time and consider the options. Stop anticipating the worst.' She looks directly into my eyes. 'We want you.'

'Hormones,' I say. 'Up the creek. Sorry.'

'You're in good company,' she says. 'I've just started having hot sweats and it's no fun, I can tell you. Look what I've had to buy.' She drops down to her handbag and rustles around its interior, pulling out a battery-operated fan which she flicks on, holding it to her face. 'It's wonderful. My best friend right now and it's given me a fantastic idea.'

'Go on.'

'Yeah. I reckon if I could invent a fan that doubles up as a dildo, I'd be made. You can bet your life *I* wouldn't go back to work. I'd go live on some Greek island for the rest of my life and drink Aperol Spritz and ouzo and get unhealthily tanned.' She waves her fan. 'And I'd have wild sex on the beach with a swarthy young waiter, with a name like Stavros. Ha! Who needs the heath? But in the meantime,' and she taps the envelope, 'this is the best thing on the table.'

2

The offers are all very fair. I can see Frank's pragmatic imprint. I've accepted what I would label as the best compromise option and I'm going back to work in a couple of weeks.

For now, I seem to find enough to do to pass the time. I've bought a sketch pad and a tray of watercolours and paint badly but I'm trying to improve. I do sudoku. I occasionally allow myself to watch daytime TV. Mainly, I enjoy reading. I've become addicted to a new kind of self-help book. I have five on pregnancy, all given to me by Isabelle. I'm still the beneficiary of her hand-me-downs. I read what each one says is happening at any given stage. They give me a good overview. It's daunting but reassuring, and they have become my bible. I've even written my own Ten Commandments, which I've posted on my fridge:

1 Eat for two not three. Just because you're pregnant doesn't mean you're entitled to eat pastries and chocolate
2 Take regular exercise but don't overdo it

3 Do your pelvic floors even when you don't
   want to
4 Remember to take your daily dose of folic acid
5 Find a good antenatal class and remember to
   book it at around 20 weeks because they get
   heavily oversubscribed
6 Think positive! You will get to 20 weeks and
   you will get to those classes at 30 weeks
7 Do not panic every time you feel a twinge
8 Do not keep imagining you feel a trickle
9 Do not keep expecting to see blood in your
   urine or one day you will
10 Do not keep checking your phone in the hope
   there might be a text from Harry

I know, I know. I'm not proud of the last one. But
I'll get there.

I've taken out a membership at the local gym on
Finchley Road which has a massive pool and I go
swimming every other day. I've read it's the best exercise. And soon I'll have another scan. I can't wait for
the next one. If I had my way, I'd probably go for a
scan every week for regular reassurance. But I read
that too many scans are not best for the baby so I just
have to reassure myself.

Isabelle has started calling me daily to check up
on me.

'I've been thinking . . .' she says one morning. 'You
should see my obstetrician. She's wonderful.'

'Why?'

'Because you're nervous and I think she'll put your mind at rest.'

'That's really kind, but I'm being very well looked after by my own hospital.'

'Don't be ridiculous. You're on the NHS. She's on Harley Street. You won't have to schlepp over here, if that's what you were thinking. You can manage Harley Street, can't you?'

'Of course I can.'

'So when shall I book the appointment?' The thing with Isabelle is, even when she's trying to be nice, it feels like she's bossing you around.

'Isabelle, it's not necessary.'

'But I want to do this for you. Let's call it my treat.'

I laugh. 'Is that what a treat is for me now? A visit to the obstetrician.'

'I'll take you out for tea at Claridge's afterwards,' she says. 'Come onnnnnn.'

'That's so generous of you but, honestly, I'm much more relaxed about it than I was.'

I'm not, but I don't want to visit some expensive Harley Street person who will only insist on all manner of tests, like the amniocentesis. Dr Mackenzie suggested I have it but I steadfastly refused. He's easy enough to manage. Isabelle's lady will no doubt be able to twist my arm – she's paid to – so, even though I'm sure she means well, it's not what I want.

'Seriously? Just one itty-bitty appointment. And then tea. Claridge's. Yummy.'

'I'm watching my waist, remember. Your instruction.'

'Oh, for goodness' sake, Jennifer. Why are you being so difficult? Why won't you let me be involved?'

I stare at the phone. 'Is that what you want? To be involved.'

'Of course!'

'Well, why didn't you say?'

'I just did.'

I smile. 'I'd love that. But you do realize being involved does not mean Harley Street. It means coming to Hampstead and braving the NHS.'

'You make me sound such a snob. I'm not. We all know the NHS is up shit creek and Brexit is not going to save it.'

'Fine. Forget it then.'

'OK. I'll come to Hampstead.'

I laugh out loud. 'Great. Come to my twenty-week scan but be prepared for a long wait. Timing is not their forte.'

'You're going to wait for your twenty-week?'

'Yes.'

'Seriously?'

'Isabelle! Do you want to be involved or in charge?'

'All right. Point taken. Give me plenty of notice. I'll drive you,' she says. 'And I'll bring my Kindle.'

3

I'm back at work. Full-time for now, then a three-day week after my maternity leave. It's a good arrangement. Walking back into my office for the first time felt very weird. It smelled different. Putting my things back in place helped me reclaim it: my photos, including a selfie with Isabelle and family from Christmas in a new frame, my stash of mints, a jar of my favourite pens and highlighters, my stapler, the ruler I never use but has followed me since school, and a little succulent plant, the sort impossible to kill. They make my desk my own again. I slowly get back into the rhythm of my old routine, glad to have my team around me. They all came by during my first day back and congratulated me on my pregnancy, accepting it without question as the reason for my absence.

Being around people, attending meetings, dealing with recruitment, readdressing job descriptions and all the other usual HR preoccupations has been good for me. Stopped me focusing too much on myself. But I'm not going to lie, sometimes evenings can feel quite lonely.

I guess that's how it's going to be until I have a baby demanding my attention, when I won't have a second to think. And I remind myself that I can feel equally lonely in a relationship, with someone sitting right next to me. Still. Being rational doesn't always make it any easier. If I really want to torture myself, I wonder if I'll ever meet someone again, knowing that the likelihood of a man taking on another man's child is slight.

For some reason, Saturday nights are the worst. That's when I'll pull out a bar of hazelnut chocolate that I've tucked away in a secret stash as though I'm hoping I might forget where I've put it. No chance. Sometimes you have to break one of your own Ten Commandments and forgive yourself.

Tonight I'm halfway through a bar when my phone rings. It's Olivia. She's on her own this weekend too. Dan's on his stag. I'd invited her over but she thought it would be good for her to prove to herself she can still 'fly solo' and she hadn't become some sad co-dependent.

'Are you busy?' she says.

'Very!' I say. 'I'm doing my pelvic floors. Actually, I'm eating chocolate.'

'Do you think you could spare me an hour if I come round?'

'Sure. And I'll spare you a piece of chocolate if you hurry.'

Dan's stag is in Ibiza. It doesn't bear thinking about. Eight middle-aged blokes let loose on party island. I did offer to make Olivia a hen do, but she said she couldn't imagine anything worse.

'I promise there'll be no pink cowboy hats, or "Liv's Hen Do" T-shirts.'

She rolls her eyes.

'And, hand on heart, I won't ever book you a stripper.'

'The fact that you're even saying that makes me want to gag.'

No hen do for Olivia then, and I can't say I'm disappointed.

I open the door to her pasty face. 'Aw, Liv. Are you lonely?'

She ignores my comment, walks straight past me into the kitchen, fishing a bottle of wine out of her tote. 'You drinking or are you being good?'

It's as if we're flashing back to the moment I told her about my 'osis'. It seems a lifetime ago and yet the memory of that intense sadness rushes straight back into my stomach. I swallow. 'You OK?' I say.

'No,' she says pointedly. 'Are you joining me or not?'

'Wow, you're scaring me. OK then. Half a glass to keep you company.'

'Thanks,' she says. 'I've had enough of drinking alone. It's no fun.'

'How long's he been gone? Two days?'

'That's not the point.'

I watch her pour the wine. Her face is taut with tension. I realize she's been crying and I think she's about to cry now. 'Let's sit down,' she says, and I follow her into the sitting room.

We sit opposite one another. She picks up her glass. 'Down the hatch,' she says and guzzles it down like water.

'Is there a problem, Liv?' I ask.

'Just a minor one.'

'How minor?'

'I don't want to get married.' She looks back at me, her eyes daring me to challenge her. 'There you are. I've said it.'

For a moment I'm speechless. I take the tiniest sip of wine. I'm not taking any risks, no matter how tense this is going to be.

'You sound as though you've already made up your mind.'

'I have. It's not that I don't love Dan. I just don't want to get married to him.'

'Does Dan know?'

'No. You're the first person I've told. You're always the first person I tell.'

'Ditto.'

I weigh up what she's said, wondering if it's classic pre-wedding nerves or if something's happened that she hasn't told me about.

'So cancel,' I say. 'No one's twisting your arm.'

'My dad will go crazy if I cancel.'

'No, he won't.'

'Don't you remember? He said he'd been saving up for my wedding my whole life. He'll kill me.'

'Well, at least you won't have to go through with the wedding.'

She forces a laugh.

'What about Dan? Won't he want to kill you?'

'I can deal with Dan. Oh God!' she groans. 'What have I done? What was I thinking?'

I'm amazed she feels this way. She's never mentioned any doubt before. 'You were thinking what you've been thinking since I've known you. That you've always wanted to get married, that a legal commitment is everything and that you've never been happier than you are with Dan.'

That dismissive laugh comes up from her throat again. 'That's true. But suppose marriage ruins it all? I mean, if it ain't broke, don't fix it, right? And it ain't.'

'Which is exactly why you're getting married. Because he's wonderful and you're terrific together and it's what you both want. Why should a piece of paper change that?'

She sighs deeply. She reaches for the bottle and tops up her glass. 'Don't worry, I got an Uber.'

We sit, looking at one another in silence because I can tell that Olivia's mind has drifted somewhere far away; she might be looking at me but she's not present. And she seems very drunk.

'I haven't heard from him since he's gone on the stag,' she says suddenly. She rocks slightly in her seat. 'Not a fucking word.'

Bingo! I swirl my wine in the glass. 'Is that what this is about?'

'No! No,' she objects. 'I'm not that lightweight. But suppose it's indicative of how things are going to be. That we get married and he starts to take me for granted.'

'Oh Liv,' I sigh. 'There could be a million reasons why he hasn't phoned you. He's on a stag for a start. In Ibiza. He's probably drunk—'

'Isn't that when you send multiple *I love you* texts? Like hundreds of them?'

'Is that what you want? I can't think of anything less attractive.'

'Oh!'

'How many have you sent?'

'Not been counting. But one itty-bitty reply from him would be nice.'

'I'm with you on that. But does that mean he's now fallen into the official "taking you for granted" category? Come on. Let's be real here. Maybe there's some great explanation. Although I'll put money on it that he's hammered. I mean, that is the point of a stag, after all.'

'Oh, stop making his behaviour sound acceptable. You'd be exactly the same as me.'

'Definitely. I don't deny it. I'd hate it. And I can't think of anything worse than a bunch of drunken middle-aged men. Bleugh.'

She looks back at me, a reluctant smile forcing up her downturned mouth. 'Really? You think that too? We're not being judgemental? After all, I am half sozzled myself.'

'Oh no,' I say. 'It's not the being drunk I hate. It's the blokey gang mentality that takes over. That's the turn-off.'

'Ha! Yeah. Especially when one of the blokey gang should have bloody texted me.'

I get out of my chair and move to sit down in front of her. 'Liv. I'm with you. Honestly, he should have texted. But it doesn't mean you should cancel the wedding. It means that when he gets back, you're going to tell him that no matter what, he should always text you back – at least once – and that he should never, ever take you for granted. And then you're going to have the most amazing make-up sex. OK?'

'Not really . . .' She lets out a loud burp. 'Oops.' She flaps her hand in front of her face. 'I cried about this all last night, you know. I haven't slept a wink.'

'I didn't want to say anything but I kind of guessed. You feeling any better? A glass of wine done the trick?'

'You mean a bottle,' she says. 'And yeah, it's helped. Until I get sober.'

'Or he does. You do know he'll call, don't you?'

'Yes, but that doesn't make the silence OK. Why do they never get that?'

'If I knew the answer to that, Olivia, I wouldn't be sitting here now, pregnant and single.'

'Being single is so much less complicated.' She yawns.

'Sure,' I nod, yawning with her. 'But who says less complicated makes you happier?'

4

'Happy birthday to you!
Happy birthday to you!
Happy birthday, dear Jennifer.
Happy birthday to you!'

The waiter puts the cake down in front of me and I blow out the candles. The women around the table clap heartily.

I take the knife and plunge it into the chocolate sponge.

'Make a wish,' says Olivia.

'You'll know what I'm wishing for,' I smile.

'I'm wishing that for you too,' says Isabelle. 'I can't wait to see that scan.'

'Are you going?' Olivia says.

'Yup,' she smiles proudly. 'Braving the NHS.'

'Rita says your baby's going to be just fine,' says Anna Maria. 'You can widen your wish spectrum.'

Isabelle leans in to my ear. 'Who is this Rita woman she keeps talking about?'

'Her reiki healer.'

'Jesus! I thought it was her lover!'

Anna Maria is looking at Pattie's palm.

'You see that line,' she says. 'It means you're going to meet someone and he's going to be the perfect man for you. A spiritual man.'

'Beggars can't be choosers,' says Pattie.

Anna Maria looks back at her, horrified by her contempt. She examines Pattie's palm again. 'And you will have two children. No. Make that three.'

Pattie scoffs and retrieves her hand. 'He's not a spiritual man, Anna Maria, he's a bloody miracle worker.' She pulls her fan from her bag, waving it furiously around her glowing face.

Anna Maria sucks in her cheeks. She knows exactly what she was doing. No one mocks the offer of a spiritual man.

We're at the Wolseley not just to celebrate my birthday but also because I want to celebrate these women. To thank them. I look around the table, committing this moment to memory because it's special. Because I never expected to have another birthday. And because these women are the best, most supportive, loyal friends a once-dying woman could wish for.

I divide the cake into generous portions. 'You all have to eat it. We're celebrating life and I'm not accepting any of this dieting nonsense from anyone. Not even the future bride. You're thin enough, Olivia.'

The wedding is back on. Not that it was ever off. Turns out Dan had had his phone confiscated by his best man as soon as he arrived at the airport. No surprise there. And no surprise that Olivia decided to forgive him. I don't think she ever told him she had considered cancelling.

'You look great, Olivia,' says Isabelle. 'A bit drawn, maybe, but that's understandable.'

'Isabelle! She looks fabulous,' I say.

'And I agree, it's just she's got that pre-wedding gaunt look.'

'Take no notice, Liv. Whatever your look, it suits you.'

I place a piece of cake on each of the tea plates in front of them. Isabelle pings on her glass with a fork.

'Happy birthday, Jennifer,' she beams, holding up her glass. 'To my wonderful sister.'

I'm chuffed.

'Hear, hear,' they say.

She carries on. 'To think she used to be such a boring old goody-two-shoes.' She blanches. 'Sorry! She hates that. But look at her now.'

'What's that supposed to mean?'

She dips her chin at me, as if I should know what it means. 'It means I'm proud of you. You're brave and gutsy.'

'Why, thank you, Isabelle!'

'You are. You're the bravest and we love you,' says Olivia, and the others nod in agreement.

I feel strangely overwhelmed. 'On that note,' I say, 'I need to pee. How many times in a day does a pregnant woman need to pee?'

'At least twice, so far. But I'm not counting,' says Olivia.

'I think you'll find it's three times. But I'm not counting either,' says Pattie.

'Anna Maria,' I say. 'Would you care to give your estimate?'

'I don't think I've noticed you leave the table once,' she says. 'Your aura is so present.'

Isabelle flashes me a look that says, Is she completely mad?

'She's kidding,' I say.

I wander through the restaurant one more time, squeezing round the outside tables, slowly negotiating the stairs down to the all too familiar Ladies' Room.

I push open the door, expecting the room to be empty, but standing in front of the basins, looking at herself in the mirror, putting on lipstick, is a large woman I instantly sense is familiar.

She turns her head, casually checking the intrusion, and jumps out of her skin, dropping the lipstick which rolls into the sink. Her mouth falls open, one red lip, one smudge.

'Elizabeth,' I say, mirroring her shock. 'How are you?'

'Jennifer?' She looks me up and down. 'Is that really you?'

I check myself. 'I think so,' I say.

'Are you *preg-nant*?' She elongates the two short syllables, conveying undisguised disgust.

I'm wearing a figure-hugging floral dress. At seventeen weeks my bump is now undeniable.

'Yes,' I say. 'Either that or I have a bad case of wind.'

'Oh God,' she groans. 'I guess I should have expected that kind of reply from you.'

She turns away momentarily, picks up her lipstick, checks the tip, tuts and finishes painting her lips. I'm standing there like an idiot watching her, deeply uncomfortable in every sense, needing to pee more than ever but somehow held rooted to the spot.

'How's Andy?' I say. 'Is he here?'

'He's at football.' She smacks her lips together, puts the lipstick away and tucks the snakeskin clutch bag under her arm ready to leave. She looms over me, posturing. 'I don't mean to be rude,' she says. 'But aren't you meant to be dead?'

I stall. 'I think you'll find that is rude,' I say.

'Oh really?' she says. 'Really. You think that, do you? Well, I think you're pretty rude, actually.' Her mouth is tight and cruel with its slicked red coat of paint. Maleficent without the charm. 'I mean, don't you think you could have let us know you were still alive? With child,' she adds.

I laugh, emboldened by her lack of grace. 'If you were even the slightest bit interested, don't you think you should have called me?' She pushes every single one of my buttons.

'We were dealing with stuff. It was a difficult time. But we're OK now.'

'And so am I,' I say. 'I'm very OK. My diagnosis was a mistake.'

'Pah! Don't be ridiculous. No one makes that kind

of mistake.' She rolls her eyes and squares up to me. 'Ohhh,' she says. 'I see it all now. You were never dying, were you? You were *preg-nant*.'

'I'm not going to justify myself to you, Elizabeth. You can think what you like.'

'Well, Andy and I are happier than we've ever been. So stay away from him.'

'Why would I come near him?'

'You wrote to him, didn't you? Begging him to come back. Begging him to take care of you in your hour of need.'

'Is that what he told you?' Her eyebrows arch. 'Did you never read the letter yourself?'

Her eyes pop out on stalks. 'Oh my God!' she screams. 'It's not *his*, is it?'

She's so exasperating. I want to slap her into a conscious reality. 'Elizabeth,' I say. 'It's not his, nor would I wish it to be. I divorced Andy a hundred years ago. He's all yours. I have absolutely no interest in him. And if you want bad sex with a serial philanderer, then you've chosen the right man. I moved on and the last thing I want to do is listen to your needy, paranoid crap.'

She's gawping at me, speechless. My bladder is fit to burst, but this feels too damn good.

'I wish you nothing but the best, Elizabeth, but you're going to have to face facts. I do not covet my ex-husband in the way you coveted him when he was my husband. But my bladder isn't going to hold on for much longer and I don't want to piss on you the way you've always pissed on me. So please excuse me. Ciao!'

I push past her into a cubicle, lock the door, scramble to find my knickers, whip them down and my bladder cheers with relief. I sit there, my head in my hands, listening for movement outside. Go, Elizabeth! I plead in my head. Go! There's the longest silence and I know she's still there. Hovering. Waiting for me. Desperate to have the final word.

'Just go, Elizabeth,' I say. 'I told you. Get over it.' I'm not going to back down, even from the inelegance of a toilet seat.

There's a whoosh of the door. She's gone.

I regain my composure, come out of the cubicle, wash my hands and look at myself in the mirror. I grin in triumph.

I did it. What I've wanted to do for years. I told her more to her face than I put in the letter she'd never read and got the pleasure of witnessing her reaction. What could be better? I smile back at myself. Well done!

I return to the table and the women stare at me as if I've been gone for hours.

'Where have you been?' says Isabelle. 'You've taken for ever. I was about to come and find you. We were getting worried.'

'I bumped into Elizabeth,' I say.

Olivia clasps her hands to her face. 'Oh my God! I think we saw her leave. She was blustering loudly for her coat. Left in a real hurry, some poor woman in her trail.'

'Must have been her,' I say. 'Good! I bothered her.'

'What happened?' says Isabelle.

I blow on a clenched fist as if I've delivered a proper punch. 'Well, you'd all be proud of me. I was brave and gutsy and I told her exactly what I thought of her.'

'You're on fire!' says Pattie.

'She was so rude, she deserved it. I left her speech-less.'

They give me a little round of applause. 'Bravo!'

'Andy's going to get a shock when he hears I'm still alive. And *preg-nant*.' I laugh. 'Do you know, she actually had the nerve to ask if it was his.'

'Good God!' says Olivia. 'That woman has no idea about anything, does she?'

'She does now!'

5

It's early morning and several blankets cold. It's the Sunday after my birthday and I'm still feeling celebratory. It was such a good lunch. Joyful. And now I have time to be lazy in bed because I have an excuse to loll around. I'm gazing at my belly under the duvet. A moment's peaceful contemplation.

My phone rings, breaking the spell, and I feel for it by the side of the bed then bring my hand back under the warmth of the duvet, glancing casually at the glow of the screen. It's Emily. It's EMILY! I sit up immediately and pull myself into some kind of reasonable shape, finger-combing my hair, as though she might catch me looking like a pregnant sloven.

'Emily!' I say, brimming with excitement. 'Oh my God, Em! I'm so pleased to hear from you.'

'I'm sorry, Jennifer, it's Michael. There's no good news, I'm afraid.'

I feel myself go cold.

'We're turning off her life support later today. We thought you would want to know.'

I'm overwhelmed with emotion but he's being so

stoic about it, I stay in control. 'I'm so sorry. Please give my love to Marion. I feel for you both. How is she coping?'

'She's not. The whole thing is unbearable. You think you're prepared. You've had months to grieve and contemplate the worst. But now it's here. It's simply agonizing. But she's a brave woman.'

'I'm so, so sorry, Michael.'

'We'll let you know arrangements. I'm sorry to be the bearer of bad news.'

The disconnect resounds cruelly in my ear. He's gone. The phone slides from my hand. 'Emily!' I whisper. 'You poor lost soul.'

I curl up on my side, warm tears trickling down my face. 'Oh my God!' I say out loud. 'Emily is about to die.' My body is trembling. The hairs on my arms sit up. 'What did she do to herself? Why? Why? Why? Was her life really that bad?'

I place my hands gently on my stomach. 'Baby,' I say. 'I want you to know how loved you are. Even now. Even when I don't have a clue who you are, or what sex you are or who you're going to be . . . You are loved. Don't you ever forget that. And if you should ever hear that you were a mistake, and someone will no doubt say something because people can be unkind, then I want you to know, we all make mistakes, and you were the best one I ever made. You will be loved all your life. I'm going to make sure of that. All your life, you will know your mummy truly loves you.'

I sense the sobbing build, slowly, silently until it

takes hold of me and I roll over and cry into my pillow, feeling my baby pushing against me. 'Poor Marion. Poor, poor Marion. A mother should never have to bury a child. Oh Emily! What were you thinking? Suicide was not in your Deathopoly plan.'

I fumble around the mattress and retrieve my phone. I dial Isabelle.

'Pick up!' I say. 'Pick up, Isabelle!' But it goes to voicemail. 'Call me, please,' I say.

I dial Olivia. She picks up straight away.

'Oh Liv,' I sob.

'What's wrong?' She waits for a bit, allowing me to settle. 'Please tell me, Jennifer. Please tell me what's wrong.'

I grapple for my voice. 'It's Emily . . .'

'What's happened?'

I come up for air and grab a tissue then blow my nose. 'Sorry, Liv. They're turning the life support off today. She's going to die.'

'Oh Jennifer. I'm so sorry. Truly I am. I'll come round now,' she says. 'I'll be there ASAP.'

I pace the room waiting for Olivia. It feels like an eternity before the bell rings. I open the door and we throw ourselves at one another, baby in between, crying in each other's arms. I tell her it should have been me and she tells me not to be so ridiculous, Emily made her choice a long time ago.

Suddenly I feel a pain. I push away and bend forward, holding my sides. I'm getting cramps in my stomach.

'Ow!' I say, stretching towards the wall, trying to pull myself out of it.

Olivia acts startled. 'You're not having the baby, are you?'

'Better not be. Way, way too early.'

'Lie down, for God's sake.' She hurries me over to the couch. 'I'll get you some water.' She rushes to the kitchen then rushes back and hands me the water. I drink it slowly and lie back down. 'Don't panic,' I say. 'I'm going to be OK. It was only a cramp.'

'You scared me.'

'I scared myself. Oh Liv. Poor Em.'

She nods. Her eyes are genuinely sad, which makes me feel even sadder. We sit quietly together, holding hands.

After she leaves, I go back to bed, feeling lonely and miserable. This is definitely a day for staying under the duvet.

The phone rings. I answer absently. 'Hi, Isabelle,' I croak.

'Jennifer?' A man's voice.

I check the phone. 'Andy. Oh my God, Andy, have you heard the news?'

'Yes!' he says, sounding massively upset.

'It's terrible, isn't it?'

'I thought you'd be pleased?'

I jolt. 'Why would I be pleased?'

'You're *preg-nant, Jennifer.* Isn't that what you've always wanted?' He says it with the same distaste as his wife. 'I think you need to explain what's going on.

One minute you tell me you're dying and the next you're *with child*. I never thought you'd try and hoodwink me like this, Jennifer.'

'Are you kidding me? Hoodwink you? After all your lies. Well, I haven't hoodwinked you. I was told I was dying and then I was told it was a mistake. If you'd have let me speak that night you came round, I would have told you everything.'

He goes quiet. 'Didn't I let you speak?'

'You know you didn't. You were wrapped up in your own little domestic soap opera.'

'Nonsense. If you'd have said something, I'd have paid attention.'

'Why do I always have to be the one to say something? Why doesn't it ever occur to you to ask?'

'Well, I'm asking you now. What did you tell Elizabeth? She's been acting like a lunatic. She's so angry at me. As if your baby is mine.'

'I told her the truth.'

'Shit, Jennifer!'

'Not about you feeling trapped in your marriage. I told her the truth about her. That's all. She'll get over it. Anyway, Emily's about to die or maybe she has already,' I say. 'That's why I thought you'd phoned.'

'Emily? As in Michael and Emily?'

'Yes. She attempted suicide but she failed. She's been in a coma for months. They're turning off the life support today.'

The horror dawns on him. 'I'm sorry. That's awful.' His voice sounds appropriately sombre. 'I haven't

377

been in touch with them for years. Not since our divorce. Poor Mike.'

Grief is tugging at my heart. I want to get off the phone. 'I've got to go, Andy. It's been a horrible morning.'

'Sure,' he says. 'I'm sorry, Jennifer. I'm sorry for everything. I was a shit.'

'Oh, don't flatter yourself.'

He splutters. 'Anyone who doesn't allow his ex-wife room in a conversation to tell him she's not dying is a shit.'

'Yeah,' I say. 'I'll give you that.'

'And you're pregnant. So whose is it?'

'No one you know.' There's a silence, as if he thinks I'm going to tell him. 'Bye, Andy,' I say, and disconnect.

6

Emily's funeral takes place very quickly. In a way, she's been dead a long time, she deserves a swift burial. And it's sunny – as though she's telling us she's finally happy.

Michael, in a dark grey suit, white shirt and skinny black tie, is in pieces. A man destroyed. I feel desolate for him. He was always so supportive of Emily. You have to admire his tenacity. She wasn't easy. But no one ever said love was easy.

The place is teeming with people. Lots of faces I recognize, some more familiar than others. Isabelle has come with me for support. Olivia and Anna Maria have come too. Emily was our friend. We are united in sorrow. Hard feelings no longer have a place.

Her mother is dressed entirely in black. She's wearing a huge black hat and sunglasses. She looks like a film star. I have to duck beneath the hat as she gives me a distracted hug, my stomach nudging hers.

'I'm so sorry,' I say.

She removes her sunglasses and dabs her eyes. 'You're pregnant,' she says. 'How wonderful.' Which is kind because I can't imagine that's what she's really thinking. She stares at my stomach. 'Nothing matters for me any more,' she says. 'Not now. But for you new life brings hope. I'm so pleased hope still exists. I wish you all the luck in the world. Be happy, Jennifer,' she says. She glances at Isabelle.

'You remember my sister, Isabelle,' I say. 'And Olivia and Anna Maria.'

'Hello, Mrs Champion,' they mutter in turn. 'So sorry for your loss.'

'Kind of you to come.' She smiles graciously, replaces her sunglasses and moves on.

We walk down the long path away from the cemetery feeling numb, the sound of loose stones crunching under our feet.

Anna Maria has driven Olivia. I warned Olivia against it, but she decided to accept the lift.

'You in the car park?' Isabelle says.

'No, it was full, we're outside.'

'Us too,' I say, and we carry on walking.

Anna Maria's car is parked on the bank, literally outside the cemetery gates.

'How on earth did you get away with parking there?' says Isabelle.

'I told her that,' says Olivia. 'We're lucky you haven't been clamped.'

'I knew it would be fine,' says Anna Maria. 'Who's gonna clamp you outside a cemetery?'

We kiss each other goodbye and Isabelle and I walk hand in hand up the hill towards her car.

'Thanks for coming with me,' I say.

'God, that was horrible.'

'Funerals aren't much fun at the best of times.'

'True, but she was so young.' She squeezes my hand. 'And I kept thinking, what if it had been you? My heart would have exploded. I don't know how Marion kept upright. Or Michael.'

'Drugs. Did you see the size of their pupils? How else do you cope?'

'Mum was definitely drugged up at Dad's funeral.'

'Mum was drugged up at the smallest opportunity.'

Isabelle laughs. 'She was, wasn't she? She was always pushing her Valium on me. If ever I was uptight with one of the kids, or with Martin, "Here," she'd say, "have one of these." As though they were Smarties.'

'Maybe they were to her. Maybe back in the day our entire street was on them the way everyone's on Prozac now.'

'You too?'

'Oh no,' I say. 'Why? Are you?'

'Not Prozac but something similar. Only a low dose, though.'

'And Martin?'

'Yeah. Same. You look surprised! I'm more surprised you're not. Most people I know are on something.'

God, I think. Is Olivia on something? Is Anna Maria's demeanour down to a happy pill? It never even occurred to me. I have such an aversion to drugs, it's not part of my thinking.

'Do you think Mum popped Smarties to help her

cope with Dad?' I say. 'Maybe that was why they always seemed so happy.' I laugh to myself.

'Who knows? Too late to wonder now.'

I shrug. 'Well, at least we've come out of it OK.'

She sniggers. 'What, two fuck-ups at a suicide's funeral?'

A wide grin stretches across our faces and we burst into laughter, falling about. 'Oh stop it,' I say, holding on to my sides. 'We're meant to be mourning Emily. This is *so* wrong.'

'Emily will be laughing with us.'

'No, she won't,' I say. 'She never had much of a sense of humour.' This irreverence only adds to the hysteria. 'Maybe we're laughing to stop ourselves from crying?' I'm crossing my legs; laughter is now a major threat to my dignity.

'Oh, I've had it up to here with crying,' says Isabelle, her hand sweeping over her head, the gaiety beginning to subside.

'Me too,' I say. 'Have you seen Barry at all?'

She rolls her eyes. 'I seem to bump into him practically every day, in a way I never used to – and not on purpose, I can assure you. My heart still skips a beat. It hasn't got the message yet. What about you? Any news?'

'No. Nor do I care.'

'Yeah, you do!'

'Honestly, I don't. I've finally come to accept that he was never right for me and I'm OK with that.'

Isabelle's expression says she thinks otherwise.

'Why don't you believe me? It's true. I've learnt what I should have learnt years ago: to trust my intuition. I've finally realized I don't have to subjugate who I am so I can be part of a couple. That if I don't fit, no matter how much I wiggle and squeeze, I'm never going to. And I'm OK on my own. Genuinely. I'm not just saying that to make myself believe it. And that makes me feel powerful.'

'That's a very big statement. What about being with someone for the baby?'

'Well, that's not going to happen, is it? So I might as well make the best of it. And I will. Somehow I'll blunder my way through parenthood same as everyone else.'

'Jesus. You've become mighty philosophical.'

'Yeah, I'm a Buddha,' I say. 'The size of one anyway.'

We climb into the car and strap on our seatbelts. Isabelle throws her bag behind her on to the back seat.

'This might sound odd,' she says. 'But this whole awful drama has done us good. We've both learnt. Thank you for that.'

I nod. 'Funny how the worst thing to happen to you can sometimes end up being the best thing.'

She looks across at me and puts her hand on mine. 'Yeah. True. But can you shut the Buddha up now!'

7

Why is it that when you're expecting something to happen it never does and when it's the last thing on your mind, that's when it happens? The doorbell rings but I'm not expecting anyone so I'm tramping around in a big old sweatshirt and tracksuit bottoms. I look a mess, but I don't care. I quite like not having to bother. I pad to the door and peer through the spyhole then quickly duck, hiding from view as if my iris can be detected.

Shut up! I think. If it isn't Harry.

'What do you want?' I say, shifting a few inches to the right, standing up and checking myself in the mirror on the wall by the door.

'Can I come in?'

'Why?'

'Because I want to see you.'

'Sorry, we're closed today.'

'Oh come on!'

'Why?'

'I want to apologize.'

'Correct password!' I say, quickly finger-combing my hair.

I open the door and there's a weird moment when we're just standing on opposite sides of the threshold, staring at one another. I don't move. I'm like a pregnant barrier.

It's the beginning of March and the weather is still harsh. He looks cold. He shoots an unsubtle glance at my stomach. 'Am I allowed in?'

'Door's open,' I say and step aside.

'Thanks,' he says, his face all meek. He manoeuvres carefully past me. 'You look good.'

'Don't flatter me. Do you want a cup of tea?'

'Only if you're making.'

'I'm not.'

'Ha! I suppose that's a no then.' He hovers in the hallway. 'Can we sit down anyway?'

'Sure,' I say.

He takes off his coat and scarf, hangs them over the bannister then moves into the sitting room, slapping his upper arms, trying to get warm. I grab his scarf and pass it to him.

'Thanks,' he says.

He sits down on the sofa, perching on the edge as if he knows he's unwelcome. I sit opposite him in the armchair, straight-backed. I feel like a sack of potatoes trying to look like a stick of celery.

'So,' he says, shifting his feet. 'I wanted to see you . . .' He pushes the hair away from his face. 'To say sorry. I've been thinking about you. About us. A lot. About how things ended at Christmas and I don't feel good about it. I behaved very badly.'

I'm trying not to react. If he thinks I'm going to make this easy for him, he's wrong.

He swallows, realizing he's on his own in this performance. He arranges the scarf, tying it a bit tighter around his neck. Like a noose, I think.

'I appreciate now what you must have been going through. I thought my being there for you was a generous gesture but, you were right, it was misguided. I don't know what I was thinking. I could have been there for you as a friend, if you'd wanted me. From a place of honesty. But I chose one of deception. And when you discovered the doctor had made a mistake, I had to come clean, which made it all seem some kind of dirty, cunning ruse. But it wasn't, Jennifer. That wasn't what was intended. I'm really sorry.'

I'm enjoying this. 'So you believe me now? That it was a mistake.'

'Of course I do. Everything I said at Christmas was just knee-jerk. I couldn't understand how you could be so angry with me when I had been nothing but decent. Or so I thought. So I hit out. But on reflection, you had every right to be angry. It was an ill-conceived idea.'

I'm still waiting for the pay-off. 'Is there a "but"? Because I'd rather know now and quit while I'm ahead.'

'No. There's no "but".' He clears his throat. 'I've been thinking about a lot of things. Re-evaluating my life.' He looks at the floor, then sidelong at me. 'I'm not with Melissa any more.'

'I've heard that one before.'

'This time it's true.'

I hold my nerve.

His mouth pulls awkwardly and he looks around, locks his fingers together, arms aloft stretching out his shoulders. 'It really is over, Jennifer. I came clean with her,' he says.

'Are you looking for applause?'

'No. Of course not.'

'What happened, then?' I don't need to know, but this is irresistible.

'I told her exactly what had happened between you and me. She wasn't impressed. Threw things and left.'

'Sausages?'

'Plates, actually. I guess she wasn't thrilled with where our supposed decent gesture took me. Funny, eh? You think you're being Superman and end up being Lex Luthor.'

'That's about right,' I say.

He clears his throat. 'So, I'm going to take myself off. Go travelling.' He looks at me as if he's hoping he's finally earned my approval and I've been placated. 'I need to find myself.'

'That's brave.'

'Thank you.'

'It's not a compliment. Suppose you don't like who you find?'

He's momentarily thrown off-kilter. 'You're funny,' he says. 'I always liked that about you.'

'I wasn't being funny.' I hate behaving like this, but he deserves it.

'Oh,' he says. That reflex of clearing his throat. 'Anyway, I'm giving up work. I've had time to reflect. I hate the man I've become. I used to love art for art's sake, that's why I do what I do. But it's no longer about art. The people I curate for don't care about the beauty, or the meaning, or the craft in the paintings I buy for them. They care about the price tag. Or whether it goes with their furnishings. They care about what it tells the world about them. And I'm no better. But I do want to be better, Jennifer. I want to change. I'm nearly fifty. That's fucking old! My life's a mess. You brought that into sharp perspective.' He takes a breath. 'So I need to start this process of change by making peace with you.'

He's paddling furiously, but I refuse to fall for his slick patter.

'You don't believe me, do you?' he sighs.

I shrug in a gesture that says, Does it matter any more?

'I don't blame you,' he says. 'I wouldn't believe me either. I guess I'll just have to prove myself to you.'

'Not to me, Harry,' I say. 'I'm not part of this any more. You need to prove yourself to you.'

He taps his hands on his thighs and looks around the room, as though hoping for his muse to appear. He needs back-up. 'I understand,' he says. 'But I still wanted to say sorry.'

He's starting to sound as though he means it. Or maybe he's slipping back under my skin.

'Thanks,' I say.

He gives a half-smile. 'I know you're not convinced,' he says. 'But I don't want you to think badly of me . . .'

'I don't, Harry. Honestly. Thanks for coming round.' I stand up. 'I really ought to be getting ready. I'm going out and . . .'

'Of course,' he says and he stands up too. He's right to suspect I'm trying to get rid of him but it saddens me. I may no longer love him but I can't hate him, either. And I don't want to hurt him. I know he means well and I've made him supplicate enough.

'Hey,' I say, dropping my guard. 'No hard feelings. Life's too fleeting. I know that now.'

'We both do,' he says, and I nod.

His face breaks into a sad smile. 'Hug?' he says. 'For old times' sake?' He opens his arms for me to move in to. I hold my breath, not wanting him to infiltrate my heart, but he doesn't. I'm more in control than I realized. We hold each other for a long minute, two people, once intimate, both acknowledging that part is over.

'Good luck,' I say, stepping back. 'I hope you find the person you're looking for.'

He grins. 'I'll send you postcards. Keep in touch. I'd like to hear your news . . . about the baby.'

'I'll put an announcement in the classifieds.'

He stares at me in that disconcerting way. 'I'm quite jealous, you know.'

'Of what?'

'Of you. Of him, whoever he is.'

'You'll get over it as soon as you pack your pass-port.'

He puffs his cheeks. 'Are you still angry with me?'

'No, Harry. There's no anger left.' I lean forward and kiss his cheek. 'Get on that plane and go find your-self. Leave the rest behind. That's the point, isn't it?'

He puts on his coat. Hesitates. Looks back at me with genuine sadness. 'I'm sorry I fucked up. But we're friends now, aren't we?'

'You should know the answer to that, Harry.'

He smiles with his eyes. 'Yeah,' he says. 'I guess we'll always have that movie. Goodbye then, Sally.'

8

I'm sitting at the Belfast sink, the enamel crackled and chipped but still beautiful, peeling potatoes. 'What are you going to make with these tonight, then?'

'Probably mash again,' says Mrs Mumford.

'If I was a cook, I'd make something for you, but I think you probably make a better job of it yourself.'

'Oh, you do more than enough for me already,' she says. 'Anyway, you shouldn't stand for too long. Not in your condition.'

'Ha! That's funny, coming from you.' She has terrible arthritis in all her joints. Her fingers are gnarled with it, hence I'm peeling her potatoes because she no longer can.

The first time I knocked on her door to offer to fetch her shopping, she looked at me with wary suspicion.

'Are you from Social Services?' she says.

I guess they must be the only legitimate people to visit her. It makes me sad. I laugh awkwardly. 'No, Mrs Mumford. I live down the road. Just over there.' I point towards my house.

'Oh yes, dear,' she says. 'I've seen you. Are you all

right? Do you need something?' She's staring at my bump.

'Actually, I was wondering if you needed anything? I'm going shopping and I could tag your list on to mine.'

She clacks her false teeth. 'That's very kind, dear. But I'm a bit nervous of strangers, what with everything you read.'

'I do understand but . . . you know where I live. I promise you, I only want to offer a bit of help.'

'Wait there.' She shuts the door and I stand on the step feeling foolish for a few long minutes, wondering if this wasn't a stupid idea, until she appears again and hands me a short shopping list scribbled in pencil on the back of an old envelope. She gives me a £5 note.

'I promise I'll be back.'

To her obvious surprise, I return with her shopping and a small amount of change and she decides I am trustworthy enough for a cup of tea.

'I'll make it,' I say.

'I may be eighty-seven, dear, but I can still make a pot of tea. You've done quite enough. You should be putting your feet up. Look at you.'

She makes an excellent pot and puts a few biscuits on a plate. She asks what my husband does and I tell her I'm not married and she looks surprised. Now, having got to know one another, she'll occasionally bring up the subject, saying she thinks I should find a man. She thinks I'm a bit foolhardy.

I get her shopping every Friday. I peel her potatoes

then we sit and chat over tea and cake. She loves the Battenberg I buy her. She tells me off for spoiling her. I love that she can feel spoilt by such simple things and I'm glad I finally knocked on her door and made the offer I had intended to suggest for so long.

To be honest, it's not totally altruistic. We are company for each other. She tells me wonderful stories about her life, how as a young girl she used to polish the silver for some grand family in a stately home in Norfolk, which was where she met her husband. He was the chauffeur. So very Downton. I could listen to her for hours.

And now, as each week passes, there is joy in the fact I'm getting bigger and contrarily I'm also getting my energy back. My baby is kicking. It's been kicking for several weeks.

Isabelle was with me for the first kick. She was helping me sort out the spare bedroom and get it prepared as a nursery.

'Isabelle, come here!' I shout from the landing. She looks up at me, drops the black bin liner she was taking out to the bins and charges up the stairs. 'Quickly. Put your hand on my stomach. The baby just kicked. I felt it!'

'Jesus, you scared me.' She stands with her hand on my stomach and puts my hand on her pounding heart. 'Feel that,' she says.

'Focus on my stomach.' We're waiting but there's nothing. 'I promise you I felt it kick.'

She smiles. 'Best thing, huh! That first one.'

'Shhhh. Wait. It's going to do it again. I know it.'

She jumps. 'There it is!' Her mouth drops open in wonder as if it's her first time too. 'Hello, baby!' she sings. 'Well, you have a mighty fine kick.' And that was the moment we agreed she should be my birthing partner. I want her to be involved for as much as possible.

It's certainly going to be interesting if her attendance at my twenty-week scan is anything to go by. I almost regretted allowing her to come.

'I don't want to know the sex,' I say to the sonographer.

'Why not?' says Isabelle, horrified.

'Because I don't.'

'But everyone wants to know.'

'No, they don't. You want to know.'

'Sure I do. I'm normal.'

'Isabelle,' I say. 'If you're normal, then the Pope's Jewish.'

She laughs. 'We're all Jewish,' she says. 'Somewhere along the line.'

I catch her looking rather too closely at the screen. 'Stop it!' I say. And she gives a sneaky smile. 'I'm looking for balls,' she says. 'I'm hoping for balls.'

'Balls or no balls, I'm hoping for healthy.'

The sonographer smiles. 'I'm not giving anything away but it's all looking pretty good to me,' she says.

At work, even though I'm absolutely fine, they all fuss over me as if I'm their pet goat, making sure I've got water and tea and that I don't outstay my welcome.

Seeing the care in their faces, I realize I was truly missed. It's given me an inner confidence in myself I didn't realize I had. It's as if I've been allowed to read my own obituary and it said the most beautiful things.

The high point, of course, was walking down the aisle, three tiny bridesmaids at my hem, behind Olivia and her father. Seeing her standing together with Dan, holding hands, entrusting themselves to an unknowable future, I couldn't help but cry. It made me want to believe in love again. But I'm always a sap at weddings.

The inevitable questions were asked.

'Where are you having it?'

'Royal Free.'

'Do you know what sex it is?'

''Fraid not. Don't want to know.'

'Where's the lucky father? Is he here?'

'I'd like to know the answer to that question myself.'

'I'm sorry?'

'It's OK. He's not here. In fact, I'm doing this alone.'

And I'd smile and leave it at that. For them to wonder. For them to gossip. Because I don't care what they think and I'm proud of that. If Olivia's wedding had happened sooner, I might have answered those same questions differently. Or hid in a corner to avoid them. But thanks to making peace with Harry, with Isabelle, with all of them one way or another, I've finally made peace with myself.

How it all ends

Today is a beautiful spring morning. My house is warm. Not just because it's a beautiful day but because I have a new boiler. Why did I ever procrastinate? As though I wanted to punish myself because in my heart of hearts I knew I was a coward. But now I've discovered I can be brave I feel I deserve to be comfortable.

The sun is shining through my windows and I can hear my mother's voice in my head. 'It's sunny. Go outside in the garden and play.' And, for ever the obedient daughter, I decide to take myself out for a walk across Primrose Hill.

I grab a large coat that wraps round my middle, my long knitted scarf, and put on a pair of sunglasses, slinging my bag over my shoulder. I only have to wait a few minutes before the arrival of the C11 bus that takes me to the top of Primrose Hill Road. Today is a good day. It smells of warmed grass, the trees are no longer naked but bursting with leaves. New life.

I breathe in deeply, feeling almost dreamlike. It's Sunday morning and everywhere is waking up slowly. I spot a father, his baby strapped to his front, and mothers pushing prams, holding their toddlers by the hand, and I'm happy to think I'm going to be part of their club.

I slowly climb the path towards the top of the hill and stop, slightly breathless, to take in the London skyline. There it is. Clear as a bell, in all its streamlined, razor-sharp glory. Standing proud in its own space, away from the crowded hub of the Gherkin, the Walkie Talkie and the Cheesegrater, is the Shard. It no longer pains me to see it. It no longer upsets me to think of Harry, something I thought I would never be able to say. It's good to know we can recover and move on.

I leave the path, enjoying the pleasure of walking alone, basking in the sunshine. I take off my sunglasses and shade my eyes to take a good look around. 'Hello, world,' I say, and I think of Anna Maria and Rita and talking to the energy and that strange time when everything seemed so daunting and out of kilter and final. Time heals. Corny but true.

Eventually, I decide to wander down the hill to the stretch of shops and cafés along Regents Park Road, thinking I'll grab a cup of tea somewhere. I amble down, through the open gate out on to the street, turn the corner and wait to cross. It's quiet, perfect, as though the world is entirely taken up with the beauty of the day.

I start to stroll across the road when WHOOSH! From nowhere! The air around me sucks in and there's a pounding through my ears as the screech of a car roars towards me.

In the vivid sensation of that moment, I know that this is it. That I have been reprieved from dying but not reprieved from death. In those few seconds I realize I have been looking back, allowed to feel good about my life before it is cruelly snatched away like a repossessed gift. The short-lived months of my unborn baby feel like a brutal joke as I stand frozen in time, waiting to feel metal against bone, overwhelmed by the knowledge that this merciless, cruel end is my destiny.

Then BOOM! The air changes. With that same sense of out of nowhere, I feel the hand of fate push me from my freeze frame into fast forward. I'm practically thrown towards the opposite side of the road.

'What the FUCK!' shouts a voice somewhere in the distance of my out-of-body haze. 'You crazy lunatic driver!'

The voice shakes me from my intense vision of death and I'm drawn back into my body, alive! Held by the hand that saved me.

'You OK?' he says. He looks back at the road, now permanently scorched with the inky swerve of skid marks. 'Jeez! That was some close shave. No way should that lunatic be allowed on the road. Must have been some crazy rich kid or—'

He turns his attention to me. I'm shaking. I want to keel over. I wrap my coat around me like a blanket.

'You need some water,' he says. 'Come and sit down.'

I can barely speak. I nod. He leads me to one of the tables outside a café but before I can get near it I throw up, spattering his trainers.

'I'm so sorry,' I say, wiping my mouth with the back of my hand. 'I'm so sorry.'

'Sit down and put your head between your knees. You're in shock. I'll get you some water and a paper bag for you to blow into.'

'Or put over my head.'

'I'll be back in two with supplies! You'll be OK?'

'Yeah, yeah. I think so.' I'm saying this to the pavement, my head between my knees. My sunglasses slide off my slippery nose and I let them lie there, in front of me. No energy.

I see his trainers return and slowly roll back up. He unscrews the top of a bottle of water and hands it to me. He's tall, with long hair that curls over his coat collar and a big bushy beard. He's holding some brown paper sandwich bags.

'Thanks,' I say, guzzling the water, aware that he's watching me closely. Studying me. I put down the bottle and smile at him and he nods his head, as if he's waiting for something.

'Thank you so much for saving me,' I say. 'I can't thank you enough.'

His scrutiny continues. Overly intense. Uncomfortable. More than general concern should allow. Then it dawns on me. My skin prickles.

I reach down for my sunglasses and quickly slide them on. My hands are now shaking uncontrollably. My whole body follows. It's him. The guy from the heath. With a beard. He's saved me.

He whips off his jacket and puts it over my

shoulders. 'You need to get warm. Maybe best move inside?'

'No, no,' I say. 'I need fresh air. I'll stay out here.'

He pulls up a chair and sits down next to me.

I feel tongue-tied and gauche, not sure what to say. 'I can't thank you enough,' I repeat, teeth chattering. 'Really. I thought I was a goner.'

He nods. 'I thought you were a goner too,' he says. 'I'm glad you're still here. And all in one piece.'

I look at him and smile. Now I know he knows.

There's a long, loaded silence.

'Yeah,' I say. 'It's me.'

He laughs. 'It damn well is you, isn't it?' he says, beaming.

'Good beard,' I say. 'Is that a disguise?'

He laughs and passes his hand over it in a loving stroke. 'Just laziness,' he says. 'I'm a hipster manqué. Nice sunglasses. Your disguise didn't work.'

'Never been my forte.' My teeth are still chattering.

He sits back and looks at me sideways on. 'Are you feeling better?'

I laugh. 'What? You mean apart from the shakes and the vomit?'

'Are you going to vomit again? Because, if so, I'll move my feet out the way.'

'I'm so sorry!' I say. 'I feel awful. But your feet are safe now.'

'That's a relief.' He's still staring at me, his eyes burning for candour.

'You want to know how come I'm still alive, don't you?'

He tilts his head. 'I'm glad *you* said that!'

I drink some more water. 'I wasn't lying to you. It wasn't some kind of sympathy ploy and it certainly wasn't a come-on. I really had been given a terminal diagnosis.' He's looking at me as if he never doubted it. 'For a couple of months I was preparing for the afterlife or the void or whatever. But my doctor's surgery made a mistake. They gave me the wrong test results.'

'Wow,' he says. 'That's some kind of mistake!' He leans forward, horrified. 'And to think, you nearly blew your second chance.'

'I did, didn't I? Thanks for sparing me. Sorry about your trainers.'

'It could have been worse.'

I nod.

I gulp down more water.

He drums his fingers on the table. 'This is a bit weird, isn't it?' he says. 'A bit formal . . . considering.' He laughs.

'A little bit.'

'How are you feeling now?'

'Better, I think.'

'Fancy taking a walk with me?'

'No funny stuff?'

'No funny stuff,' he says.

'You can have your coat back now. I'm OK.'

'You're sure?'

'I have several layers.'

I stand up. I'm wobbly. And then I feel it. A sudden cramp, more intense than ever before, and I lean over the table, holding on to my stomach. 'Shit!'

'What? What's wrong?'

'Nothing. Just . . . well . . .' I'm trying to breathe. '. . . I have a cramp.'

'Here. Breathe into the bag.' He opens up one of the paper bags and thrusts it over my mouth and nose.

I hold on, my hand over his.

'Slowly,' he instructs.

I slow down my breathing, feeling woozy with pain. In. Out. In. Out. The bag expands and contracts.

Eventually the pain starts to ease.

'It's OK,' I say, slowly straightening up. 'It's gone. That worked.' I let out a sigh of relief and let go of his hand and he scrunches up the paper bag and puts it in his pocket.

'You were starting to scare me,' he says. Then I see his eyes fall to my stomach and his expression changes. 'Don't you think you ought to get to a hospital?'

'No, no, I'll be fine. Honestly.' I pull my coat across my stomach. 'Shall we go for that walk?'

'I think we should.' He looks wary. 'No more cramps?'

'No more cramps.'

'OK then. But you'll let me know if anything changes.'

'I think you'll know.'

We cross the road, vigilantly checking every which

way for cars and lunatics, back through the gate into the park.

'I don't know your name,' he says, with a hint of embarrassment. 'We never exchanged names, did we? We didn't bother with minor details like that.'

'I know. Funny that. I'm Jennifer.' I look across at him.

'Leo.'

'Leo,' I repeat. 'Hence the good hair.'

'You believe in that stuff?'

'No.'

'Thank God!'

A group of women walk towards us.

'Morning!' they say.

'Morning!' we reply in unison.

'Lovely day.'

'Yes,' we say. It feels almost familiar, as though walking together is what we do.

'So what do you do, Leo? Isn't that always the next question everybody asks?'

He takes my hand and slips my arm through the crook of his. Totally easy in himself. 'I'm a writer. I freelance. For TV. Radio. Anyone who'll have me, in fact.'

I'm quietly thrilled. A creative, I think. My child will have the gift of creativity. I'll take that! I examine his face side on. He has a kind face, good nose. His hair is still long and shaggy. Maybe even longer, and he seems warm and open even behind his dark beard. In my recklessness, I've chosen well.

403

'And you? Are you working?' he says. 'Or are you just a lady-in-waiting?'

I cough awkwardly. 'You mean for this?' I say with as much casual dismissiveness as I can muster.

He nods.

'Well, I'm waiting for this but I'm still working. I'm in HR.'

'How many weeks?'

'Oh gosh. I've been in HR for years.' I laugh at my mistake and he laughs too. 'That's not what you meant, is it?'

'No,' he says.

I fumble. 'Erm, twentyish, I think.' I'm flannelling, obfuscating – well, lying actually – hoping it will put him off the scent and the timing won't register.

'You were so accurate about your death – seventy-nine days, if I recall – but on this you're kind of -ish -ish.'

'God! You remember *that* detail.'

'Hard to forget.' He smiles. 'That wasn't exactly an everyday conversation. Pretty memorable.'

'I guess it was,' I say.

'So you and the father, you're together? I think that's the next question everybody asks.'

'Why is that?' I say. 'Why does that matter so much?'

'I don't know,' he says. 'It probably doesn't any more in this age of anything goes. You don't have to answer if you don't want to.'

He deserves some kind of explanation. If not the truth, then at least something to quell his curiosity.

But the words elude me. I've not come prepared. I don't want to lie but the alternative is too terrifying.

'Actually,' I mumble. 'It didn't work out.' Not a lie. A half-truth.

'I'm so sorry. That's shit.' He shakes his head. 'Men!' he says and I laugh awkwardly.

We continue walking, quietly taking in the surroundings and I'm so aware of him, aware of his smell, his warmth, his tread.

'You with someone new, then?' he says, breaking the tranquillity.

'You're very inquisitive.'

'I'm a writer. I'm interested in people.'

'No,' I say. 'I'm doing this alone.'

'Entirely? The father not interested at all?'

I nod non-committally.

'You OK with that?'

'Yes.' I hear myself say it out loud and it feels right. 'Yes, I am!'

He's scrutinizing me again. 'You're cool,' he says. 'Good for you.'

'What about you?' I venture. 'Are you with anyone?'

'No,' he smiles. 'I'm like you. Doing this alone.'

I laugh. Probably a bit too eagerly. I'm aware of how pleased I am to hear he's single. Then pull myself into check. No expectations! I shouldn't get too pleased.

'I love this view,' he says. 'Could stare at it for hours. In fact, sometimes I do. Just stand here and stare. Let the world rush over me. It clears my mind. Opens up my thought process.' He turns to look at me. 'I've thought about you a lot, you know.' I feel my eyes widen. He tilts his head. 'Does that make you feel uncomfortable?'

'A little.'

'Well, I have. You certainly made an impact. I've often wondered what happened to that woman on the heath with the great body and the gorgeous face who was too young to die.'

'Now that does make me feel uncomfortable.' I feel my cheeks colour. 'Well, now you know.' I hold my hands wide open as if to say, Here I am.

'May I?' he says. He puts his hand out, waiting for permission.

THIS IS SO INTENSE.

'You may,' I say, and in that crazy intimate moment, feeling the warmth of his hand on my belly, on his baby, I want to tell him. I so badly want to tell him the truth.

He looks at me as if in awe, then steps back. 'Amazing,' he says. 'I saved two lives today. Superhero me!' He goes into Superman pose and I laugh with relief. He's stopped me from blundering in.

'So, Superman. Have you got kids?'

'No,' he says. 'One day, though,' he adds. 'For now I'm enjoying being an irresponsible creative. No obligations. No ties. It suits me. I can fuck beautiful women in the park and watch as they walk away. And then I can save them.' He says this with a flourish of his hand, then catches my look. 'I'm kidding,' he says. 'Don't worry. You're the only one I've ever done either of those things to.'

I raise my eyebrows. 'As a rule, I don't go around throwing myself under people or cars either.'

We continue our stroll and my arm slips back into his. 'So,' I say, taking a leap of faith. 'When you wondered about me, what did you . . . wonder?'

His face becomes thoughtful. 'Well, since you ask . . . I wondered how you were and how you were coping and then . . . I'd remember how you leaned forward and kissed me.' I shiver unconsciously. 'I'd replay that one in my head, a lot. I liked the way you took me by surprise. I'd think about how your mouth felt, and your body, which was wonderful.' His eyes flash at me, enjoying my reaction. 'And I'd think of your smell and the sensation of your skin as we rolled around.' I hear myself sigh as I allow the memory back in. 'And then I remember the cigarette we smoked together. In fact, I do that one a lot – I've given up smoking, don't you know! Thirty-four days, five hours, six minutes and . . .' He checks his naked wrist. 'Eleven seconds of total agony. You see how precise I am! None of your pregnancy vagueness.'

'Oh, well done. Congratulations!'

'Thank you,' he says, taking a low bow. 'So, thinking of you made me feel happy . . . and sad at the same time. But now I can think of you and just feel happy. It's good to see you. To see both of you.' He laughs.

I sense the power of our strange connection and feel my emotions soar. It couldn't have been just a one-off. Because now he's saved me. Surely that must mean something? Surely it's a sign. But maybe it means nothing. Maybe life is nothing more than a bunch of coincidences.

'So what are you writing at the moment?' I ask.

He makes a kind of ha! sound. 'I'm writing about a guy who meets a girl who tells him she's about to die and they have the best sex ever and then they part and he wonders what happens to her.'

'That's a good story,' I say, aware he's playing with me. 'How does it end?'

'Like this,' he says, pointing to the two of us. 'I think this is a pretty good ending, don't you?'

'Seriously though,' I say. 'What are you really writing?'

'I just told you.'

'Honestly?'

'Why would I bother to lie?'

'And is this really how it ends?'

'I don't know,' he says. 'I was going to make him wander the streets looking for her but obviously never finding her. Knowing she must have died. Then maybe he'd meet some other woman who would help him forget.'

'Not so keen on that one.'

'Nah. Me neither. So, I was a bit stuck and came out for a walk to clear my head and *voilà*! There you are. Still trying to die. And I save you. So, thanks to you, I guess I have my ending.' He looks at me. 'What do you think?'

'I like it,' I say. 'Everyone likes a happy ending.'

He smiles hesitantly. 'So tell me, why wouldn't you give me your phone number before?'

I think for a moment. 'Because my mother told me never to speak to strangers.'

'Did she forget to mention not to fuck them?'

'She forgot to mention a lot of things.'

He half laughs. 'So will you give me your number now?'

'You're not serious?' I say.

'Why wouldn't I be?'

'Because of this.' I point to my bump.

'So?' he says, as if my pregnancy is no more of an impediment than a spot on my chin.

'OK, then.' I reach for my phone. 'Give me your number. I'll dial it.'

I type in his number and we're both standing there looking at our phones, waiting. My heart skips ahead of itself. My baby kicks as though it's willing me to tell him.

As his phone rings, I feel a sharp pang of guilt. I know I have to say it. NOW OR NEVER. It's only fair. I look up at his open face with a huge surge of sadness knowing I'm risking blowing this potential friendship, but I have to. My new rule of candour, voicing what needs to be said, now, in the moment, no matter how uncomfortable, has to be adhered to. Besides, he's been so up front with me, I have to give him the chance to run for the hills.

I speak into the phone as though he's not standing right next to me.

'Hi, Leo.'

He plays along. 'Hi, Jennifer. Thanks for calling.'

'Thanks for saving me.'

'You're welcome.'

I take a deep breath. 'Leo, there's something I feel you should know.' Beat. 'I'm pregnant.'

'So I see.'

'Yes, but—'

He puts his finger to my lips. 'It's OK.'

'But—'

'All in good time,' he says. 'You have to build up the tension. Keep back the big reveal and leave the audience guessing. And you have to trust I know what I'm talking about. That I'm a decent writer.'

A tingle of excitement runs down my spine like a charge of electricity. 'Right,' I say, swallowing back my revelation. 'I'm prepared to do that. Good talking to you, Leo.'

We ring off, grinning at each other.

'So now I have your number,' he says. 'Thank you!'

I smile.

'And, one more thing, Jennifer—'

'Yes?'

He hears my sharp intake of breath.

'Thanks for the happy ending.'

Epilogue

BIRTHS

2 July to Jennifer Cole and
Leo Granger, a daughter,
Primrose Hope. 6lbs 12oz of
miracle. Mother recovering well.
Doula Isabelle getting there.
Please direct any flowers to her.

Acknowledgements

As I write, I have yet to hold an actual copy of my book in my hands but when I finally do, it will be like holding an Oscar – it's been that big a dream. This is my acceptance speech:

I would like to thank:

Celine Kelly, who when this novel was a germ of an idea, made me believe it was a good one and encouraged me to write it. My friend and mentor, Joanna Briscoe, who offered to read the first few chapters and ended up devouring the entire manuscript, then placed me in the skilled hands of Sophie Wilson. Thanks again to Joanna for recommending me to the woman who would become my longed-for agent, the magnificent Felicity Blunt at Curtis Brown. Felicity, your genius in nailing this book's title and placing me with the best publishing houses has allowed me to call myself by my other favourite title, 'author'.

Also at Curtis Brown, thank you to the inimitable Gordon Wise for insisting never to represent me, not wanting to risk our friendship – I never liked you anyway! To Lucy Morris, the best surrogate and guide, and to Melissa Pimentel and team who took me into territories beyond my wildest expectations. Thanks go to Kristyn Keene Benton at ICM, New York for your work and support across the pond.

Here comes the Gwyneth moment (sobs): I have been blessed with three outstanding professionals: my talented, incisive editors, Susanna Wadeson at Transworld, and Pamela Dorman and Jeramie Orton at Pamela Dorman Books/Viking Penguin. Your guidance, care and keen observations have helped craft this book into a far, far better one. Other people who have contributed to the general loveliness of this book include my copy-editor Anne O'Brien, and the ingenious designers Beci Kelly and Marianne Issa El-Khoury. The Oscar is yours too!

My writing journey started long before this novel. Over the past ten years and several courses, I have had the privilege of meeting fellow writers, some of whom have become lifelong friends. Thank you to my special gang: Val Phelps, Sadie Morgan, and the much-missed-but-never-forgotten Grace French, for your support and love, and for the weekends of laughter, food and wine and the very occasional writing exercise.

To my friends who have kindly been my readers, special mention goes to Genevieve Nikolopulos, who has doggedly read almost every manuscript I've ever written. To Rebecca Lacey: Becs! Who knew your wise piece of advice would inspire the book that became *the one*? Thanks, too, to Judy Chilcote, Basi Akpabio, Bert Tyler-Moore, Rebecca Rimington, Melanie Sykes, Kim Creed, my cousins Joanne Millett and Julia Schwarzmann, Louise Roberts in Sydney, Martin Olson in LA, and to Lynzie Rogers in New York, who championed me when silence might have served her better. Hero!

I am fortunate to have many special mates who have stood on the sidelines, cheering me on. Among them Janet Ellis, Patrick Finnegan, Juliet Blake, Rosie Phipps, Georgia Clark, Nicola Kelly, Nina Myskow, Amanda Hellberg, Vicki McIvor, Tracey Cox, Lesley Goldberg, Peter Thompson, Lloyd Millett, Francesca Cantor and my regular cohort Marc van Schie – always there at the significant moments of this journey – thank you all. Shout out to Wayne Brookes, the first industry person to truly believe in me. To my lovely ex-neighbour Eleanor Fea for her HR guidance, I hope I got it right. And to Federico Andornino, whose friendship, enthusiasm and advice are *inestimabile. Grazie!*

And now to my sons, Alexander and Joseph. I know with every rejection over each passing year, you wondered why the hell I was putting myself through the pain. Thank you for keeping the faith. I am proof that failure is merely a stepping stone. Tenacity is all.

And Mabel. Dog lovers among you will understand how special this mixed-breed wonder is in my life.

Mabel has been curled up next to me the entire time I have pawed (yes, I know!) over this manuscript. She is my laughter tonic and always the most pleased to see me. Yes, Mabes, you can have a treat.

And now I'm being given my cue to leave the stage. *drops mic*

About the Author

Author photo © Karla Gowlett

Melanie Cantor worked for many years in PR and as a celebrity talent agent. She has dabbled in interior renovations, which led to her hosting the TV series *Making Space* on Channel 4, in which she tidied up people's messy houses. She now concentrates on writing; *Life and Other Happy Endings* is her first published novel. She has two grown-up sons and lives in London with her dog, Mabel.

Ring 15.10.20